6/30/2011

P9-BXZ-866

2010

SHORT

SHORT

CORTRIGHT MCMEEL

THOMAS DUNNE BOOKS

ST. MARTIN'S PRESS

NEW YORK

This is a work of fiction. All of the characters, organizations, and events portrayed in this novel are either products of the author's imagination or are used fictitiously.

THOMAS DUNNE BOOKS.
An imprint of St. Martin's Press.

SHORT. Copyright © 2010 by Cortright McMeel. All rights reserved. Printed in the United States of America. For information, address St. Martin's Press, 175 Fifth Avenue, New York, N.Y. 10010.

www.thomasdunnebooks.com
www.stmartins.com

Library of Congress Cataloging-in-Publication Data

McMeel, Cortright.
  Short / Cortright McMeel. — 1st ed.
      p.   cm.
  ISBN 978-0-312-59431-2
  1. Floor traders (Finance)—Fiction. 2. Energy industries—Finance—Fiction. 3. Commodity exchanges—Fiction. I. Title.
  PS3613.C58537S56   2010
  813'.6—dc22

                                                              2010035898

First Edition: December 2010

10   9   8   7   6   5   4   3   2   1

For Sharbo, *sempre misterioso*

ACKNOWLEDGMENTS

Alex Glass, a great agent. John Schoenfelder, who took a chance on me. Brendan Deneen, who saw me through.

Michael Langnas, friend and editor.

Tristan Davies, mentor.

Eddie Vega, seafarer and poet.

John D. Spooner, Farrell Warner, AK, Sweendogs, Cooper "Chicken" Darnell, Jean Charbonneau, Swezey, Jen Ward, JF Connolly, Pete Scott, Shawn Belschwender, Hunter, Bill Thomas, Gary Wilson, Gordon Witherspoon, D'Arcy Carroll, Ron Zanoni, "Uncle Bud" Patton, Cecil Bennett, George Clark, Price Wetherill, Allen Grossman, Ken Poulin, Patrick "Hoss" Marable, TD, Davarryl "Touch of Sleep" Williamson, Helen Schulman, Andrea Dupree, Mike Henry, and Sean O'Kane.

PART ONE

Love no one, work, and don't let the pack know you're wounded . . .
Stupid, disappointed strategies.
Hazel wind of dusk, I have lived so much.

—*Illlit*, Franz Wright

TRADING FLOOR

A haiku of fat.

Hutchinson: Three-egg omelet. Double sausage and potato. Order onion rings.

The breakfast list went out.

Miller: Double egg over easy, bacon and tomato on Asiago bagel.

Churchill: Bacon, ham, egg, and cheese on English muffin.

Large: Three pancakes, butter & cream cheese. Side order bacon.

Greenblatt: Two-egg omelet. Chorizo and cheese. Hash browns with applesauce.

The list traveled around the energy desk. A gray Formica tablet of biblical proportion, the desk was forty-five feet long. It housed six traders* per side, twelve in all. The senior traders at Allied Power were veterans of the commodities circuit. Most of them had made their bones in big utilities or on the Mercantile Exchange in New York. Of the younger traders, two showed promise. One was a mathematics prodigy who had come up fresh from Caltech. The other was a kid named Gallagher from a Minnesota utility. The list complete, Andrews, the boss, passed it to Sami.

* See Notes on Trading, page 285.

The traders looked up at the mounted flat-screen TV with shifty eyes and quiet interest.

A wild bull was running amok in Kansas City. A train transporting cattle had overturned and one maverick had escaped unharmed, charging off into the urban landscape. The havoc wreaked thus far included a few broken rear-view mirrors, the dented hood of a Cadillac, three resultant fender benders, and a five-mile backup to the city-bound lanes of Route 70. A live broadcast from CNN showed the scene, an indignant brown bull taunting commuters as he lowered his head and wagged his short stumps of horns at them.

The traders snorted with contempt. The story said it all. The bull market had gone crazy and now apparently it had no fear for the bull was off in Kansas City, trampling on the hood of some hayseed's car. Andrews didn't laugh, though. He was hungry and thinking of yesterday's botched order.

—Sami, make sure I get double cream cheese this time, demanded Andrews.

It was midmorning on Allied Power's trading floor in Boston. 8:30 A.M. Brokers were already shouting down numbers on squawk boxes even though the New York Mercantile Exchange wouldn't open for another hour and a half.

Gallagher, whose broad forehead and round, cherubic face made him resemble an overgrown toddler, sat at his desk, sipping a carton of chocolate milk. Andrews looked at his newest acquisition and furrowed his brow. Traders drank coffee, black.

Natural gas futures had shot up forty cents overnight. Gallagher allowed himself a tight grin. Miller, the trader who sat across from him, said:

—You got your poker face on, Joe.

Gallagher said nothing. His smile was the smile of a simpleton.

Large, who was Gallagher's neighbor to his left, said:

—He's long as balls.

Andrews stood up and glared across the desk at his young protégé. As broad as Gallagher was, Andrews's powerful girth encompassed two of him. Andrews could have easily made the minimum weight requirement to wrestle sumo in Tokyo. Breakfast was on his mind, but when big money was being made it had a sweet smell of its own, one that trumped even food.

—How long are you, Joe?

—Long, he said.

—Shut it down before you give it all back.

—Natty's going to the moon, said Gallagher. —I'll sell when it gets to nine dollars.

—Wrong answer, said Andrews.

Since Gallagher had signed on, he'd had an impressive run and Andrews decided to take the young trader under his wing. He had only one doubt about the newcomer: how he'd take his first loss. In Andrews's mind trading was about two things, taking profits and enduring pain. Gallagher had not yet shown he could take the pain. Gallagher nodded at Andrews, signaling that he would exit the position. Then he sipped at his chocolate milk.

Andrews was at his core a family man. Taciturn, moral, occasionally sentimental after twelve beers, his desk was covered with beach and ski vacation photos of his three children and his wife, a striking brunette. An industrious Midwesterner, he was the first to arrive on the desk, last to leave. And while dedicated to his vocation, Andrews's passion lay with his religious beliefs: Chicago Bears football. His place of worship was his den, every Sunday sitting on the couch in front of his TV, baptizing his thirst with a new cold beer every commercial break. As for actual religion, Andrews believed that was a niche market reserved for women and children. When his Iowa-born Lutheran wife worried for his immortal soul, Andrews would respond that his status as a taxpayer absolved him from sin and any of the other apparent character flaws he might happen to possess.

Andrews and the other traders knew very little about Joe Gallagher save that he recently came up from their version of the minors. He seldom drank with them when he first started, and after one night when Gallagher had drunk too much, he never drank with them again. Andrews had certain insights into the nature of his understudy that the others lacked. He was walking by Gallagher's desk one day and saw a small piece of paper taped to his desktop. On it were cryptic words, words that no trader should tape to any desk:

Both the victor and the vanquished
Are but drops of dew,
But bolts of lightning:
Thus should we view the world.

Many of the other traders left Gallagher to himself. Being a superstitious lot, they suspected from his brooding nature that the residue of a recent misfortune clung to him like bad mojo. Andrews alone reached out to him.

—I don't know if you saw the memo, said Andrews. —We drink coffee here, not milk.

Gallagher nodded, remaining silent. Andrews patted down his cowlick of thick blond hair above his brow with the palm of his hand. It was a habit he had when perturbed.

After this the men got back to business, the business of taking other people's money. Hurricanes, weather, gas draws, nuke plants coming online, nukes coming offline, coal barges and rail transport disruptions, transmission lines that caused price congestion between the hubs, and then again with the weather. On top of all that, one had to throw crude oil insanity in the mix, the terrorists and psychopathic nuke-wielding leaders with a taste for shoving lit firecrackers in the ass of geopolitics. Predicting gas, oil, and electricity futures was an easy job when you happened to be right. It was also easy when you were wrong: You got fired.

Gallagher finished his chocolate milk and pulled up the commodity news service CQG, which also provided natural gas and crude oil trend charts. There was a record amount of gas in the ground. The economy was sagging because the Republicans were fighting wars that no one believed in. Record supply, waning demand.

It was there, while sitting at his desk, that Gallagher felt his third eye coming on. It was a thing he told no one about: Looking at the nat gas bar chart, he sometimes heard a music from the up ticks and down ticks, which arranged themselves like notes on a score. Gallagher gazed about the room and felt a truth that no one yet realized. The market was going to rally, a chocolate milk epiphany.

Still, he had to convince himself. The art of trading lay in good judgment and constant adjustment.

He looked at the candlestick charts: the monthly, weekly, and daily charts all lined up with bullish hammer patterns. As the price of gas ticked higher on the Intercontinental Exchange, an electronic trading platform known as "ICE," Joe had the feeling he imagined a general might have before a decisive victory. Tomorrow and the next day were irrelevant. The battle was now. Others were bleeding on the battlefield. His heavy cavalry and tank divisions rolled over them, massacring legions, driving them into the dirt.

Taste it, as his broker would say.

Take them to the woodshed.

Blood on the walls.

As gas rallied, his adversaries who had sold to him at much lower levels suffered as electronic dollars, their lifeblood, went pouring into Gallagher's trading book. He tried to wear his invincibility with an air of grim silence like he'd seen Andrews do. Andrews, always adept with football analogies, had a line about how to act when making money. He likened it to a trip to the end zone:

—Act like you've been there before.

—Here's the goat, said Miller, shaking his head.

—Sorry, said Sami, out of breath, holding a cardboard box with eleven white paper bags.

—Beatings, said Miller. —You being late every day isn't the way to get off breakfast detail.

—He's pledging for life, chuckled Large.

Sami walked around the desk passing out the breakfast sandwiches. As he handed them out, Sami would recite each order with an exasperated optimism.

—Miller: Double egg over easy, bacon and tomato on toasted bagel!

—Churchill: Bacon, ham, egg, and cheese on English muffin!

—Large: Two pancakes wrapped with cream cheese, bacon side!

—Hutchinson: Double sausage and potato three-egg omelet. Side order onion rings!

Gallagher, who was too cheap to order take-out, was eating his second peanut butter on a bagel, which he'd brought from home. Sami went down the rows reciting and handing out the orders, wondering the whole time why he bothered to get an MBA from Yale. This bullshit was the kind of attitudes that his Pakistani father had warned him about.

Sami gave his least favorite coworker, Andrews, his order last. Once this task was done Sami returned to his desk, and got back to work, thinking, defeat is only temporary.

Today it was not.

—Yo, Goat. What the hell? said Andrews. —I ordered double cream cheese on these. You blew it again.

Sami stood up and approached the angry veteran trader. Andrews held out the bag and without another word handed it over to Sami. As Sami made his way off the trading floor toward the elevators, he heard Andrews bellow:

—Pledging for life.

As Andrews lambasted him, Sami moved toward the door of the trading floor. Gallagher held out his hand and took the breakfast order from Sami.

—I'll go get it, said Gallagher, standing.

Sami put a hand on Gallagher's back.

—Thanks, Joe.

As Gallagher left the floor, Andrews shouted:

—Two goats are better than one.

When Gallagher returned with the two double cream cheese and bacon bagels, he noticed the absence of chatter. Leslie Moran had wafted in and taken the buzz of the trading floor to zero. She worked in legal and usually her presence signaled evil tidings like Sarbanes-Oxley regulations and time-consuming HR seminars on trading ethics. However, her beauty quieted the traders, although she did cause some like Dave Vern from Mississippi to scratch themselves and others to sniff the air for her scent. The traders tried to make her something of their own and secretly they called her Max Gen. This referred to "maximum generation," a phenomena that occurred on extremely hot summer days when all available power units on the grid had to run to cover demand. On this morning Max Gen was wearing a tight-fitting white blouse. A whisper went across the desk.

—Joe, said Miller. —You see Max Gen today? That shit is printing.

With the prospect of making a killing in the market, Gallagher was keeping to himself. As Max Gen breezed by, his head was the only one in the row that did not turn her way. He was thinking about covering his position. The markets were not always rational, and often moved violently. They were after all a product of the people who traded them.

Thinking about the violent, irrational nature of traders, Gallagher recalled that day seven years ago when he had just started in the biz, working in the pits of the MERC in New York. It was a cautionary memory, a visceral illustration of the emotional nature of markets and how sometimes the machinery that comprised the market could go insane.

Some Greenpeace activists had attempted to disrupt the oil market, to make a statement against fossil fuels and the damage they caused to the environment. Gallagher was just a runner at the time. The activists were mostly average-sized, bearded men. They had the wiry tough builds possessed by rock climbers and mountain bikers. The activists were not weaklings. They came in with their placards and protest signs and two had bullhorns and they were chanting slogans about oil companies and capitalism.

For a moment it seemed as if they were going to break up the trading that day on the exchange. But once the pit traders and brokers realized it was not some TV gag but an invading foreign body trying to disrupt their work, they reacted efficiently and violently, like a market that has decided to run or plummet and not stop until there were bodies lining the meat locker. The traders shoved the activists off the steps and hurled them into the center of the ring.

The red-faced, hypertension-afflicted traders kicked and punched anyone who tried climbing back out of the pit. Then the real devastation began. Traders began ripping their own computer screens and phone sets off the walls of the exchanges and began hurling them, along with garbage cans, full bottles of soda, coffee mugs, anything they could get their hands on, down onto the heads of the Greens. One activist was carried out on a stretcher with part of his skull showing.

Gallagher recalled the look in the pit that afternoon. Men's eyes were glazed over with something that was usually reserved only for special times when there was an extreme bull rally or a bear plummet. In the pits, everything was hyperreal. You were only alive in moments of pleasure or pain. Euphoria or terror.

Now, today, as the money poured into his trading book, Gallagher felt as if his survival depended on remaining calm. He took a deep breath. Thinking about the brutalized activists always reminded Gallagher of how not to act. Markets punish ignorance and feed on fear, he told himself.

Ten-thirty A.M. After option expiration the market quieted down. All the cash traders were in their midmorning lull and, along with the term traders, awaited "the nooner," or the midday weather report that took the newest satellite models out to a fifteen-day forecast.

The meteorologist, Bill Rector, had the most thankless job on the trading floor. When he was right, he didn't get paid. When he was wrong, large fat men who were losing millions of dollars wanted to destroy him. Today he had been wrong again about the upcoming blast of heat rolling across the Plains states, known as a "heat dome."

Meteorologists had their own lexicon of doomsday terminology, something that could penetrate even the thick skulls of nonscientists. In the summer it was the dreaded heat dome and in the winter it was the "polar pig." Yesterday in the weather meeting Rector had promised that the heat dome would dissipate as it moved east into a low-pressure system traveling north out of the Gulf of Mexico. But the low-pressure system had skated due west and pushed the heat dome even farther east.

Andrews had been hoping against hope that Rector's "heat dome" would get diverted by the system in the Gulf. Now, as gas and power prices skyrocketed, most of Andrews's traders, who had been somewhat short, were ready to unleash their fury on Rector. The clever, rail-thin meteorologist was no novice to the trading floor. For the nooner weather chat he sent down his new minion out of Nebraska, a well-meaning, gawky kid named Sykes who had a haircut that made him look Amish.

Sykes started his nooner with the backpedaling, relativist technique that the meteorologists used when they were wrong. It was probably similar to the modifications and excuses of misconstrued meaning that had been employed thousands of years ago by witch doctors and oracles. Only instead of a couple of chicken bones scattered across the floor, Sykes had the religion of science to legitimate his tale.

—Although the models indicate a short-term display of warmth across the eastern half of the U.S., we believe they are not taking into consideration a moderate system that should disrupt the current pattern and allow for a shot of milder weather than the models are calling for.

—Is the heat dome coming? asked Andrews. —The guys want to know. I want to know.

He popped a pork rind in his mouth and shot the weatherman a questioning look.

—Well, of course, the new models have dropped our confidence a bit from yesterday because the timing of the system in the Gulf has slowed down as well as taken a more westerly direction. . . .

—"Heat dome" my ass, cried Miller. —Y'all are PNL terrorists.

Like every trader, Miller lived and died by his PNL, profit and loss.

—Where is Rector? He told us this system was going to ice the fucking heat. Now the only trader on this desk making money is the guy who's been selling you guys down the river, said Andrews, pointing over to Gallagher.

—Mr. Rector is taking an early lunch.

Andrews was speechless. A murmur went up among the traders. They despised cowardice. Rector was expected to come down and take his medicine.

Like an industrial crane slowly rising to its full height, Andrews stood up. Something was going to happen.

—Turn around, he told Sykes, pointing at the far wall.

Sykes did so, believing he was being told to look at some weather pattern on the mounted plasma TV.

Andrews heaved his huge leg forward and kicked Sykes square in the ass with a scuffed brown shoe.

—Deliver that message to Rector, said Andrews. The older traders laughed and the more politically correct younger guys just stared ahead.

Without looking back Sykes darted from the trading floor.

That afternoon the sky was clear and the sun came through the windows of Allied Power's twenty-story building, casting the corner office on the tenth floor in a soft, fuzzy light. Spiros Nikakis, managing director, the head of power trading, was still sweating from his midmorning run. He was a married man of fine tastes, ranging from wine tours in Napa to office closet gropings with slim-hipped secretaries of Indian and Latvian descent. He ate smoked turkey on plain pumpernickel for lunch and his breakfast consisted of one hard-boiled egg, no salt, and forty chin-ups on the crossbar in his office. For the board and the CEO, he reserved his Savile Row Saddam Hussein gray pinstripes and a slightly effeminate tone of voice, which differed from his usual foreman's growl. He looked at the computer screen and clicked "send" on his e-mail that called for a floor-wide meeting of all traders.

Any day with a meeting was a bad day. At best the meetings were adept performances where Spiros tried to keep his gruff audience awake by balancing the delivery of boring addendums and to-dos with witticisms and racy anecdotes. At their worst the meetings brought veiled threats and bad news: potential corporate buyouts, the latest firings, compliance seminars, or sensitivity training. Today Spiros announced that he was heading up the corporate ladder. A replacement had already been chosen.

—There's been a lot of talk. I might add that this talk has all been positive, said Spiros. —As you all know, Allied is a growing company. Growing in many ways. We're expanding our trading now to NOx and SOx emissions and weather derivatives. Our profits in our staple energy commodities are strong. The trading group has been key to utilities' success.

Traders were glancing around the table at one another. When Spiros came out with abstract statements followed by a buttering-up job, it meant something big was going to be announced.

—Our next step is to grow our leadership. That is why we're bringing an industry leader to head up the new expanded trading desk, said Spiros.

—Who is it? someone called out.

—It's Randall Jennings. Former head trader of Dynesty and Travista.

Andrews put his half-eaten stale cookie back on the plastic dessert tray that was at the center of the conference table. A few groans arose from a group of traders out of Spiros's direct line of vision.

—No matter what you've heard of him, and I'm sure you've all heard some good and some not so good things about him, rest assured that after a lengthy executive search, he was deemed the trader best suited for this job. In short, I think you're all in good hands.

More and louder groans came from those hidden in the periphery. All of the senior traders excepts for Andrews had sounded off. Andrews had to remain silent, composed. He was the one being replaced. Andrews could feel the eyes of the room upon him. Part of the job description was bearing defeat gracefully.

—Now, now, let's keep an open mind, said Spiros, spreading his arms wide. —It's done.

IN THE CARDS

That night none of Gallagher's friends were drinking at the Colony Inn. Gallagher sat down at the bar, ordered a beer, and began reading the book he'd been carrying around the past few days, Richard Rhodes's *The Making of the Atom Bomb*. Many patrons at the Colony Inn did not understand reading in a bar. It seemed to defeat the purpose both ways. To them it was like smoking while jogging, though none of them were joggers. The patrons kept to themselves, which was why Gallagher thought of it as a good place to read. It was a row house bar and rooms upstairs could be rented hourly, so it was technically an "inn." The only downside was that the interior remained gloomy despite the Christmas lights that were lit up year-round.

After reading a few chapters on the life of nuclear physicist Enrico Fermi, and putting away more than a few beers, Gallagher left the inn and drove home to Chucktown.

Everything Gallagher did, he reasoned, was to make his wife happy. Celina was an artist. She didn't want to live out in the suburbs and languish in a country club world. Gallagher was one of the few traders who lived with his wife near the city. His two-family townhome was located in Charlestown.

The alleyway before Gallagher's house was called Krakow Lane. During the day it echoed with laughter, the bouncing of soccer balls, and the sounds of children playing games. At night it was a stark and quiet street, the burnt-out lightbulbs of the streetlamps never having been replaced.

That evening it was too hot to remain inside a house with no air-conditioning. On Krakow Lane three men were sitting on the front stoop of a row house, drinking beer. Their six-packs sat below them on the sidewalk. Gallagher could not help himself, he was still thirsty and he wondered if the beer was cold.

Gallagher approached the three men, swaggering and rubbing the back of his head with his palm, trying not to seem like the ultimate mooch. One of them, a teacher at Carver High who lived two doors down from Galla-gher, recognized him. The teacher had small, myopic eyes that seemed even smaller behind the thick lenses of his tortoiseshell glasses.

—Have a beer, he said, holding one out. —It's Joe, right?

Gallagher nodded as he drank. Celina was out with some of her friends. Gallagher figured he had time for one or two pops.

The teacher introduced himself as Perkins. The other two men were Fred and Billy Helms, middle-aged brothers who lived together and worked for the city. Gallagher beamed at them drunkenly after he was introduced. They were both going bald, wore tie-dyed T-shirts, and their arms were covered in faded green-ink tattoos. The older one, Fred, wore an impressive, well-groomed, Fu Manchu–style mustache. In Gallagher's mind they looked like fried roadies for some Southern rock band like Lynyrd Skynyrd or Molly Hatchet.

The Helms brothers had seen Gallagher around the neighborhood. His oafish size made him hard to miss. They had both noticed Gallagher's wife and had shared the same thought: What was a beauty like that doing with someone who looked and acted like Gallagher?

—Have a seat, said Fred Helms.

He produced a bent blue fold-out chair from out of nowhere. It was his house that they were drinking in front of.

Celina Gallagher was dreaming of the ocean, Hiroshige's tumultuous blue-green waves. She often dreamt of what she had painted during the day. She had been deep into Japanese woodcuts for the past two months trying to perfect the aqueous curves of an angry sea, but the wood would not yield. She couldn't translate the grace of the waves from the carving knife to the wood block. Occasionally, Joe sat silently in her studio and watched her work, scratching away at the wood. His presence did not bother her, but it did not improve her art.

She opened her eyes. It was Joe calling up from the kitchen.

—Where are the cards, baby? Where did I leave the cards?

Celina could tell he was drunk. She turned over in bed and stared at the ceiling. Upon waking, the familiar late-night feeling was there. It felt at first like a jolt of panic—as if time was running out. Then this panic became like a weight on her chest. It bore down into her and a heaviness coursed through her whole being, as if her blood was made of liquified lead. She was still an unknown artist. She was living in Boston. And she'd just turned thirty.

—I found them, she heard him call out as she forced herself to get back to sleep.

It was hours later. Celina felt her heart beating. Someone was downstairs in the house. She thought it must be Joe, but a chair squeaked on the dining room floor and she heard a voice, not her husband's. Celina went to the bedroom door and listened. The voices got louder and there were more of them. She tried to think where her cell phone was so she could call the police and then thought that she must get to the roof, to escape.

—We can stop playing if you're not paying attention, exclaimed a voice.

—You're not listening, yelled another voice. It was Joe. He was slurring and unable to contain his joy.

—Enrico Fermi did it, he was saying. —Enrico Fermi did what I'm talking about. He made the whole thing come together. The radioactive U238 jammed into the tube. You got to listen to understand.

Celina heard the shuffling of a deck and the *thwap!* of cards hitting the table as they were being dealt. She crept to the stairwell and peeked over the banister, getting a limited view of the front end of the dining room. She could see Joe in his work clothes with his back to her. They were drinking and playing cards. There was a bottle of champagne on the table. One of her Tiffany vases was also on the table. It was being used as an ashtray. She looked at her watch. It was two in the morning.

—Where's the pisser? If you don't mind, asked a bald man with a mustache that drooped down the sides of his face. He stood up and placed his cards upon the table. Some moments later she heard the sound of the toilet flushing.

Celina stared down the dark hallway that led to her bedroom. She was thinking she should creep silently back to her door. If Joe heard her, he would want her to come down. Instead, she stood there, listening.

There was a black-and-white photograph of a Greek fishing village on the wall. Celina's friend who took the picture was an architect who worked in Athens. Celina felt a pang of jealousy as she looked at the photo.

—I'm a scientist. A scientist of cards, she heard Gallagher say. He was guzzling whiskey from a wineglass. Gallagher laid down his hand and then pulled the pile of poker chips toward him with one swoop of his forearm.

—Shit, chuckled another, slimmer bald man. —Joe actually won a round. He must be cheating.

—Get the cotton out of your ears, boomed Gallagher. —Enrico Fermi.

—I've heard enough about him, said the skinny one.

—Ever heard of Hiroshima? fired back Gallagher. —That's what I'm talking about!

Celina heard everything. She knew what was going on. Gallagher would read a book and if he admired it would somehow work that book into all aspects of his everyday life. Right now he was reading that book about the atom bomb.

A beer bottle clinked as it was set upon the table.

She locked the door to her bedroom. Her husband would be sleeping on the couch, alive or dead. But that was him, her husband, Joe Gallagher, she thought, a soul whose acts of idiocy were larger than life. He was a doomed Romantic construct. A fool.

She pulled up the covers and went back to bed.

Downstairs she could hear the men laughing.

MILT THE BROKER

Every day after the close, traders and brokers would emerge from the New York Mercantile Exchange like a herd of water buffalo, weary, staggering, and driven by thirst. The Admiral's Cup was the bar where the traders went to guzzle cheap beer and eat salted peanuts out of a huge, oaken keg that sat in the corner. Nut shells littered the floor. Conversations at the Cup tended to be loud, much louder than normal bar chatter. This was because many of the traders were hard of hearing from years of shouting in the pits. Partial deafness was not uncommon from constant exposure to extreme decibel levels that occurred daily in the rallying and falling markets. One man named Milt Harkrader spoke louder than anyone at the bar, but not because he was deaf. Milt wore a cowboy hat and steel-toed wingtips. The hat was for after work, his unwinding hat, the essence of his tobacco-chewing Texas persona. The steel-toed wingtips were for work. If things got ugly around market open or close, the shoes were good for staking out his place in the trading pit. Shin wreckers, he called them.

Milt, like many other ten-gallon-hat-toting brokers in Manhattan, heralded from New Jersey. He needed the hat more than most because his hairline now began behind his ears. Milt had always been a loudmouth. Sometime after his divorce he had to have his jaw wired shut, the outcome of a late-night brawl that had occurred at a 7-Eleven in Rahway. This helped

Milt develop a new respect for strangers but didn't stop him from talking so loud in bars, especially around his coworkers and other people he suspected wouldn't take the time to kick his ass.

That Friday Milt Harkrader stood in the Admiral's Cup, exhausted and smelling like green onions. He was talking to two screen clerks and pointing at a fat trader who was leaning against the bar.

—You know who should get a big bonus this year? Milt told the men. —That guy's belt, because that thing is fucking *working*.

The younger of the two screen clerks chuckled. The older one said in a deadpan tone:

—Harkrader loves being an asshole.

By nine o'clock that night Milt was alone in the corner by the keg of peanuts, nursing a beer. He was glad when his screen clerks had finally left the bar. He was getting tired of entertaining them. Now alone, left to his own thoughts, the sinking feeling in Milt's guts became more pronounced. The past week's botched orders flashed through his mind, a run of bad luck, a five-day curse. He was on the verge of losing some of his better clients. He rolled the beer bottle between his hands, as if summoning a genie from a magic lamp. But nothing came out except for more beer.

On Sunday Milt found himself in Atlantic City, standing by a craps table at the Sands. He was thinking how he just needed one break. He needed the clouds to part, so he could be allowed to grasp onto that one ray of sunshine, that one beam of hope.

As Milt shook the dice, he felt the hard metal in his shoes against the top of his big toe. Besides the cowboy hat, his steel-toed wingtips were the last vestige of glory days machismo that Milt still allowed himself.

The croupier gave Milt a smarmy grin beneath a wispy, tan mustache.

—Slapnuts, said Milt as he rolled the dice.

Seven. He crapped out. Again. He swore he saw the dealer sneer.

—Hey chicken shit, yelled Milt. In a sudden motion he spread his arms and spilled the drink of the gambler standing next to him.

—Yo, buddy, said a man in a purple Baltimore Ravens sweatshirt.

—Taste it, slapnuts, said Milt, trying to provoke the man. —Nice fucking sweatshirt.

The man backed away and Milt could see the security guards in their cheap suits already closing in.

For a gambling mecca, Atlantic City had pathetic strip clubs, something to do with the zoning. No beaver shots and the dancers had to have green cards. The city elders wanted AC to be a family town. They imagined beaches, boardwalks, cotton candy, and roller skaters. Stumbling out of the Sands with a few remaining twenties in his wallet, Milt made his way across the gray, trash-strewn streets of AC to the only decent go-go bar in town, Club Chubby.

Last time Milt came to Club Chubby he had befriended a six-foot-tall dancer. He had just come from a title bout featuring two out-of-shape heavyweight fighters. They had spoken briefly at the bar before she went on for her set. She had an interest in prizefighting and, as it turned out, took kickboxing lessons.

On the way in a young bouncer gave Milt a disapproving look. Milt wondered if he was the one who'd thrown him out on his previous visit.

Club Chubby was a dark parlor shot through with the purple gloom of halogen lights. Rows of fake bookbindings lined the walls to make it look classy like a study from the eighteenth century. As soon as Milt took a seat, a server wearing a tight bodice top and fishnet stockings came over and took his order.

—Is Zorra around? Milt asked.

—Huh?

—Is Zorra around?

—No one around named Zorra.

—Six-foot-tall blonde? Takes kickboxing?

—You mean Nora, she said.

—Nora. Is she here tonight?

—She went to Georgia. Her daughter's in the National Cheerleading Finals.

Milt grunted his disapproval and then got up and left.

Making his way back to the bus station through the empty streets Milt came upon a newly planted tree, about as wide around as a large grapefruit. He hugged the base and pulled up with all his might. The moist earth gave. He heaved again. Slaveship rower. Enraged Cyclops. The tree came up with seeming ease. He carried it over his shoulder walking through desolate parking lots.

As he approached the bus station, he hurled the tree into the street. It landed roots first on the pavement, shedding dirt, and stood upright for one moment before falling on its side. Milt had come from New York to AC on the train, business class, with money to spare. Now two thousand dollars poorer, Milt wallowed in a fit of gambler's self-loathing. His punishment: a return home by bus.

The Atlantic City Bus Terminal at 3:00 A.M. was a graveyard of sleeping drunks and penniless gamblers. The meandering glass-eyed bums were the only ones with a hint of dignity.

Passed out on a bench was a trader who Milt often saw at AC, ape-man, Ryan Hogan. Sitting beside him was some sustenance: a can of root beer, a bag of cheese curls, and a pack of beef jerky. Hogan had been trying to concoct some kind of cheese curl beef jerky sandwich when he keeled over.

Milt went over and finished off his cheese curls. Parched, Milt took a sip of the root beer. Only the root beer didn't go down so well, because it wasn't root beer.

—Chew spittle, gagged Milt.

As the bus pulled out of the station Milt felt a fever coming on. His forehead beaded up with tiny droplets of perspiration. The back of the bus where Milt and Hogan were sitting reeked of exhaust, BO, and the antiseptic from the latrine.

—Jesus, said Hogan, still groggy. —What a fucking night.

—Get smoked?

—No, not at the tables. I got shook down at the hospital.

Hogan's tale was sordid after-hours nastiness. Milt's eyes flickered with interest as the pit trader relayed the story of a potbellied whore. She had driven Hogan to a cheap motel in her broken-down Dodge Dart with imitation white tiger-skin seat covers, sharing a bottle of gin and telling Hogan the story of how she had evaded a murder/rape attempt by a Chinese serial killer. An hour later, midcoital transaction, in a motel with a vibrating bed, the whore received a call on her cell phone. It was an emergency that involved her son being rushed to the hospital for a late-night asthma attack. While waiting for her out in the parking lot, still ready for her to make fully good on services rendered, Hogan got approached by a pock-faced man with skinny arms and a shamrock tattoo on his neck. The man announced himself as the whore's husband. He didn't pull a knife or a gun. He just stared down the bigger man, made his intentions known, and relieved Hogan of his wallet. The disappointed trader leaned back in his seat.

—I guess I had to hand it over, he said.

—The guy had the moral high ground. Pimp or husband, explained Milt.

—Still, six eighty in cash, said Hogan.

—I like the girl's style, responded Milt. —A *Chinese* serial killer.

—Guy left two twenties in my wallet and said "For the bus."

—Taste it, said Milt.

Three hours later, at six o'clock Monday morning, Milt's alarm clock went off. At first he didn't respond. Then he said in a calm voice, addressing the alarm clock and the empty room:

—Fuck you.

Milt drifted off to sleep for some period of time, dreaming of two sick lions being stalked in the empty stands of a football stadium by a ferocious and powerful-looking green-eyed tiger. When he finally awoke he vaguely remembered the dream and had an uneasy feeling in his belly. Milt then got out of bed and took a long shower. Stepping out of the shower, he looked in the mirror at the saggy jowls beneath his chin. He put his hands around each side of his rotund belly. Monday, he thought, a school day. Before getting on the PATH train to the city, Milt decided that he couldn't make it through the day unless he had a beer in him. Something to ease the cotton-mouth and pain behind his eyes and general ache of alcoholic malaise that creaked throughout his worn body. At the station package store Milt bought a Budweiser tallboy, a distinctly American beer to start the workweek off on the right foot. He boarded the 8:15 train with the beer wrapped in a paper bag. During the commute Milt sipped away at his breakfast and watched the underground tunnel pass by him in shafts of flickering light and darkness. When the train came to the end of the line, Milt let out a soft belch and, feeling somewhat better, crushed the tallboy and placed it under his seat.

Milt was sweating by the time he got off the elevator at the forty-ninth floor of One World Financial Center. He made a halfhearted hustle through the glass doors of NYMB. He hadn't even made it down the row to his desk on the floor when his boss, Dartmouth Collins, known as the Commander, waved him over to the corner office. The offense of being late was not in the Commander's wheelhouse. However, chronic lateness, of which Milt was guilty, certainly might hit the radar. Milt walked into the office. The Commander sat behind his desk and shot the cuffs of his forest green Fendi suit. The six-foot-three, well-pressed Commander stood in stark contrast to the booze-reeking, bald, run-down Milt who shambled into the corner office looking like someone who'd recently come down with a bad case of the flu. The Commander's tanned, tennis-player good looks, fine scent of expensive cologne, and coiffed mane of ash blond hair were all punctuated by a crescent-shaped scar that ran from below the Commander's earlobe to just above his right eyelid, allowing him to emanate a hint of worldly menace. Milt, however, was not intimidated, assuming the scar was obtained while shucking lobster or other shellfish at a New England clambake.

—Have a seat, Milt, said the Commander, not offering a handshake.

Milt slumped into the chair and, smelling his own breath, realized he needed a breath mint.

—Who do you cover at Allied Power? asked the Commander, nodding his head pleasantly. Milt immediately knew that he wasn't in trouble for chronic lateness, and relaxed, taking a cavalier tone, relishing the experience of being in the corner office and not being braced for underperformance or some HR infraction.

—The young buck over there. Kid's making waves. Name's Joe Gallagher. One of my best clients.

—Right, that's his name. You've done well by him. Your numbers are back up where they belong, stated the Commander, flipping a paper clip adroitly between his fingers.

—I've brought him along, said Milt, trying to take a little credit. —Got a very solid relationship.

The Commander put down the paper clip.

—There's some big news today. If you'd come in on time you would have heard it.

Milt nodded his head, acknowledging the jibe.

—Randall Jennings is back in play. Allied Power hired him on Friday.

—Fascinating, said Milt.

—That's right, said the Commander. —Your Gallagher trades the Texas region.

—Yes. ERCOT, corrected Milt, using the technical term for the region.

—Jennings is going to be able to swing a big stick now with Allied Power behind him and he loves ERCOT; little, illiquid hub he can bash around. Gallagher will be his boy. Randall will run it and squeeze it. Lots of commission for you, Milt: a real chance for you to shine if the kid makes you his top broker.

—I'm on it. I'm on a plane to Beantown this week to wine and dine the kid.

The Commander shook his head.

—I don't think so, Milt. Gallagher is a young guy, right? Tell you what. You fly him down here. Show him a good time in the city. Make him your buddy. And, Milt, spare no expense.

Milt coughed and then winced like he had to use the facilities.

—And Milt, you're getting in with the kid to eventually get in with Jennings. You know that, right? He's the big fish.

—I got one problem, said Milt.

The Commander was already turning around to read the *Journal*. He didn't want to hear it. When the excuse came, it was more pathetic than the Commander expected.

—It has to be next week, though, stumbled Milt. —I forgot. I got some personal days this week. I'm going to Florida to see my son while he's on spring break for school.

The Commander opened up the *Journal*.

—Next week then, but book it with Gallagher today, said the Commander in a resigned, tired voice, contemplating if he should take a sad sack like Milt off the account.

MILT IN FLORIDA

A seagull was perched on the railing outside the bar of the Don CeSar, a famous pink Spanish stucco hotel. It peered in through the bay window, its orange eyes unblinking, as if looking for someone. After some time the bird hopped from the railing onto one of the empty tables on the balcony. The bird stood there for a moment and then, seeming satisfied, walked in a circle.

Milt tilted his silver-gray Stetson back off his forehead. The seagull, strutting on the balcony table, let out a contemptuous squawk. Milt watched the bird and threw a handful of bar cashews in his mouth. Sounds like he's begging for money, thought Milt. The bartender stood with his back turned to Milt, fiddling with a bottle. Milt frowned at the man's cheap imitation snakeskin belt.

—That shit can't be sanitary, chimed Milt. The bartender turned around. His face was weather-beaten and tanned except where the rolls of fat met on his neck, leaving two white strings of flesh untouched by the Florida sun. The bartender had made a sloppy piña colada, turned his back on Milt, and hadn't refreshed the bowl of cashews.

—Can I get you another drink, sir? asked the bartender.

—You guys always let the birds shit on those outside tables? Because if that's the case, I don't know if I'm coming in here anymore. I mean maybe this glass I'm drinking from was crapped in just the other day. I could catch a serious disease. Or worse.

—The gulls are a part of the ecosystem down here, sir. And I assure you we wash everything down twice at the end of the night.

Milt silently contemplated the bartender's answer, gauging it for any smart-ass remarks or taunts. Milt nodded his head slightly. The bartender had made an attempt at manners. Still, Milt decided he didn't like anyone who used the word "ecosystem."

—How about another piña colada with a decent amount of rum in it? And try not to fill it right to the top. It spills and I hate that coconut sugary shit all over my hands.

Milt looked through the bay window. White crests of waves disappeared into the black surf, only to rise again. The fronds of the palm trees whipped about in the wind like frantic tails. The sky seemed darker than usual, crowned with looming clouds. Milt looked back at the table on the balcony. The seagull was gone.

Milt's ex-wife, Debby, was ten minutes late. She refused to let Milt take her to dinner in the main dining room. She insisted instead that they meet in the bar. After all, in her reasoning, they had first met in a bar and she could afford to split the bill there. She didn't want to give Milt any ideas that she was fishing or hard up for cash.

Debby wore her one nice work suit, a chocolate brown Ralph Lauren, matched with a pair of tweed shoes. It was her lucky suit. She sat next to Milt at the bar. She had intended to shake Milt's hand as a gesture of professionalism and friendship but Milt slid a drink in front of her.

—Drink this, he said. —I've been here two hours schooling our boy here on how to make a piña colada. He finally got one right.

Debby could already feel his hands in his words. They slithered over her like they were groping her. Milt had that effect, she thought; he could feel you up by merely offering you a cocktail.

—Nice to see you, too, Milt, she said.

—Sell any condos today? asked Milt.

—Work sucks, baby. Can we talk about Aaron?

Milt raised his own glass.

—To the boy then.

Debby hesitated and then picked up the drink.

—Cheers, she said. —To *our* boy.

Milt tried to flag the bartender down for some appetizers. He'd seen some coconut shrimp and raw blue point oysters on the menu.

—Milt, we'll eat after.

—Like last time, he said, and put his hand on her thigh.

Debby shook off his hand and let out an exasperated sigh. She pulled out some paperwork—an application, a brochure, and some information leaflets. Then she handed them to Milt, inundating him with paper.

—These are for you. This is Aaron's new school. It's expensive. Twenty-five K a year.

—Whoa! You're not dropping this shit on me now. On my one weekend to visit the kid.

—You ask him tomorrow. The public junior high school down here is bad. It's not Newark or Detroit but it's bad. And, well, Aaron's not adjusting.

Milt tugged at his belt buckle.

—It's because his stepdad is a redneck, racist cop. Ignorant fuckhead.

Debby could feel the anger coming off Milt like a red steam. She wanted to defend her husband, Curt Long, a state trooper, a decent man with none of Milt's vices, but she needed Milt. She needed his money. She touched the back of Milt's hand. He calmed instantly.

—What do you want me to say, Milt?

—What's wrong? asked Milt. —Is he failing out? Or is he getting his ass beat?

Milt knew the answer. He felt himself shrinking in his stool until he was three inches tall. His son, his skinny, bright, funny, sarcastic kid catching beatdowns from bigger, stronger, meaner kids.

Debby said something too soft for Milt to hear. All the alcohol in his system was either going to make him very brave and great or he was going to weep like a baby. He put his fist into his hand.

—I'll fucking kill all those motherfuckers, screamed Milt at the top of his lungs.

—Hey! shouted the bartender from the end of the bar, hunched over a martini shaker. Two or three other patrons stared up from their drinks.

—My wife's cancer has been misdiagnosed. She's going to die, said Milt loudly. —I'm sorry about the F bomb.

A few people mumbled "sorry" back to Milt and Debby. They kept staring for a moment, out of morbid curiosity, wondering if Debby was the woman marked for death.

Milt refocused on the task at hand. He leafed through the brochure: St. Paul's Episcopal High School. There were pictures of students in white lab coats and safety goggles holding beakers above a Bunsen burner, an artsy shot of a modern library that looked like a spaceship, a photo of male students dancing in tights, a nice sports panorama featuring a football field, track, and eight tennis courts. The last picture was the kicker. They had a planetarium.

—A planetarium, said Milt, stunned. —How about that?

—Milt, baby, Debby said, touching his hand again. —Aaron needs this.

—I'd like to go and kill just one, just one of those kids that are picking on my boy, said Milt, putting down the brochure. —But your boyfriend would probably arrest me.

—You know, Milty. You're his daddy, said Debby, ignoring the comment about her husband. —Aaron knows that.

Milt grabbed her hand and picked it up. He kissed her knuckle.

—I used to be your daddy.

Debby pulled her hand down, still clutching Milt's. It was waist level, the handshake she'd been looking for on greeting him.

—Can you do it, Milt? Can you promise this?

Milt wasn't going to make the mother of his child beg, although he was trying to find a way quickly before the interview ended to somehow interest her in a drink, a conversation, a walk on the beach.

—Done, he said. —It's already paid.

Debby picked up the brochure and sundry papers and stuffed them in her bag. She got up from the stool and stood stiffly in front of Milt.

—You were a cheat, Milt. But you're a good father. I got to give you credit for that.

She felt if she were honest and upright, she could inspire some honor in the man.

—I was a cheat. Now I'm lonely and middle-aged. Won't you come for a walk on the beach with me? It'll be like the boardwalk in Wildwood. Only nicer.

Debby fixed her stiff peroxide blond hair with one hand.

—No, Milty. That is not going to happen, she said.

Milt lifted his drink. For a moment he considered humility, saying something witty and self-deprecating, that his ex-wife might appreciate his maturity, be proud that she had given birth to his child. But he imagined her state trooper husband with his long, narrow face and blank expression, the dead, gray, close-set eyes that displayed a vacancy somewhere beyond stupid, and he chose instead to please himself.

—Give my best to Robo Cop. He carries a gun but he can't pay the bills. All cock and no balls, said Milt, putting his drink to his lips and already eyeing a heavyset fifty-year-old redhead who had just rolled into the bar.

At eleven o'clock the next day Aaron requested that Milt take him to his favorite lunch joint, Cawley's Cove. It was a hamburger shack right on the beach just a five-minute stroll from the Don CeSar. Milt and Aaron sat down on one of the wood picnic-style tables complete with rust-colored chipped paint. It was a dive compared to the other faux French Riviera cafes of St. Pete Beach with their wrought-iron chairs, cream-colored embroidered napkins, and little white fences keeping out the sand from their patios. No, his boy had chosen the one beach shack that most resembled the places where he'd spent summers eating zeppole with Milt on the Jersey Shore.

—Dad, you look like a total tourist.

—You don't like my shirt? Tommy Bahama is the thing back home.

—I'm talking about your cheesy flip-up sunglasses. And your nose is all white. You got to rub in the sunblock more.

—I need my nose, said Milt. —I can be uncool for a day. Skin cancer lasts a lifetime.

Aaron slurped at his Coke and nodded. Milt figured Aaron's stepdad didn't have many good one-liners. Milt hoped he'd come up with at least two or three more keepers for his son to repeat ad nauseam to Debby and Trooper Long. Milt bit into his cheeseburger. He was in the middle of chewing his way through an aggressive-sized bite when he saw her, the redhead from last night, walking toward him and his son. In the light of day her legs were twice as large as he remembered and pocked with cellulite that moved on its own.

—Hi Milt, she called, waving.

He raised his hand and waved it like a drowning man, a salute of the bewildered. He choked down his burger and took a sip of Coke while trying to remember her name.

—Heya, Kathy.

—You guys just having some burgers? This place is my favorite. I've eaten lunch here each day.

Her eyes were bright blue and seemed a touch mournful shrouded in the shade of her wide-brimmed straw hat. Her hair fell to her shoulders. It was an iridescent scarlet with purple highlights when the sun caught it at a certain angle. Milt introduced his son and Kathy leaned forward and shook his hand.

—I'm taking my son up to Epcot today, explained Milt. —We got a little bit of a ride ahead of us.

—Such a beautiful day. Too bad you have to spend it in a car.

Milt nodded in agreement, but said nothing, his mouth full again. Kathy stood there for a moment stroking a hand over a freckled shoulder, as if caressing a sunburn. When Kathy looked toward Cawley's menu board, Milt made a hand gesture for his son to finish his hot dog.

Before she could tell Milt that she was staying for another three days, he and his son were already by the trash can, disposing of their waste. Milt made a big deal of shooing away the hornets and did not turn to face her.

Milt and his son made their way up the beach back toward the hotel. They walked for some time in silence. The echo of the surf rumbled across the glinting white sand.

—I didn't know we were going to Epcot today, Dad.

Caught in an improvised lie, Milt made the best of it.

—It's a haul. But I thought you always wanted to go there.

—Oh, man, said Aaron. —You bet. Curt says Epcot is for losers. No way he'd ever pay for gas money from St. Pete.

—Losers worry about gas money. We're going to fucking Epcot, said Milt, secretly reveling in the fact that he'd delivered yet another classic one-liner that was sure to be repeated.

He put out his hand and his son high-fived him. Then Aaron took two bounding leaps over the hot sand. His skinny legs moved with an athleticism that Milt had not formerly seen in his son. Aaron plopped down in front of Milt and threw a light jab at his belly. Milt deflected it with a hairy forearm. But the kid has no jab, thought Milt sadly.

—Who was that lady, Dad? Did you meet her at the hotel?

—She's my maid, said Milt. —This must be her day off.

Milt bought his son a beer in Germany but some greasy-haired kid fresh out of his teens in his German Epcot Staff alpiners hat appeared at their table and confiscated Aaron's mug. The manager of the tavern, a middle-aged man in khaki pants and white oxford shirt with the Epcot logo, came over a moment later and told Milt that if he tried it again he'd be asked to leave the park. Father and son sat at the faux Bavarian bar table, eating their brats.

—The world's gone pussy, said Milt.

—Dad, I'm not twenty-one. It's illegal. What did you expect?

—This is over your head. This is all about insurance companies and legal torts and shit. You'll see when you get older. But don't worry, I'll buy you a beer in China. Nobody knows this, but the Chinese make good beer. It isn't heavy like this shit.

—Dad, they'll kick us out.

—I'd like to see them try, said Milt.

—This is Epcot, said Aaron. —I bet they have photo imaging with face recognition technology. Besides, Dad, at the very least they radioed your description ahead to the other stations. With that shirt and your cowboy hat it's not like you are low profile.

Milt flicked his son's left ear with a snapping middle finger.

—What's wrong with you? I'm trying to buy you a beer, huh?

Milt took a sip from his foamy mug.

—I got to figure out how to pay for that school. Yah. That St. Paul's. You going to make it worth my while?

—I'd like to go there if you and Mom can afford it, said his son.

—Just do good when you get there. And remember me when you're a lawyer. I'm going to need someone to look after me in my twilight years.

Milt bit into his bratwurst. Some of the juices squirted out onto his shirt and some ran down his chin. He wiped his face with the back of his hand.

—You know that wrinkle you have on your forehead, Dad, said Aaron.

Milt munched and with his thumb rubbed the single deep, straight crevasse above his brow. It looked like someone had attempted to sharpen their ax on Milt's skull.

—My friend, Zach, saw a picture of you and he said your wrinkle looked exactly like one that Pablo Picasso had. He thought you looked intense and wondered if you were an artist or something.

Milt washed down his brat with some more beer. After two gulps, he pointed at his son with a thick finger and said:

—Don't you butter my ass with Pablo Picasso. I don't want no con jobs.

If I send you to this school, you're going to go to college and get a real job: doctor, lawyer, banker. You flake out on me and I'll beat your ass worse than those kids at Tampa Junior High.

Milt put his hatbox with the Stetson in the overhead bin. He then plunked down in the aisle seat and massaged his temples. Someday he'd retire here in sunny Florida and be near the kid and the palm trees and the white sandy beaches. Milt decided that if he had the money, he was going to live at the Don CeSar. It was a rococo pink Spanish castle; a Vegas-inspired atrocity. Milt liked the idea of living in the four-star pink hotel. It suited a man who wore a silver-gray cowboy hat and had an affinity for baggy Hawaiian shirts. Those poor shits in New York City who choked through life with the gray smoke in their eyes, barraged with scampering rats, insolent pigeons, maniac cabdrivers, the screech of trains, the blaring of sirens, the ugly crush of humanity rubbing and pushing and fighting one another as the roaches thrived and sat perched on the back of your chair, mocking you, as you ate dinner in an expensive four-star restaurant. Fools, thought Milt. Then imagining a single palm tree, he was overcome with happiness and shut his eyes.

Ten minutes or so after takeoff, Milt opened his eyes. Without hesitating, Milt pushed the flight attendant call button. She appeared almost immediately, a tired-looking thirty-something brunette with pretty green eyes that were offset by a prematurely wrinkled mouth. Probably a smoker, thought Milt.

—May I help you? she asked.

—I'd like a Jack and Coke and also a pen and paper, if you have it.

She returned quicker than expected and Milt overtipped her. He thought for a few moments more about the Hunt Brothers. In 1979 they had effectively cornered the silver market. The economy had been ripe for a silver boom. Oil prices had been high, the dollar had been devalued due to the recession. The Hunts had speculated they could take silver up to forty dollars. They then went out and bought up all the physical silver they could get their hands on: bullion stored in banks; mining operations in Mexico, Peru, New Zealand, and Kazakhstan; as well as coins, currency, whatever. Once they commanded a big presence in the market share of the world's physical silver, they began to push the paper.

It wasn't long before all the shorts were clamoring to cover and the

Hunts pushed the futures up in their faces, ruining many speculators and sticking it to the investment banks whose traders had sold prematurely.

It had almost worked, but for the age-old maxim: Don't piss off the wrong people. The Hunts had effectively cornered the market but they'd taken the price action too far. The scheme unraveled. The predators became the patsy. First, the Hunts ran into oil tycoon Armand Hammer, who brought all his big forces to play in shorting silver. Second, the Hunts became targets of the brokerage and trading firms who were getting killed on margin though they were long silver. Too many important people had lost too much money and the Hunts' score was considered little better than stolen property. Politicians who lunched with brokerage firm partners, their fellow members at the Winged Foot Club and the Metropolitan Club, learned, over lobster rolls and escargots, of the Hunts' egregiousness, and it wasn't long before the government investigators and FBI had their snouts in the silver pot pie fiasco.

Milt felt something lodged in between his molars, a piece of food or small fish bone. He pulled his wallet out of his pocket and removed his business card. He then began flossing his teeth with the card but it didn't work, the card was too thick. Using his tongue, he tried to push the particle out, but that didn't work either.

Finally, Milt stopped trying and took the piece of paper the flight attendant handed him and wrote down some names:

Joe Gallagher=Randall Jennings (the Ghost)
Stan Couch

The Hunt Brothers had been traders. If two or more traders, in collusion, try to corner a market, they'll eventually get caught. All the price action is a result of their buying. It becomes blatantly apparent who is moving the market. But Milt was not a trader, he was a broker, the middleman who executed trades for them. If he could convince Gallagher and Couch, separately, that the other was trying to short the summer futures contract in ERCOT, they would both sell it down and send prices to new lows. ERCOT was the perfect market for this ploy, small and illiquid.

His plan was simple: Get the heavy hitters on board and then front run them with his own private account.

Milt had one big name who was already short: Stan Couch. But with Randall Jennings, otherwise known as the Ghost, behind him, Joe Gallagher would now be a factor. The Ghost would make Gallagher swing a big book. Once they both started selling the two could send prices south and create a short squeeze among the utilities, who were already net long off their generation units. Milt realized his own stake had to be sold early in the over-the-counter (OTC) market and through an anonymous third party. Once he sold a small, but still viable, portion of the summer contract, he'd implement his plan. The two big traders would crush the market and Milt would buy back at a lower price and collect his winnings.

It wasn't *exactly* illegal, thought Milt, because it would be nearly impossible for the Feds to prosecute, since it wasn't Milt himself shorting the markets. However, the plan wasn't foolproof either. If the traders spoke to each other they might discern Milt's front-running scheme. The more likely scenario in Milt's mind was that he would use his Svengali-like brokering powers and succeed in luring the two big traders into a pitched selling frenzy of coerced collusion.

The chance of them talking to each other and discerning Milt's hand at play, the one true risk, was very small in Milt's mind. Traders by nature are suspicious of each other. Furthermore, he knew that the Ghost and Stan Couch were sworn enemies who'd worked across from each other at Piedmont Power in the early days, so the chance of them speaking was nonexistent. Milt tapped his wingtips with a certain glee. He felt like the troll under the bridge in that fairy tale, *The Three Billy Goats Gruff.* Only this time, thought Milt, the billy goats are going to get milked.

Milt put the piece of paper in his pocket. He thought conservatively he could make five dollars on three "pieces" of the summer contract, which was listed as NQ on the NYMEX floor. This would equate to about a half million dollars, a humble amount that wouldn't hit the Fed radar screen. It wouldn't get him a lifetime suite at the Don CeSar, but it would more than pay for the kid's education. After all, why should Milt's good fortune mostly benefit the Commander and the other higher-ups who made off with the lion's share of Milt's commissions?

Milt sat back in his seat and drank his Jack and Coke. Then four more after that. He put down his fourth drink and felt it again, the piece of food still lodged in his teeth. Determined, he flicked at it with his tongue. Finally, more tired than annoyed, he got up and made his way back to the bathroom.

After some time spent attacking the foreign object stuck in his gum line with his craggy, bitten-down thumbnail, it came loose. Milt held it aloft between his thumb and forefinger. Under the fluorescent light of the airplane bathroom, it looked for a moment like it was a tiny, translucent fish bone. When he held it up closer to the mirror, he realized it was a single, wiry, white hair.

—A pussy hair, exclaimed Milt.

It brought Milt back to that Friday night in his hotel room at the Don CeSar. Milt was a haggard forty-one but Kathy had been much older. Maybe, Milt thought, his oldest ever. She'd had a bad back and had asked Milt to put a pillow under her coccyx before he fucked her. She also had slathered a certain gel in her vagina that had made Milt's cock turn red and tingle with a burning sensation. The gel had smelled and tasted like mint. Milt put the hair in his pocket and decided that he had wronged her by telling his son that she'd been a hotel employee. Milt thought, maybe, when he retired, he'd give her a call some day and buy her a nice dinner. He at least owed her that.

On the way back to his seat, an obese woman who had been talking loudly the entire flight stopped Milt with a soft, white hand. Her fingers were adorned with an array of rings, featuring platinum bands and exotic gemstones, turquoise and amber. She wore a brightly patterned scarf woven through her auburn hair. With her technicolored ensemble and large dark eyes, the woman could've been mistaken for a gypsy, if her clothes hadn't been high-priced designer fashion.

—You look familiar to me, she said. —Don't I know you?

Milt juxtaposed this woman in his mind with Kathy the sexagenarian redhead. They trade about flat, thought Milt. He reached for his wallet to grab the remaining business card that he hadn't used as a toothpick.

—I'm sure you know me, replied Milt, slightly drunk, extending his hand. —My name is Pablo Picasso.

OFFICE GRAFFITI

Stan Couch gave out a low growl and looked out over the Houston skyline riddled with immense buildings and modern towers. Glass, steel, and burnished chrome, the skyscrapers reflected sunrays, beams of gold, streaming like ether amid the smog. Beneath him, the streets seemed deserted and squalid, pedestrians shuffling and sweating in the sticky heat. These edifices stood glowing, sentinels of wealth, and when one looked down, the ants moving below reminded one of how far you could fall. It was the nature of a boom-bust town, Houston.

Stan Couch, head trader of Dynesty Energy, pursed his lips like a fish. His broker, Milt, told him the news: Stan's old nemesis was back in the market. The Ghost. Shades. Mr. Magoo. Or when Randall Jennings first started in the business, it was Rock Star, because of his omnipresent tinted glasses.

This would've been easier back in the old days, thought Stan. I would've just called him up and said: "You fucking whore. Back in the game for another beating?"

Stan threw his Starbucks Americano in the trash can; caffeine-laced, it was Devil's juice. Thoughts came out too fast and one couldn't control them. Stan looked out his office window and then stared down at the little card taped to the bottom edge of his screen. Psalm 148: "Praise ye the LORD. Praise ye the LORD from the heavens: praise him in the heights."

Let us praise the name of the LORD: His glory is above earth and heaven, thought Stan Couch.

—Mr. Couch, there is a call for you on line two, said his secretary Norma Lea. She poked her cheerful, pleasant-looking face through the door to his office. Her cheeks had too much rouge. Her accent, music to Stan's ears, was lilting and pleasant. In his mind she was pure Texas. Probably was a cheerleader in Fort Griffin, Stan mused for a moment before answering her.

—Norma Lea. Please take a message. I'm excusing myself from the floor for a few moments.

Stan smoothed out his pressed khaki pants with the palms of his hands. Then he centered his silver and rhinestone–embedded belt buckle with his thumb and forefinger.

When Stan entered the men's room he chose the handicapped stall. As he sat down on the toilet he clenched his fists. The Ghost was not going to beat him, get inside his head and unleash sinful thoughts. But Stan wanted to commit badness. He had a dark urge to unzip his pants and grab his privates. His mind pictured Norma Lea in the stall with him, on her knees in the piss and the stink, looking up at him with innocent, lamb eyes before committing fellatio.

Lamb. Lamb of God, thought Stan.

Stan took a deep breath and said a short prayer that was unintelligible even to him. He rocked forward on the toilet seat with his hands clasped between his knees. Stan reckoned he was praying, but if anyone saw him, they would have thought it was a man experiencing a minor fit of palsy. Stan slowed his breathing.

—The Lamb of God. The Lamb of God, he was whispering.

When the moment of prayer was over, he pulled out his favorite pen, a thick, black-tipped Sharpie. Then Stan studied his surroundings. Quickly he uncapped the pen and wrote "Jesus" on the side of the toilet paper dispenser followed by the universal fish symbol for the Lord. He bit his lower lip and regarded his handiwork. Inspired, without hesitation, he scribbled "John 3:16" on the stall's worn iron latch piece.

Stan Couch studied both his writings before capping the pen and putting it back in his pocket. So as not to arouse suspicion, he flushed the toilet and stood. Striding out of the men's room, Stan Couch felt that the Lord once again walked with him and protected him from the pulse and aura of evil men.

THE ENGLISH MAJOR

—You convicts ready? Andrews asked the cash traders.

Miller, who was pacing behind his chair and fidgeting with his thumbs, nodded. Sami pushed himself up from the desk with his two flabby arms and said "Risk" with a groan.

—Where's Shuggs? barked Andrews.

—Right here, said Shuggs, hustling back from the vending machine with a can of Red Bull in his hand.

Gallagher alone was not standing. He stared at his position report and typed numbers into a spreadsheet, as if he hadn't heard Andrews. If he had been in his usual morning mood, Andrews would've exploded at the chronically late Gallagher. But Andrews was feeling magnanimous. He had just been told by Spiros that he wasn't being fired to make room for the incoming Randall Jennings, just slotted to the number two position, a backup quarterback of sorts. Andrews could live with that.

—Gallagher? Are you going to grace us with your presence at today's risk meeting?

—Stupid is sweating it, said Miller.

—I'll see you all down there, said Gallagher, distracted.

—Don't be late. And don't get cute with Sayers again. You're not helping your cause, growled Andrews, and he strolled down the floor to the main conference room with Miller, Shuggs, and Sami in tow.

Andrews was not nervous, but he had to be on edge. He was the cash trader's go-between in navigating the mathematical scrutiny of the risk committee. Andrews's veteran crew of term traders—Hutch, Churchill, and Large—had met with the risk group earlier in the day. They were old-time bullshit artists and adept at outtalking and outmaneuvering the risk managers. The cash traders were children who lacked experience and conviction. Sayers the Slayer, former military man and currently chief bean counter, was able to bully the younger traders into smaller, less risky positions when they were unable to eloquently defend their trading strategies.

Gallagher pushed his pencil across a piece of paper. There were two ways to present his position to Sayers the Slayer: the right way and the wrong way. Each time Gallagher presented his clinical view of the electricity grid, a study of inefficiencies between different transmission hubs, Sayers would take him to task, speaking about overweight delta positions and gamma risk. Once he had dropped a description of the Black-Scholes Model in the process of ripping apart one of Shuggs's New York option positions. Andrews had said after the meeting he was positive Sayers wouldn't know a practical application of Black-Scholes if it marched up to him and gave him a full-on marine salute.

Gallagher sat at his desk, wearing a determined look on his face like someone on the verge of finishing a crossword puzzle. Hutch, who was two seats down, was picking his nose with his thumb. When Gallagher noticed Hutch looking at him, Hutch scowled back at Gallagher like it was he who was engaged in an unhygienic act.

—You're going to be late again, chief, said Hutch.

Gallagher stood up only at Hutch's suggestion.

—You're supposed to go *that* way, said Hutch, pointing to the risk conference room.

Gallagher heaved a sigh and headed down the rows of trading desks.

Hutch shook his head and in contempt pushed his glasses up onto the bridge of his nose with his middle finger. In Hutch's mind, he was showing restraint, withholding some insult such as he was exposed to in his younger trading days, such as a character-building *Yo douchebag!*

■　　　　■　　　　■

When Gallagher entered the conference room, Sayers the risk manager, a lean, crew cut–wearing, ex–Naval Supply Corps officer, cleared his throat. Suspenders had long gone out of fashion on trading floors across America, but Sayers wore a pair. They were his conversation piece with the secretary pool. Today he donned a navy blue, reasonably priced pair of suspenders from Jos. A. Bank clothiers that were decorated with small orange pineapples. The orange pineapples, Gallagher assessed, were Sayers's way of conveying a sense of whimsy, which, of course, he did not possess. The suspenders were yet another extension of his military self: a tactic, a decoy.

Gallagher surveyed the long conference room table. At the far end, seated next to Sayers, were not one, but two, of his assistants. First was Alicia, an MBA fresh out of UChicago, possessing plump red cheeks that contrasted with her gym-hardened muscles that put Andrews ill at ease. Then there was Stiles, an emaciated kid in a tie, whose facial features were so pasty that they all seemed indistinguishable. When you stared at Stiles long enough everything but his brown hair blended together. It was like looking into a bowl of porridge.

—You're late, said Andrews. —We started without you.

Gallagher viewed the table. He needed to set the tone. Put his enemies at the far end on the defensive.

—What? No cookies? he asked.

Sayers darted a look at Andrews, hoping he would quell this insubordination. But Andrews glanced around and seemed a little perturbed about the missing plate of chocolate-chip-and-peanut-butter cookies that were usually the highlight of the monthly risk meeting.

–They won't forget next time. I'll get Sami on that, said Andrews. —Okay, Miller. Continue.

The game was simple: The risk managers tried to poke holes in the energy trader's Value-at-Risk (VaR) calculation as it related to their trading strategies. In order to appease the risk group, the traders would have to reduce their position and have on less risk. It was the way risk managers avoided getting fired. They didn't care if traders missed out on huge profits. All they cared about was No Blow-Ups on their watch.

Miller had a cut-and-dry position: He was short Palo Verde cash. He had a reasonable amount of risk on, but nothing extraordinary. He didn't dabble in options or even location or time spreads, so it was a vanilla VaR calculation.

The risk managers liked Miller. He put on what Sayers referred to as "amendable and quantifiable" positions.

As Miller spoke, Gallagher saw Sayers's glare settle on him or about him, as if trying to envelop Gallagher in a beam of intimidation. The more Sayers stared at him the more Gallagher doodled on his page with his pencil. Gallagher kept glancing up from his piece of paper. Sayers suspected that the young trader was penciling a sketch of him but wasn't sure.

—We are a little troubled by this three-way locational spread that you have, Mr. Gallagher, said Sayers. —It seems counterintuitive and at minimum incurring unnecessary risk. Please explain. And forgo if you will the "dear friends and countrymen" preamble like last time.

Gallagher spoke for five minutes about the Texas transmission grid and how certain line outages would cause "congestion" between the lines. At each juncture Sayers would ask Gallagher to qualify how he was sure such and such a line would "congest." In reality one could never be sure; at best it was always an educated bet or an odds-on hunch. Just as Gallagher sensed Sayers about to lower the boom and take his position in half, he let it fly:

—The main reason I'd like to put on this spread is because we calculated the inherent risk in this exact transmission play and it's a pure Scylla and Charybdis scenario.

Gallagher took a deep breath.

It was that key point in a risk meeting: the bluff. As long as Sayers's intellectual pride prevented him from professing ignorance of the Scylla and Charybdis scenario, the fictional Scylla and Charybdis scenario would take on power and credence with each passing sentence, allowing Gallagher to legitimate his largely indefensible electricity position.

—That's the reason the spread is three-pronged. In a Scylla and Charybdis scenario, one transmission path, which we refer to as the Charybdis path, will either triple the value of the megawatts or conversely get hosed and lose an equal amount. On paper this is a fifty-fifty play that, in and of itself, is not highly attractive. However, when we add the Scylla transmission path as a hedge, the position makes sense. The Scylla path, which is the third part of the spread that you seem to frown upon, is absolutely essential. It is this alternate transmission path that operates as an insurance policy, if you will, allowing the trader to limit losses should the Charybdis path get cut.

Sayers's mouth was a straight line hiding teeth that ground into themselves.

Alicia spoke up with a hint of enthusiasm.

—Has this Scylla and Charybdis scenario worked before? she asked.

—Just last week, exclaimed Gallagher. —As a matter of fact the vanilla spread I had on last week that lost money would have made money had I executed this spread. And as you know, the following week has the same transmission outages. So this baby should work.

Sayers the Slayer played with his Naval Academy class ring, rolling it slowly on his finger. Gallagher reminded him of his underwater acoustics class at the Academy. Gallagher was the submarine slinking back and forth obfuscated by ambient noise, trying to avoid each sonar wave "ping" that Sayers sent out to triangulate his position. Just as Sayers knew about the financial markets using Fibonacci targets, Black–Scholes, and the Greeks (delta, gamma, rho, theta, vega) to assess risk, Gallagher knew, or sounded like he knew, about the world of physical megawatts and the electricity grid, of which Sayers knew little. Sayers did not doubt that the Scylla and Charybdis transmission scenario was real, but he was not one hundred percent sold on the effectiveness of the hedging capability that Gallagher professed. Still, thought Sayers, if I ax his battle plan and it makes money then I'll look like I was entirely ignorant of the Scylla-Charybdis. Better to let the Gallagher submarine run silent, run deep, and sink himself, this time.

Gallagher was still talking. He had an arrogant lilt to his voice that was distinctly unmilitary and this annoyed Sayers to no end. He interrupted the junior trader:

—Scylla and Charybdis is a go, said Sayers. —Execute at will. We'll be watching for its hedge effectiveness.

Andrews was watching Gallagher talk. He began pushing down on his cowlick. His palms were sweating. While what Gallagher was saying seemed to make sense at every level, Andrews had never heard of this term: Sillo and Karibidus. Furthermore, from the look on Miller's, Shuggs's, and Sami's faces they hadn't either. But Sayers and his assistants had bought it. And that was their job. Andrews put it on his list: "Make Gallagher explain this Sillo and Karibidus thing" right next to "Sami get cookies for monthly risk meeting."

A week later Andrews came up to Gallagher after breakfast. The Ghost was days away from his start date and Andrews had been feeling the pressure of impending doom. He felt like putting himself in a good mood, so he went to talk to Gallagher about the success of the Sillo and Karibidus spread.

—That crazy spread made some money, he said, slapping Gallagher on the back.

—It did okay, said Gallagher. —I was hoping it would've made more.

—A lot of fools dropped money this week. You did fine.

Andrews shifted his belt buckle and then scratched his chin.

—We're going to Imperial Grill. If you think you can behave yourself, I'll take you off drinking probation. I'll give you another shot.

Gallagher nodded. Then Andrews decided he'd been nice enough to his protégé.

—You never got me that report. I want it by day's end. Especially now that the spread worked, Sayers has been busting my balls to see it.

—Got it, boss, said Gallagher.

After Andrews sauntered away, Gallagher reached down and opened up the bottom drawer of his desk, which was a dumping ground for books he was currently reading or about to read. Gallagher rooted around for a few moments before pulling out a worn copy of Homer's *Odyssey*.

Gallagher paged through the epic looking at pages he'd underlined and annotated from his undergraduate days. He located the "Scylla and Charybdis" chapter. Then Gallagher walked over to the copy machine and began Xeroxing the pages from the book for Andrews and whoever else cared to learn a little about Greek mythology.

Andrews didn't look at the Scylla and Charybdis report until Gallagher had headed to the bar. Andrews knew something was wrong as soon as he picked up the report. First of all it was too long. Any report worth its salt was four to five pages in length. That was one of Andrews's rules and Gallagher knew it. Second, upon first glance, the report contained no numbers. Instead, it was just filled with words. But worse than just plain, factual words like "risk," "megawatts," and "congestion play," it contained sentences, descriptive sentences, that couldn't be processed just by glancing at the page for a second. You actually had to concentrate to read this shit. It was a story about some guy on a ship who had to choose between taking his crew down one of two routes: through the open sea and by Charybdis, a deadly whirlpool, or staying close to the shoreline where there lived a two-headed dragon named Scylla hidden in the cliffs. The Scylla and Charybdis scenario.

Andrews forced himself to read the report all the way through. He was a thorough trader. As a reader of detective novels, Andrews gauged the story-line as "not bad." As a report to hand off to Sayers, it was worthless. Andrews exhaled and tossed the pages in the trash can.

—The kid has a screw loose, said Andrews out loud. Then he leaned forward to his desktop and wrote at the top of his "to do" list:

Tell Gallagher no more ghost stories at risk meeting.

THE TRADERS'
"THIRSTY THURSDAY"

Gallagher stepped out of the office building. He was strolling alongside Andrews. Large, only five foot five and his skull the size of pony keg, took the lead. Churchill and Hutch scuffed their shoes as they walked, bringing up the rear. The formation was not unlike the old Notre Dame flying V pattern. The cloudy sky loomed above: a smudged gray, the color of pig iron. Just outside the office building on the red brick parquet was a smashed bottle of Mad Dog wine, lime flavored. The glass was scattered across the brick in gleaming shards. The traders ignored the smashed bottle and made their way across Quincy Market toward the harbor side. Gallagher was thirsty and knew that each trader had a specific drink and steak on his mind. The walk of his companions, which usually had a sublime economy to it, was now possessed by a slump-shouldered weariness. Change was on their minds. A new boss meant change. And any change that did not include guaranteed money was never welcome.

The traders entered the Imperial Grill, an upscale steakhouse that had outfitted itself with a long, sleek oaken bar. On one wall was an oversized portrait of Red Sox legend Carl Yastrzemski. Gallagher always noticed how the painting depicted "Yaz" in his silver-haired waning years, the obsequious smile he flashed in the painting, giving no impression of the mudstained gutter fighter he'd been on the baseball diamond.

If it was a grim reminder of the diminished value of fame and glory, the other traders didn't acknowledge it. "Thirsty Thursday" was the traders' ritual, a weekly feast to eat and drink to excess, especially since change was coming. Some of them knew this Thirsty Thursday would be their last.

The hostess came and seated them at a table in one of the back rooms. The manager of Imperial Grill appreciated their business, but there had been complaints about loudness and foul language in the past, so the hostesses had instructions to seat these men away from the center of the restaurant floor, in side rooms or back booths. As the traders sat down, Churchill, the Texan, continued talking.

—It's going to be a war, huh? he asked Andrews.

—We hate each other, said Andrews.

—Why the bad blood? asked Hutch.

—I was his broker back in the day, when he worked at Travista.

—He can't fire you, said Large. —You're up.

—He won't need to fire me. I'm a relief pitcher now. Riding the bench, said Andrews, scowling. —But Jennings is going to fire some fools. Right out of the gate. Bet on it.

—Who told you that? asked Hutch.

—Trust me, said Andrews.

No one wanted to think about having to distance themselves from their respected boss, Old School Andrews. Churchill even tried to get off the topic of Randall Jennings and attempted to cheer up the table. He began holding forth on the price of beef.

—What do cows eat? Corn is what they eat. But corn prices have gone way up because that shit is in demand to make ethanol. If oil wasn't so high we wouldn't need to put corn in our cars. And so the cows eat expensive corn and we got to now eat expensive cow.

The traders mumbled and nodded in agreement. The corn crush could be a spread that traded off oil prices. Each trader at the table privately speculated whether it was possible to make money from it. In the end conversation about the corn crush and its relation to oil futures brought a levity to the table; after all, it touched upon their favorite subjects: food and money.

One of the senior traders, Hutch, took a deep breath and then bent over to tie his shoes. The mood lightened and the other fat men at the dinner table moved on to another favorite topic, Craig Gide, a coworker who owned a cat.

—From what I've heard about that cat, it's a big fan of peanut butter, said Churchill, his belly pressing against the table.

Toward the end of the main course Gallagher looked over the scene. The bare bones of his lamb chops lay across his plate, which was empty but for a pool of coagulated butter and specks of mint jelly. The other plates consisted of rib eye bones that looked gnawed upon. One plate, Churchill's, looked as if it had been licked clean.

Even gorging on red meat and wine could not inspire joy. The mood was one of a last supper before execution. Some of them would be gone by the next Thirsty Thursday. They had to keep drinking.

The waiter trolled nearby, looking to refill the traders' glasses with the bottle of Cabernet tucked expertly in the crook of his elbow.

—Gin and tonic, please, Hutch said, feeling his heart rate quicken.

He had the vague sense that he had eaten too much, and a sheen of perspiration broke out on his high forehead.

When the waiter brought the G&T, filled to the rim, Hutch guzzled it.

Gallagher grabbed the waiter by his free arm. His grip was too tight. The waiter pouted but remained officious.

—Can I have another potato, please? asked Gallagher.

Churchill was built like a fire hydrant and he had the firm jowls of an overweight younger man. The whiskey had reduced his self-control and he began talking about Jennings again, this time calling him by his industry nickname: the Ghost.

—The Ghost fucking blew up at Dynesty and Piedmont. He's dangerous. Guy like that has no wife, no kids to worry about. Just roll the fucking dice and let her ride. That's his way.

Gallagher looked over at Hutch, who was going in and out. His focus waned. Then regained, tinged with ferocity:

—The stripper with the sweaty belly rolls at the Jewel Bait, said Hutch to Gallagher. —My eight-year-old daughter has the same sort of flab. Strange, isn't it?

Hutch was flailing out at the world, hoping to strike something. With an index finger, he pushed his thick glasses up on the bridge of his nose. He looked at Gallagher, as if he could provide an explanation.

Hutch had dove deep into gin-think until he came up with something that repulsed him out of his stupor.

Churchill droned on:

—I hear he's almost blind. How does he see the screen?

—He's got nystagmus, said Andrews. —It means his eyeballs quiver. You'll see. It's why he always wears tinted glasses.

Hutch was not listening about the Ghost. He was held down by a torrent of sickness. Suddenly, he stood up and burped.

—Gin is an evil drink, he said in a low voice to Gallagher. —The shit you think up is enough to secure you a free pass to Hell.

Then Hutch made his way to the bathroom. Gallagher knew that if the stall was occupied Hutch was going to have to use the sink. When Hutch was gone, Gallagher looked over the table.

—You're all drunk, he said.

—So are you, said Churchill.

—Not like you, said Gallagher. —You're drunk in the way that let the Roman legions get slain by the Visigoths.

—Here it comes, said Large.

—Tell us about the Visigoths, said Churchill.

—The Visigoths hid in the Black Forest and they covered themselves in black dirt and emerged out of the earth and slaughtered the Roman legions. And you can be drunk in two ways: the way that needs to sleep one off and doesn't see them coming up out of the dirt, or the way that you got one eye still open. You're ready for them.

—Now that is something, said Churchill, whose sense of history favored the Alamo and Pickett's Charge.

—Only one standard-bearer made it out of the Black Forest alive and reported back to Caesar Augustus, continued Gallagher.

Then Gallagher stood up on his chair. His big, stocky frame wobbled a little.

It started off well.

But before Gallagher could get going about the Mongols and Genghis Khan, the waiter pulled on his pocket and asked him to step down so he wouldn't have to be thrown out.

—Of course, said Gallagher, as gallantly as he could, before jumping down from the chair.

When the waiter came back the traders took dessert. Andrews ordered the bananas Foster and a glass of Château d'Yquem and Churchill, not wanting to be outdone by the larger man, signed on for the buttery fried ice cream concoction as well. Large and Miller, who still held on to a vague hint of their former athletic physiques, ordered crème brûlée, while Hutch and Gallagher had coffee. Andrews, who had been uncharacteristically grim and quiet throughout the meal, was now unable to hold back a smile.

—You missed Joe's speech, said Andrews to Hutch. —It had a rare quality to it. It was both educational and stupid.

Hutch, now refreshed, was back in attack mode:

—Tighten up, chief, he said to Gallagher.

The traders ate dessert in near silence. An alcohol and meat–induced daze finally overcame them. Blood and booze.

THE GHOST ARRIVES

Randall Jennings, the Ghost, had just finished his usual three-mile morning run. He stepped off his treadmill and sat in an antique Windsor chair, his elbows akimbo on its cushioned arms. He wore a black polo golf shirt emblazoned with a pink logo and black Adidas nylon sports pants. His running shoes were the latest and greatest Nike model with an extended rubber heel to absorb the shock. Next to the Ghost on a settee was a tall glass of iced tea with the usual three ice cubes. The Ghost liked his ice cubes round so he could suck on them, a nervous habit. He lived in a penthouse apartment that looked out over Boston Harbor, but he could not appreciate the view. The Ghost sat in the chair sweating and drinking his iced tea. He wiped a sheen of perspiration from his forehead with the side of the cold glass.

The Ghost picked up a remote and turned on the CD player. He resumed listening to an audiobook of James Watson's *The Double Helix*. The Ghost suffered from an eye condition called macular degeneration. He had a rare genetic form, which was accompanied by nystagmus. The latter caused the Ghost to wear his ever-present tinted glasses to hide the disturbing effect of his eyes uncontrollably flickering back and forth. His affliction made the Ghost interested in the study of genes. He'd majored in cellular biology at SMU, before changing to microeconomics his junior year. It was a trip to Kansas City where he'd visited a cousin who worked on the commodities exchange that had changed his mind: It was the sound, the mad rush of human emotions and words that were connected to market forces, economic principles, which were then translated through the language of numbers. For the first time in his life the Ghost felt truly connected to the great web of humanity. It was here on this global stage of the markets that the Ghost knew, despite his disability, he could contribute, master, and inflict, instead of dwelling back in the scientific shadows of the lab.

The Ghost also listened to all the business news stations and took in the sports rundown from Jim Rome's TV show *Rome Is Burning*. It was necessary on a trading floor to possess sports knowledge even if one could not see the games in detail. Listening to the talking heads arguing the day's controversies and tuning in to live games and evening recaps, combined with the Ghost's excellent memory, gave him an encyclopedic knowledge of the three sports that counted: baseball, football, and basketball.

When the Ghost finished the iced tea, he stood up from his chair and began stretching. Nearly six feet tall, the Ghost seemed taller because of his wiry runner's build. After twenty minutes of limbering up his muscles, so they wouldn't tighten up on him, the Ghost turned off the Watson book. He then walked across the room to his piano. The Ghost moved in a short-stepped, controlled, and seemingly effortless gait. This manner of movement, even and steady, gave one the impression of a man being whisked along by a mechanical walkway or escalator.

The Steinway piano was the Ghost's connection to the world of inner thought. His ex-wife, Cheryl, had been a concert pianist and the Ghost had come up with some of his best trading ideas listening to her play. The Ghost had no formal training. He preferred to play show tunes and piano rock, Billy Joel, Elton John. When sitting at the Steinway, he was transfixed, as if playing Chopin or Bach before a private audience in Vienna or Paris. His mind, however, was set free and would balance musical notes and mathematical figures simultaneously. It was then trading ideas would emerge. Music facilitated financial strategy.

In the middle of playing the piano the Ghost's intercom buzzed. It was the concierge asking if he could let in a "Mr. Carey." The Ghost made his way to the intercom and after a few moments responded to send the man up.

When Mr. Carey arrived, the Ghost was waiting for him. He could make out the vague image of a man wearing a dark jacket and tie.

—Good afternoon, Mr. Jennings, said Mr. Carey. He had a Boston Irish accent. When the Ghost shook his hand, he felt that it was a small, sweaty, soft hand.

—Are you going to be my driver today? asked the Ghost.

—Yes, sir.

—I'm ready to go, said the Ghost.

On their drive through the city streets, Mr. Carey began to talk, sometimes looking back at his silent bespectacled passenger. One of Mr. Carey's stories was about his former career.

—I spent twenty years in corrections and I've seen many things that would make you shudder. Murders, rapes, gang wars, you name it. I'm actually working with a ghostwriter on a screenplay about Stockpole. I'm telling you, this guy says we can't use half the stuff because it's just too brutal. Too brutal for Hollywood. Imagine that.

The car took a right turn off Charles Street across from the Boston Gardens.

—Up here on the right is the bar where they filmed *Cheers*, said Mr. Carey.

The Ghost cleared his throat.

—Mr. Carey, he said in a low voice. —I prefer quiet.

—Understood, sir. Absolutely, said Mr. Carey.

CHAMP IN THE BOX

The Ghost secured the company box for that Friday. He preferred a social setting to meet his traders for the first time. It was a two o'clock game against the Yankees. The box looked out over the third base line. There were no clouds in the sky and the sun settled over the outfield and made the grass seem a brighter shade of green.

The Ghost arrived at the box early. He wore a floppy L.L.Bean fisherman hat, thick, tinted bifocals, and a long-sleeve plaid shirt. One of the young cash traders, Shuggs, drove the Ghost to the ballpark. He walked alongside the Ghost, maneuvering him through the sea of the pregame crowd, and helped him find the company box. Shuggs thought his new boss moved pretty well on his own and that he was probably less blind than the rumors had portrayed him. Shuggs had thought from the nickname that the Ghost might've been an albino, but he had been too embarrassed to ask anyone. Shuggs hadn't expected someone who looked like a fit Secret Service agent with short, graying hair and a set jaw.

The Ghost moved slowly to the front of the box and took out a small telescope and watched as the grounds crew raked the base paths. Fans noisily spilled through the turnstiles into Fenway Park. Many of them wore Yankees hats, T-shirts, and team jerseys with their favorite player's name and number on the back. The company box had two refrigerators full of beer and bottled water; a bar with vodka, bourbon, and gin; and four Sterna-heated covered tin bins with crab cakes, hot dogs, hamburgers, and teriyaki chicken on a stick.

The Ghost, sitting by himself, put in his earpiece to listen to the game.

Soon his traders, one by one, sauntered into the box. They all introduced themselves to the Ghost as they entered. Most shook his hand. There was Gallagher, Miller, Hutch, Greenblatt, who traded weather derivatives, and Hobart, the coal trader who knew the record of every mixed martial arts fighter in the UFC, yet had the aesthetic sense to wax his dark stripe of monobrow.

—The despised Yankees, said the Ghost during the singing of the national anthem.

—Easy, said Greenblatt.

The Ghost waved a hand at his weather derivatives trader.

—Don't hate the greatness, said Greenblatt.

The Ghost was from Seattle. He was a Mariners fan.

—Where are you from in New York? asked the Ghost.

—I'm from New Haven.

—Bandwagon, shouted Miller.

Sami showed up after the national anthem. He walked over to the crab cakes.

Hutch gave Sami an insolent stare. Then he pushed his glasses up on the bridge of his nose.

—Sami, what the fuck?

—What? asked Sami, almost dropping his crab cake.

—You missed "The Star Spangled Banner." That's unacceptable. And un-American. Go get me a Bud Light out of the fridge. Make sure it's cold.

Large and Churchill, two of the top traders, made their entrance after the first pitch. No one said anything about their lack of patriotism and Sami noted this. Like Andrews, these two traders were reserved. Unlike Andrews, neither man had made any money that week. Churchill went over to the bar and came back swishing his pint glass of Maker's Mark. He walked with a slight limp, having pulled a hamstring a week earlier at the driving range. He seemed exhausted and irritable, though not beaten. Large had a glowing sheen of sweat on his large expanse of forehead from the walk over.

—Where's Gide? asked the Ghost. —I gave Gide the look and he's a no-show.

—I believe he had a ticket to the ballet, chimed Churchill.

—Or he might be grooming his cat, added Hutch.

—He owns a cat? asked the Ghost. And this comment put the traders at ease.

It was evident to everyone in the box, except for Sami, who was too busy feeling slighted, that there was one glaring omission, Stu Andrews. Even the desk goat, Sami, had been invited, but Andrews had not. Not getting the look at the box was the trading floor equivalent to a papal edict of excommunication. The older traders knew this and saw it as a sign that the Ghost would have zero tolerance for those he didn't like.

—No Blue? Large asked.

—They only got Johnnie Walker Black, replied Churchill. —You trying to drown the "whale song"?

—I'm just trying to drown period, replied Large after pouring his whiskey to the brim.

That Thursday Large had made what the other traders on the desk called "Large's whale song." These whale songs were a series of low groans commingled with muffled grunts that Large emitted when the market was exacting a singular pain on his PNL. Taken together, these sounds of distress had a kind of grumbling, but still intricate, musical quality, and while they didn't sound exactly like whale songs, there was no other real way to describe the strange sounds. So whale songs stuck.

Hobart grabbed a handful of potato chips and sat down next to Greenblatt, who was discussing his weather derivatives position. The meteorologists had told him that it was too early in the season for tropical storms, but there was some low-pressure activity off the coast of Africa.

—Way too early in the season to be talking about hurricanes, agreed Hobart. Storms concerned him because high precipitation levels could soak the coal stacks, rendering them wet and useless.

—Still, said Greenblatt. —Stranger things have happened.

The Ghost was two rows back. He did not want any talk of hurricanes. A storm up the East Coast took temperatures down and would help the Ghost's net short position that he was going to implement. But a hurricane: A hurricane, especially if it was to go in the Gulf, was unthinkable. At the very least even a small storm this early would have drilling platforms evacuated.

—Who's talking about hurricanes down there? asked the Ghost.

Large and Churchill looked at each other and rolled their eyes.

—Is that my weather derivatives trader trying to ruin my first day on the job?

—Just weather geek chatter is all, Greenblatt said, turning around, face flushed.

Large was in the back of the box, talking to himself.

—After Blue, this Black is really terrible, mumbled Large, staring into his glass.

Right out of the gate, the Yankees were up two runs. Sheffield homered with no men on in the first inning. At the top of the third Giambi ripped a triple into deep right field that sent two more runners home, a beating. A tired gloom settled over the box. They plied themselves with liquor. The bets started to fly.

The traders made markets on pitch count, hits, strikes, fouls, bunts, giving and taking odds. Although the stress of the week had worn them down, the booze and betting gave them a second wind. It was a way to kill the time and impose their trading will upon the world, even if it was limited to the small shark tank of themselves. Still, the Ghost, who listened from his top row in the box, saw it for something more, a constant training of the mind under duress, the ability to fight off one's heels, barraged by the soak of alcohol and noise and glare of a ball game; all these things impaired the ability to judge a market and make a profitable trade. And the Ghost knew that the traders who consistently won these mundane box seat bets would be among the ones that he would keep an eye on.

In the bottom of the sixth inning, the game started to turn. A rookie catcher sent up from the minors smashed a three-hundred-foot bomb over the right field wall. It sent Garciaparra, who had walked, and Manny Ramirez, who had been hit with a pitch, to home plate and tied up the game.

A cheer went up in the box. The Ghost let out a loud: "Haaaaah!" Miller jumped over his seat and pointed a finger at Greenblatt's chest. Greenblatt, the sole Yankee fan among the traders, was now glum and sedate. He lit a cigarette in the no-smoking box and said in his foreign accent:

—Bullshit. Bullshit. Bullshit.

Large, who was sitting next to Gallagher, put his finger in his drink and asked:

—Boy, did I ever tell you the story of the Bullhead Clap?

Just as Large was about to relate his adventures in the South Pacific from his navy days, a shout went up from the back of the box.

Hobart, who had disappeared for three innings, now reentered the box. He wore a stupid, drunken smile on his face. It was the look of a happy child:

—Look who I found in the pisser!

Walking in behind Hobart was a muscular black man wearing a white oxford button-down and a pair of well-pressed gray flannel pants. His biceps bulged like cantaloupes. He had a nasty-looking scar across his cheek. It looked like he'd been burned by a welding torch. But the smile he flashed was magnanimous, all encompassing.

—I brought the champ, shouted Hobart.

"Marvelous" Marvin Hagler, ex-middleweight champ and pride of the Bay State, walked throughout the box shaking hands with all the traders, who leapt up from their seats. It was as if each trader felt an urge, some superstitious taboo to reach out and grab hold of living greatness. Hobart kept slapping Hagler on the back and saying:

—I can't believe I'm touching the champ.

Gallagher watched Hagler's hand envelop his own, as if he was placing his hand into a catcher's mitt. When Hagler came to the Ghost sitting in his chair, he placed his large hand on the Ghost's shoulder, smiling his champion's smile. The Ghost stuck out his jaw in a look of pride as if the champ's appearance was a prophecy of his own forthcoming victories, a herald of things to come.

—Good to meet you, Marvelous, said the Ghost in a quiet voice.

Later on no one could remember if Hagler had said a word, but everyone spoke about how large his hand was when they shook it and how massive his arms and back were. But it was his smile, his champion's smile, that lit up the box with a triumphant glow. And later on when the Yankees came back and beat the Sox in the eighth and a drunk Gallagher knocked over the Sterna to the chicken wings and set the back wall of the box on fire, no one cared. They put out the fire and drank all the beer and the gin and bourbon. Large polished off the Johnnie Walker Black. They left the ballpark long after it was empty of fans, walking through Fenway in drunken silence thinking they had the champ's blessing, and in some unspoken way, that made them untouchable.

MILT GETS FUNDING
FROM A LOCAL

The brokers and the traders in the NYMEX pits wear yellow badges with each member's four-letter code. In the Natgas pit you have code badges like HOOK, THOR, WEED, DOPE, BABY, HASH, TRIM, and BOAT. Having a memorable badge name gives the trader or broker a psychological edge. It's all about aura and mythmaking. Lame badge names like MURF, JOEY, or LARY broadcast coward, schlub, or has-been in the same way the maverick names flipped the middle finger toward convention and beckoned greatness. It was, after all, a game about embracing risk. Four letters, however, can be tempting, even for grown men, but the exchange policy has a no-obscenities rule. Thus, famous lewd badges like SLUT, SUCK, SCRU, TWAT, and BJOK have all been removed. Only one sole obscenity badge remains, QQQQ, shouted as "Four Q," which sailed across the floor in a New York accent as "Fuck you."

Before he got hired by a brokerage house Milt Harkrader had been a local in the natural gas pit for five years. He'd had a rather mundane badge name, MILT, that matched a rather mediocre career. On the floor locals are a dying breed. Instead of working for a company and trading on their seat of the exchange, a local fronts his own money to rent a seat and trade his own book. On the floor when a minor player, a small-time broker or screen clerk, becomes a local, it is known as "going for the Brass Ring." It is a true gambler's existence. You have no salary. Every day you risk getting rolled over by huge firms like Goldman Sachs and Morgan Stanley. One such local was legendary Charley Benton, a former bail bondsman from Newark, whose badge name was SKIP, short for skiptracer.

On August 2, 1990, Saddam Hussein sent Iraqi tanks cruising through the desert toward Kuwait City. That morning futures in the crude oil pit went limit up forty-five minutes after the opening bell. The bulls were hoping for a war. Not just any war, but a war in the Middle East. If they didn't get a war, they at least wanted a conflict: troops, yellow ribbons, aircraft carriers, and SCUD missiles. War was good for business, especially in the crude pits. It ensured a price spike, and, if you were long, you made out— bandito style. If you were short, you wished the president wasn't a Texan out for blood. But as they say in trading: Hope is not a strategy. George Herbert Walker Bush was going to war.

Skip was long that day, very long. Those who were familiar with his position surmised that Skip was a millionaire many times over before the market closed. He had gone for the Brass Ring and won the rare prize. It was no surprise when a rumor circulated around the pits that anyone who knew Skip was invited to the Waldorf-Astoria to enjoy the victuals of his payday. Skip wanted to go down in Merc history and one way to ensure that was to invite the unwashed legions to bask in his glory.

From the moment the traders stepped off the gold-plated elevator onto the fifteenth-floor suites of the hotel, it was obvious that people were going to go to jail. A mirror inside the suite could be heard being smashed within the first five minutes of the party. Billy Boreland, who was totally bald except for a psychotic, single stripe of cornrow-styled hairplugs going across the top of his forehead, opened the door and greeted all entering the suite..

—The ladies are on their way, he said with gusto.

Some young brokers from Freebond were smoking cigars in the room. Billy Boreland, who had made himself the master of ceremonies, screamed:

—Have some fucking brains. At least rip that smoke detector off the wall.

One of the Freebond brokers tried to pry the device off the wall with his shoe. When that failed Billy Boreland came to the rescue and began smashing the smoke detector with a fifth of unopened vodka.

Skip was in the plush bathroom waiting for the entertainment and holding court. He cried out from a hot tub the size of a small pool:

—Clams and oysters. I want more clams and oysters and cocktail sauce and shrimp and fucking all the champagne you can carry. I'm starting to run low.

Skip sat in the oversized tub with a bottle of Dom Perignon in each hand. Empty bottles and shucked clam and oyster shells covered the tile floor of the enormous bathroom. He was wearing nothing but his cowboy hat, a hat that he had won in a bet off a friend of his, one Milt Harkrader.

As expected, sometime after 1:00 A.M. two large NYPD cops swaggered up to the front desk. The complaint was of an assault and vandalism. Apparently, there had been some kind of altercation where a gentleman who had accompanied two female strippers had been thrown into a headlock and hustled to the edge of the penthouse deck while various men could be heard screaming, "Pimp off the roof! Pimp off the roof!" Somewhere in the process a TV had been thrown out into the hallway. Although the disturbance needed quelling, the diminutive desk clerk brushed some lint off his gold silk vest and took a secret pleasure in making the police wait for an extra moment or two before he gave them instructions to Skip's penthouse suite.

It was 11:00 A.M. on a wet, gray Tuesday down on Wall Street. Milt sat at the back of the Admiral's Cup, drinking a rum and Coke, entertaining his friend Charley "Skip" Benton with a story from the old days of the exchange.

—I mean you knew Louis Caza. He was a careful guy. I think he was the one who coined the phrase: "Pigs get fed, hogs get slaughtered."

That phrase was the mantra of controlled greed that was quoted like biblical scripture by managers to green traders, warning them of gung ho aggressiveness.

—But by the end Louis was starting to show signs. I mean sure some guys get the eczema, nervous tics, and hypertension red-face, but Louis, he started getting these bags under his eyes. Each week they were getting a shade darker: the color of a shiner. I mean, Louis, he outlived the pack, yeah, he was a survivor, a student of the market, but toward that last day his face wore those losses, those sad sack pouches beneath his eyes.

Charley Benton scratched his double chin with its three-day stubble and grunted a laugh. He was wearing a hooded gray sweatshirt, jeans, and a nice pair of Italian loafers with no socks. In downtown Manhattan you could lunch out anywhere so long as you had nice shoes.

—Anyways, said Milt. —That first Monday in September. About exactly one month after you retired, Louis Caza walked into the Natgas ring at 9:59, a minute before the opening bell. I saw him. He was holding nothing but a pencil and his trade tickets just like he had every other day since his trading life began. Only today Louis Caza wasn't wearing pants, he was wearing pajama bottoms. Some young idiot who didn't know any better made a joke about it. But all the old-timers, you could see it, they got all nervous, like they all knew what was coming. Then at the opening bell Louis sat down on the edge of the ring and began to cry. He was just shaking all over, weeping. It was awful. Then the paramedics came and they carried him out on a stretcher. It was a true "taste it."

Charley Benton nodded his head. He lived in a house in Deal, New Jersey. The house had been built and owned by the rock star Billy Joel. It was shaped like a giant piano in homage to the singer's hit song "Piano Man." As Milt spoke about the grim spectacle of the "old days," Charley felt himself withdrawing into his thoughts. He had two pressing meetings that day with regard to his philanthropic work. He had to lunch with the director of Earthfirst to check up on how the NOx Emissions commission was progressing. He'd given them almost a million dollars. Then he had to make his way up to St. Luke's Hospital in Midtown where he was to greet some of the children who had benefited from the leukemia wing that bore his name. Milt was still hustling and had a line on something. Charley let Milt hold forth on Louis Caza for another minute but when Milt changed topics, Charley put his wrist in front of his face, giving his watch a blatant staredown. Milt caught the hint.

—I took the day off to see you, said Milt. —Because I've come across a pretty good call. It's a lock on the energy futures market. An illiquid hub. I know the players involved and there's going to be some price action going on in the near term.

Charley Benton could hear the sound of Milt's greed but he knew the difference in the cadence between greed and desperation. Greed always brimmed with possibility and hope, whereas desperation caused a man to hold his breath for a moment too long, as if choking on a prayer. No, Charley heard in Milt's breathing a churlish optimism. What fascinated Charley was that Milt was still there, where he himself had once been, still on the ropes, throwing punches, ducking, bobbing, and weaving: the great hustle to survive.

Charley Benton was going to go uptown and help sick children and save the rivers and streams with his dollars. And it was going to give him the feeling of humility, that connection to humanity, something close to grace. And here was Milt with a grease spot on his collar and fingernails chewed down to their nubs asking him to throw in dollars on a "sure thing."

—Look, said Charley Benton. —If you want to make a killing I can spot you a loan because I know you're good for it. But commodities don't interest me. I got the annuity. I'm done.

Milt lowered his head. It was an accidental act of deference.

—How much you need, Milt? prompted Charley.

Milt gave him a number. It was a smart number. Any higher his friend might've guffawed, any lower would have revealed Milt's trepidation about the plan. Milt could almost hear Charley's head working the numbers.

—Okay, he said. —I'll wire it to you. The day after next if that works?

Milt felt awkward, like Skip was a loan officer at a bank. Immediately, he stood and shook Charley's hand like he was a complete stranger, which, in a way, he was. As a parting intimacy Milt wanted to ask Charley if he still had the Stetson he won off Milt, but all that came out, as his friend walked away, was an obsequious:

—You still got it.

Milt wandered up to the bar. As he did, he looked out the front window and saw Charley Benton getting into a Lincoln Town Car. His driver, a slight man in a suit and tie, opened the door for him. Milt ordered a beer, which he thought would be a good way to keep his wits about him. He played out everything in his mind.

I'm glad Charley didn't go off on some tangent about the pollution in the East River, thought Milt. I would've said something insensitive that would've blown the deal.

—Too much money kills the funny, said Milt out loud.

The bartender turned around from watching TV, ESPN highlights. He had porkchop sideburns and a ponytail. His small black eyes squinted down the bar at Milt, talking to himself.

—What did you say?

—I said, said Milt, brandishing his glass, —pigs get fed, hogs get slaughtered.

After some six beers and an escalating argument with a customer on an issue of politics, the bartender threw Milt out.

—See if I ever come back, Milt screamed as he left. Milt had uttered that exact same sentence at many bars. It was one of his favorite farewell exit lines.

Milt headed north up Broadway. It was a beautiful day and he had nothing better to do. He walked with a feeling of accomplishment. He had a plan. He had funding. And he still had the uncanny ability to get kicked out of a bar before noon.

After twenty blocks or so Milt became tired. He put his hand inside his pants pocket and discovered that he had forgotten his cell phone. Milt stumbled into the Blarney Stone Pub on the cross street at Twenty-ninth. A dim throwback to the old days of smoke-filled blue-collar bars, there was a greasy spoon buffet at the front, where a sickly looking cook spooned out $4.99 lunch platters of mac and cheese, mashed potatoes, mangy sauerkraut, pork sausages, and watery meatloaf.

Harkrader took a stool at the bar and began to methodically celebrate with shots of Jameson's whiskey. Eventually, he was watching the television without comprehending it. Some hardhats came into the pub on their lunch break. Milt went into the small wooden phone booth at the back of the bar and called his ex-wife.

—Milt, she said. —Nice to hear from you.

—I love you, goose, he whispered into the phone, thinking of her coming down a water slide in a black bikini one summer in their early days of marriage. Whiskified, and ill prepared for the emotions coming over him, Milt felt the greed-mongering troglodyte of his soul come blistering forth. He fought back the desire to cry. He braced against the wall with a steel-toed wingtip.

—I got the check for St. Paul's, she said.

Someone put a quarter into the jukebox and T-Rex's "Bang a Gong" sounded in the background.

—Milt, are you at a bar?

—Business lunch, slurred Milt. The music in the background was not the kind played at business luncheons.

—Milt, you've been drinking.

—No, he said, his voice sullen, soaked.

Then there was silence on the other end of the line. Milt searched for the words but his head was ringing. He couldn't determine if he couldn't speak because of alcohol or because of regret.

—No. No. Goose, I'm not, was all he could say before his ex-wife hung up the phone.

Milt went into the bathroom and ran cold water from the tap. For five minutes he stood in front of the mirror and alternated splashing the frigid water on his face and staring at himself in the mirror. When he saw the spark of recognition mixed with a touch of gutter-fighter anger come back to his eyes, he wiped off his face with some paper towels and went back to settle his tab.

By eleven o'clock that night and five bars later, Milt had staggered farther uptown to buy a hot dog from Gray's Papaya. As meat sauce from the chili-dog dribbled onto the front of his shirt, Milt caught sight of a limousine that was driving up Broadway. He flagged it down and the limo pulled alongside him. Milt got in and gave him directions to his apartment in Hoboken. When Milt looked up front he noticed that the driver looked familiar. It was Louis Caza, "Pajama Bottoms" himself. Even through his haze of drink Milt recognized him. But somehow Louis Caza had changed. Thinner, perhaps. But it was not that Louis was thinner. It was that the dark circles from under his eyes had disappeared. The ashen pallor in his face had vanished, replaced by a ruddiness blended now in its olive tones.

—Where to, friend? asked the driver with a grin.

Milt sank into the comfortable leather seat, not believing that the man whom he had just spoken about hours before was now driving him home. Milt thought he should make a joke of it. It would make the whole thing more sane, less like a delirium tremens nightmare. Perhaps Louis Caza would remember him. But when Milt scooted up to tell his joke, he got another look at the driver's face. It had changed completely. And while the driver in the black felt paperboy cap resembled Louis Caza, it was not him. Milt inhaled the fresh scent of a new pine air freshener and splayed out on the leather seat. With one hand he gripped the door handle tightly. Nausea set in. When Milt closed his eyes, the world began to spin around him.

—How'd those Mets do? pled Milt, hoping for something to buoy his spirits.

The driver didn't answer. Milt didn't expect him to. After all, he thought, it's only Caza's ghost.

THE GHOST IN ACTION

On Jennings's first official day of work he appeared on the trading floor an hour before anyone else. He carefully clocked who came in first and who came in last. From his perch at the center of the trading desk, he sat with his monocular and zeroed in on the movements of the traders. He could tell who was going to be fired and who was not before he even looked at their spec books. Profitable guys walked upright or swaggered knowingly. When they noticed Jennings, they acknowledged him with a nod or even the odd salute. Losers were a bit harder to ferret out but not much. They usually walked with their head down or had a carefulness to their stride as if surrounded by some giant, invisible bubble that would pop if something unexpected came around the corner.

Jennings had once seen a horror movie about a demon that could taste fear. The more afraid his victims were the better they tasted. Jennings's mouth contorted—unleashing a ferocious grin. Craig Gide had stridden onto the trading floor wearing a tight-fitting blue and red bicycler's shirt. Despite the brazen color of the outfit, Jennings saw a serpentine slink to his walk and when he glared at Gide, the senior trader pretended not to notice and looked away. Jennings pictured the fear-tasting demon and was thinking:

—I smell fear.

At a quarter to one, just after lunch, Jennings walked into his executive office with the glass window and the fake ficus tree in the corner. He had practiced this walk for a few hours the previous weekend so it would seem completely natural. He had the number of steps to the glass door memorized. All his trading he would execute at his desk on the main floor in the middle of the action, democratic, just one of the guys. But for conferences, where privacy and often sensitivity were required, the office was necessary. Jennings summoned Gary Wynert, the head of Human Resources, to his office. Wynert had the look of someone who had done at least two cycles of steroids: the simian ridge, protruding brow, sparse hair, and a look of perpetual anger plastered on his waxen face. He was affectionately called the Executioner by all the traders. This was not just because the Executioner looked like he could rip your head off with his bare hands, but because he was HR's axman, present at every trader firing.

The first trader called into the office was Andrews.

ANDREWS GETS
SIZED UP

The reason why the executives brought on the Ghost to replace Andrews was murky. The trading floor was up money. They were having a good, but not great, year; what is known in the business known as a *solid* year. Andrews was everything shareholders would want as a head of trading: honest, respectable, no suspect extracurricular activities, a veteran with more than a few notable victories. The rumor was the CEO, now approaching a youthful seventy years of age, had an ambitious wife. She was his third, a former daytime TV soap star, who had acquired a taste for the high life. They already owned ranches in Colorado and a beach home on Cape Cod, which was featured on the cover of *Yankee Living*. Still, she wanted more, even bigger things for her husband. So, the traders reasoned, the way for the CEO to get paid was to bring in a big name and sell the company. The Ghost was that name, famous and controversial with the industry, a trader who'd blown up big but who'd also made it rain, and gotten executives paid. The brass, ravenous for upside, smiled upon this.

The hatred that the Ghost felt for Andrews was of a special variety. No head trader climbs to the top without having his own unique form of motivation. The Ghost throughout his career had not just been motivated by the usual greed but also by hatred of certain coworkers, usually other alpha traders.

His hatred for Andrews was all-consuming. It originally derived from a rumor that Andrews, as a broker, had started everyone calling him the Dungeon Master, indemnifying him as a nerd. Andrews's nickname had struck home more than he could've known. The name had brought back painful memories for the Ghost: sitting in a musty attic with three other friends; unathletic, socially awkward, acne-ridden boys, spending hours in the midst of various role-playing games, *Gamma World, Top Secret,* and, of course, *Dungeons & Dragons.* While other kids took drugs, played football and baseball, got laid, and saw bands, Randall Jennings was in an attic rolling twenty-sided dice, insisting to his friends that his "character" always had to be a wizard or a druid. His teens were dominated with fighting orcs and storm giants, winning gold pieces and earning experience points. Though it didn't seem especially bad at the time, by his sophomore year of college memories of those years had become excruciating. Andrews had reopened this wound and earned the Ghost's enmity.

When Andrews walked into the office, the Ghost sized him up. His powerful frame was slightly bigger than the Ghost remembered. Even the rumors about Andrews were big. The Ghost didn't bother to say hello; he addressed a grapevine tale that he'd always wondered about: a relationship Andrews had with a professional wrestler.

—Is it true you were friends with Big John Studs? asked the Ghost.

—No. We weren't friends, said Andrews.

—You knew him though?

—Back when I started on the floor in Chicago, Studs lived downtown and hung out at that same local bar as me.

—What did he drink?

—He would order a fifth of Hennessey cognac and it was as big in his hand as a sixteen-ounce Coke is in yours or mine.

—Cognac? asked Jennings.

—Sometimes he'd have a bottle of Scotch after. For dessert. But he always drank the Hennessey. He liked cognac. Even though he was from Texas.

—Interesting. I would've lost money on that, said Jennings. —Did he tell you that wrestling was fake?

—He only talked about wrestling once when he was drunk. He told me Hulk Hogan was a pussy.

The Ghost held a printout of Andrews's trading positions in his hand.

The Ghost knew if he failed to meet expectations, Andrews was the only one who could replace him. The second string quarterback waiting in the wings. Andrews had the respect of the higher-ups as a very solid performer. Furthermore, Andrews was the biggest threat to any legally questionable trading strategies that the Ghost might employ to make money. Andrews both had the reputation of being morally unimpeachable and knew the accounting systems and volatility curves by heart. He was most likely the only one smart enough to ferret out any possible discrepancies.

Finally, there was the fact that Andrews was the prototypical bull, a gung ho American—a buyer who believed in driving a big, gas-guzzling SUV, purchasing his wife four-carat diamonds on anniversaries, eating four-inch-thick rib eye Imperial Grill dinners. Andrews believed in the process of eternal consumption, progress, and expansion: the more, more, more and up, up, up of things. A hundred years ago, he would have been a railroad baron.

Andrews, his rival, had not only wronged him, he was a current threat and, as bull to the Ghost's bear, a philosophical foe. For the Ghost his hatred of Andrews was complete. And every time he smelled the salty pork rinds which invariably covered Andrews's fingers, he was filled with repulsion and loathing.

The Ghost moved the piece of paper squarely in front of him under his dome magnifier, so he could see the numbers clearly. Andrews was long Midwest power futures at the Cinergy hub. Of course, he was sizably long.

The strategy to bankrupt Andrews's Cinergy hub position would be two-pronged.

One, the Ghost would enlist the brokers, inform them of Andrews's position, which they would in turn share with Andrews's counterparts at competing firms in the Cinergy market. These traders would then short sell the market against Andrews's long position. As for the brokers, they would back the Ghost's play over Andrews's. The Ghost did more size, which meant more commissions, meaning the Ghost paid them, and the repeating monkeys, as he called brokers, would do his bidding.

Two, the Ghost would utilize some in-house help in selling down the market to make Andrews tap out. This would be necessary in getting Andrews fired. The Ghost would need two accomplices so it couldn't be traced directly to him. He'd need the help of Allied Power's Midwest origination manager, who was known as "the Colonel." He was the trader responsible for selling excess power off the gas and coal plants in that region.

As a backup plan, a second shooter would be necessary. The Ghost imagined he might use the kid, the ERCOT trader, Gallagher, to execute a short Cinergy spread at the appropriate time. It would be a speculative short push, to really drive the prices down and stop Andrews out for the final kill.

MILT AMONG THE CZARS

Milt rapped his knuckles on the black marble tabletop and pushed the Stetson up on his forehead to let it breathe a bit. Joe Gallagher was a half hour late. Traders could be late, brokers could not.

Once inside the Club Ivan, Milt stared at the impressive floorshow on the stage at the center of the room. The 1950s-styled Vegas long-legged dancers kicked their thigh-high boots up past their shoulders. They were adorned with such Tinseltown fanfare as nipple tassels, sequined panties, and crowns made from ostrich feather plumes. An overweight Elvis impersonator stood at center stage. He looked like an imposing ruin in a rhinestone-speckled white jumpsuit, part shuddering alcoholic, part gyrating cock bulge. He sang "Hound Dog" in a deep, guttural Moscow accent. Milt shook his head at the scene. He had come to play cards, not see the King mocked by a Commie cabaret. An attractive blonde took him to his table and he sat as the unseemly act came to an end.

At the table next to him two men with the huge, thick frames of power lifters toasted one another with flutes of champagne. Their expensive suits glistened with silvery threads under the dim lights and seemed as if they might rip at the shoulders when the men raised their arms. Huge platinum watches that could be mistaken for manacles glittered on their wrists. The one facing Milt had a shaved head and an expressive, steroid-bloated face, red and meaty like beef tartar. Milt rapped his knuckles on the tabletop and then flipped his wrist and looked at his own watch. He was on his second helping of caviar. Milt picked up his silver-handled mother-of-pearl spoon and took another taste of fish eggs. It was Osetra Malossol from the Caspian, unique for its colossal-sized beads and mild palette. It tasted something like the salty spray of the sea, but seductive, mermaid on the tongue, an edible art form, aquatic cunnilingus. Milt considered the blinis and toast points topped with crème fraiche as bastardizations of the experience like pouring Coke in your Woodford Reserve, so he left those alone, pushed toward the side of his plate.

A moment later the waitress returned, serving Milt a complimentary shot of Stolichnaya in a tall, thin shot glass.

—Why thank you, said Milt.

—Not me. The manager, she said. —He likes Texas.

She gesticulated with her hands, pointing to Milt's hat.

—He wants to know what kind?

—Stetson, el Jefe, said Milt.

The waitress threw back her head and her blond hair waved to one side. Then she laughed.

—Stetson, L-Heavy, she said, mispronouncing "jefe." —Cool.

Milt spooned some more caviar in his mouth and let it sit on his tongue until the fragile eggs dissolved, leaving a thirsty, oily residue behind. He washed it down with some vodka. Chilled and harsh, it delivered a blast of Arctic truth, in the form of meandering thoughts. Milt counted in his mind the number of Texas hold 'em, five-card stud, and seven-card poker games he'd played. He thought of river card draws that had made him and had ruined him. Seamlessly, his thoughts turned to football and he pictured games in Baton Rouge, Austin, Kansas City, and South Bend where he'd been and the touchdown passes caught with seconds on the clock. He thought of NASCAR finishes in Daytona and twenty-foot putts missed by inches at Pinehurst. His gambling and obsession with cards and sports had taken him all across America, his passport to the hallowed halls, domes, arenas, casinos, and courses. Milt tugged at one side of his neck. His fingers sunk into the soft jowls. He looked down at his shoes with the laces tied on the sides. Then he looked over at the czar in the silver suit. The man gleamed with an unholy zeal like he wanted to fuck a dozen whores, strangle a hundred men, and deadlift a thousand pounds, simultaneously. It occurred to Milt that this man with the lusty, seared red face and the Asiatic eyes and folded lids that looked like someone had grabbed the man's cheeks and stretched his face across the width of a frying pan and then pinned the excess skin somewhere out of view still possessed the warm spot. This was that place where consuming and winning and profiting was never enough. It never got you hot, you just got warmer and warmer until you began to glow. Only the czar had it in the way no one but a new American can have it. The man had probably seen much, but as an American, he was a newborn, newly infected, newly inspired. Milt felt twenty years older than the man who could've passed for his father. He sat drinking the vodka and let the cold thoughts come. He wanted to pull out his wallet and look at a picture of his boy but he kept his hands on the table. Milt wondered for a moment when he'd stopped being a true gambler, which exact event it was during his time as a father that dulled his instincts. They probably just dissolved over time, he thought.

Yet Milt needed to make his score, move to Florida, and live the dream. He needed to be here in some fake New York version of Russia to play broker and take Joe Gallagher, a goofball who liked to play cards, against some real players who would impress the kid. With young traders, reasoned Milt, you feed the vices. With older traders, you feed the vanity. Milt hoped he still had what it took to grease the Gallagher kid and win his soul. He'd done this so many times and now he was tired, sagging. Milt felt like an old baseball player in his last season, only more bloated and out of breath. Perhaps he'd order a coffee.

MEETING OF THE MINDS

On the train ride down to New York Celina slept and Gallagher read. He was devouring the pages of a biography, *Doc Holliday*; the gun-fighting, gambling dentist who saw his notoriety become legend when he shot down two men at the Gunfight of the O.K. Corral. Doc was of an aristocratic family from the antebellum south, an Ivy League–educated dentist, fluent in Greek, Latin, and cards, who contracted tuberculosis at an early age. In search of a panacea for his disease, Doc sought out the dry climate of the Southwest. As it became more apparent to the would-be dentist that he would not live long, he decided instead to live hard. Doc Holliday wore a diamond stickpin on his lapel and carried a straight razor concealed in an easy-access pocket of his gray silk vest. Gallagher consumed pages and forgot himself, letting the book and the jostle of the train whisk him into another world. When he stepped off the Acela Express at Penn Station, Gallagher was in a hypnotic daze. He kissed his wife good-bye. She was headed to some art event in Brooklyn.

Originally, Gallagher bought the bio of Doc H. to get in the gambler's mind-set, as the Doc was a legendary faro dealer and poker player. But the more murderous side of Holliday's life infected Gallagher's mind. He got into a cab and on the way to Club Ivan practiced drawing and shooting an imaginary pistol. He knew that everything would come off all right with the card game, as long as he did not drink whiskey.

This was a business meeting. Gallagher sheathed his imaginary six-gun and composed himself. Milt could furnish him with information about the players in the ERCOT market. If Gallagher played it right, he could intimate that Milt would receive large commissions in exchange for revealing the positions of the two other large traders in Gallagher's sandbox, mainly that of the nine-hundred-pound gorilla, Stan Couch of Dynesty, who was notorious for putting on "size," or having a large futures position. But first the meeting would be a fine dance, actually making the broker believe you were his friend instead of merely his client.

Be classy, he thought.

When Gallagher appeared at Ivan, Milt was sitting at the table drinking a cup of coffee. Gallagher locked onto Milt's Stetson. Somehow the ghost-gray hat, the lush, velvety seediness of the club, the impending poker game, and everything Gallagher had read about Doc Holliday fused together in his mind. He had no choice but to embrace the evening.

—Order me a whiskey, said Gallagher, sitting down.

—This card game should be good, said Milt to Gallagher, rubbing his hands together, again perusing the menu.

After his second whiskey Gallagher started speaking in a Southern accent.

—I have one request tonight, my portly friend, said Gallagher. —I'd be mighty thankful if I could don the lid.

Milt did not understand. Gallagher repeated the statement in plain English.

—Your hat, sir. I want to wear the hat.

Milt pointed to his own hat in disbelief.

—This one? he asked.

—None other, said Gallagher in a voice not his own.

Milt scrunched up his face as if he had stepped on a thorn or was trying to answer a question on a subject he was clueless about, say fractals or the game of chess.

Milt didn't want to hand over el Jefe. Besides, it was *his* hat.

There were many parts to being a broker that Milt liked. He liked sleeping soundly at night with the clean, risk-averse conscience of the middle-man. He liked schmoozing the client, comping big-ticket dinners, golf outings, Vegas junkets, deep-sea fishing. But when it came down to it, Milt was a man bought and paid for by the traders he serviced. They were always right, he was always wrong. Commodity traders all had an ugly ego—it was what let them believe they could take money out of something as volatile and amorphous as electricity, a product you could not store and one whose value literally depended on the weather. Milt had seen many traders come and go. Milt's one point of pride was that he had been a broker for far longer than most traders remained traders. However, Milt had taken verbal beat-ings from nearly all his clients, as they waged war against the market and thrashed Milt for missed trades, cuffing, or wide bid asks. The abuse barked over the squawk box was what every broker had to tolerate if they wished to survive. Milt took his medicine like a good dog; the railings and yammer-ings of "fuck you" and "fuck off" and "suck my cock" and "shut up," "suck it up" and "you fuck up," and then of course the worst of all, insults that bore implications, such as "you're boxed," "in the box bal life," or "I'm hanging you." But through his brokering years he'd built up a calloused ear and a colder eye. And every day after work like a turtle peeking its head out of its shell, Milt would don his beautiful Stetson, have a few drinks, and his ego would reemerge unscathed. Each hat had its own persona and, Milt believed, was capable of attracting different women to him. His current hat seemed to work well with older women, especially redheads and blondes.

Milt gnawed at his lower lip in order to avert a sneer. *This was his hat!* He picked the Stetson gingerly off his head and placed it on Gallagher's head.

—Tonight, you're the King, said Milt.

—I'm feeling the hat, sir.

Milt looked at his client. Gallagher never before addressed Milt as "sir" and he was speaking differently. His client's burly presence seemed to have taken on a strange air of arrogance and feigned nobility. Milt thought, I'll play along, roll with this and it'll work to my advantage.

Milt pushed the plate of remaining caviar toward Gallagher, who scooped the black seedlings onto a blini the size of a silver dollar and cov-ered it with a swathe of crème fraiche. Gallagher knew ahead of time that his behavior was going to get away from him. But he still had a strategy: ob-tain information. Milt was the broker. Let him be the babysitter. Let him believe he was in control of the evening. Milt would settle into the easy routine of being the rational person and would believe the young Gallagher to be the impressed and impressionable pawn.

I just need to know what direction of the market Stan Couch is coming from, thought Gallagher. Have Milt tell me to my face what Stan is doing and then make up my mind whether or not Milt is lying.

Gallagher cracked his knuckles and spread his wide, flat hands on the table in front of him.

—Who is playing cards with us this evening? he inquired.

—Marat, the manager, he set up the game for me. We're playing against two Chinese guys, both small-business owners, and a lawyer from Midtown with a WASP-sounding name. Marat says they're all wannabes, especially the lawyer.

Gallagher sat back in his chair and fitted the hat so it sat a thirty-degree angle off his forehead. He then leaned forward and rubbed his smooth chin over the back of his hand. It was uncharacteristic for the low-key Gallagher, acting like a dandy and trying to be elegant and smooth. Milt wrongly attributed it to the powers of el Jefe.

My hat has put Gallagher out of himself, above himself. This will work, thought Milt, I'll get what I need to know out of the kid because the old el Jefe is working its magic. He's going to forget himself.

As Gallagher was chewing his blinis, carefully like a gentleman would, Marat the manager came over and introduced himself. He was a tall, lean man with a crew cut. His dinner jacket looked a size too big and unlike most of the men in Club Ivan, Marat didn't emanate a gangster vibe.

—I was hoping to see your cowboy hat, he said.

Gallagher took it off and handed it to the young Russian. Marat turned it over and inspected the hat brim. Gallagher sensed the ability of the Stetson to bridge time and space. The alcohol blurred reality and made it easy to discern the cosmic powers of the hat. El Jefe was wide brimmed, large, and brash, though the color was subtle, somewhere between precious platinum and a hovering phantom. It was a beacon for some and lent itself to certain situations: gunfights, fistfights, knife fights, card games, cheating at cards, whore wrangling, whiskey swilling, and business negotiations. Whoever wore the hat, possessed that inscrutable edge.

—Stetson, said Marat. —This is the best. This is the Beluga caviar of cowboy hats.

He put it on and pulled it down too low over his eyes.

—This is how I wear it, yes?

—Sure, said Gallagher. Milt registered a grin. The hat was money. He was proud of it like it was a son or a famous ancestor.

The Russian looked back at the foyer to the restaurant where two attractive brunette waitresses smiled at him and waved. Marat grunted and leered. Then he returned the hat back to Gallagher.

—Yes. I like this hat, he said. —By the way, gentlemen, if you want I'd like to offer you some shots of Stolichnaya on the house before you go upstairs for your game.

—We'll take them. Thank you, said Gallagher.

—It's best to stay sharp, said Milt, wanting Gallagher to stay sober enough to win at cards.

—It's not polite to refuse a drink, said Gallagher.

Milt tried to reel Gallagher in by talking shop. Sure enough, after ten minutes and two more shots, Gallagher bit:

—So, Milt, asked Gallagher. —Who's shorting all my ERCOT summer?

When Milt heard Gallagher speak the words, he almost giggled.

—Stan Couch is short, lied Milt. —He's selling it all.

Gallagher pursed his lips, holding back anger. Stan Couch was the one trader who could short squeeze Gallagher out of his length. But was Milt lying?

—You know your new boss, the Ghost, is a big fan of ERCOT. Of shorting it, said Milt.

—So I've been told.

—You know what they say, said Milt.

Gallagher waited.

—The trend is your friend, cooed Milt.

—If I swim downstream instead of upstream, I'll need someone to keep it on the down-low.

—With you and Stan on the same side I don't think the utilities can remain solvent. Why fight a sell-off when you can profit by it?

Gallagher took a big scoop of caviar and swished it around his mouth like it was a fine wine. Milt saw his eyes become glassy.

—More whiskey, said Milt.

There was a trading saying: Fish on. It meant your fish was on the hook. The greedy thing that lived in Milt's belly was happy. He was snaring Gallagher and soon he'd have Stan Couch.

FOLD

Marat escorted Milt and Gallagher to the back of the club. The three men ascended a cramped stairwell that had a pungent, rich smell, hints of cherry tobacco. Milt and Gallagher entered the room. Marat announced them:

—Mr. Milt Harkrader and Mr. Joe Gallagher.

The pair teetered near the doorway for a moment. Four people sat at a round wooden table with patient expressions on their faces. Gallagher noticed the wallpaper was red velvet. The color hurt his eyes.

Gallagher grunted his way through the introductions. The Manhattan lawyer wore a powder blue polo sweater. His face was memorable for his nose, a grotesque knob peppered with small anthills of raised pores earned from years of drinking gin. The two Chinese businessmen Milt had mentioned turned out to be a Korean man, who wore sunglasses, and his well-dressed wife. The dealer had sunken eyes and a build so slight he could not fill out his tuxedo.

The game was Texas hold 'em. The dealer shuffled the deck. His fingers were long stalks connected by joints. They moved with an insectlike efficiency.

Gallagher won the first hand with a pair of threes.

Milt winked at his client and mouthed the word "balls."

A few hands later, a surly Gallagher looked over at the Manhattan lawyer.

—You son of a Yankee whore.

—I beg your pardon.

—You winked at the dealer.

Milt saw where it was going. This was one of those rare times where a broker could take advantage of a situation and prove undying loyalty to their trader, a moment where careers were made.

—I saw it too. You fucking fink, sneered Milt.

The dealer, whose English was suspect, knew enough to realize that two players at the table, who were initially very drunk, were now belligerent.

The lawyer stood up. He pointed at Milt.

—Outrageous, he said.

Milt upended the table, sending a maelstrom of drinks, cards, chips, and cigar butts flying through the air. Gallagher knocked the dealer aside as he ran from the room. Milt bumped into the stout Korean woman with his belly, knocking her off her chair onto the floor. Gallagher huffed as he bounded down the stairs, four steps at a time. Milt was already out of breath when they hit the main floor. The two of them fled through the club like purse-snatchers. One of the large Russians in a sharkskin suit waved a spit of lamb kebob at them, as they stormed by.

Milt was wondering when they were going to be tackled by the club goons. He wasn't paying attention and tripped on a step. He stumbled forward into the foyer, knocking over the coat check girl's tip jar. It fell onto the floor and an array of bills spilled out. She retreated backward into the closet, her breasts heaving in her low-cut dress. She let out a small yelp.

Marat was at the bar talking to a customer.

—What is it? he shouted at Milt, as the trader and broker barged through the front door and spilled out into the warm city night. They ran for two blocks before Milt collapsed against a lamppost.

—Flag a cab, he said.

FAMOUS

When she got out of the cab Celina wondered if she was in the right place. The address was a building, an industrial hulking structure made of red brick. It sat on a deserted stretch of treeless avenue by the East River. Across the street was an auto body shop with a fenced-in lot crowned with razor wire, protecting stacks and stacks of used tires. Twenty years ago this would've been somewhere in SoHo, thought Celina. But the Wall Streeters had moved in and the artists had fled to Brooklyn.

The loft was on the second floor of the redbrick building. Celina could hear the rumbling murmur of the party above. Of course, only a few cars had been parked out front because most everyone had taken a cab, except for the artists, most of whom had taken the subway.

Phil Persimmon in a cranberry sweater vest greeted Celina at the door.

—You're back, said Phil.

Celina forced a smile.

—Actually, just visiting, she said.

She made her way through the crowd, nodding politely at some people she'd never met. They weren't artists. They were too well dressed, ornamental twenty-something girls, gallery cheese, or from the Christie's and Sotheby's crowd. Celina then sipped red wine and settled into a conversation with two of her best friends from Yale, Billy Jameson and Petra Bernier.

They had all been studio partners in oils back at Yale as MFA students. They had taken to painting derivative works of the New Objectivists, George Grosz and Otto Dix. Celina had reworked the prostitute with purple panties from the Grosz painting called *Suicide* into a self-portrait that won her the Peggy Guggenheim award and the scholarship money that came along with it.

—I'm relieved I still know somebody, said Celina, lighting a cigarette.

Billy Jameson wagged his shaggy mane at her.

—We're not somebodies, he said.

—He's just annoyed you're smoking. Billy has allergies, remember? said Petra.

—No. I'm fine, said Billy Jameson.

Celina looked around. No one was smoking. She noticed the distinct smell of sawdust. The wooden floor had been swept clean but the smell was there, the lingering industrial past. Celina took one last drag.

—Still a hater, said Petra, smiling.

—Hating Boston, said Celina, stubbing out her cigarette with her heel.

—You're not missing anything. There is nothing happening, said Billy Jameson. —Everyone has boring jobs and no one is showing except for your best friend.

—The boy has a piece at the Whitney, said Petra. —I'm sure you heard about that.

Celina had read about it. As jealous as they all were, it was too huge and depressing not to talk about.

—When you knew him he was in a band, right? asked Petra.

—No. He was a DJ.

—Now he's a "genius," said Billy Jameson.

"Genius" was a word scorned by artists. It was the anachronistic language of the art auctioneers, gallery owners, and other hucksters of the art world. Art was a for-profit commodity and "genius" was the sales tagline for the uninitiated.

Billy Jameson took a sip of his beer and tried to distance himself from his obvious envy.

—Has anyone actually seen the work? asked Celina. She enjoyed needling her peers.

Petra worked as a greeter in a SoHo gallery and Billy Jameson was a self-employed Web designer. Celina felt comfortable among her old friends.

The feeling of being in a nexus of the art world among artists made Celina feel as if she had woken up from a deep sleep. Her eyes and ears took in the various energies and bits of conversation, the tittering of industry minions and the smug, leering eyes of the wealthy buyers, professionals, middle-aged men in pressed pants. She was normally so far away from this and the room began to pulse. Celina was aware of the hunger sweeping over her; the appetite, so long suppressed, returning now.

Celina said she had to get a drink and left her former classmates to work the room. At least a dealer had enough faith in her work to put it on the walls of his gallery. Fuck Web designing, thought Celina, I'm a painter.

She reached into her purse and lit up another cigarette. And fuck Phil Persimmon too, she thought, navigating toward the bar.

She sipped away at two champagnes, her second one brought to her by a former classmate who was in the film division. He'd mentioned his name but Celina immediately forgot it. He was dark-haired like her husband but even taller and with finer features, so Celina figured he was nice to stare at. Besides it didn't look good at a party to be drinking alone, she would trade up for company when the chance presented itself.

—Yo, said someone from behind Celina. She knew who it was at once: Toulee Nesbit. Celina turned and faced him. He was still slender but instead of the close-cropped hairstyle she remembered he had long dreads as she'd seen in his photo in *The New York Times Magazine* article.

—Yo, replied Celina, deadpan. —And how is the artiste du jour?

Toulee smiled, tight-lipped, exuding the confidence and wariness brought on by fame.

—Have you seen Sasha in these past years? asked Celina.

—No, said Toulee, not wanting to talk about Celina's ex-roommate and his girlfriend during their time as undergrads at Brown. He wasn't being forthcoming so Celina asked him about his piece that was at the Whitney.

As he spoke about the piece, Celina painfully recalled a photo of it she'd seen in the *Times* article. Toulee was a political artist. He'd juxtaposed photos of beautiful, thin models with obese teenagers from East L.A. and Iowa and painted slogans over them.

Toulee finished talking about that piece; he went on to talk about his new work. It was inspired, he said, by his experience in an earthquake in L.A.

He touched Celina's shoulder as he spoke to her. Celina felt him looming. He did a sort of anxious dance, impatiently scuffing his paint-speckled

Timberland boots against the wood floor. It had always been there, every time he'd come over to the freshman dorm room to see Sasha, looking intensely at Celina when he passed by her, as she sat on the couch out in the common room watching an episode of *X-Files*. But instead of a slouching unknown, he was now a famous artist. Toulee no longer stared at the floor as he once had.

He feels he's entitled to me, thought Celina.

As he weaved the tale of his art, it became apparent to Celina he had no intention of asking about her work. When he did, two drinks later, finally say "How about your stuff? Are you still at it?" it came off as perfunctory. The requisite preliminary line that laid the groundwork to take her home.

Instead of letting Toulee know that she was still painting, still alive and showing her work in second-tier Boston, a mean pride like a rush of dark waters flooded through her and she said:

—I'm like the rest of the smart ladies, said Celina bitterly. —I went off and married a Wall Street boy.

—Really?

—Didn't you read in *The Times*? He's the one who made the markets crash.

For a moment she imagined her comment to be an affectation in a duel of vanities among artists. But then she realized it for what it was: her father's strategy. An immigrant, born in Lebanon to a shoemaker, his own textile business had grown from long days and a cold industriousness. And always his words, confident and angry, rang with the wisdom of the self-made. *It's always good when someone in business thinks they're smarter than you. It just means if you work harder you'll probably beat them.*

Toulee glared at her, wondering for a second if it was a joke.

—He makes the clouds rain bolts of thunder, Celina said. —We live in a giant castle.

Toulee's eyebrows receded up on his forehead.

—I'm messing with you, Toulee. I live in Boston.

He looked down at her finger and saw the ring, the medium-sized rock that had cost Gallagher two months' salary. Toulee recovered and flashed Celina a taut grin.

—But you are a banker's wife, he said, trying not to sound too smug.

—Actually, she said, blowing cigarette smoke into the musty air, —he's a commodity trader.

GALLAGHER SHORTS

THE MARKET

When Hutch entered the trading floor ten minutes late, the armpits of his white button-down shirt stained yellow, still squinting from his headache, he headed straight for the vending machines. He was seeking out his daily hangover cure: a can of grape soda and a pack of Cheetos. He fed in his dollar and pressed the button. Silence. No grape soda. His backup was Dr Pepper. If there was no Dr Pepper this morning, Hutch considered putting his fist through the machine. The Dr Pepper clanged down into the pickup bin and Hutch raised an eyebrow.

—Your lucky day, chief, he said to the vending machine and then moved on. As he sauntered down the trading floor he stopped in front of Gallagher's desk.

—You look happy, he said sarcastically.

—Blue-hairs are expiring and I should be getting paid, shot back Gallagher.

Hutch slurped from his soda and laughed.

The first thing Gallagher had seen when he opened his Reuters page on his computer was the headline:

Record Heat Wave in Texas Kills Ten in Nursing Home

He scanned the article just to make sure. Abilene, Texas, temperatures surged north of 109 degrees Fahrenheit with seventy-five percent humidity. A line outage made the nursing home lose its power. Ten patients died of heat-stroke.

Gallagher had been long, but Andrews had made him take profit and exit the position. Gallagher realized that it was part of Andrews's disciplined trading strategy: *You can't take a loss on a profit*. Still, as a result, he had missed out on the largest run of the summer contract in recent history. Disappointed that the money train left the station without him, Gallagher felt a little reckless.

Sell into strength. The summer futures market had run seven dollars on a prolonged heat event in the Southwest. It's the perfect selling opportunity, thought Gallagher. The longs in the market were in a full-on frenzied bull run. If Milt was right and Stan was short then the two biggest trading shops could stem the stampeding longs. But if Stan panicked and covered his short, closing out his position, Gallagher could be out of a job.

Gallagher was warily eager as he pushed a button on his squawk box, summoning his hungover broker in New York.

—Milt, you got any market on summer ERCOT?

No answer. Then a crackle of static came over the box.

—Seventy-eight bid, intoned Gallagher's broker.

—Where's the offer?

Seconds passed.

—HPL just came in with an eighty bid. Still no offer, barked Milt.

—I'm an eighty-two offer, said Gallagher.

—Mine, said Milt. —They'll do one hundred megawatts.

HPL was in panic mode and had immediately lifted him.

—A hundred done, said Gallagher. His short position was now in play.

Gallagher was relieved it wasn't Stan Couch on the bid. Selling short had a different psychology to getting long. There was a patience to it. You sold and you waited for the market to buckle like a bad knee.

An energy bull market was more like a cavalry charge. You bought, and if the market weakened, you bought more, until everyone started buying, because the traders out there could smell the money and the market had nowhere to go but up. When a market rallied you felt you could hear the canons and thunder. Not so when it puked.

Andrews sauntered over.

—Selling summer? You've made all your money being long.

—Sell into rallies. Isn't that what the book says?

Andrews chewed at his lower lip.

—There is no book.

—That's my point, said Gallagher. —There's no blueprint to this shit.

—Being short summer, said Andrews. —That's the short that ends careers. Or makes them.

Then Andrews made a face like he'd just smelled an unpleasant odor.

—But I'm not the play-caller around here anymore, he added in a tired voice. He turned and walked back to his desk.

THE COLONEL

When Daniel Haupt, the Midwest origination trader, first came on the desk he would execute what he termed drive-bys every day around noon. This entailed him walking down the row of desks that showcased the administrative assistants, who were mostly women. At first, there was no concern. Haupt had chiseled features and the dark, good looks of a C-list action hero. But with each successive drive-by the rumor mill festered. Word was that every day Daniel Haupt would return to his seat on the desk after these drive-bys and keep a list of who was wearing what each day; that he would study the list and try and predict what each woman would wear the following day.

People took to calling him "the Colonel." Haupt liked this title because he thought it was the recognition of his former status as a United States Marine. What he didn't realize was that Hutch, one night out drinking, had remarked to all that Haupt's strange, purplish birthmark on his neck had the same shape as a chicken drumstick from Colonel Sanders KFC's extra-crispy fried chicken recipe. Like so many names on the floor, once dropped, it stuck. From then on it was "Colonel" to his face, and "Chicken Neck" behind his back.

The Colonel, being in origination, was not one of the top earners. Origination guys were like the used car salesman of the power desk. Unlike the market wizards who traded volatility and financial futures, trying to beat a nameless, faceless market, the Colonel had actual clients, good old boy utility traders whom he called on the phone and chatted up every day, bullshitting about NASCAR and Big Ten football. The Colonel would sell actual physical megawatts from the companies' natural gas and coal units in Minnesota and Iowa where the weather tended to be cooler in the summer and the prices cheaper and then move that power down south, where it was hot and the prices higher, and collect the arbitrage. The dangerous part of the game was in moving the power. The Colonel had to go out ahead of time and buy transmission from the power lines that routed the power down south. Sometimes the firm transmission wasn't there and you'd have to buy nonfirm "tranny," and often on hot days your power would get cut and then you'd still be short power in the south and getting rolled. The worst-case scenario was what was happening this summer, hot only in Texas, where he couldn't move his power across the constricted transmission lines. The Colonel knocked on the door to the Ghost's office. The Executioner had left for a bathroom break, so it was just the two of them in the room.

—You wanted to see me?

—They call you the Colonel. Why is that? asked the Ghost, turning around from his flat-screen where trades flashed in green on the electronic market.

—Because I was a marine. Actually I was only a captain, but I'll take the promotion.

Jennings blinked behind his tinted glasses. He already knew the "Chicken Neck" story.

—You're in trouble with HR. Did you know that?

—No, answered the Colonel.

—You filed an expense report for two thousand dollars and you didn't have the good sense to check the name on the receipt: the Pussy Den.

The Colonel exhaled and swatted his hand against his forehead. Most of the strip clubs in Boston and out Route 9 used politically correct pseudonyms on receipts, like HGS Tavern for Club Blonde or Z Street Club for the Jewel Bait; not so with the Pussy Den apparently. He whispered "fuck" under his breath. The Ghost, whose ears were highly sensitized from his impaired vision, heard this.

—Your immediate boss, Pelazzi, wants you fired, added the Ghost.

The Colonel looked across the desk at the Ghost with a blank expression, his hands on his knees, a prisoner awaiting sentencing.

—Anyways, I told HR and your boss that it was my tab and you kindly picked it up for me. The matter has been dropped.

The Colonel sucked at his tongue. The Ghost heard greed in the Colonel's heaving sigh.

—What's the biggest bonus you've gotten working in origination?

—Sixty K.

—I can do you much better than sixty K.

The Colonel's face remained blank.

—You like strip clubs, don't you? asked the Ghost.

—Who doesn't? spouted the Colonel, becoming suddenly alert.

—I hear you own a boat?

The Colonel shrugged.

—Take me for a cruise on your whaler this weekend. We can talk about your future. Sixty K bonuses will be a thing of the past for you.

—How about my expense reports?

—The word "pussy" should not appear on the expense report of a professional trader.

The Colonel snorted. He couldn't help himself. He always liked the sound of that word, even when it was used as a threat.

HUTCH GOES HOME

Miller was heckling his broker over the squawk box.

—Yours you! he said.

—I'm sorry, big guy, but this guy flaked on the trade. What you want me to do? pled the broker over the box. —The guy's a bird. He flaked. It's not my fault, honest.

—Bring me value, taunted Miller.

—Are you going to hang me?

—Bike rack, said Miller.

—What? simpered the broker, voice crackling in static.

—Bike rack.

—What's that?

—That's back in the day. You, me, at the bike rack after school.

—Come on. I bring value.

—My ears are hurting.

Miller clicked the off switch to TMB Brokers on his squawk box.

—KO, he said. —That right there is how you deal with those whiny motherfuckers.

Miller nodded to Hutch, who sat to his right on the trading floor. Then they both looked over at the Ghost and the Executioner, both sitting in the corner office with the see-through glass walls. Four traders had been in there today and two had come out escorted off the floor by security. The termination process had the precision of a well-oiled machine. The gloom that settled over the floor was rife with inevitability, and the traders had that dull-eyed look about them like those awaiting an execution, either as victims or spectators. The ideology behind it was simple: the sound American practice of capitalism and meritocracy. If a trader was whacked, it was his own damn fault. It was the efficiency of the thing that troubled Gallagher. It goes down so quick, he thought. Gallagher couldn't decide, as each doomed trader walked back to the Ghost's office with its clear glass walls, if it was more like a mob killing or a hog killing. He decided since it was done in plain sight it was more like the latter, though with more paperwork.

—Think he's done yet? Miller asked Hutch.

—He's just getting started, chief, replied the veteran trader. Hutch wore a look of existential calm, but inside he felt a gnawing worry.

—Jesus, said Miller. —We should be okay, though. The Colonel survived.

—The Colonel made it through! I thought for sure he was going to put a bullet in Chicken Neck.

Hutch was worried about the stories he'd repeated concerning the CEO, Miles McDuggin. When McDuggin started he went on a grand tour of the energy fleet, visiting all the New England coal, gas, and oil plants. When he arrived at one coal unit, his helicopter landed on a small strip of lawn that was six stories below the operator's control room. Never having been in a coal plant before, McDuggin had no idea that the single stripe of tinted glass six stories up was the only set of windows in the facility and that behind them was housed the tiny, compact office of the sergeants that ran his plant. When the chopper touched down McDuggin stepped out and unzipped his pants. CEOs don't have to use bathrooms like normal employees, so he began taking a whiz. Only as he did so, the helicopter started up again, and the rotors kicked up a breeze that blew McDuggin's stream of urine back all over his pant legs. The operators in the control room witnessed this and the story circulated through various channels of upper and lower middle management until it hit the trading floor. Hutch had immediately called all his friends who worked with him in the pits on the Mercantile Exchange and by the end of the next day the company's stock had been sold off 3 percent because the Street was wise that there was a new CEO who pissed into the wind. Hutch was worried that McDuggin might have heard in his multiple trips to New York, while talking to the big banks, that one trader in particular was the gleeful source of this story to all the trading floors in the city. Now would be a perfect time to opt for his revenge. Under the guise of the Ghost cleaning house. Maybe, maybe not. Still Hutch felt a sheen of perspiration on his upper lip. The taste of ash was at the back of his tongue. His breath was labored. He'd have to take the cigars to zero starting tomorrow.

When Craig Gide, a native of Antwerp, got up from his desk and solemnly marched toward the corner office, silence washed over the floor. Heads turned as he passed by. Gide was a senior vice president with some mediocre years to back him up. He had three consecutive lousy quarters to his name recently. Although despised as arrogant and a dilettante, an owner of cats, a fan of Chardonnay, bicycling, square-toed shoes, and possibly ball gags, it was believed that Gide had nine lives. Each time in the past when he had lost a lot of money, there was an excuse. After one blowup, he came in every day for the next five weeks wearing a leg brace. There was no explanation about the brace, but the tribal and superstitious traders supposed that when Gide was not fired that it was the leg brace itself that had protected him. When enough money is involved grown men will attribute magical powers to something as mundane as a leg brace. However, after each blowup, Gide would come back and prove the naysayers wrong by earning a little bit of money, before the next big blowup. Each time he made some money, he was promoted. As if the higher-ups had blowup amnesia. Many traders like Andrews and Large and Churchill who did nothing but make money hypothesized that the higher-ups liked and could relate to Gide. He had a business degree from the Sorbonne. He spoke four languages. He wore fancy clothes. He had a thirty-two-inch waist and his platinum wristwatch, made in Switzerland, told the time in New York, London, and Hong Kong. And now as Gide marched toward the Ghost's office without his bicycle outfit or leg brace to protect him, the trading floor held a collective breath.

Doug Lawrence, the laconic, ex-NSA man and head of security, appeared. He was standing by the door to escort Gide off the floor. Gide held his chin up and stood erect as he walked out of the Ghost's office and down the row past the trading desk. Three-quarters of the way to the exit, he touched his index finger to the corner of his eye. Even though it might have been a slight itch he was scratching, he went down in trading floor lore as the only trader who cried on the trading floor. One week later the story recounted in the bar would have it that he was bawling like a baby as he strode down the aisle.

The Ghost could be seen from his glass-walled office following Gide's walk of shame without seeming to see him. His mouth wore a smirk that looked like it could mask sadness or rage with equal capacity. As soon as the exit door closed behind him and Craig Gide was gone forever, the entire trading floor did not applaud the departure of this universally loathed trader, no wisecrack was made, no cheer went up, no sigh of relief was breathed. The Ghost was not done and no one felt safe.

As Hutch was sitting there he felt a shock of pain run down his arm. Then his chest tightened up. God damn grape soda, thought Hutch. He grabbed his arm and then tried to raise it, a failed salute. Clasping his elbow and letting out a heavy breath, Hutch slid out of his chair and onto the floor.

His last thought before light flooded his eyes was the vision of "The Rumble in the Jungle" poster in his bedroom, of George Foreman hunched down tight in mid bob and weave, ducking one of Ali's lightning-fast jabs, a look of determination, pain, and rage in his swollen face as he struggled in vain against a greater fighter.

The Colonel was over at the printer picking up his positions report and was walking back to his desk when he came across Hutch on the ground clutching his elbow with a pained look on his face. Thinking Hutch was drunk and had banged his elbow when he slid out of his chair, the Colonel stepped over Hutch's body before continuing back to his desk.

The paramedics arrived within ten minutes and attempted CPR at the scene. When Hutch made no sign of being resuscitated, they carried the unconscious trader off the floor on a stretcher. Churchill and Large, his two best friends, followed helplessly in tow. When one of the paramedics almost tripped on the carpet while transporting the burly Hutch, a great gasp rose up within the room. Stan Lawrence held open the door for the paramedics, as they rushed out. Then the trading floor was quiet once again. On Hutch's computer screen his e-mail in box was flashing. The unopened message was from the Ghost. It asked Hutch to see him down in his office.

At 4:00 P.M. a companywide e-mail was sent out, that Hutchinson had died of a stroke at Johns Hopkins Hospital shortly after he arrived. A father of four, William Hutchinson was forty-one years old

One of the company lawyers was hanging out by the desk of Saul Jacobsen, a portfolio manager of the coal plants.

—Forty-one, sighed the lawyer reading the message over Jacobsen's shoulder.

—He was not a healthy man, said Jacobsen.

Churchill and Andrews could be heard two rows down on the trading floor simultaneously shouting at the brokers over their squawk box.

—Give me that fucking piece of Cal 07 or I'll fucking box you for life, screamed Andrews.

—Jesus Christ, I give up! That shitbird always pulls his fucking bid, shouted Churchill, yelling about something completely different.

The lawyer and Jacobsen regarded the red-faced traders and the lawyer audibly swallowed.

—It's like Hutchinson never died, he said in a hushed voice.

Jacobsen looked at him matter-of-factly and said:

—When a trader dies, nobody cries.

PART TWO

MILT SHOOTS FOR PAR

A young caddy at the pro shop told Milt there was an alligator in the pond on the ninth. He smiled and tipped the lid of his Calloway visor. The kid's a clown, thought Milt. But after Milt saw an armadillo scamper out of a hole in the ground on the second and watched an elderly man peppered with small welts limp past them on the fourth, shaking his head and saying: "God-damned Africanized bees," he began to wonder. As he approached the half-way point on eight, Milt's ball was hidden somewhere in the dry, yellow thatch of rough ten yards off the fairway.

His client, Stan Couch, stood in the middle of the fairway, legs shoulder-width apart, back straight, arms relaxed and slightly bent. Just as Stan swung his four iron, Milt quickly fished a Titleist out of his pocket and dropped it in as nice a patch of combed-down crabgrass as he could find.

This was much more than a game of golf to Milt. Now that he had locked Joe Gallagher into his front-running scheme, he needed this outing with Stan Couch to be a fine performance in the art of brokering. It would have to start with Milt not sucking so bad at golf that his client would lose respect for him.

—Found it, Milt called out.

Stan Couch remained poised in his finishing stance, frozen with his arms raised above his chest and his golf club balanced behind him. Stan's head moved ever so slightly as he watched the flight of his ball. His erect stance, the elegance of his swing, and the gleaming length of graphite club arced across his back made Stan Couch seem taller than he actually was.

—Hallelujah, he cried out.

—What's that? You on the green? shouted Milt, squinting into the sun, looking to get a bead on Couch's ball, which had just vanished into the perfect blue sky.

Stan turned to Milt, his face still wearing a smile that remained there as if transfixed by a plastic mold. His teeth, Milt had already noted, were irritatingly white.

—No, Milty. That one is in the cup—another birdie. The Lord is in my corner today.

There was a small egg-sized sweat stain at the center of Stan Couch's checkered golf shirt with the Sharks logo. It seemed like a controlled, even polite, blot of perspiration that evoked both physical fitness and ascetic industriousness on this ninety-five-degree afternoon at Rosewood. Milt, on the other hand, had a large blotchy lake of perspiration that had spread across his golf shirt like a disease. The cottony fabric stuck fast to his belly.

—All right, Milty. Go for it, buddy, said Stan Couch, watching. —You're due for a bogey, maybe a par if you get lucky.

So far on the day Milt had yet to score even a double bogey. Milt licked the salty moisture lingering on his upper lip and without thinking about his underwear riding up on him, feeling guilty about his fifth or sixth time cheating with a dropped ball, or flinching at armored rats or wincing before the sight of angry, grandfather oil tycoons, Milt let loose with a swing that made him feel weightless. The club face connected square on the small, white orb—and although Milt wobbled some on the finish, there was the sound of an effortlessness hit—a surprising metallic *pop!* that seemed to always have its own unique, even magical, echo.

The ball careened in a low line drive arc, caught a fortunate bounce by the bunker, and hopped like an athletic cricket across the green, coming to a rest inches from the cup. Milt stood there in awe of his shot. He was sure that he himself could not have made it. Was this the Milt who loved the doglegs because it was easier to cheat? Was this the Milt whose lower back pain prevented him from following through on his drives? A vague feeling of elation evaporated and an ignoble giddiness crept up his spine that made him want to start drinking immediately.

—MOTHERFUCKER! cried Milt, realizing he was going to par the hole.

Stan Couch nodded his head at his broker. It was a damn fine shot, Milt's best all day. He was even going to congratulate Milt on such a fine shot, but Milt had ruined the moment with foul language. Stan made a note to himself that next time Milt visited him here in Houston, they'd go to a different course. Stan was a member here at Rosewood Country Club.

When they approached the green, they saw the closeness of Milt's ball to the edge of the cup had been an illusion. The ball was perched atop a tough decline almost two feet away. The decline and curvature of the green increased the trickiness of the shot. Milt uttered a sole "damnit" and Stan Couch was surprised by such defeatism. Brokers have to be defeatist I suppose, thought Stan, their livelihood belongs in another man's hands; "cheery skies" is the sales pitch and contempt is the reality. Milt licked his chops. He was not to be denied. With a putt that was graceful and controlled in its own shabby way, Milt knocked the ball in from twenty-two inches out. Milt's golf game had finally lived up to his ten-gallon Stetson. Despite Stan Couch's various references to God and Christianity and his refusal of alcohol from the girl in the beer cart and his lack of colorful language, Milt celebrated his par by going into his golf bag, pulling forth his driver, and announcing:

—Nine's next. I'm going to go shove this club up that gator's ass. I might even make a pair of boots out of him.

STAN COUCH'S XANADU

Milt sat out on the patio under a large umbrella and gazed over the expanse of Stan Couch's backyard. Just yards from the deck was an elliptical-shaped swimming pool decorated with ruby red Spanish tile that gave the water a deep purplish color. Beyond the pool was a row of five finely trimmed hibiscus trees. Milt felt they gave the landscape a Mediterranean feel. Behind the sculpted trees, obscured for privacy but not completely out of view, was a strange white dome. What is that? wondered Milt.

Milt had suspected from seeing the inside of Stan's palatial house that he was childless. His wife was an attractive Mexican woman who spoke English with a thick accent. Milt surmised she was either an ex-stripper from Stan's pre-AA days or a nice girl whom he met at church in his current life as a recovering alcoholic. He had seen an oil painting of Jesus in the bathroom hanging above the green marble sink, and the son of God had looked very Hispanic with the dark twinkling eyes of a mariachi, a healthy tan, and a nicely coiffed head of coal-black hair.

It was Stan himself, not his wife, who brought the pitcher of lemonade out onto the patio. He poured Milt and then himself a tall glass. Stan then gingerly placed three ice cubes from a silver bucket with a pair of tongs into each glass. Milt noted how everything from his golf swing to the placing of ice cubes into a glass was the picture of deliberate care and efficiency of movement. That's what it must be like being sober all the time, thought Milt.

Stan took a sip of his lemonade and gestured to the pool.

—Take a dip if you want, Milty.

—Nah. It's nice just sitting here relaxing, taking in the scene.

Two chickadees perched on the top of a lawn chair moved their heads like small, mechanical toys and chirped in agreement.

—God has been good to me, since I sobered up.

—I can see that, said Milt. —Trading has been going well then.

—Trading success only came after I got on the Program. I mean I had money before, but I was heading for failure. Now everything is as I always pictured it.

Stan put down his glass on the table and laughed out loud.

—Right down to even my golf game. Now that is a miracle.

In his slyly professional way, ever calculating, Milt the broker went to work and mimed genuine interest, curiosity. Like a guilty sinner before a reformed saint Milt's body played the part. He slunk back into his cushioned patio chair with an ingratiating, humble face that let Stan Couch devolve from reverie into sermon. Stan first spoke about meeting his wife and how she'd given him hope. And then went on to tell how the Program gave him the tools and eventually how he'd converted to the First Adventist Church and that he was on his way, in the struggle of his days, toward working to becoming saved. He asked Milt about his own Catholic upbringing. Milt spoke about it in a quiet, reserved way and dropped certain uninventable details like the fact that he still used his rosary beads to validate the legitimacy of his belief. Milt realized this discussion was the key to Milt's own earthly salvation.

As Stan spoke and praised the Lord and his life and his wife and his luck and his house and his pool and his job and his country and his faith, Milt bore inside his own belly an evil, yellow-fanged, greedy, ugly, growling demon, even more hungry and obscene than usual. Milt felt he saw Stan's preaching for what it was, a selfish need to exorcise guilt by saving others.

—I like the way you put it about the prodigal son, Stan, said Milt. —Makes me think.

Milt sighed, feigning relaxation. He crossed his legs and leaned forward slightly, speaking softly, in a confessional tone:

—Since my divorce Jesus has really gone from my life.

—And he will take you back, Milt. But you've got to make sacrifices. The sauce puts a roadblock in God's plan.

Then Stan told Milt in further detail about the Program: all twelve steps. He'll get Milty's soul, thought Milt, and Milty will get my suite at the pink, beautiful Don CeSar.

Milt had reasoned that as one who believed in goodness and good fortune and good luck and America's success and zeal as part and parcel of the whole works, Stan was a natural bull. But being from a utility background, Stan was used to selling power and believed the price of electricity was often hyped by the premium put on it by the big banks from New York speculating on shit they really didn't understand: he was a bear.

—The New York financial boys and their cronies at the hedge funds, said Stan, holding up his lemonade. —They may be bulls, but they are un-American. The bulls have a self-serving optimism, which is founded in sleaze. They are, Milt, sinners who think the market is going up and that they are going to Heaven.

It's a crusade, thought Milt, squelching the desire to click his heels together.

—They are wrong on both counts, said Stan.

Getting Stan to sell on into Gallagher's and the Ghost's existing short ERCOT summer futures position was going to be easier than he thought. If God wanted the market to puke, then puke it must! Like the beautiful sound of his perfect golf shot, Milt heard the sweet sound of success in Stan's market homily.

Toward the end of the afternoon when the sun faded into the bright pink clouds beyond the haze of Houston's horizon, after talking together quietly for hours, Milt asked Stan a question.

—What is that tent-looking thing over there behind your trees?

—Oh that, said Stan. —That's a yurt. It's an enclosed tent with AC, and paneled floor where Josifa does her yoga.

—A yurt, repeated Milt.

—It's great. The latest thing in H-town. Comes from the Mongols, actually. They lived in them as nomads on the steppes. Easy to put up, easy to take down, and lots of space.

Milt's gizzard of a chin folded up on itself, as he bobbed his head up and down in agreement. All the way from murderous Mongols and Genghis

Khan to Texas housewives, stretching their thighs. Milt understood why Stan Couch thought Jesus was winning the war on Satan's slaves.

The next morning Milt woke up shivering in his hotel room at Quality Inn. With an exultant *ugh!* Milt executed a labored ninja roll across his mattress, sprung out of bed, took two steps to the room's thermostat by the window, and turned off the air-conditioning. Milt wasn't used to the Texas heat, a dry, ravenous heat that withered the skin and scorched the lungs. Then Milt recalled the dinner with Stan at the steak house. He smiled and patted his belly: victory. His shivering was a result of overdoing it on the AC, not the booze. In honor of his teetotaler client he'd only had a few glasses of wine, no hard stuff. He and Couch had gone to Morton's, and each ordered the Valhalla, a 22-ounce rib eye steak, and talked about the market. At the end of the night, while spooning some crème brûlée topped with blackberries into his mouth, Milt had merely alluded to the fact that Allied Power had begun to implement a short position in summer ERCOT.

—The fucker is going to squash it, said Stan, his dark eyes flashing with anger.

—I was just saying that . . .

—Shut up, Milt. Shut up and listen to me.

Stan then confided to Milt that he'd been wanting to get very short. He didn't want the Ghost beating him to the punch. Stan had just been waiting for his moment. But now it was happening.

—This next week I'm going to short the summer and September contracts, exclusively through you. Get me bit players, small utilities. Or sleeve the trades if you have to. I don't want Allied on the other side of any trades. They can't know we're front-running them. We'll get off a minimum of one hundred and fifty megawatts a day. And, Milt, I want discretion. If I find out that my name comes up as a market seller, you'll be fired on the spot.

Stan had taken longer to divulge his strategy than Gallagher, but then again Couch was the kind of trader who once his mind was made up rode that position to settlement. Couch, by nature stubborn and pessimistic, a trader who swung for size, was key to the success of Milt's plan.

All the pigeons were in the coop.

THE GHOST AND THE
EXECUTIVES

McDuggin, the CEO, and Williams, the president, had invited the Ghost to the venerable Olympia Club. The sit-down was a Thursday luncheon to go over trading strategies for Allied Power's third quarter: the essence of which was how the energy desk was going to make one hundred million dollars.

At the club the Ghost was greeted by a formally dressed doorman, whose black coat bore elegant, gold-embroidered epaulets. The Ghost made his way carefully up the steps, holding on to the brass handrail. The front hall spilled out into a lounging area. The room had a spacious, domed ceiling and black-and-white tiled floor. On the back wall a dusty, life-sized portrait of a glum, unsmiling George Washington sat astride a warhorse. The Ghost felt lost in the dimly lit room. He spun to the left and, in doing so, bumped into a large marble bust. The Ghost peered at the stern, hook-nosed statue. The desk captain noted the small collision and cleared his throat. The Ghost glanced over in the direction of the front desk and gave the desk captain his name. The man had a small salt-and-pepper mustache that looked like toothbrush bristles. It twitched when the Ghost said he was meeting members McDuggin and Williams in the dining room for lunch.

—Sir, do you have a tie?

—A tie, repeated the Ghost, in his own mind being fair and giving the factotum one chance to back off.

—Yes. A tie. There's a dress code in the dining room.

The Ghost removed his dark-tinted glasses, revealing his nystagmus-afflicted eyes. Dull blue, they palpitated, flicking back and forth like something robotic or insectoid. His eyes seemed to scan the desk clerk in a gridlike pattern. The clerk nervously poked at his mustache. He was trying to come up with words, the right words, proper, inoffensive words, and he was struggling. The Ghost waited. Judging from the obeisant tone in his voice, the desk clerk began to suggest something, a noise issued from deep in his throat, a sort of placating sound that was going to accommodate this surly guest, and before he could come out with it, the Ghost looked at the clerk with the calm, piercing gaze that a prison warden reserves for the lowliest inmate.

—Don't be rude, said the Ghost. —I'm a guest of Miles McDuggin. I'm nearly legally blind. Would you please show me the way to the lunchroom.

—I'm so sorry, sir. Please, right this way, stammered the desk clerk.

Miles McDuggin was a swiller of expensive Scotches, a silver-haired club gentleman who still was able to pull off the easygoing blue-collar air of a joke-telling union rep. Roger Williams, the president, sat beside Miles McDuggin with his hands in his lap. He was the first African-American admitted to the Olympia Club. He had the reserved demeanor of a diplomat and an aristocrat's sense of the immaculate: crisp, starched white shirt, pants perfectly pressed, shoes impeccably shined. Williams possessed that great power of true executives—inscrutability. The Ghost knew less about Williams but felt he understood him better. An Ivy Leaguer, Williams had less to prove than McDuggin. Hence, he was more reasonable, but twice as unforgiving.

Neither man had ever traded for his livelihood and for that reason the Ghost harbored an innate trader's mistrust of them. There would always be jobs for these executives. But the trader making his way down the hall, the man without the tie, once he was bounced for the second time, rarely ever got a third title shot.

The Ghost was escorted through the clustered dining room to the executive's table. Hustling waiters flitted about with serving trays like nervous water striders skittering on the surface of a pond. The desk clerk navigated the Ghost through the labyrinth of the lunch crowd without incident and considered it a victory.

McDuggin and Williams stood and each in turn shook the Ghost's hand. The Ghost didn't mind that the executives had seen him escorted. He liked to encourage the idea that he was brilliant, a blind savant, a man capable of playing championship chess when the board in front of him was merely mist and shadows.

—I recommend the crab bisque, said McDuggin upon sitting.

The easiest thing for him to eat was a sandwich. These places always had a B.L.T.

—B.L.T. sandwich sounds good, said the Ghost.

—No bisque, Randall? inquired McDuggin, arching his eyebrows.

—Not today, said the Ghost.

Williams played the straight man and after some small talk and an order of shrimp cocktail for the table came right out with their concern.

The Ghost anticipated the first strike and in defense grasped his glass of water.

—We're wondering about something. And we're not here to tell you how to do your job. But there is a concern.

The Ghost bought himself time by steadying his hand for a moment, pretending to almost spill his glass of water, which wavered in his tenuous grip. The meeting was, as he suspected, an ambush. He knew it wasn't going to be about macrotrading strategy. The Ghost was surprised that Andrews acted as quickly as he did going behind his back and warning the brass of the large short position.

If they weren't concerned about him upsetting his water and causing a scene they would have been zeroing in on where his tie should be, and would've had the upper hand. The Ghost smiled, putting down the glass safely, reassuring them. Their attention thus averted, the Ghost called their bluff.

—You're wondering why we're short everywhere and why Andrews is long?

The Ghost licked his lips.

—It's my contention that Andrews is going to get destroyed.

—And he shares the exact same view, said Williams. —That you're going to get killed. And that the position that the rest of the trading floor has on, that was spearheaded by you, is too aggressive of a short.

—First of all, Andrews is too conservative. Second of all, I would've fired him already but he hasn't lost any money yet, so I've kept him on.

—Randall, I think what Roger is trying to say is that we just want you to know that part of your job as head of the trading desk is to make money, yes. But we want to avoid any unnecessary . . .

The executive hesitated. He was searching for a word other than "blow-ups."

—Drawdowns, he said finally and held his hands up in a defensive posture.

Normally, corporate didn't delve too far into the position of the trading book. It was something they knew little about and preferred to let the numbers speak for themselves. The Ghost now saw the setup. The executives had been alerted to the risks of his sizable short play. It had, of course, been Andrews who'd done an end run and complained directly to Williams and McDuggin. Now, either the Ghost's short position would pay off and make $100 million or Andrews would get his old job back. So easy for the executives. They got to pit their top two guys against each other. If the Ghost didn't deliver, well, he'd at least been given a nice lunch in a fancy club with two gentlemen executives and been properly forewarned.

Andrews had been so by the book, thought the Ghost, so prosaic in his strategy. His own destruction of Andrews would be a calculated, brutal, and clandestine affair.

—Blowups only happen when you're unhedged and on the wrong side. We're neither, said the Ghost.

—Williams here will follow up with the risk committee to make sure those hedges are in place, said McDuggin. —Now may I recommend the crème brûlée for dessert.

A lackey from the front desk came up and whispered something in Williams's ear and handed him a white note card. He read it slowly, deliberately. When he was done Williams looked up at the Ghost and said:

—Sorry about the mix-up with regard to the dress code. We'll address that for the next time.

—It's no problem, said the Ghost. —A tie has never had anything to do with me making money.

The executives both let out an uncertain chuckle, wondering if they had been insulted. The Ghost, his palpitating eyes invisible behind his glasses, hidden from the executives, smiled at McDuggin and Williams, figuring he had at least played them to a draw.

THE MARINER

The Colonel and his wife, Stephanie, waited at Long Wharf Marina for the limo that would be bringing the Ghost. It was early Saturday morning and the sunlight glinted off small patches of oil in the harbor, dirty rainbows. Brown bay water smacked against the sides of the boats. Moored in their slips, this fleet of stinkpot yachts, whalers, cruising vessels, and the odd sloop or J-28 jostled about impatiently like dogs begging to be taken for a walk.

The American flag flapped lazily, the breeze came off the bay south by southwest. The Ghost said he would be there at one. His limo service dropped him off at twelve fifty-two. For the Ghost punctuality was a form of respect.

—The weather is good, Stephanie, said the Colonel. —So there's no excuse for getting seasick.

The Colonel helped the Ghost on board the whaler.

—I'll need a life jacket, said the Ghost.

Upon the Ghost's command the Colonel went aft and pulled some life jackets out from under a flip-top seat.

—It smells like gas, called out Stephanie.

—The marina is soaked with diesel.

The sound of the clanging halyards put the Ghost into a sailor's reverie. Soon he'd be free of land, sea bound. He loved boats, the powerful sound of the waves, the salty blasts of ocean air, even the impertinent squawk of sea-gulls.

As the Boston whaler headed out of the marina, its twin Evinrude engines churned. Bobbing up and down in the boat's crested wake were soda cans, cardboard, a headless sea duck that had been hit by a speedboat, and other debris. The Ghost saw none of it. He pulled his red baseball cap with its weathered brim down over his forehead. He knew he was surrounded by industrial structures, fossils of a once booming port city; a defunct fort from the revolutionary war; the near ancient sea-worn docks, some of which must have plummeted into the bay leaving only the stark skeletons of black pilings poking up above the surf. But standing there beside the Colonel he could just concentrate on the whipping wind and sea spray, the smell of the ocean and the sun warming his back. He could almost convince himself that the faint smudges he saw in the distance were a glittering expanse of open blue water.

When the whaler passed the shipping lane docks with their massive Caterpillar cranes, the Colonel became animated.

—Notice how those cranes are the only things we've seen that aren't rusted out. It's because the container ships still deliver cargo here.

—They're beautiful, said Stephanie.

The Colonel told Stephanie she'd better go up to the bow because she'd get a better view of the city when the whaler cruised out of the harbor. The Ghost stood by the Colonel, who manned the console. The ex-marine captain explained his boat, the Northstar M84 navigation system equipped with GPS, chart plotter, and fish finder. The Ghost listened intently.

—We'd run aground if we went that way, said the Colonel, pointing.

As the whaler sped across the water, the Ghost jarred the Colonel's confidence by reprimanding his daily "drive-bys" of the secretary pool. Then the Ghost said:

—I'm going to make you a lot of money, Colonel, if you're willing to work for me, began the Ghost. —So just listen for a bit and if you like what I say just shake my hand when I'm finished and then I'll know you're with me.

The Colonel had no idea what the Ghost had coming next, if it was a threat or a trap or a promotion. He stood there, stung by sea spray, waiting for the proposition.

The Ghost enjoyed the motion of the boat, veering along its course.

—You're going to help me, said the Ghost at last.

—What do I have to do?

—Have you ever heard of a wash trade?

—No, said the Colonel.

—It's simple. You and I will transact, buy and sell, between the trading arm and the origination arm: in-house trades. I keep the winners and we'll delete the losers, passing profits from origination to trading. The rate-payers will pick up the origination tab and trading gets paid.

—So I lose money and you make money, said the Colonel.

—Exactly, said the Ghost. —We won't be greedy. We'll basis over about one hundred and fifty K a month.

—What happens when I get fired?

—No one in origination gets fired. If your boss gets cranky about losses, we'll give you some positive numbers that month and then back to business. If Pellazi fires you, in like a year or so, I'll hire you on our desk. You'll be getting paid to lose. I'll give a bonus double what Pellazi ever gave you. Plus, you're on my expense account.

The Colonel nodded. Then he frowned. The Ghost could tell what he was thinking and addressed his fears.

—What's my upside in screwing you over? You could get us *both* fired. We're going to be a team. Besides, I've looked at your daily trades. You've been stealing from Pellazi. Probably for years. We both know he's an idiot. And now you're going to get really paid.

The Colonel put out his hand.

The Ghost raised a finger. The look behind his dark glasses bored into the Colonel's forehead.

—One more thing. You are *also* going to help me get rid of Andrews. When I tell you to sell all the length off your units, you do it. And then sell some more. I'm just going to wait for the appropriate time when I can squeeze Andrews out of his long position. So you just sit on the desk and wait for my word.

The Colonel felt his chest unclench. He straightened himself up, standing taller and prouder.

Just before noon the Colonel pulled *Outage* to the end of a small estuary on the North Shore. The estuary spilled into a secluded cove whose shoreline was shrouded by a thick forest of oak, birch, and evergreen trees. What few houses spotted the landscape peered out from the woods like abandoned forts, hidden in the brush.

—Don't these people have lawns? complained Stephanie Haupt.

—It's a good place for a swim if you want, Stephanie, said the Colonel from behind the steering console. And then:

—I'll throw the anchor overboard. We're breaking for lunch.

Stephanie Haupt spread out a red-and-white-checkered blanket on the deck and put out two large Tupperware bowls. Inside one were baby back ribs smothered in Kansas City Sweet sauce and cooked in apple juice. The second container had German potato salad with stone-ground mustard. The Colonel played bartender and handed out bottles of beer. Besides the drumbeat of a woodpecker's beak against a faraway tree, the cove emanated quiet. As they began their feast, the Colonel toasted to the Ghost. His wife heaped their paper plates with food.

—Do you need some sunblock? asked Stephanie Haupt. —Daniel doesn't need any. He's part Cherokee, that's why he has that nice, dark head of hair.

The Ghost let the cold beer wash back down his throat. He felt the sun beat away on his exposed neck.

GOOGLE

The Ghost had a lunch meeting with Gallagher the following day. He sat in front of his computer, which was a closed-circuit TV, which allowed him to magnify the screen font to match his impaired vision. He typed the name "Joseph Gallagher" into the Google search engine. The Ghost enjoyed gathering intelligence via the Internet. It always amazed him how the most innocuous details were sometimes the most telling.

The name Joseph Gallagher was not an uncommon one and brought up too many hits. Even "Joe Gallagher Boston" made for a long night of scrolling. The Ghost scanned each hit, moving his specially made ball and turret mouse with the base of his palm. There was Joseph Gallagher the union lawyer. Joe Gallagher of the Gaelic Hurling League. And yet another: this one was a picture of an overweight African-American city alderman.

Finally, the Ghost came across two hits that could be his Gallagher. They were Amazon.com book reviews. The two reviews were of science books by the author Michio Kaku: one on wormholes and the other on dark matter. He painstakingly read them, word by word. The reviews were moronic.

The third hit he pulled up was an article from the Boston free weekly newspaper *On the Town*. Gallagher's name appeared under the image of a color photograph. It was Joe Gallagher looking large and oblivious, standing next to a woman with dark hair who wore a distracted, aloof expression on her face.

The text underneath the photograph read:

Boston artist, Celina Gallagher, featured at the gallery opening. Standing with her is husband, Joe Gallagher.

Gallagher's wife threw the Ghost off a bit. He had not expected Gallagher to be married to a serious artist. She had won awards and fellowships.

When the Ghost finished reading the article about the local art gallery's first of three exhibitions, he gnawed at the back of his thumb. No revelation came to him. For a moment it bothered him that a clear-cut image of Gallagher hadn't emerged. Unlike the Colonel's pure greed, Gallagher's motives still evaded the Ghost. Yet staring at the screen, at the picture of Joe Gallagher and his wife, the Ghost realized all he had to do was pay a visit to the gallery. Maybe purchase some art.

PIZZA PARLOR

Angelo's pizzeria was on the edge of Little Italy next to Vassino's, the gelato and pastry shop. The woman who owned it liked Gallagher because he always fed the pinball machine quarters as he waited for his order. The only other person who seemed to use the thing was her son who played in between deliveries.

It was a bright summer day and the air was crisp and dry. Gallagher sat at an outdoor table with the Ghost, a large pepperoni pizza between them.

—How about *The Shining*? asked the Ghost.

Gallagher bit into a piece of pizza and nodded his head as he chewed.

—A classic.

—*I Spit on Your Grave*?

It was bid and answer on one of the Ghost's favorite topics, horror films. He'd explained to Gallagher that horror movies were the only genre he watched in his youth, because the dialogue, the screams of horror, the sounds of violence, and the eerie musical scores allowed him to enjoy the movies despite his impaired vision.

Gallagher was aware that this interview was much more than a question of knowledge. It was a test of *ainos*, the Greek word loosely translated as: those who share a forgotten tongue. Gallagher himself thought of *ainos* as a tribal thing, a way to ferret out pretenders or legitimate comrades. The way one answered the questions, the methodology of thought, gestures, and speech patterns were just as important, if not more so, than the actual answers themselves.

—I saw it drunk in high school. Don't really remember it.

—How about *It's Alive*?

—With the mutant baby. That was cool.

—Here's one I'd be interested in your opinion: *The Evil Dead*?

Gallagher put down his soda and rattled the ice in his cup, as if this one required a little extra consideration.

—*The Evil Dead* was stupid, said Gallagher finally. —Horror movies aren't supposed to be funny.

The Ghost raised his hand, as if halting the conversation to make an important point.

—You're right. *The Evil Dead* does not hit the radar.

The Ghost picked up a slice and bit into it. Gallagher could tell that the Ghost had relaxed a bit. Gallagher realized that this was a head fake of sorts. Letting up the pressure was a tried-and-true sleight of hand that made the interviewee feel at ease, that *ainos* had been achieved, when in reality it was merely that the second, more challenging phase of the discerning process had begun.

—You should go rent *I Spit on Your Grave*. The director of that movie understood human nature. He would've made a good trader. His timing was flawless.

Gallagher, whose sense of irony was not always the most finely tuned, did not miss the fact that the more intelligent man in this conversation wanted to talk about B horror movies and not trading or highbrow science or history. Still, Gallagher felt he'd held his own, and prepared for the second stage of the interview.

The Ghost gave his cash trader a glaring, inquisitive look. One last question:

—How about *The Evil Face*?

Gallagher shook his head.

—Never heard of it, he conceded.

The Ghost drank the remainder of his soda dry, making a sucking sound through the straw.

—That's because it was never made. That was me seeing if you were full of shit. I don't like liars.

Gallagher laughed out loud. He laughed because he was a liar.

—What's so funny? asked the Ghost.

—I was going to say, "Never heard of it but that's a lame title," lied Gallagher.

The Ghost grinned. Then he let loose a drawn-out noise from the back of his throat that was his mode of laughter.

The Ghost wiped some cheese from his chin with a napkin.

—The bosses gave me some target numbers, the Ghost said to Gallagher, leaning forward in business mode. —And I need five to ten million from you this year.

It was a stout number. Gallagher nodded.

—There are two ways to guarantee this number.

Gallagher pursed his lips and listened.

—First, I notice you are short summer ERCOT. So you agree with my first point—the direction of the market. Second, there are ways of making sure we stay solvent . . . or, don't post huge losses.

Gallagher placed his soda on the table.

—There will be times when the market moves against us. I want you to defend against that. On those days, you'll mark the curves in our favor. If it goes against us badly, just call Milt at the end of the day and execute a trade out of the money. That way Milt can report the marks as unchanged, and our position won't look underwater.

Potential jail time was not part of Gallagher's trading methodology. He began to have an uneasy feeling like an amoeba was entering his bloodstream.

—Believe me, said the Ghost. —Milt will do what you say. He wants your business. We're his biggest customer.

—Why mismark ERCOT? asked Gallagher. —It's such a small hub.

—It's a key hub in my plan. It's going to be a multiregion coordinated play, a long squeeze.

The Ghost took a bite out of his pizza crust and gave Gallagher a confident look.

—We've got people on board, said the Ghost. —Take the Colonel, I mean Haupt. Even though he's in origination, he'll be adding to our bottom line. You should work with him. Maybe work some transmission deals with him from the Midwest to ERCOT.

Gallagher speculated that the Colonel's cut was small. No doubt the Ghost had gotten him cheap.

—Certain people aren't on board with the team, he said, still chewing the crust. He swallowed, licked his lips, and almost sneered as he said:

—They're long and wrong.

Gallagher realized it was Andrews who was the target. He'd read *On War* and missed it completely. Andrews was the one who was going to be dealt with by the Ghost's manipulation of the political instrument.

—We need to make our numbers, continued the Ghost. —To make one hundred million you need to put on size. To defend size, to protect your chips, you need an advantage. This is how it works in the Big Game. Can I count on you?

The Ghost stuck out his hand in a fist. He raised it for Gallagher to tap with his own, the knighting of a squire. Their knuckles collided.

Gallagher felt his chest tighten. His first thought was would he be asked to do something that would undermine Andrews? Smear his old boss's credibility? Thinking for a moment, Gallagher decided to offer up something that would cost him nothing but at the same time prove his loyalty.

—I can do one other thing for you, said Gallagher.

—What's that?

—The Colonel hasn't been able to get anything done with Northern Lakes Power. Since he's part of the bottom line now, I can introduce the Colonel to my old boss, Peter the German. I think if he plays it right, the Colonel might be able to work a physical deal with Peter.

The Ghost nodded and said matter-of-factly:

—We'll see.

—Thanks for the pizza.

—Don't mention it.

POLKA BAND

Peter the German was known as "the man who smiles" by the secretary pool at the utility. His coworkers called him "Mysterious" Pete. Every day he wore a plain denim button-down shirt to work. Then one of the dispatchers had seen Pete at a casino in St. Cloud wearing a yellow suit that matched his blond mustache, while carrying a monkey-headed cane. This story circulated around the utility and the nickname "Mysterious" Pete soon followed. But to Gallagher, who had sat with Pete for hours in his ice-fishing house on Lake Minnetonka, drinking, talking politics, every once in a while pulling a walleye or a northern pike up from the line dropped through a hole in the frozen floor, it was Peter the German, because he was of German stock and he drank beer like a German, which is to say he put away pint after pint without seeming to get drunk. This was an amazing feat to Gallagher, who felt the urge to start telling lies after two beers and scale trees or fire escapes after five or so.

Gallagher and the Colonel sat across the table from Peter the German. The bar was High's Polonaise in St. Paul, Minnesota. Gallagher had chosen High's as the place for the meeting. It was a long, dimly lit hallway of a bar connected to High's restaurant that featured Cuban fare. That night there was a special on fried cheese curds listed on a blackboard by the cash register for $2.95. At one end of the bar was a small stage where a two-person polka band was making music. Playing the tuba was a rail-thin man with a sparse red beard and half-closed eyes who looked like the weight of the instrument might tip him over. By his side, on the accordion, was an energetic middle-aged brunette, wearing the traditional German dirndl. She swayed back and forth under the lights working the squeezebox. Gallagher could see that her red-cheeked face glowed with perspiration. There was something robust and genuine about her that made Gallagher remember the aspects of Minnesota he missed.

Dancing enthusiastically in front of the band were three lesbian couples and one lonely drunk man who meandered as if lost at the edge of the dance floor. While not a lesbian bar per se, High's Polonaise attracted these all-women couples, especially on polka night. Gallagher had chosen High's for this exact purpose. The Colonel was a ladies' man. Gallagher realized if the Colonel's eye wandered during the conversation, Peter the German might get annoyed. High's Polonaise on polka night, he reasoned, would be as safe a place as any to insulate the Colonel from his libido.

Gallagher was pleased that the meeting was going better than he'd imagined it would. The Colonel and Peter did not hate each other yet. And, as Gallagher suspected, without any distractions, the Colonel was focused on the conversation and even offered up some insights about transmission plays and line outages that seemed to impress the usually reserved Peter the German. Peter even spoke about looking at one or two of the term deals that the Colonel proposed. Gallagher viewed the Colonel as an opportunist, willing to cut some corners, and he knew Peter the German to be a savvy operator more than capable of allowing those corners to be cut in the interests of closing a profitable deal.

—You know, Colonel, Peter here is an expert poker player.

Peter the German leered at Gallagher.

—I've seen him hide a card in his sandwich, continued Gallagher.

The Colonel tilted his head and raised his eyebrows, feigning to be impressed. Gallagher noted that the Colonel was a first-rate sycophant.

—Indeed, said the Colonel.

—If you know Joe, said Peter, —you know he's full of it.

—I know Gallagher, said the Colonel.

—Do you play? asked Peter the German.

—Off and on, said the Colonel.

—Next time you come, I'll have you out to the ice-fishing house. Bourbon, cards, and walleye.

When Peter the German invited the Colonel to his ice-fishing house, Gallagher chalked the meeting up as a certain victory. Gallagher would achieve loyal soldier status from the Ghost for this. He decided to give into a celebratory mood and indulge.

He ate the first bowl of butter-soaked mussels in under three and a half minutes, the second in four, the third in just under five. Looking at the healthy woman on the accordion, working the squeezebox, put a hunger on Gallagher. As he shucked the mussels, butter splashed on his shirt, the table, and his dinner partner to the right, the Colonel. While on any given day other traders on the floor could probably beat Gallagher for total food consumption, Gallagher had a gift for speed eating. He ate with abandon. His stomach, assaulted, was in a state of shock and unable to register the feeling of being satiated. He shoveled shellfish and spilled beer down his throat at a frantic pace. To better suit his purpose, Gallagher imagined himself in a time and place where the eating mores dispensed with cleanliness, hygiene, and manners. A time in history more given toward banging on the bar with your pewter mug; a time when the furniture was sturdier, sturdy enough to support, say, a grown man dancing on a table.

Gallagher belched and wiped the swathe of butter from his upper lip.

—Man, that's good, he said.

Finally, Peter the German addressed his old friend.

—So, Joe, do you miss us?

Gallagher's eyes were glazed over with food lust. He was contemptuous that anyone was talking to him, requiring anything more of him, since his work was essentially done. Gallagher looked over his shoulder and took in the bar: the throng of dancing women, the polka band duet, red-faced and sweating under the lights, the hapless drunk mooning about at the edge of the stage. There was something sad and loud and true at High's Polonaise. It was there waiting for him. He wasn't sure what it was but he knew it was not here at the table discussing "business," and that it lay farther on down the bar, nearer to where the smudged light percolated through the hall like some Neanderthal cave or castle dungeon. Gallagher believed he was on the edge of it: some adventure where he would inflict himself upon the world and raise his cup and talk loudly until someone forked over a wise saying or challenged him to a contest.

Gallagher scratched his head and tried to recall Peter the German's question. When he did he made his answer short:

—Hell no.

Gallagher picked up his mug of beer and stood up.

—You going to the bathroom? asked the Colonel. He gave Gallagher a glum look, trying to communicate his displeasure. He noticed that his new Brooks Brothers shirt had butter stains all up and down his right sleeve.

—No, said Gallagher. —I'm going to dance with the ladies.

—Some batch of ladies, commented the Colonel, being politic, thinking in his calculating way, You never know this guy Peter may have a sister who's a bull-dike.

Peter the German looked at Gallagher and let loose that smile for which the secretaries had named him.

As Gallagher walked down the length of the gloomy bar toward the dance floor, both Peter the German and the Colonel followed him with their eyes. When he was out of earshot, Peter the German said:

—His second week here in Minnesota he ended up in county lockup. I bailed him out.

Then the Colonel saw Peter the German lean forward and look past him down the bar toward the polka band. The Colonel turned around to see what Peter the German was gawking at. It was Gallagher. He stood in the middle of the dance floor. With one hand he gave a salute and with the other he poured a full glass of beer on his head, as if extinguishing a fire.

—I guess he likes the polka music, said the Colonel in his dry voice.

—The problem with that boy, said Peter the German, shaking his head, —is that he thinks when he dies someone's going to give him a Viking burial.

ANDREWS EATS A JAB

Andrews was angry. He was always angry. If he was up a million or down a million it was the same, because no matter what he was angry. His anger in the face of market highs and market lows was his shield. What seemed to the outside world as a perpetually angry man was in truth Andrews at the bottom of a fish bowl, calm, looking up at the tempestuous waters above. Of course it wasn't all an act. There was a lot to be angry about: pestering brokers, taxes, young traders waxing their chests and getting manicures. His doctor's appointment was up there too: some insolent thirty-something MD talking smack about hypertension, diabetes. Somehow they were connected to egg sandwiches. He liked his daily breakfast sandwich. So he was angry. But if he wasn't angry, he couldn't be really, truly happy and protected from the storm that swirled above him.

So he took another bite of his bacon, egg, and cheese sandwich.

When Gallagher marched into work Andrews was taping another picture of his family onto the bottom of his computer screen. It was a beach scene from the Andrewses' trip to Kennebunkport, Maine. The background sky was cloudy and gray and the wind must have been up because all their hair was blown back and their brightly colored sweaters were pressed against their bodies.

Andrews, the seasoned pro, the veteran, was usually above the insults that were hurled back and forth between the traders. His diminished position in the hierarchy had left him suddenly open to attack. Only last week Churchill had noticed that the heavyweight Andrews had "blown out" his loafers, the shoes having literally come undone at the seams. In the past Andrews wouldn't have cared and would've gone on wearing the shoes. But as things were, he couldn't afford to be made fun of and had gone out that day and purchased a new pair.

The second assault on Andrews's authority had come over the lunch order. The catered lunches were controlled by Andrews and had consisted of a rotation of subs, BBQ pork and ribs, cheeseburger day, Italian Thursday, and meat-lover's pizza Friday. Andrews had been out sick and the younger traders had staged a revolt. They had stepped in and ordered take-out sushi. When the Pink Shirts, as Andrews called them, tried to keep sushi on the menu, he gave it the kibosh. He also made comments about how wearing a pink shirt, getting manicures, and wearing square-toed shoes should all be banned. However, the very next Thursday sushi appeared at noon. When Andrews pressed the secretary who had countermanded his order, she told him in a quiet voice that the Ghost had done so.

This morning's first comedic barrage came from Large, who was making a bid-ask two-way on Miller's wispy hair that was on the verge of a comb-over.

—Your hair is in need of a Code Red, said Large. —Right now the market on your wig is Cobweb *at* Seaweed.

Andrews, who had a nice full head of bristly, blond hair with his trademark cowlick, was going to join the fray when he thought the better of it. I'll stay below the radar, he thought.

Andrews was opening up a new BlackBerry he'd received from the IT department. He was trying to program it, pushing the small letter key buttons with his oversized fingers. Miller noticed this.

—Hey there, Andrews, Miller said. —How're you going to type on those tiny keys with those Porky Pig fingers of yours?

Churchill and Large began to hoot with laughter. Andrews waited for their silence.

—That's easy, he said. —I'm going to use your pencil-thin dick.

More hoots of derision and laughter. Other traders peeked over their flatscreens prairie-dog style to see who was getting made fun of and to find out what the joke was.

Andrews was pleased that though he was reduced to combat on a third-grade level, he could still hold his own.

THE K-WAVE

The Eight's was the restaurant where Andrews went to watch football when he wanted to get away from his family. Gallagher sat on a wooden stool at the bar, waiting for Andrews to show. Gallagher hadn't slept well. His hair was flattened against one side of his head. His face was unshaven.

Five sets of glowing TV screens, neon lights above the bar, reflected off the shellacked countertop into Gallagher's tired eyes. He drank a tall glass of draft beer. It tasted like tap water gone bad. When the bartender came around again, Gallagher pushed the grease-stained menu to the side.

Andrews startled Gallagher when he appeared behind him, practically shouting in his ear.

—You look like crap, he boomed. A few heads of concerned parents turned from the seated dining area. The Eight's was a family restaurant during the day. At night it became a popular bar.

—If we're going to talk shop, I'd rather have you drink chocolate milk, said Andrews. —Your tolerance for alcohol is struggling.

—Your wings are coming. You like wings, right? asked Gallagher.

Andrews frowned.

He had called Gallagher on Friday night and arranged for the meeting, The Eight's Restaurant, noon at the bar. Gallagher was relieved that

Andrews had set the meeting. The Ghost's complete domination of the floor loomed over everything. Gallagher harbored thoughts of rebellion every day. He wanted Andrews to act as War Chief, even if he was a deposed one.

Andrews grabbed the menu off the counter and studied it gravely, as if analyzing an annual report. He perused it for a few minutes and said finally:

—B.L.T.s are stupid. It's a stupid sandwich. I mean it's not really a sandwich. It's like a salad with bread and mayo. There's nothing there.

Gallagher stared up at one of the TVs. The Sox were playing the Devil Rays and losing. Lowell had hit a line drive into deep left field. He was rounding first base, looking out of breath.

—Let me guess. You won't be eating any wings? asked Andrews.

—I'll have a few, said Gallagher, showing loyalty through food.

Andrews ordered a Jack and Coke. He heaved a sigh and said:

—There's no pride in this market. All our counterparties are birds.

—Liquidity is drying up, agreed Gallagher.

—I'm getting nickel-and-dimed to death myself. Plus my brokers are useless.

It was Andrews's standard fare. He loved to complain about brokers. He had been one himself at the beginning of his career. Andrews couldn't bring himself to forgive them for his time served.

—The Ghost is turning the whole book around and getting short, continued Andrews. —He's getting stupid short. He thinks natty's going to come off hard after the spring peak.

Gallagher took a long pull from his tasteless draft. Even the foam seemed stale.

—He's been talking about the K-wave, continued Andrews. —I'm sure you've heard?

—I've heard.

—You know what it is? It's some crazy macroeconomic theory. His whole short is based on this commie technical guru, continued Andrews.

—Kondratieff, said Gallagher, who'd done his homework. —He was Stalin's chief economist. He invented the K-wave: the theory of sixty-year economic cycles.

Stalin's economist had predicted the Great Depression among the Western powers. When Kondratieff spoke about the economic inefficiencies of

Communism, Stalin sent him away. He perished in the gulag. But it didn't matter: All his predictions came true.

This fed into Andrews's belief that the Ghost was at heart anti-American, but instead of confirming this to Gallagher, he just said:

—It's crazy wizard shit.

—The Ghost likes Kondratieff because he's a fatalist. There's no free will in the K-wave.

—You read too many books. The point is the Ghost did the same shit back when he blew up at Dynesty, said Andrews, shifting on his stool. —Only then he was touting something called Mosaic Theory. Bottom line is I'm so bulled up I can hardly see straight.

—So you got to trade your mind, said Gallagher. —Or you got to trade with the boss.

Andrews gnawed at his tongue inside his mouth. To him Gallagher seemed sometimes ebullient, and other times aloof. Andrews chalked it up as the schizophrenia of one who is both an alcoholic gambler *and* someone who drinks chocolate milk and reads books.

—I hired you, said Andrews. —Don't follow the lemmings off the cliff.

Gallagher pushed his beer away from him.

—I'm trying to figure a way out of this, but it hasn't come to me yet. If I reverse my ERCOT position, he'll fire me.

Andrews nodded.

—What's more, admitted Gallagher, —he has me mismarking the forward curve to make our losses look less ugly.

—You're going out on a limb, telling me this, said Andrews.

—And you know he's cozy with the Colonel now. You're long Cinergy and the Colonel has those power plants. He's long too.

—I'm wary of that, said Andrews. —I see that selloff coming from a mile away. It's all about who can stay at the table longer.

—Not if they're cooking the books, protested Gallagher.

The bartender came over and put a plate of twenty steaming wings in front of Andrews.

—He's got almost the whole shop riding the short bus, said Gallagher. —I've got to figure a way to get off.

Gallagher looked straight ahead at the shelf full of liquor bottles.

—Want to get drunk?

—Not with a lightweight like you, said Andrews.

The big man stripped two wings to the bone and then licked his fingers clean.

—They think you've lost it, Andrews, said Gallagher.

—And what do you think?

—I'm just a lemming.

—Always sell the short bus, said Andrews, not smiling.

WEATHER DERIVATIVES

The name of the artist was Nils Wundermetz. His paintings consisted of chaotic scenes of protest reminiscent of Eastern bloc countries. Large canvases with themes of barbed wire, German shepherds, riot police, book burnings, peace rallies splashed with bright rainbow colors in homage to the energy inherent in carnage and bloodshed.

—I like the one with riot police, said Gallagher. —They look like space aliens in their helmets.

—It's such crap, said Celina.

Gallagher looked at the other people meandering throughout the exhibit. He didn't think the paintings were as bad as Celina said. At least they were about something: something real and violent.

Celina touched Gallagher's arm, alerting him.

—Here comes Howard, she said.

Howard Schiller owned three art galleries: two in New York and one in Boston. His galleries in Manhattan sold high-end turn-of-the-century European second-tier Impressionists, artists on the periphery of the masters. These businesses made him wealthy. His Boston gallery featured up-and-coming contemporary artists and unknowns. It was not a profitable venture but it kept Howard's finger on the pulse of what he deemed the edgy scene. Most importantly, though, the Boston gallery allowed him to not feel that he was nothing but a picture pimp for Wall Street money. When Howard Schiller spotted Gallagher and Celina he gave out a little wave. He was wearing a cream-colored poplin suit with a white silk scarf draped around his neck, aviator style. Gallagher figured the scarf was an inevitable fashion casualty of the art world, just like a barbecue stain on a shirt was to the trading floor.

Howard introduced himself, patting Gallagher on the shoulder, saying in a deeper voice than expected:

—I feel like I know you already from the charcoal portraits.

Then he turned to Celina, pivoting on tan suede Italian loafers, and hugged her briefly. She smiled at him and put a hand on one side of his shiny, bald dome. Gallagher pigeon-holed Howard Schiller as an old money patrician, a too-elegant man of the world type, between forty and fifty years old.

Howard spread out his arms, showcasing the room:

—Can you believe it? he said happily. —Nils just keeps getting better.

Gallagher watched as Celina gauged the expression on Howard's face and listened to the tone of his voice. She brushed her hair back and turned her face to the paintings so Gallagher could not see it.

—It's incredible, she said.

—I love Nils's work, continued Howard. There was a slight British accent to his voice even though he grew up in western Maryland. —I always have. He's got such muscle, such bold passions.

Celina turned, facing Howard, and let her wide green eyes settle on an article of his clothing.

—I know, she said. And though she spoke with enthusiasm and sounded like she was going to continue praising the artist whose work she secretly hated, she stopped short and said nothing further.

Howard bent forward like a German commandant with a robotic bow, inviting Gallagher to join them for lunch at the museum cafe.

—No, said Celina. —Joe understands it's business. He just likes to make sure I'm chaperoned. He'll meet me after.

—I'm just going to walk around, said Gallagher. —Look at the art. There's enough of it to keep me busy.

As long as they'd been married, and as long as Celina had put up with Gallagher's exaggerated stories, bullshit anecdotes, half-truths, and outrageous confabulations, he had seldom seen her lie. That she had done it with such calculating coolness, while being both blasé and laconic, shook Gallagher up a little.

He walked on through the rooms of the museum in sort of a bored fog. All the paintings seemed the same. The African masks blurred into the Indonesian headpieces became faces on Eskimo totem poles. Gallagher passed by a jowly, white-haired security guard, stooped shoulders, his mouth slack almost drooling from boredom. Gallagher felt the museum closing in, and was going to walk out and go to the park.

The work of art that stopped him was a Chinese scroll. The hieroglyphs of Chinese characters that ran up and down the side of the picture told the story in symbols that were unintelligible to Gallagher. But the scroll itself depicted a scene that those in the trading world knew well. The scroll showed a blue wave rising out of the ocean like a great wall, the frothy crown churning water the only inkling of its capacity for destruction. Below the wave was a fleet of boats, most likely merchant ships bearing cargo to a nearby bustling port town, meekly lying in wait for its Maker. The picture told the inevitable story of the world markets that humans did not like to contemplate. It was a tale about weather, commodities, and the end of civilization, or nearing the end. Tumult, upheaval, and destruction.

Gallagher took a few steps back until he could clearly view the tsunami wave. It formed a market equation in his mind. The storm equaled profiting off disaster, instead of being victimized by it.

Weather derivatives, said Gallagher.

Days ago, Greenblatt, the chain-smoker and Caltech chemistry genius, had explained the odds and risk profile of a new exotic commodity called weather derivatives. The OTC product speculated on heating degree days in the winter, cooling degree days in the summer, as well as the seasonal precipitation levels.

Greenblatt, drinking a Pellegrino and lounging on his leather couch in a bright yellow Adidas track suit, had said:

—You know who takes the other side of the trade: the producers, the worriers. It's the farmers, commercial real-estate guys, and the insurance companies. Those who want to lay off risk from disaster scenarios. Super hot or cold temps or the lack of precipitation; shit that kills crops or hurricanes that ruin buildings, all so they can keep their crummy jobs. I'm there to take the other side, and for this service they pay me a big premium.

Greenblatt was getting paid by those afraid of the wave. His counterparties were those in the merchant ships, the port town, those bound to protect fixed investments.

Greenblatt had explained while cleaning out his quartz ashtray that he diversified his risk over an array of different weather and precipitation products, so if the disaster premium came in on one, he would still get paid on the rest. Greenblatt was hedged against the tsunami scenario.

—Pure Occam's Razor, Greenblatt had said with an air of serenity. —The suckers pay to alleviate risk and the house gets paid. Odds are every six to seven years I'll get wiped out by a huge disaster, but then I go to another firm who will hire me because they'll see my five years of huge profits.

Gallagher found Howard Schiller and Celina sitting at the bar in Museum Cafe. Howard was putting down his martini glass as Gallagher walked up. The art dealer tipped his hand to Celina as if he were holding an invisible fedora perched atop his bald head.

—Adieu, he said to her. Turning to Gallagher he half-drunkenly saluted him:

—Your wife has accepted for you.

—Howard's sister is having a party out in Wellesley. We're invited, explained Celina. She wasn't quite so drunk, though her legs hung down from the bar stool in a relaxed fashion that meant she'd had a few.

Gallagher yawned, exposing the teeth in his mouth.

—Sounds fine, he said and put his hand on Celina's thigh.

Howard embraced Celina and shook Gallagher's hand.

—Good meeting you, he said.

—Do I like Howard? asked Gallagher when the art dealer was gone.

—You should. He's a fan of me.

—Is he British?

—No, actually. I don't think he is.

—I thought he might be British, said Gallagher.

—You don't like him, said Celina.

—I do like him, said Gallagher emphatically.

Celina readjusted the clip that held her hair up in a bun. She glanced at her husband.

—That's because you like everyone.

THE T.U. (TIGHTEN-UP
SESSION)

The Colonel munched on a cruller. His meeting with the Ghost had gone very well. The Colonel had presented to the Ghost a side deal. It was a physical transmission play in the Midwest, low risk, is how the Colonel sold it. He would put the trade in the Ghost's book, and, if the trade made money, as the Colonel knew it would, because it was illegal, he'd take fifty percent of the profits for himself.

—What do you need to make this happen? the Ghost had asked him.

—I need to visit someone, a contact in Minnesota, to see if this can happen.

—Gallagher's contact, corrected the Ghost. —Give me some color. What's he like?

—He's a utility guy, likes to duck hunt. North Dakota would be the best place to take him.

—Go duck hunting then. Just don't lose any big money on this play of yours.

—Worst happens is it's a wasted trip.

As the other traders rolled in, no one paid much attention to the Colonel. Of late, he was always strutting his stuff, shouting or bragging more than usual. It was his way of advertising his alliance with the Ghost. However, this morning the Colonel was almost giddy, being louder and more abusive than usual. All the traders who sat down assumed he was crushing a broker who had misquoted a market or cuffed some of the Colonel's numbers or fumbled the execution of a trade.

—You're a disgrace, shouted the Colonel into the phone. —That's exactly what you are. You're a disgrace to your family. Does your mother know that her son is a fucking disgrace?

Sami put a small wad of tissue in his right ear as he sat down on the desk next to the Colonel. A few traders saw this and sniggered.

The Colonel listened for a few moments and then lit into his prey:

—I didn't call you. You called me. You attempted to do your job. I ask you one simple question about your product and you didn't know it. How fucking stupid do you think I am? Do you think I am some ratfuck shitball who has the time to sit here and listen to a moron, a disgraceful moron who hasn't even taken the time to know his product, his business? This is the real world and I am trying to help you. You have a wife and kid, yes? Two kids. Well, those kids are going to die if you can't feed them. And you can't feed them unless you have a job. And how can you have a job if you don't know fuckall about your product?

The Colonel breathed and made a face at Sami. It was his *I'm educating this moron* face. He took another bite of egg sandwich while pretending to listen to the voice on the other end of the line.

—Okay. Okay, said the Colonel. —Now learn your fucking product. No, I'm not going to give you any business because if you're listening to me I am helping you. I am saving your children from starvation. You can't make money if you don't know your product. So understand it. Do some homework. You had homework in the fifth grade, right? Well, read up on that shit. And if you ever call me again and you don't know what you're selling me, I'm going to call you a fucking disgrace and give you this beatdown all over again, understood? Okay? Yes. Thank you too. Have a nice day.

The Colonel hung up the phone.

—Which broker was it this time? asked Sami.

—That was no broker, said the Colonel. —Just some tool trying to get me to switch over to Verizon.

EXPENSE ACCOUNT

The Colonel never wore his wedding ring. His wife, Stephanie, was a handsome woman of old New England stock. At the wedding all the Colonel's friends had been jealous. Seven years and three kids later, they were no longer jealous. Stephanie was starting to resemble her mother.

But Stephanie was far from his thoughts as the Colonel sipped his ginger ale and observed the beautiful women among the men in suits who milled about the bar at Club Lex.

His eyes flitted about the room. He had discerned more than a few females who looked good, but one couple caught his attention right away. A tall, slender brunette in red leather pants, a white blouse, and black pumps was standing next to a statuesque redhead with a porcelain perfect face. The prospects looked good.

As the ginger ale fizzed at the back of his throat he took in his competition. There seemed to be three types of males, but only two categories: lions and jackals. One type was the entourage of short, dumpy, swarthy men that wore rings or a fancy watch, some kind of gold on them, most likely of Middle Eastern or Mediterranean descent. Then there were the fragile ones, older, thin haired, pasty white men, politicians, partners of law firms, ad execs who although in various states of middle age, all still seemed ancient like vampires. The Swarthies and the Vampires seemed to be accompanied by the more attractive females, who were universally tricked out with expensive ice that glowed radioactive blue, illuminated by the black light. Then there was a small host of men, fellow hunters like himself, their eyes narrowing and scouring the room. Posers, younger men in designer suits and tight-fitting silk shirts, either maroon or black, accompanied by a variety of scantily or provocatively clad women: hos.

Beside the Colonel in a strapless black dress looking not elegant enough to be of Boston elite society and a touch too thick in the ankles to pass as a high-class escort or a twenty-something hottie stood Debra Nunzi, a raven-haired Venus with pouty lips. She grasped onto the Colonel's hand a bit too tightly. She was a receptionist at his health club, and, as she told the Colonel the first time she met him, she liked the finer things in life. Her husband, a computer technician, seemed in so many ways a horrible mistake.

The Colonel had picked her up for the evening in Quincy Market and then driven her straight to their hotel, the ornate Bella Luna, with its rococo lounge. And why not since this soiree was all courtesy of the Ghost? As soon as they'd tipped the bellboy, the Colonel had thrown her on the bed and they'd had a passionate session. Once Debra had showered and dressed, the Colonel took her out to a sushi restaurant where she'd tried hot sake for the first time. It had tasted like tea spiked with grain alcohol, but she had liked the high: It made her giddy and flirtatious. It also allowed her to endure the Colonel's plodding conversation. His idea of a fascinating story was bragging about how he handled himself on the obstacle course at Quantico.

—Next time we should meet in Florida. It'd be cool to have sex at Disney World.

—No, Daniel. I can't take a trip. My husband is already the suspicious type as is.

The Colonel guffawed; insulted by the suggestion that he might be intimidated by her IT dork husband.

—He can film us if he wants.

—Next topic, said Debra.

The Colonel sat there sulking. He popped an edamame bean in his mouth.

But as always the Colonel made up for his lackluster dialogue by attending to his mistress's needs. Between bites of California roll and dragon roll, he told her all the things he was going to do to her. Then she leaned across the table and whispered one thing she wanted done that he hadn't mentioned. She thought it would shock him. But it didn't; he smiled and said:

—You bet.

Debra was annoyed by his cavalier tone and wondered if he'd already done that before.

—Don't be so grumpy, she said.

—I'm not.

—Prove it.

—Do you want to fuck again before we go to the club?

—How about you finger my pussy in the cab on the way there?

The Colonel finished up his ginger ale and looked down to make sure Debra had finished her gin and tonic. He needed to get her past her social, babbling phase of drunkenness.

—Baby, there are so many gorgeous people here. Where do we start? It's just overwhelming . . .

—Let's go to the bar and get you another drink, the Colonel said, savoring one last glance at the redhead and brunette.

He maneuvered onto the bartop with a gentle but real force, his broad head bent forward. He stuck out a hand and waved down the bartender. As he did so, a languid accented voice behind him said:

—Say, I've been waiting on that bartender for some time.

The Colonel turned and faced the man. He was a lanky, wispy-haired blond man whose Adam's apple was a size too big for his rather thin neck. The Colonel pegged him immediately as a beta-male. But his blue blazer and a white handkerchief in his breast pocket hinted at class. Sure enough, standing beside Mr. Class was a wide-eyed pert little nymph, her auburn hair in ringlets and her small nose turned up ever so slightly as if she could cast a spell like Samantha from *Bewitched*. The girl's strange beauty was owl-like and unveiled itself completely when she spoke. The Colonel caught only her name, Fiona.

—What's your accent? I like it, said Haupt.

—She's from Liverpool, said Mr. Class politely, shaking the Colonel's hand. —I'm Nigel.

—I'm Daniel from Oklahoma.

And then Nigel reached across the Colonel and raised his eyebrows in approval, clasping Debra's four fingers.

—It's nice to meet you as well, he said to Debra. Then turned to Fiona and said:

—They're very American, aren't they?

—Did you play football, American football? Fiona asked, eyeing the Colonel.

—No. I was a marine.

—But you're from the South. I lived in Dallas for three years, said Nigel.
—And I much prefer the South to the North. Let's have a toast.

The Colonel raised his glass unsure of what kind of toast this was going to be. But Debra, eyes glazed with titillation and savage enthusiasm, grabbed the Colonel's ass and squeezed as if to signal Haupt, *This is the couple.*

—A toast to excellent Americans and not the sort I have to deal with here in Boston, said Nigel.

—And to the marines, said Fiona, chiming the Colonel's glass.

The Colonel clinked glasses all around and wondered at the ease with which his iron-pumped biceps could magnetize, appropriate, and still deliver the goods.

The Brit took himself out of the triangle when he sat in the front seat of the cab. The Colonel sat between Debra and Fiona in the back. He could feel it as the warm air wafted through the windows and the bright lights from restaurant signs, bars, and cafes illuminated Newberry Street by the Boston Garden. There in the cavelike and secret gloom of the cab the two women pulsed with the kinetic energy of fright and sexual longing.

The Colonel took control. Nigel was explaining where his hotel was when the Colonel leaned forward.

—The Luna, he said to the driver. And then to Nigel: —The Luna. Trust me.

He then leaned back, looked down at Fiona, and with an American goofiness raised his eyebrows up and down at her. The Middle Eastern music that blared with a strange fervor on the cab's sound system made his action even more incongruous and funny. Fiona giggled.

—Have you ever been with another woman? asked the Colonel.

Fiona shook her head.

—Neither has Debra, said the Colonel.

He looked to his right at Debra and then to his left at Fiona and said:

—I think you two should make out. Right here. Just get this out of the way right now.

Fiona leaned forward in her seat and gnawed at her upper lip as she stared across the gray shadows of the cab to where Debra sat, already perched forward, her white teeth visible, exposed by her silent smile.

The kiss was tentative at first, as if both women expected a small electric shock. Then Fiona's thin lips yielded to Debra's widening mouth and hungrier tongue that inserted and retracted with curiosity. At once both women's hands went out to each other. Fiona steadied her diminutive form by placing her hand on Debra's shoulder. Debra cupped her own hand against Fiona's rib cage just beneath her breast. The Colonel thought it would be just one kiss, but whether they enjoyed it or were afraid to insult the other by ending the exchange, the women continued on. At some point the Colonel deftly took Fiona's free hand that was poised in the air like something that was lost, and guided it to the inside of his pant leg. The hand let itself be placed. Then with almost reptilian efficiency Fiona's hand of its own accord felt along his shaft until it became obvious to her what it was and how large it was so that she pulled away from the kiss and stared down at the Colonel's leg, still gripping through the pants, to make sure what she was feeling was real.

—This is going to be fun, said Debra.

Fiona, embarrassed, let go of the Colonel's thigh.

—He's very large, said Debra in a husky voice.

The Colonel sort of laugh-grunted and Fiona called out to Nigel in the front seat.

—Our friend has quite a willy.

Nigel, who had been aloof and staring out the window, poked his face around the headrest.

—I don't, I'm afraid, he said. —But I can go on forever.

—Nigel has staying power, Fiona agreed awkwardly, sounding as if she had been taught the phrase.

—You missed it, said the Colonel. —The ladies had quite a makeout session just now.

—Well, well, said Nigel, beaming.

—She's a wonderful kisser, said Debra.

Nigel smiled a fretful smile.

The Colonel spoke in a low voice to the two women, as the mysterious, frantic-sounding music conjured up foreign visions: sandstorms, cloaked harems, minarets.

—I want to see both of you kiss like that, said the Colonel, his voice blending into a whisper. —I'll take Fiona from behind, Debra, and watch you kiss her like that. And he can take you at the same time. Would you both like that? That's what I'm seeing in my mind when we go back to the hotel.

Fiona nodded and again furtively bit her upper lip. She had her hands in her lap now and she felt a trembling inside her.

—Daniel, said Debra, and then something in a whisper.

—Yes, he said.

—Just like we talked about, she said.

The Colonel said nothing and took one of Debra's breasts in his hand and searched for her nipple. He found it and did circles with his thumb.

THE TRACK

The man in the purple suit sorted through his betting slips. When he'd scrutinized the final ticket, he let them all fall to the floor, his hard face expressionless.

—That guy has lost like six straight, said Large.

Large stood up and waved his ticket in front of Gallagher's face.

—This phenom here, he said, pointing to himself, —is going to collect on his third in a row while your broke ass buys me another beer.

But the way Large said it, it didn't come off as bragging. Besides Andrews, Large had been on the circuit the longest. He'd seen it all and even his putdowns had a world-weary wisdom to them that made Gallagher feel lucky to be on the receiving end of his insults.

Beer in the VIP bar was seven dollars for a draft. Large was not wrong. Gallagher had five bucks in his pocket.

Large was Gallagher's track buddy. One Friday a month they'd skip out on work to go to Suffolk Downs and bet the ponies. Originally from Kentucky, Large had grown up around horses and was a natural bettor at the track. He liked to go to the paddock between races and look over the horses. He studied the horses' legs and flanks, talking about musculature and definition. He had theories about nervous ones that spooked easy: They ran better on a dry track. While horses with shorter calf-to-flank ratio had better times in the mud. Gallagher put down the *Daily Racing Form*. No matter how much he analyzed the racing data, handicapper's picks, past times, jockey ratings, he couldn't string more than one or two wins together. Gallagher went to the bar and bought Large and himself a beer apiece. Then, as an afterthought, he ordered himself a whiskey and charged it.

Large came back from the betting window and sat down with a groan. He took a sip of his beer and looking at Gallagher, said:

—You flat broke, ain't you?

—I got five bucks.

Disgusted, Large peeled a twenty off his roll of bills and, pointing to Gallagher's whiskey, said:

—Go buy me one of those what you got. And keep the change.

When Gallagher returned Large had his ear tilted toward the foursome two tables over. Whenever Large and Gallagher came to the track, the same four men, balding, middle-aged track fiends, sat at their usual corner table, drinking and getting loud. Large was somewhat jealous that someone could spend more time at the track than himself. He constantly was wondering what the men did for a living that gave them such a life of leisure. With his face flushed and almost as red as a tomato, Large leaned forward and said:

—The fat guy over there. The leader. He runs a painting outfit. I should've guessed that: union guys.

The union guys were drunk and they were all speaking at the same time, talking over one another. Gallagher couldn't understand what they were saying among their conversational rumble. It was as if they possessed their own language.

—I can't make out a word, said Gallagher.

—That's because you don't speak carny.

Sitting at a table next to the bar was an old man; the gray skin of his face was blotched with small red scabs and covered with a translucent oxygen mask. He wore an Irish tweed cap and sat in his wheelchair, staring at the large-screen TV. The oxygen tank was bound to the back of his chair. One of the four union guys, a dark-haired, barrel-chested man in a red Hawaiian T-shirt, got up from their table and went over to the old man. He said something to the old man and then put his finger up to the bartender for a drink. Leaning forward, he took the oxygen mask from the old man and turning to his crowd of friends, he waved at them, while taking deep hits off the respirator. Then he gave the oxygen mask back to the old man and brought him a beer from the barman.

The man in the red Hawaiian T-shirt beat his chest once as he walked back to his crew.

—Better than Viagra, he said.

Large stared at the table and laughed silently.

—Eye-talians, he said finally, picking up his *Racing Form*. Gallagher was looking through the race stats himself. After a few moments, Large said:

—Who we got in the next race?

—Look at the four horse.

—What about him?

—The name. Hurricane Jane.

—Stop, said Large. —Don't even go there. This is my day off. I'm winning. And you just spoiled my day.

Large was the only other trader besides himself and Andrews who were nervous about the house short position. While the mild temperatures were helping their position, the NOAA weather model had come out predicting an active hurricane season, which would drive gas prices up, and electricity would run with it. Dave Rector, Allied's meteorologist, had assuaged the trading floor's fears in a special Hurricane Outlook meeting, saying the NOAA was wrong and that wind shears off the Sahara Desert would blow dust into the jet stream and crush any chance of tropical storm development. Upon hearing Rector's analysis, the Ghost had pumped his fist in the air, because to exit out of their current huge short position would have cost them near ten million dollars. Large had later joked to Gallagher, calling Rector's wind shear theory Operation Desert Storm.

Large let out one of his patented "ughs," which made it sound like he had indigestion but in reality was him concerned about a trading position. Then he said:

—Wind shear, my ass. If Rector's wrong, it's going to be a CAT 4 cluster-fuck. Let's go to the paddock.

It was drizzling outside and the air was humid and musty. The dirt floor of the paddock smelled like mulch. A few trainers were walking their stallions around the ring, letting the reins run slack. One jockey in a blue and white harlequin pattern racing shirt brushed at the coarse black mane of a chestnut-colored horse.

—That's him, the six horse, said Large. —Look it, his calves are just as long as his flanks. And his hooves are on the large side. That's a pure mud horse.

—The track isn't mud yet, said Gallagher.

—By the time they're off, it'll be wet enough. What's his name?

Gallagher glanced at his *Racing Form*.

—Rum Runner.

—Money, said Large, standing on his tiptoes as he high-fived Gallagher.

Gallagher took one hundred dollars out of the ATM and bet it all on the six horse to win. Large bet somewhat more to win and then put another twenty down on a trifecta. They went out into the grandstand and stood in the rain. Rum Runner went off at four to one.

On the drive home Gallagher looked at the wad of twenty-dollar bills sitting beside him in the passenger seat. A euphoria came over him as he maneuvered the car out on the freeway.

Gallagher had a thought that he could apply to protect his trading portfolio. He would hedge his bets and likewise put on a trade that would "run in the rain." If the hurricanes came in the Gulf and disrupted the rigs, this would drive gas and power prices to the moon, bankrupting the house. But the storms as they moved north from the Gulf would also dump rain and send ninety-degree Texas weather to below seventy-five degrees and the weather derivatives would plummet with the temp drop. Gallagher thought, I'll hedge my power short by shorting the weather derivatives. It sounded crazy, hedging a short with another short. But as Gallagher played out the scenario in his mind, it wasn't just the whiskey talking, the logic held.

If the hurricanes come through the Gulf, I'll get paid, he thought. And he patted the wad of bills next to him on the front seat like it was a complicit pet.

Some ponies were made to run in the rain.

THE COLONEL IN
NORTH DAKOTA

In the predawn darkness the hunters could hear the beating of the ducks' wings as they passed overhead. Hunched down in their blinds they waited for a moment and then stood up, taking aim with their shotguns. The five ducks swooped down across the hunters' kill zone with such speed that they seemed just a blur of moving shadows. In an instant the hunters fired: an orange-yellow muzzle flash lit up the shooters' faces in the dark blinds.

Around noon the truck came. It rumbled over the broad valley, jolting and creaking like an old tank. Young Hoffmann, the guide, got out and inspected the ducks lined up in the grass.

—Not bad, he said, counting them. —Eleven.

The hunters helped the young guide put the decoys in the back of the truck. Back at Hoffmann's farm the hunting party gathered in the barn. They called it the barn but it looked like an airplane hangar. The men, tired and hungry, lounged on worn, musty-smelling couches and scarred wooden chairs that bore notches from the buck knives of bored hunters. The concrete floor was covered with muddy boot tracks. On the wall there was an old, yellowed poster advertising the Minot Rodeo and Roundup. Young Hoffmann went in the kitchen with game shears and fillet knives and began skinning the ducks, while the hunters lunched on ham on rye sandwiches.

After a midday nap the hunters went for beers at Holsteins. It was a thirty-minute drive to the bar. Holsteins was nothing but an old farmer's cabin from the pioneer days built in the middle of a floodplain with nothing else in sight except for fence posts and flat land that extended all the way to the horizon.

Inside it was lit up with faux kerosene lamps. Against one wall was an ancient, rotted wagon wheel. Above the bar hung a collection of tomahawks that were fixed to a plank with bent hobnails. The tomahawk handles were unlaquered wood and the ax blades seemed tinged with rust. The Colonel wondered if they were real. The bartender was a middle-aged blonde who had a solid Midwestern beauty coupled with a stare of resignation and contempt that gave her a maternal aura. Each man in turn noticed her good looks. Most of the hunters took seats at the big tables. The Colonel, Peter the German, and Young Hoffmann sat three across at the bar. Peter the German was the Colonel's client, a generation dispatcher from Northern Lakes Power.

—Hunting pheasant tomorrow? asked Peter the German.

Young Hoffmann nodded, sipping at his beer.

—I'm telling you right now. I'm not going to stand post. ·

The young guide stared at the Colonel for a moment.

—I got clipped once, said Peter the German, scratching at his chestnut red beard.

A lanky hollow-cheeked man with bluish circles under his eyes, sitting at the far end of the bar, began to hoot:

—Wooohooo.

He looked at the three hunters sitting at the bar.

—Wooohooo, he hollered a second time, even louder.

Peter the German called the attractive bartender over.

—What is our friend at the end of the bar so happy about?

—He just got out of jail. He was in for a year, she said.

—Buy him a shot from me. To shut him up.

—He's at least part Indian. I'd leave him alone, said Young Hoffmann.

Though the Colonel's late mother had been half Scotch-Irish, half Hungarian, the Colonel and his father told everyone she'd been a full-blood Cherokee. The Colonel failed to mention his imaginary heritage tonight.

The customer drank the whiskey Peter bought him and came over.

—Thank you. I'm Hill, he said, sticking out his hand.

—The bartender said you just got out of jail, said Peter the German in his matter-of-fact way.

—You bet, said Hill. —One year and three months and I kept my cherry.

—Traffic violation? asked Peter the German.

Hill took a step back. His mouth hung open revealing brown, crooked stumps of teeth, and a wet, black wad of chew stuck to his gum line like a leech.

—No, friend, said Hill. —Murder. I killed my wife.

Peter the German sat motionless. The Colonel leaned forward in disbelief. Young Hoffmann pushed his beer away from him and excused himself.

Hill told the story. He'd caught his wife with a meth addict from Bismarck, outside in the parking lot of a roadside motel. It was spur of the moment. He ran her down in his truck. The judge had ruled it manslaughter.

Two drinks later Hill grew surly. Peter the German was also surly, but in a quiet way. He was chastising himself for buying a murderer a beer and for not listening to the advice of Young Hoffmann. The anger of the man called Hill was like the bouncing ball of a roulette wheel and it settled on the Colonel. —You don't look like much, he said.

—Turn your back on him, Dan, said Peter the German.

The Colonel turned away from him, expecting to be hit with something. The blond bartender appeared and said to Hill:

—It was such a nice place where you were. You want to head right back where you came from?

Hill's features softened, going from ferocious to haggard and tired in an instant. He looked like a man unaccustomed to his own demons.

—Time to go, Hill, she said. Her words came out firm but had a protective aura to them, like those of a nurse steadying an invalid. Hill came to for a moment and scratched his black greasy hair above his ear.

—Yup. I got to go before I hurt somebody, he said and left the bar.

The Colonel had never seen a fight diffused so quickly. His attraction to the bartender increased tenfold.

—One year for murder, said the Colonel when Hill had gone.

—Technically, I was right, said Peter the German. —It was a traffic violation.

The pheasant hunt had not gone well. Rain had poured down and flooded the draws, soaking the fields where the pheasant nested. It was slow going through the mud and the birds were scarce. The hunting party quit early and headed back to the Sportman's Roost to shoot clay pigeons. While a few of the group were outside engaged in a shooting competition, Peter the German sat in the living room on a three-legged stool by a gas-lit fireplace. The Colonel was at the table, wiping down the choke of his Mossberg with a dry rag, talking to Peter the German about a plan where they could both make some money.

—The problem is, said Peter the German, —the way you want to do it. By having me overdispatch my gas units in the Day Ahead Market, and flood the power lines with megawatts; it will crush the real-time prices.

The Colonel listened, as he reinserted the choke in the muzzle.

—There's a record of all that. If I really overdo like you want by turning on all or most of my gas plants, not only is my manager going to get on my ass, but FERC is going to have me on their radar: Peter Mueller over-dispatching units. *Now why would he do that?* They'll ask themselves. *Let's check his bank account. Hmmmm.*

—So no interest? asked the Colonel.

—I didn't say that, did I? I only said the way you want to do it, the old-fashioned way of manipulating the lines by scheduling too much power into them, don't work so well. At least not with me being the one who pulls the switch.

—I got a plane to catch in a few hours. How else could you game it? asked the Colonel, growing impatient.

—Now I've been thinking of what you said, Peter the German went on. —And there is a way to fix it so we could make some big money off line congestion. But it won't work like you think. No loading the lines or with-holding megawatts day ahead.

Peter the German's lower lip came up over his mustache and pressed down on it.

—Simple fact, though, Dan, is I can make the prices go up. But you probably don't want to know how I do it. It can be done is all you need to know.

—Just tell me. Otherwise I have a plane to catch, said the Colonel.

Peter the German leaned forward over the burnished oak table and he stared at the Colonel's face closely, his blue eyes straining to see any kind of weakness, hesitation.

—I'm going to fly a prop plane over the transmission lines at four A.M. and drop a fifty-foot length of chain on them. That chain conducts the

X-line, power going in, to the counterbalance Y-line, power going out, and it'll short out the whole damn interface.

The Colonel's jaw almost dropped. Then he became indignant. He thought of saying, "I wanted you to flip a switch and here you want to conduct an act of terrorism." But the Colonel didn't say that, instead he composed himself.

—You can do that?

Peter the German flashed a mysterious smile.

—Who do you think sets all the forest fires?

The Colonel shot him a look. He didn't like puzzles.

—You know those blazes in California, the ones that go for hundreds of miles and take out whole valleys? It's out-of-work firemen who set those fires. I know because my brother-in-law is one. They light the fire and then get the call. At thirty bucks an hour plus overtime pay, it's worth it. You got to get paid somehow. It's the American way.

The Colonel made a "come on" motion with his hand, wanting Peter the German to get to the point.

—Well, by the same token, when the power lines go nuts and someone makes a killing being long that hub, you might say once or twice before it's been people you and I know dropping chains across the lines.

Peter the German chuckled and slapped the Colonel on the back.

—The Wall Street boys aren't the only ones with tricks up their sleeves.

—How long a run time? asked the Colonel. He wanted to be the one in control of the conversation.

—It's a minimum of twenty hours before that line is fixed, explained Peter the German. —And anybody who owned cheap megawatts at the Minnesota hub that day would be rich, because there wouldn't be any way of power getting imported into Minny. Prices would be sky high.

—How high is sky high? I need numbers, said the Colonel.

—Four or five hundred dollars a megawatt hour. With no cheap coal or combined cycle gas imports, they'll have to turn on the oil units.

The Colonel whistled. Then regaining composure he asked:

—For how long?

—Like I said it'll be twenty hours or so before they fix the line, but prices printing over the peak of the day at those levels will be five, maybe six hours.

The Colonel did the calculations in his head.

—That's going to be some real money, he murmured, already thinking he didn't want to share fifty percent of that number with the Ghost.

—We can only do this one time. So make sure you got the position on, Peter the German told him.

—Right, said the Colonel, drawing out the word, elongating it, as he handled the Mossberg carefully and put it in the gun case.

—Then there is the method of my payment, said Peter the German.

—It has to be cash, said the Colonel.

—Cash is fine, said Peter the German. —And, Dan, I want fifty grand up front: win, lose, or draw. You can even take it out of my percentage, if it all plays out the way we want it.

—You'll get your fifty and if this works I'll give you the rest in Vegas and put you up at the Hard Rock myself.

Standing up, Peter the German went over to the Colonel and shook his hand.

BULLISH

The cocktail party was out in the suburbs north of Boston: home to rolling hills, green lawns, rustic barns with cast-iron weather vanes, and antique cars parked in winding, gravel driveways. Howard Schiller's sister, Laura, lived in a medium-sized white colonial with navy blue shutters, a redbrick chimney, and a wraparound porch. Her ex-husband, the owner of an outdoor supply store, had provided her with the house. She'd just given birth three months earlier to a child with her boyfriend, a stockbroker by the name of Phillips. Motherhood agreed with her and Laura Morgan still entertained, often.

Gallagher had only been there five minutes when he wanted to leave. He was bunched up against a bookcase talking to an MIT genetics engineer. The engineer had a high-pitched voice and dried crab dip in his goatee. He was explaining to Gallagher what had gone wrong with the sheep cloning trials. It had to do with their DNA. Gallagher enjoyed reading about the discipline of science, but was invariably let down when meeting scientists. When the engineer's wife came over he introduced her to Gallagher. She had her own homemade jewelry Web site, and handed over her card.

Gallagher found himself in the bathroom, breaking out in a sweat. He looked down at the toilet seat. Someone had urinated all over it like it was a stall at the ballpark. Gallagher wiped it clean with a monogrammed hand towel. He didn't want anyone in line for the bathroom to call him out. Celina was on display in the solarium. She was there with Howard's two other artists. Both, like Celina, were attractive females; together they formed a collection in and of themselves. They all stood somewhat near their paintings in the sunlit room. Ostensibly, they were trying to make what Gallagher had learned from Celina was termed in the art business as a social sale.

Gallagher splashed water on his face.

—No bid for you, he said evenly, looking at himself in the mirror.

Gallagher walked out into the kitchen to make himself another Southside. Howard Schiller was holding court, talking to a young, professional couple. The wife was thin with platinum hair and the fit body of a yoga devotee. The expression on her face was one of curiosity. She was either wondering who Gallagher was or she was intrigued by Howard Schiller's sales pitch. The husband wore beige but his gold watch sparkled. His white oxford shirt was starched and his pants were creased. Gallagher would've bet money that he was a lawyer or the recipient of a trust fund, or both.

—Here is Celina Gallagher's husband, Joseph Gallagher. I was just telling the Blakenships here about your wife's paintings.

He raised his eyebrows at Gallagher. It was like some salacious code that left Gallagher feeling at a loss, that he was out of his depth and had somehow miscalculated this market. Gallagher raised his glass and walked on.

He's too old to make a play for my wife, Gallagher thought, reassuring himself, drinking as he walked.

Celina was not in the solarium. Gallagher found her in the archway where the living room led into the den. She was talking to two men, one about Gallagher's age and size and the other smaller and younger who wore wire-rimmed glasses and possessed the slight but tawny tough of a marathon runner.

Both of the men ignored Gallagher until Celina went to her husband and took him by the hand. The younger skinny guy was called Kirby and Gallagher barely caught the name of the larger man. He'd muttered it and had stared Gallagher down just a little and his handshake was on the aggressive side.

Gallagher finished his first drink and knew he was being sized up. The archway was a sort of a cocktail party nether zone; situated between the crowded living room with its rows of bookcases, Chagall prints, and bright yellow upholstered sofa and chairs and the gloomier, testosterone-laced den, which was empty of people and featured a stuffed wood duck on a driftwood mount, a brass-rimmed globe, and an antique double-barrel shotgun in a glass case. The vibe here of these two men paying attention to his wife was clearly not Art Showing. This was something else, thought Gallagher, deciding there was potential here, for what he was not sure, but it was now worth staying.

—You were telling us about ballet school, said Quint.

Gallagher picked it up after a few more moments. He heard the greed in Quint's voice and saw it in Kirby's stare. Gallagher recognized it immediately. It was a bull market.

Markets have moods just like people. At work Gallagher had been in a selling mode for some time and was currently in tune with the essence of a bear market, the nature of which was contempt. In a bear market you would short a product because you thought it was overvalued. When you laid into it, it was like slaughter: You took the price of something and you killed it. But Gallagher was just as familiar with a bull market, which was about wanting and ownership. When you really wanted to own a commodity, you bought and bought; until you ran the price up. Then, in full buying frenzy, one could never own enough.

The nature of a bull market was a hunger and greed that becomes insatiable. The big rally is what changes man into animal, intelligent trader into lemming. All booms in the history of mankind have this characteristic, the price spike, the ultimate cost of blind ownership that bankrupts the multitudes.

Gallagher found himself sniffing out how the scene would unfold, as if he was honing trading instincts. His conclusion: This market too was getting away from him. Celina was tipsy, her guard let down. Gallagher knew her first reaction was to maintain that veneer of politeness at all times.

—Can you still do one of those things you were describing? A grand plié? asked Kirby, the muscle beneath his eye twitching slightly.

—No. I couldn't, she said.

—Come on. You can still do it. You're in great shape, said Quint, his tongue sticking out of his mouth for a moment.

Celina looked at her husband. Gallagher seemed poised like he was about to do something. A part of Celina relished the attention, the jealousy.

—I could try, she said, still waiting for the look on Gallagher's face to turn to disapproval. When it did not she said:

—Stand back. Give me some room, kicking off her shoes.

Quint reached down and moved the shoes to the side of the archway. Gallagher bristled at this but then focused on his wife.

She put her heels together, perfectly balanced, then spread her feet apart, the strength in the arch of her foot supporting the whole of her body. Then Celina's knees bowed out gracefully in twin arcs, when something popped. It was a distinct sound, the sound of a seam bursting. Celina's pants split at the crotch.

—Oh my God, she gasped when she realized what had happened.

Kirby gawked with fascination. Quint let out a possessive, mean guttural laugh. Gallagher went to his wife and put his arm around her, because she looked like she was going to lose her balance from shock or embarrassment.

—Show's over. Get your coat and let's go home, he said.

Celina went to the upstairs guest bedroom that had been converted to a coatroom. She saw her jacket and Gallagher's dirt-stained Patagonia draped over the headboard. Then, tired, somewhat drunk, and still mortified, she flopped onto the day bed, resigned to the fact that she didn't care if anyone saw her splayed out over the coats and jackets, the tear in her crotch exposing a glimpse of her panties.

She was thinking about the man named Quint. He had spoken to her in the solarium. He was not particularly intelligent, but neither was he dense. He owned his own building company and had made it apparent that he was more interested in her than her work. Celina had been taken off guard by his honest approach. Also, he had been polite, polite enough, though he had that hard, dull, empty stare of say, maybe, an ox. Earlier, when Celina came out of the bathroom, Quint had been in the hallway and he'd extended his hand as he said hello when she passed and it had touched her or more brushed up against the side of her hip. She had turned back around to give him a punishing look but he was entering the bathroom. Then when she was on the edge of the cocktail party, Quint had been sitting alone in a leather chair in the den, as if this were his home and his chair, though he sat looking straight ahead with a disconnected stare. In her mind she decided that the hallway incident had been accidental contact. He noticed her in the archway and addressed her by name. She had hesitated and he'd said:

—I'll buy your painting.

He'd said it so pathetically that she went over to him. It had been a trap of sorts. Quint asked to see her hands. He wanted to see what the hands of a painter looked like and he had grabbed them and turned them over, as if they were not her hands but things he was inspecting to buy. His grip was firm and impersonal. That was when the smaller man, Kirby, had come up. Instead of being put off by Kirby, Quint seemed humored by his presence. He glanced at Celina in a knowing way, as if they had somehow shared a private moment. It was all so coarse, so imbecilic. And her husband had come and he had sensed it all and she'd drunkenly humiliated herself and been sent upstairs to fetch her things.

Celina lay back on the mountain of coats and spread her legs slightly. What if someone came in and found her like this? They'd just assume she had passed out. They would not guess that she was lying there, an artist imagining anonymous scenes of women who fucked strangers at parties in coatrooms just like this one.

THE RED LION

The Red Lion Pub was a gloomy English pub near the State House on the back side of Beacon Hill. The antique brass sconces near the front door bathed the ceiling in a smudged grayish light. The thick smell of lard, coming from a shepherd's pie, put Andrews in a foul mood. He was sitting at the bar. He looked at the man next to him eating the shepherd's pie and, sizing up his cheap suit, weak chin, and two-day stubble on a gizzard neck, decided he was a government worker.

Andrews drank a Guinness and eyed a bowl of peanuts just out of reach.

Gallagher appeared behind him.

After exchanging pleasantries, the two traders began speaking in quiet, humdrum voices about their positions, the direction of the market.

—You called this little meeting, said Andrews abruptly. —Why don't you tell me what it's all about?

—I think I have it figured out, said Gallagher.

—You think you got something figured out, said Andrews.

—Can I sell this before I hear it? Because whenever anyone in the history of the world says that they got something figured out either they're lying or they're selling me something.

Gallagher sat on his stool. He knew Andrews wasn't finished.

—Did Einstein say he got the shit figured out? No. He just said "E=mc squared, idiots." So if you want my attention, my respect, give me a formula, a spreadsheet with something real on it.

Gallagher, knowing he had only a few moments before Andrews lost his temper, came out with it.

—Weather derivatives, he said. And he told Andrews the plan to hurricane-proof his portfolio. Andrews himself had learned a little about the new exotic product when it first came out. As the boss at the time, he had to learn enough about the new derivatives product to assign the right trader to cover that market. Andrews reasoned since there were so few players in the weather derivatives market it would be a very illiquid product and he'd do better to put someone on the job with greater analytical skills. Hence, he'd chosen Greenblatt.

After Gallagher finished explaining his plan, Andrews washed down some wings with a swig of black stout. His pint glass was smudged with hot sauce.

—I see what you're doing, said Andrews, licking his thumb. —You think the Ghost won't be upset when you cover your power short and then roll it into being short Texas weather derivatives?

—I'm not going to cover my entire power short, said Gallagher.

—If the hurricanes come, what is going to happen to gas, even if the fuckers don't land in the Gulf?

—Gas will go up.

—When gas goes up what is going to happen to the power you are still short?

—It will go up too, said Gallagher.

—You might make some money on the weather derivatives, but you'll lose as much, if not more on the power.

—That's the thing, said Gallagher. —Greenblatt told me the risk is mis-calculated in the system. It will look like I have one to two million of risk on the weather but it's more like five to ten.

—You want me to get out of my length and put on some weather derivatives position that our risk group can't calculate. All so the Ghost will spare me?

—You might not get rich, said Gallagher. —But you'll be out of your power position, and when the Colonel sells the plants and the Ghost mis-marks the curve, you'll be solvent. You yourself said it's all about staying at the table.

—No, said Andrews, raising his voice. —Breaking even for me isn't surviving. I need to win. And look at this gas, the stochastics are shit, but it isn't going anywhere. You want to win, you find a way to get long, and stay long.

Andrews looked up at the TV. Being an English pub, the Red Lion often showed soccer and rugby matches. At that moment the broadcast was Arsenal versus Liverpool.

—See that up there on the TV, said Andrews, beads of sweat rimming his upper lip.

—That is soccer, he said spitefully. —Those little guys running around in shorts, kicking a rubber ball and shit. That is not a sport and those guys aren't athletes. No one is getting hit. Nothing is at stake.

Andrews heaved himself up, standing straight in his stool. He shifted his weight as he turned to face Gallagher. When Gallagher spun on his stool to face Andrews, hoping to reason with him, Andrews poked him in the chest.

—What you're doing with these weather derivatives is you're being clever. You want to make money in summer power, you take a position and you ride it. The Ghost is short. I am long. You. You're playing soccer.

Gallagher thought about these words. Then, deciding he could do no more to help save his mentor, he reached across the table for a hot and spicy wing. Andrews smacked his hand away.

—Wings are for athletes only.

CAPE HATTERAS

NYMB, the venerable brokerage house that employed Milt Harkrader, rented a seventy-foot yacht and took its best customers on a poker cum booze cruise off the coast of Coral Gables, Florida. The year before it had been five fishing boats filled with traders trolling for yellowfin tuna a mile off Cape Hatteras, North Carolina. But some intoxicated oil trader had taken a spill on the slippery deck astern and impaled himself on a gaff. Hooks, gaffs, fishing line, and live fish with teeth didn't seem to go hand in hand with bourbon-swilling city folk, even if they were playing at being deep-sea BassMasters, so the CEO of NYMB settled on something that would keep the goons inside while providing an exotic scenario: poker at sea, a barge sitting at the dock so no one would get seasick.

Milt was on board with the program, preferring gambling to seasickness and fishing, which amounted in his mind to a sore back and hard work. And when he excitedly pitched the booze cruise to his biggest client, Stan Couch, he was crestfallen when Stan, the new AA Stan, took a pass.

—I'd love to go deep-sea fishing again, but a gambling barge is no longer my thing.

■   ■   ■

Milt cursed softly as the North Carolina surf pounded against the beach-head. Whitecaps appeared and disappeared, their foamy crowns dotting the dark sea. Milt walked along the beach and looked out across the dunes. In the dim light of the dawn they seemed like gloomy misshapen heads with spare patches of hair like on a cancer patient. The patches of hair were nothing but yellow-green saw grass that whispered angrily as it whipped about in the wind. Milt finished up his bacon, egg, and cheese McMuffin and headed over to the van in the hotel parking lot.

Milt's boy, Aaron, was standing in front of the van looking wet and cold in the morning mist.

—What a day to go fishing, huh, Dad?

—I'm meeting a client at the dock. Not just any client, my biggest client. So you talk about nothing but sunshine and roses. Positive mental attitude, you got that?

—Yes, Captain.

Milt threw his breakfast sandwich wrapper on the ground and then got in the rental van. Once inside he made sure his cooler with the beer was in the backseat.

—Get me a beer, he said to his son.

—Are you allowed to drink and drive here?

—This is North Carolina, boy, said Milt in his best Southern sheriff twang.

Milt was late for the push-off time. He sped down the causeway nearing eighty. He slowed it up a touch when he remembered his son was in the vehicle.

—Dad, why did you rent a van if there is only the two of us? asked Aaron.

—Because we might catch a big fish. And if we do, I'll get it stuffed and you can hang it up in your dorm room.

—There's pretty huge waves out there today, Dad. Think they'll let us fish?

Milt looked out at the ocean. Ten-foot swells rose up and crashed into the shoreline. Milt bit his lip. He searched his fishing vest and pulled out a packet of Dramamine.

—Here, take one of these, said Milt, handing his son the packet of pills.

—What should I wash it down with?

—Here. Take a sip of my beer. That'll get it down.

—Hey, Dad. You're not supposed to take this with alcohol. It says it right here on the package.

—You ever been deep-sea fishing before?

—No.

—That was a rhetorical question, lectured Milt. —Listen, this is a dangerous sport, a manly sport. You got to be on your toes. You don't want to be down in the hold puking your guts out, especially in these seas. You can never let the client show you up. Now take that pill.

In defiance his son washed the pill down with three large slurps of beer. They drove on in silence until they were in sight of the marina. Aaron sitting in the passenger seat turned to Milt.

—Dad, he said, —I feel better already.

—Hey, no comedy routines.

—It wasn't. I feel good. I feel ready.

—Good, get good and ready, said Milt. —Because this is going to be educational.

The captain and Stan were standing at the dock in front of the fifty-five-foot fishing boat, talking about the weather. The first mate waved hello from the boat; he looked like a high school fullback, a young man not yet filled out but broad with a flattened nose and when he smiled you expected him to be missing a tooth. He was unhooking the painter line as the engine, ready to go, sputtered in neutral. Diesel exhaust fumes hung in the light fog. Aaron coughed.

After Milt introduced his boy to the two men, the captain stroked his chin with his calloused hand.

—It's ten-foot seas out there, he said. —I won't go out in anything over twelve. But we can try ten as long as it stays like this or better.

The captain then stopped midsentence. He lowered his arm and pointed a finger at Aaron. The boy noticed a faded tattoo on the captain's bicep and then the forearm, roped with muscle.

—Have you ever been deep-sea fishing before?

Aaron shook his head. Unlike Milt this man sounded like Aaron expected a captain to sound: grave and soft-spoken.

—Stan here is ready to go. But Mr. Harkrader, I'm not going to take your boy unless he is up for it, said the captain.

Milt looked at the whitecaps slapping the dock and jostling the boats in their slips—even roughing them up. The open ocean would be even worse.

Here was his out: the high road, saving his greenhorn son. Before Milt could answer for him, Aaron said, looking at his dad:

—I can do it. I want to do it. I want to catch a fish.

He said it with such naked desire that the captain and Stan Couch felt a surge of admiration for the boy, making them nostalgic, remembering their own first trip out on the seas; and since they were both true fishermen they also were superstitious and a virgin voyage was a thing of good luck; perhaps they'd catch a bluefin today.

Milt, whose dad had never taken him fishing, who had never liked fishing or rough seas or any sort of physical discomfort, was still stuck on what the captain had said about twelve-foot waves being too dangerous. Wait, thought Milt, we're only two feet away from dangerous. What does that make the waves now? Dangerous minus two.

The clouds loomed and seemed endless, a mass of gray tinged in their center with a menacing black, the color of charcoal. There was no rain yet but on the horizon, distant showers, patches of mist and shadow hung low in the sky.

— Cumulonimbus, said the first mate, checking the fifty-pound line on each reel. He pointed up at the sky. —Storm clouds. The fishing boat pitched forward in the swarming seas. Aaron was holding on to a railing next to his stern bench seat. He watched as the first mate with perfect balance hopped up onto the transom and checked the outrigger lines. Milt and Stan were seated in their swivel turret fishing chairs looking like bloated ticks as the chair harnesses pressed into their life jackets. He offered a contrast to the captain, because the first mate liked to talk.

—This fifty-pound line is the next best thing to steel wire, he said. —You hook even a bluefin, it should hold.

—What about a shark? asked Milt.

—Shark's got some sharp teeth, sir. Would depend on what kind.

Milt turned around and waved to his son.

—Beer me, he said.

—You might want to take it easy on the drinking, said the first mate. —Rough seas today. Not wise for more reasons than one.

Milt had no intention of catching a fish. The most important thing was that his client had a good time, which meant if Milt hooked a fish, he'd let

Stan claim the glory and reel it in. Aaron appeared with a tallboy and handed it to his dad. Milt took the beer and winked at his son, letting the boy in on a shared secret—that the first mate didn't "get it." Two hours passed. The boat chugged along the horizon parallel to the surf to reduce the rising and dipping motion. However, waves crashed against the port side of the boat sending a cold bitter Atlantic sea spray into the stern, soaking the fishermen.

—Cap is nice and dry up there on the flying bridge, said the first mate. —How you men holding out so far?

Stan Couch let out a low grunt.

—I'm good, said Milt and looked back at his son, hoping Aaron remembered his advice earlier in the van about never letting a client show you up. Milt was on his third beer and felt happy because it was Stan who looked green. Milt looked out at the sea: the gunmetal blue-gray ocean seemed peaceful when he stared into its depths. Except when he honed in on the crests of waves, frothed up with a rabid foam. Soon the inherent violence of the ocean played on Milt and he felt up for a fight. If I hook a fish, thought Milt, I'm going to take it. Besides, Stan looks like he couldn't drag in a minnow. That's when Stan's line fell from the outrigger in a fanciful arc and went taut when it hit the water. The line buzzed on the reel, as the rod tip was yanked downward.

—You're on. You got one, said the first mate, jumping up on the companionway to get a view of the fish.

Stan hit it right off, jerking the rod back over his right shoulder.

—Not yet, said the first mate. —Run the line out a bit. Give this bitch some room to breathe and then hit him.

—What is it? asked Milt.

—It's got zip to it, he said. A yellowfin. Good size. Eighty pounds, maybe.

The first mate jumped back down to the deck and checked the rod butt, making sure it was fit snug into the gimbal socket. Stan braced against the fish as it ran, his feet pressing into the chair's running board. The first mate called up to the captain.

—We hooked a yellowfin, cap.

Stan fought the fish with calmness and resolve. He'd let out the line and wait. When he felt the pressure let up, he'd pull back on the rod, using his back and his legs. Then he'd start reeling it in, lowering the rod, and then pull it back up, arching his spine, contracting his shoulder blades.

—That's good form, Mr. Couch, said the first mate. —You got a good feel for him, don't you?

Stan Couch nodded and bit into his lip. He was thinking that outsmarting a fish was all about being a contrarian just like timing the market: buying into weakness, selling into strength. The swells pummeled the side of the craft, making it sway port to starboard. One monster wave stared them down for a moment that seemed like forever.

—Incoming, shouted the first mate.

The dark wall of water hit the boat, as it dipped, and crashed onto the stern deck, coming down onto the men, hitting the fishing chairs with the force of a punch. Stan was gritting his teeth and hanging on to the rod. His knuckles had lost their color long ago.

—Reel this thing in and let's go home, said Milt. —This is getting stupid. He was officially wet and drunk and angry.

—He's making progress, said the first mate. —We'll hook him soon, I'd say.

Milt looked back at his son. Aaron had not gone belowdecks. He was clutching on to the companionway rail with everything he had.

—Jesus, cried Stan suddenly. The rod dipped down violently, as if the line had gotten wrapped around the propeller. The reel spun like a top. The line made a whizzing sound like a band saw.

—Oh shit, said the first mate. —Want me to take it?

Stan's hands trembled. He nodded.

—It got strong all of a sudden, crooned Stan, passing the rod. —He's been playing possum.

The first mate steadied the butt in the gimbal as he took the rod. Jumping into the chair, he harnessed himself in a whir of movement and began the wrestling match.

Milt caught a glance of Stan's palms as he bent over in pain; they were raw with a white, puffy blister forming at the thumb joint.

—It didn't get stronger, said the first mate, as the line hissed. —We got something bigger on the line. I think a shark took the yellowfin. He looked at Milt.

—You want to try to reel it in? Chances are the line snaps.

Milt grabbed the rod from the first mate with his white soft hands good for grasping donuts and egg sandwiches. He'd had enough beers where the idea of defeating some massive creature was something that appealed to him; an idealistic notion like getting into a bar fight and winning. However, Milt's legs were cold and cramped up in the calves. Before getting into a prolonged battle Milt knew he'd have to stretch them. He'd unhooked his harness long before, in one of his many runs to the cooler, as it made the life jacket straps tug at his gut. Milt stood up in the chair.

—Don't, was all Milt heard.

The boat dipped. Milt wobbled for a moment, grasping the rod to his chest for counterbalance. Then in an uncanny moment, where bad luck, nature, and physics collide, Milt, attached to the fishing rod, went airborne like a missile. He was pulled with such force that he landed twenty yards from the boat and hit the ocean with barely a splash. The first mate stood there, his mouth open. Stan and Aaron sat next to each other, huddled on the stern bench seat, wondering if what they'd just witnessed was real: a two-hundred-and-thirty-pound man jettisoned into the sea. The captain, who looked over his shoulder just as Milt went under, heard what he thought was a fantail clap of water, and assumed he'd missed the yellowfin breaching.

The feeling of flying through the air, unbound, looking sideways at gigantic waves, was replaced quickly by the initial shock of hitting what felt like concrete. Submerged in a dark world, cold and muffled, with water rushing into his eyes, nose, and mouth, Milt felt some presence pulling him to some deep, unknown destination, colder, more desolate, and yet more peaceful. It was very cold, sleepy and profound like some hidden cosmos was revealing itself to Milt the broker. He was hurtling downward, whisked like someone chosen. Attached to the rod like a piece of bait, Milt was unaware that the reel handle was hooked to the chest strap on his life preserver. Dragged deeper and deeper, the force of the coursing water distorted his face, making it appear he was trembling. In his own mind Milt saw himself with a child-like smile, zooming through the depths to oblivion with a nonchalant peace that he would later mistake for courage and the notion that he had stared the Executioner in the face and had not blinked. His legs and arms flailed. In a lucky moment his hand knocked loose the reel handle from the life vest and Milt floated toward the surface, the waves crashing above him.

The first mate began screaming "Man overboard!" as Milt hit the water. Up on the bridge, the captain killed the engines. A moment later his red face appeared looking down from the flying bridge.

—What the fuck happened?

—He got hooked. His rod got caught in his life vest, said the first mate. One of the captain's eyes winced shut. It was an evil look. He was too angry to even ask about the harness.

—Cap. Something real big pulled him right over the side of the boat, said the first mate.

—Get up here. Now! screamed the captain in a hoarse voice.

The trawler engines sputtered back on and the boat came about. The first mate began shouting out at the ocean for Milt. The echo of rolling waves heaving in the ocean, the machine-gun patter of approaching rain made the first mate's calls seem futile. Aaron and Stan Couch had stayed aft and both scanned the horizon, one to port and the other starboard. Stan could hear the boy, shouting "Dad! Dad!" into the howling wind. The boy's voice kept cracking as he called out, breaking into a high-pitched shriek that seemed almost animal in its panic and desperation. Stan himself called until his vocal cords hurt. As the sea lifted and dropped the boat, Stan's body lurched, as he slipped on the wet deck. He prayed to himself. The boy screamed on.

Finally, the captain spotted Milt floating in the waves, bobbing like a helpless buoy, his orange vest and his pale face bloated from a lungful of seawater. He sounded the horn and saw Milt's head turn. *The man was alive!*

—Man to starboard, he cried, pointing. —It's a fucking miracle.

The first mate scrambled down the ladder and without being told went belowdecks for the gaff. When he reappeared the captain was shouting out commands.

—Go to port. I'm circling. Go fucking portside.

The boat bounded through the dark seas and approached Milt. When they got close enough the captain timed a small wave. Milt floated in on the back of it and almost crashed up against the side of the boat. The first mate braced the hooked end of the gaff under his shoulder and dipped the long handle into the ocean toward Milt, who floated nearby, yet each foot could've been a world away.

—Swim. Swim to it, he called out, knowing that the captain had once again killed the engine so Milt wouldn't get chopped up in the propeller.

Milt, looking dazed, began to swim. He shot out his hands and grabbed the gaff just as another wave lifted him up toward the boat. The first mate caught the back of Milt's life jacket as he floated upward with the crest of the oncoming wave. Stan Couch leaned halfway out of the boat and grabbed one of Milt's legs. Then as if the sea vomited up something inedible, Milt's body was lifted by the surging wave and spilled onto the deck with Stan and first mate in tow. Milt's head gave out a crack as his skull hit the gunwale. The first mate looked up and saw Milt, soaked through and pale, a translucent white, lolling on the deck with his sagging jowls quivering, and he thought of mollusk or squid flesh. The first person on top of Milt was the boy. Milt was coughing and sputtering, his lips blue, and his eyes red-rimmed from the sea. The boy was hugging his father, clutching onto him, when the captain yelled to the first mate from the bridge:

—Pete. Make sure he's breathing. Then get him fucking below. And get those wet clothes off him.

The first mate had to peel the boy off his father. Stan Couch put a hand on Aaron's shoulder and Aaron moved away as the two stronger men carried Milt belowdecks. Aaron, who was in shock, did not know his father was alive until he went down into the hold and heard his father's teeth chattering. Milt laid on the teak floor, a shivering mass, being stripped naked by the first mate in a clinical fashion, as one scaling a fish.

When Milt was bundled up in a polypropylene sleeping bag, resting comfortably on the captain's bunk, he finally spoke:

—Ocean is cold, he said. —Colder than it looks.

ANOTHER ONE
GETS AWAY

By the time the craft reached the dock the seas had become calm and shafts of sunlight peeked through the breaking clouds. Milt, Stan, and Aaron were in the hold, listening to the captain rail into the first mate. The swearing and lambasting was as creative and brutal as that heard on any trading floor. Milt, wrapped up in towels like an Egyptian pharaoh in a sleeping bag sarcophagus, listened and admired the captain's turns of phrase, storing in his memory one or two keepers. All three, Stan, Milt, and Aaron, felt bad as the tirade ended with the first mate's dismissal.

—You're through, shouted the captain. —You're through working for anyone on Hatteras. You didn't strap the man in and that's the fucking end of you.

Once they arrived at the marina, the captain apologized and told Milt there was no charge. Then he apologized again, his face looking like a time bomb as he tried to hold in his anger, as he shook the men's hands. The first mate was nowhere to be seen. Aaron wondered if the captain had thrown him overboard, but said nothing.

Stan and Milt walked down the pier away from the boat with Aaron two steps behind. Milt was wearing a dry pair of the captain's clothes, jeans and a Cape Hatteras Chum Fest T-shirt.

Stan turned back to Milt's son.

—Sorry we didn't get you your fish, he said.

—It's cool, the boy mumbled.

Once they were at the van, Aaron ran around to the passenger side and got in. Stan held Milt up for a moment by placing his hand on Milt's shoulder in a brotherly fashion.

—Milt, he said, and paused.

Milt was prepared for a religious speech of some sort. But he had not provided Stan with a fish, so the least he could do was let his client feel that he had come closer to God.

—I'm leaving the business, he said. —Quitting trading.

Milt almost dropped to a knee.

—I was hoping this would be a fond farewell. This trip. But as so often with you, it was something else.

The Atlantic wind coursed through the parking lot as its perverse howl sounded from beyond the breakers.

—My wife and I are going to be working at a mission in Guatemala.

He stuck out his hand and Milt took it. The urge to punch Stan in the face came quickly and both of Milt's fists tightened. But a man who has spent his entire career surviving on a diet of bruised ego and battered feelings doesn't give it all up for a career-killing moment like the one Milt envisioned and then just as quickly dismissed. Punching a trader would be a deathblow, reasoned Milt, but still, I brokered for his ass for over seven years, I deserved more of a heads-up than this. The prick. Take a shot.

Milt shook his head. It was all Gallagher now. A scary thought, everything hinged on one trader.

—I could've taken Joe Gallagher on this trip, said Milt in a half whine.

—You're going to be okay, Milty, said Stan. —You know everyone in this industry and everyone knows you. Plus, I put in a good word for you with my replacement.

—Who's that? asked Milt, resisting the urge to spit, yet trying to look appeased as he hoped it was someone who he liked and knew.

—Angel Pedroia, said Stan.

Milt had met Angel once, when he was a junior trader. Milt had spilled a beer on him half by mistake. Still, Milt needed Stan's blessing to even have a shot. So here he was, the man who had wrestled sea beasts and the drowning depths, with his head now bent, gazing at the dirt, shuffling his feet, unable to stare down a lesser man who was looking at him with a straight face, while pissing on his shoes.

THE SANDPIPER

After Stan had left Milt kicked the side of the van so hard that it left a dent. On the ride back to the hotel Aaron told Milt that he was glad he didn't die. Then the boy nodded off to sleep. On the way through the town of Cape Hatteras Milt saw the Sandpiper bar and decided that he'd come back for a well-needed drink. He ate supper with Aaron in the local restaurant next to the hotel. They both had crab soup and fish 'n' chips. While Aaron lifted a piece of key lime pie off his plate with a fork, Milt said:

—Don't tell your mother about this. If she knows we were out in bad weather she'll make sure they lock me up.

Aaron nodded. He'd heard this speech many times. He enjoyed analyzing the different variations his father tacked on with each new scenario. When Milt was done he patted Aaron on the head like he always did when the boy was much younger, when they were still a family.

—You head up to bed now. Watch a movie or something. You must be exhausted, said Milt. —I have some business to attend to. I'll be up in an hour or two.

Milt walked into the Sandpiper. It was a fisherman's bar with clean, wiped-down wooden tables and a pool table with salt stains on the green felt. Even inside Milt could smell the fresh scent of the ocean, and that was perhaps, Milt thought, what made all seaside bars seem clean. Within two shots of whiskey the dim lights overhead glowed in that special way that Milt was used to when he was drinking in a safe place, a good bar, the kind that makes you happy like a second home. Milt sat there up on a stool in the middle of the bar. He was drinking and reliving the feeling of being underwater and hurtling toward the bottom of the sea. It was like falling but somehow less terrible. Milt promised himself he was going to hold the experience close and not debase it by bragging or concocting a cheap yarn.

Milt played two games of pool and lost against a kid named Willy, the first mate on a boat called the *Broadbill*. He was making some shots and happy that he hadn't given in to the desire to tell the kid about his adventure. Midway through the second game Milt noticed two twenty-something girls in ECU sweatshirts enter the bar. They were both varying degrees of bleached blond. The bigger one took off her sweatshirt and the tight black T-shirt she wore beneath made her look to be the taller, more impressive of the two. She was in Milt's sweet spot, only about thirty pounds overweight.

Willy raised his eyebrows at Milt.

—That one is easy pickings, he said and smiled.

Milt then bonded with Willy, telling him the story of being pulled overboard. Only the way Milt told it the shark ripped him out of his harness.

—Must have been a mako, said Willy. —You're lucky to be alive.

It wasn't so much that Milt liked Willy that he told him the story, more that he was just practicing a version to work on the big blonde. Milt lost the second game on purpose and made his way to the bar. Milt drank patiently for some time. But when none of the other ten or so men in the bar approached the duo, Milt sauntered over and bought them a round.

On closer inspection, as Milt had guessed, the big one was the prettier of the two. Her name was Meghan. She was apple-shaped with thin arms and nice, tanned legs. Her mouth was turned down at the edges in a pout; her eyes were a brilliant, shimmering, Caribbean blue. Milt could not stop looking at her. To Milt she possessed a sour-faced Teutonic beauty. Drinking whiskey, Milt forged on, entertaining.

—This mako dragged me into the depths, he was saying. —And all I could think of was not letting go.

Then Milt stepped back and looked at Meghan, a full once up and down.

—But in the end I was beaten. I lost the battle.

—You look like you're okay to me, said Meghan. She flashed a smile.

It wasn't two more rounds of drinks before Milt grabbed her heavy thigh and she put an arm around Milt's back. Her friend had faded to some other corner of the Sandpiper. Milt's tongue, whiskey soaked and still tasting of the sea, groped her mouth. Milt felt twelve, fifteen, twenty years old. Between sloppy kisses, Milt disengaged himself and said to her:

—Fuck the Executioner.

His chest swelled as he wrapped his arms around her. Sometime later the bartender cleared his throat and Milt paid the tab. Meghan then held out her hand and tugged Milt by the fingertips toward the door. He felt lighter than air and remembered floating on the stormy seas. And he walked out the door believing that anything was possible.

Pete Nelson, former first mate of *Baptizo*, wandered into the Sandpiper around midnight. He'd already had a pint of rum, while packing his bags. He'd been fired because some novice hadn't hooked himself in. He came to say his "good-byes" to his friends; other first mates and fry cooks and off-duty barbacks and bartenders who worked on Hatteras and hung out at the Sandpiper. He fully believed his captain, Sam Cooke, would have him black-balled by Monday.

When he told the story of his day to his friend Willy Frazer, Willy got an excited look on his face.

—That guy. That guy was just in here. From New Jersey. Big, bald guy like Tony Soprano?

—That's him.

—He told everyone he was strapped in, said Willy.

—He wasn't a bad guy, said Pete. —Just an idiot. He almost died in front of his kid.

Willy put his lanky arm around his friend's neck and pulled him close.

—Dude, he said. —He just got snagged by the Sea Hag. She just walked out the door with him ten minutes ago.

—The fucking Sea Hag, repeated Pete. —Oh no.

—He better hope she's not having an outbreak.

—Guy like that, said Pete, —he's hit worse.

THE WEATHER HEDGE

It was Friday morning and most of the traders were hungover from the previous night's drinking debacle. Gallagher called down to Milt on the squawk box.

—Where's summer?

—Same as yesterday, yawned Milt.

—I want to buy some summer, wrote Gallagher to Milt on his instant messenger. He wanted to buy on the down-low without attracting the attention of his deskmates. Buying back your shorts was tantamount to treason against the Ghost's religious K-wave belief that the markets would soon plummet.

Milt didn't respond, his IM remained blank. Gallagher could feel the vibe through the box. It was as if Milt didn't want him to buy back his shorts. Did Milt know something? Gallagher hesitated.

—Summer ERCOT offer is kind of high, said Milt over the box, revealing Gallagher's position to those around him on the desk.

Buy me 250MW NQ ERCOT, typed Gallagher on his instant messenger. *And keep this on the down-low.*

The electricity and gas markets had been static for over a week. It was the perfect time to quietly cover most of his short position. The Ghost wasn't in the office and the market volatility was zero.

—Hey, stupid, said Miller to Gallagher, hearing Milt over the box. —Don't be a bird. Why you fooling with it? You want to be short, stay short.

Like everyone else except for Andrews, Miller was short energy futures. He traded the California market.

—You know what I'm doing today? asked Miller. —I'm going to ninja roll out of here at two o'clock and going to go home and lounge. The Patrón Silver will be printing.

Miller, who sat across from Gallagher, was in the process of rearranging his desk. Of all the superstitious traders, their desks crammed with good-luck charms, blessed mementos, and family pics, Miller's was a shrine to his various passions and fears. On his desk stood a small Gadsden "Don't tread on me" flag and a framed old newspaper clipping that showed Ronald Reagan astride a horse, giving a thumbs-up sign. Then taped to the rim of his computer screen was a piece of gambler's wisdom:

> *Always sit with your back to the wall.*
> —*Luke Short*

The redheaded, Fresno State ex-fullback was bored. Days like today where nothing was going on reminded him of sitting in the locker room after a football game, instead now he was lounging on the desk, tired and listless. Miller removed a wad of dip from his mouth. He regarded Gallagher with a suspicious eye and put the soggy tobacco plug into a paper cup.

—Stupid, what you up to? he asked. —You ain't got no poker face.

—I'm not doing shit, said Gallagher. —I'm going to take a walk and go talk to Greenblatt.

—That Communist, said Miller, referring to Greenblatt's left-wing politics.

Greenblatt was deep into writing a regression analysis of a program that spit out odds on different weather derivative markets. Gallagher stood in front of him for thirty seconds before Greenblatt noticed he was there. Greenblatt's seat on the floor was situated near the quants and the risk management group. It was away from the energy desk and thus Gallagher felt he could speak to Greenblatt and not be in the presence of suspicious ears.

—I want to go short the Dallas August weather, said Gallagher.

Greenblatt pulled up the screen and quoted the market:

—K5 is 610 at 629.

—K5? asked Gallagher.

—That's the ticker for Dallas.

—Make me the best offer.

—I'll put you at 619. You'll get done there. How many pieces do you want?

—Six pieces, said Gallagher.

—That's wood, said Greenblatt, nodding as if impressed. —The system values the risk at like $1.8M but in reality it's more like you got four to five million on the table.

Greenblatt looked at Gallagher. He was shaking his head, his eyes glazed over with knowing stoner wisdom.

—What have you got going on, dude?

Gallagher admired the chain-smoking Greenblatt. They had brewed a batch of pumpkin ale together and the Caltech genius had explained how to add chemicals to give it hallucinogenic properties.

—Let's just say I'm not drinking Rector's Kool-Aid. Everyone is overboard short. What if we do see a hurricane?

—But going outright short Dallas? That's some balls.

—Not if I'm already short the power. If the hurricane comes in the Gulf my power will lose but Dallas will get wet and my weather short will get paid.

Greenblatt flung himself back in his seat and clapped his hands together and started laughing.

—That's a dynamic fucking hedge. I like it. You'll be the only energy guy who doesn't get fired, he said. —It's the fucking Cult of the K-wave down there.

—Andrews is long, said Gallagher.

—So I hear, said Greenblatt. —But we're in the staying alive game.

Greenblatt drummed the edge of his desk with a pen, doing calculations in his head.

—I like your odds, he said finally.

Gallagher didn't leave. He stood there watching Greenblatt work the market with his broker. The weather trader glanced up at Gallagher and read his mind.

—You want me to keep these in my book? I'll basis them over to you when August goes prompt. That way the Ghost can't stop you out.

—Sure, said Gallagher.

Walking back down the row, Gallagher felt conflicted, like he had both committed a crime and bought an insurance policy.

ART GALLERY

John Shuggs accompanied the Ghost down Berkeley Street. It started to drizzle. The misty rain and the humidity and the soot in the air settled on them like a filmy paste. It was a Wednesday night and the downtown streets were deserted.

—How can you fuck up a lobster? asked Shuggs. —You throw it in a pot, boil it, and you're done.

The Ghost liked Shuggs to accompany him out in public, a second pair of eyes.

—I'm putting a bullet in Ruth Chris, said the Ghost.

Outside a building under the streetlight was a spidery-limbed woman smoking a cigarette. Her legs were so skinny they seemed birdlike in the distance.

—This must be it. Freakshow, whispered Shuggs, as they approached.

—Easy, said the Ghost. —I'm here to make a transaction, not crush beings.

The door to the gallery had chipped red paint. A white shade hung in the front window. The rumble of a party could be heard going on behind the door.

—Do we need to buy tickets to get in? the Ghost asked the girl.

She looked at them and blew out a stream of smoke.

—Just walk right in, she said.

Shuggs opened the door.

—She wasn't too friendly, said Shuggs.

—She's probably an artist, Shuggsy, said the Ghost. —Artists don't *help* people. They create art.

—Sure. I guess so, agreed Shuggs.

They moved slowly down the hall. Entering the main gallery, the two traders saw a dimly lit room packed with a mass of people standing in front of paintings illuminated by floodlights. In the back of the room elevated on a small stage an electric guitar, bass, and drum trio played a funk version of Jimi Hendrix's "Voodoo Child." Out of the gloom a girl in a Vegas-style cocktail waitress outfit, fishnets, and four-inch pumps quizzed them:

—Champagne? she asked over the music, offering a tray of cheap bubbly in plastic flutes.

They each took a glass. Shuggs muttered something to the Ghost, but the Ghost couldn't hear it over the din.

—Red Bull, said Shuggs loudly. —Think they got any Red Bull?

Shuggs was from York, Pennsylvania, and drank twelve Red Bulls a day, and although his favorite movie was *Star Wars* he liked to think of himself as someone who could take care of himself in a fight.

The Ghost told Shuggs to get them some cheese. There was a table full of four cheese plates; each looked greener, moldier, and more exotic than the next. Shuggs came back. The Ghost finished his piss champagne and handed Shuggs the empty cup, who threw it in the trash can.

—Walk me down to the other end, Shuggs. And don't disappear on me. Lots of bodies. It's like a fog for me.

Shuggs looked around uncomfortably like an ex-girlfriend might be stalking him.

—I wish they had some Red Bull. Might take the edge off. A lot of mutants lurking, he said and stalked off.

The Ghost made his way through the crowd as best he could and nudged within reach of each painting. He really couldn't see the art, but he enjoyed eavesdropping on the conversations.

Some viewers stood in front of a set of pictures.

—It's striking, said a woman.

The woman was in her forties. The Ghost made out the vague features, a square jaw, saggy jowls. A clone of a downtown frappuccino-drinking insurance agent. Her clothes were art critic: black blouse, gray suit pants. Next to her was a tall, thin, bald man. The Ghost could not see him clearly in the low light, but from his voice judged him the equivalent of a prissy French aristocrat.

—I agree. It rejects the rote, tired rhetoric of overt transgression, said Howard.

The Ghost leaned forward to hear better. The small crowd felt the Ghost's presence and moved to the side so that he could view the painting. It was a massive canvas: in its middle were gray, red, and black blotches. The Ghost saw blur and shadow.

The same way Elliot Wave theoreticians spoke of IV down waves and II up wave corrections and traders who believed in Japanese candlestick theory spoke of evening star and dark clouds and hanging men, these people were speaking of art. None of them knew which way the market was going but they felt happy and safe and intelligent knowing and espousing accepted theories. The Ghost surmised from the woman's words that the painting was shit even though he could not see it, because in art, figured the Ghost, as in trading, the futures market always moves in ways that are slightly different from the modes that came before it. People can succeed by predicting the market in ways that the scholars and theoreticians never recognize from their tried-and-true pattern calling. The best guessers made the best traders but you could always tell shit because the academics flocked to it.

The Ghost blinked. The three steak house vodka sodas were coming on like a toxin. He was feeling like a poisoned, radioactive Russian spy. He moved on to the next one. A hundred-pound whisper of a girl twirled her auburn hair and gave him a cat-glowing glance that he could not see. The Ghost stood next to her as she gazed at a medium-sized canvas oil painting.

She looked at the Ghost and said:

—It's called *Waiting*.

—I have very bad eyes, he said. —Can you please describe it for me?

She told him that it was a pair of Amazonian muscled legs in a spread-eagled V framing the painting and a vista beyond her muff: a neon blue sky and gray mountain range beneath. The Ghost sat there listening, mesmerized. The Ghost felt himself drawn in by the girl's words as if being sucked up and then floating between the legs and mountain range as if on a magic carpet. He knew it was of course the martinis and bad champagne but the light blazing on the painting called *Waiting* made it very real for him, the feeling that he had forgotten his blindness.

—No one's bought it yet, said the girl.

—Did you paint this? asked the Ghost.

The girl shook her head.

—I wish I had, she said.

—I'm buying it, he said.

The girl coughed. It was wet out. She held her flute of champagne with both hands, as if she was going to shatter at any moment.

—How much is it? asked the Ghost.

—It says right there on the wall, she said, pointing. —Three thousand dollars. By Celina Gallagher.

Celina was staring at her dealer, Howard, as he talked up the bad painting of another artist. Just beyond him she noticed a man in dark glasses, bent forward, scrutinizing her title plaque. Celina realized it was Randall Jennings, her husband's boss. At first she was embarrassed, afraid that the painting somehow would be used as a joke against her husband at work. But she remembered that he was sight impaired. She went to him and grasped his hand.

—You're Randall Jennings. My husband's boss? asked Celina.

—Yes. And you are Celina the artist, said the Ghost. Celina laughed in a way that told him she was not pretentious.

The Ghost turned back to her painting and looked at it again. He waved at the picture with his hand as if slapping the background noise of the party away so he could speak and be heard. Celina was expecting a polite, if innocuous, compliment from her husband's boss.

—It's been described to me and I'm buying it, he said.

Celina couldn't help but feel moved, as the Ghost gazed at her painting. It inflicted upon her some affection for the man. She had no way of knowing that his feeling was concocted, a sprinkling of seedlings to feed a larger purpose. She saw his reaction to the painting. Her work had broken through.

—I sent your husband away to Vegas, said the Ghost. —So I came down here to invite you out on a coworker's boat this Saturday. But instead I'm buying your art.

Celina smiled meekly but said nothing.

—You should come, though. Some of the wives will be there.

The Ghost smiled slightly at Celina.

Shuggs and the Ghost strolled down the sidewalk outside the art gallery. He was thinking about catching the late-night HBO show *Taxi Cab Confessions*. His sneakers splashed in small puddles as his boss whistled quietly in the rain, as if he was pleased with himself.

—You buy anything? asked Shuggs, talking just to talk.

—I made a transaction, said the Ghost. —One where I bluffed the man and not the hand.

The Ghost was a nocturnal being. The night was the only time he gave vent to philosophies.

They walked another hundred yards before coming to the intersection of State Street and the Boston Common. Shuggs stood there at the corner, waiting for the light to change. The Ghost looked back over his shoulder at the young trader and said:

—One day, if you ever learn how to trade, Shuggs, you'll know the difference.

VEGAS

When Gallagher opened the door to his suite at the Bellagio, he saw that the Colonel had placed his luggage on the bed closest to the bathroom.

—Of course, said Gallagher.

He went over and heaved the Colonel's bag off his bed onto the satin sheet of the far one. Along with himself and the Colonel, the Ghost also sent Churchill to the Day of the Trader conference in Vegas. Andrews was the only one who had made money of late but the Ghost wasn't giving him a look at anything. Gallagher guessed why the Ghost had sent the Colonel, greasing him up for the big unit selloff. The Colonel is probably rooming with me to convince me to come back into the K-wave fold, thought Gallagher.

Gallagher unpacked in a slow, deliberate manner. Gallagher conserved his mojo. He needed to focus his gambling energies into a pinpoint—so that everything seemed simple and clear. The Colonel's luggage even being in the room was a disturbance, an imbalance.

After all his clothes were folded and put away in the drawers, Gallagher stripped down and went into the bathroom. The showerhead was a brass that was polished so brightly it could've passed for gold. The Colonel had not yet used the bathroom and all the towels were clean and crisply folded. He had his pick of unused towels, or, more precisely, a lucky towel. Gallagher got out of the shower, contemplating the towels hanging from the rack. He looked them over carefully. He eyed one that seemed to sit as if the maid had taken extra care and diligence in hanging it perfectly.

—This one's good, he said, grabbing the lucky towel.

In the middle of getting dressed, Gallagher noticed that a single mint wrapped in gold with a Bellagio seal imprinted on it had been placed on the pillows of each double bed. He went over and inspected the one on his bed. He unwrapped it and took a bite.

Then Gallagher began getting dressed, putting on jeans, a clean white oxford shirt, and a blue blazer. In the blazer's inner pocket he put a worn paperback copy of Von Clausewitz's *On War*. He'd go to the bar and read the book if he lost a lot of money quickly. It was Gallagher's way of stemming excessive losses.

He sucked his teeth with his tongue and decided the mint had been delicious. He went over to the Colonel's bed and took his.

HARD ROCK POOL

The Colonel took care of business first. Carrying a small blue Gold's Gym bag, he navigated the beach chairs and traffic of tan bodies to find Peter the German lounging poolside in a cabana at the Hard Rock. The spot had been the Colonel's choice.

Peter the German's alert eyes devoured the hard body bikini set. He was a voyeuristic connoisseur. It was bright out by the pool; the midday Las Vegas sun beat down everything with a blinding light, as if aware it had to compete with the midnight sparkle of the casinos. The imitation palm frond fan whirred lazily above them in the cabana.

—Look at all the fresh-cut grass, said the Colonel.

—Kids call it the Brazilian 'kini wax.

A waitress came by and delivered their drinks. When she left the Colonel asked:

—MinnHub printed five hundred dollars for five hours. You did it. Want to tell me how it went down?

—I'd be happy to paint the scene. What a pretty picture it was. Peter the German described that early morning in Minnesota when he flew his Ultra Light over the 500 kV lines on the Eau Claire Arpin transformer that connected Minneapolis to Chicago.

—Did I tell you how it was a beautiful morning? Cold and gray with ice crystals hanging from the pines. But it wasn't too windy. Perfect for flying. I swooped down about twenty feet above the lines and dropped the chain right on them.

Peter sucked his mojito through his small cocktail straw.

—Boom, he said. —Sparks lit up the sky behind me and I heard the transmission lines melt. It sounded like a huge, gigantic bug zapper as soon as the chain hit. Man, what a sound.

The Colonel looked out at all the lithe bronzed bodies congregating around the tiki bar.

—I didn't even need to take another pass to see if I hit it. I knew they melted outright when I heard that sound. I just kept flying.

—I don't have to ask the question "Did anyone see you?" said the Colonel.

—It was four A.M. No one saw a thing. The nearest farm to those wires where the chain hit was twenty miles away.

The Colonel glanced at Peter the German's face, looking for any trace of fear or nervousness. There was none.

—I imagine that was what it was like being a World War I flying ace, dropping grenades right into the trenches, up close and personal, said Peter the German.

—It worked. We got paid. Now I imagine we shouldn't talk about it, said the Colonel.

After a moment of silence Peter the German looked at the Colonel's small blue Gold's Gym bag underneath his chair.

—There's a lot of money in there, he said. —Can I trust you to watch it if I go to the bar for a drink?

—I'm leaving soon, said the Colonel. —This isn't a social call. Peter the German looked out over the fleshy scene of the pool and grew contemplative.

—You know I had a great-uncle in World War I. Flew for the Kaiser in the air corps. Said to have been friendly with Baron von Richthofen.

—That right?

—The Red Baron, said Peter the German.

The Colonel took off his sunglasses and gave Peter the German a blank stare that said: *I don't care.*

—You're not the only one who is ex-military, said Peter the German.

Peter the German rang the button on the cabana wall for service. Then he got up from his beach chair and stretched. He bore the thick, hirsute trunk of middle age, but his legs were thin as a ballerina's.

—Order yourself another drink, said Peter the German. —I'm going to the pool bar to mingle. You watch that bag.

The Colonel lay back on the chair and closed his eyes. He listened to the thrum of voices echoing across the pool and the steady blare of rock and roll presiding over the scene. Kid Rock's "Bawitaba" was the last thing he heard before he drifted off into a restless sleep.

The Colonel was having a nightmare that the Feds were handcuffing him and throwing him into the back of a white Buick LeSabre. Peter the German woke up the Colonel, nudging him by his shoulder.

—You awake?

The Colonel blinked a few times and then yawned. His back was stiff from the beach chair. Peter the German was smiling. He held up a silver-gray felt cowboy hat that had water dripping from the brim.

—Look what I found, he said, showing the hat off to the Colonel.

He put it on his head.

—It almost fits.

—Where'd you get that?

—At the pool.

—You won it? asked the Colonel.

—No, said Peter the German. —Some jackass at the pool bar was drinking hard and talking a blue streak of bullshit. He was *trying* to hit on some ladies, except he couldn't keep up the pace under that sun. Finally, he passed out. Fell right into the pool. Raised quite a big commotion too. Lifeguards, a few customers at the bar; they all fished him out. Some guy gave him mouth to mouth.

—Amateurs, said the Colonel.

—When all was said and done, his hat was still floating near my bar stool.

—You mean your hat, said the Colonel.

Peter the German twisted the end of his blond mustache between his forefinger and thumb.

—That is precisely what I mean.

GOOD-LUCK CHARMS

Milt was standing by a fake palm tree in the Voodoo Lounge talking to a tall options trader from VBS. It was a brunch held by Milt's brokerage firm. Gallagher didn't recognize any of the other traders there. As Gallagher walked over to Milt he noticed a flat-screen TV playing an old Elvis movie, the King in a boat wearing a captain's hat. The rest of the bar was pure Manhattan lounge, low lights, zinc bar, modern décor. Gallagher couldn't figure out the theme.

The tall guy talking to Milt traded options. As Gallagher approached he saw that the trader wore silver cuff links on his purple Façonnable shirt. One cuff link was a small bear and the other was a bull: bull/bear cuff links, standard Wall Street pretension.

—Gallagher, said Milt, turning. —You ever met Herman?

Herman looked young to Gallagher, young and from the city. From his contemptuous smile Gallagher would have bet money that Herman the options trader drove a Lamborghini, and that he leased it.

—No, said Gallagher.

Gallagher had a Scotch. Milt drank wine with his prospective client and moved the conversation to a ridiculous fish tale about hooking a twenty-foot mako shark off Cape Hatteras. The options trader in turn told an account of blasting doves out of the air in Argentina with a double-barreled custom-made Benelli. When Herman took a bathroom break, Gallagher said to Milt:

—So you are a sportsman nowadays?

—You kids are into guns and fishing, said Milt. —I blame it on the Nature Channel.

He thought about confessing to Gallagher that since he'd lost Stan Couch, business had suffered. Milt needed to rebuild his base with some younger traders, up and comers. But he knew better than to whine to his meal ticket.

—Well, I'm done schmoozing with Herman, said Milt, smashing his fist into an open palm. —Let's go play games of chance.

Gallagher surveyed the scene of the MGM's main floor as they descended the escalator. The pure oxygenated air that prevented sleep, a caffeine inhaler, hit his nostrils with welcome familiarity. He listened to the rows of slot machines: the bell-ringing, bleep-spewing, carnival din of the slots, spinning, whirring, change-spitting and coin-devouring one-armed bandits who were being stared down by dead-eyed zombies, blue-hairs, and cancer survivors trying their luck with the worst odds in the casino: taxes for poor people.

—Poor bastards, said Milt, looking on, as if reading Gallagher's thoughts.

Forty-something, heavily mascaraed cocktail waitresses scurried between the crowds, toting trays jam-packed with drinks. Beyond the slots were the blackjack tables and beyond them in the back of the room, the deep end of the pool, out of sight from the escalator, were the arena-shaped craps tables, their destination.

—Where's el Jefe? asked Gallagher.

—Lost it today, said Milt, rubbing his puffy eyes. —I had a few midmorning cocktails at the Hard Rock pool.

—That was a lucky hat, said Gallagher.

—I don't want to talk about it, said Milt.

He tapped the rubber railing of the escalator.

—It's bad luck to talk about good-luck charms, said Milt after a second.

—It's only bad luck to lose, responded Gallagher.

—But there are reasons behind losing, said Milt. —You win or lose long before you even hit the tables.

—Let's not talk business, said Milt out of the blue. —I want to focus on the dice.

—Just one question, Milt. Then we gamble. Why are you giving the Ghost color on my directional trading? asked Gallagher.

Milt stood there stunned. I've been dry-gulched, he thought.

—Kid, said Milt, taking two seconds to recover his footing. —You got a boss. I got a boss. Dartmouth Collins covers the Ghost and shit rolls down-hill. My boss braced me. I never even spoke to the Ghost.

Gallagher let Milt keep talking. He was talking fast, selling, digging his way out of a hole.

—You're my main guy, said Milt. —I wouldn't ever throw you under the bus. You want to buy or sell. Don't matter to me. I just bring you the markets.

Gallagher didn't need to hear any more to know Milt was lying. He decided then and there he was done with Milt, but seeing as Milt was a good guy, he'd let him enjoy the conference. Milt knew nothing of the weather derivatives hedge so Gallagher still believed he was up a chess piece on the Ghost.

—It's forgotten. Let's hit the tables, Milt, said Gallagher.

Gallagher put his hand on Milt's shoulder, a friendly gesture. Too friendly for the usually cool Gallagher, thought Milt, who felt a chill, an alcoholic sweat coming on. The walls were closing in.

THE COLONEL AND
HIS MANSERVANT

The Colonel pulled out onto the Las Vegas strip with the top down. It was ninety degrees, zero humidity: two strippers away from beautiful, thought the Colonel, scratching his birthmark behind his ear. Sporting a new high and tight military haircut that glinted blue-black in the noonday sun, a pair of Ray Ban Aviator sunglasses, a button-down gray silk short-sleeve shirt, and acid-washed jeans, he drove with his left arm hanging loosely out the window like he didn't give a fuck. The cherry red El Dorado chugged with a lazy coughing murmur down the street doing a mean ten miles an hour, as the Colonel gazed at the spectacle of castles that passed by him in a parade of decadent majesty: the Aladdin; the MGM; New York, New York; the Bellagio; the Luxor; Caesar's; and on down the strip to the minor venues like Hooters and Gold Dust. The car was rented from Chester's Vintage Automobile for two hundred bucks a day. The Ghost assured him any expense within reason would be written off. For the work he was doing for the Ghost, the Colonel decided he would push toward the unreasonable side of reason. A mile or so down past the casinos, the Colonel pulled into a strip mall that featured a modern architectural feat of glass and white clay tiles; it looked like some NASA project gone awry. The Colonel parked his car in front of a storefront that read ESTEEMED VALET.

The décor inside Esteemed Valet was that of a high-end spa lounge like the ones the Colonel's wife frequented in Boston. Big leather chairs sat facing a large framed Andy Warhol print of a neon pink and inviting Marilyn Monroe. A rock slate waterfall built into the wall gurgled peacefully. A Japanese vase with pussy willows stood on a table with an assortment of magazines like GQ, *Playboy,* and *Maxim.* New Age music that sounded like a waterfall or bubbling brook only served to disorient the Colonel as he tried to place which sound was which. The Colonel walked up to the girl at the front desk, a chunky, ham-armed redhead.

—Daniel Haupt. I'm here for my midget.

The concierge glanced up at the Colonel, adjusting her tortoiseshell glasses. The guy, she thought, looked like a serial killer or border patrol agent on vacation, it was a toss-up. She looked back down at a chart.

—You're Daniel Haupt. Okayyyyy, said the concierge with skepticism.

He nodded. She picked up a phone and turned her back on the Colonel as she spoke into the receiver. Hanging up the phone, she said:

—His name is Eduardo. Please have a seat. He'll be right out.

—He's a bartender, right? He has a kit and everything. Booze included?

—He's a martini mixer, she replied, explaining. —That's his specialty. And, yes, he brings a martini kit: shaker, ice, stirrer, lemon rinds, olives, whatever you can think of in your martini, he has it.

—No beer, though? questioned the Colonel, removing his sunglasses to get a better look at her strawberry-colored freckles that spread across her nose. He wondered if she was from Tennessee or Georgia, she had that healthy look about her.

—He's a martini mixer, said the concierge flatly. —No beer. Just martinis.

The Colonel squinted at the concierge. She had a pretty face. The Colonel leaned forward to see if she had a smell to her. The concierge took a small step back and instinctively folded her arms across her chest. Wanting to engage the woman, to look at her, take her in, the Colonel asked her a question, the first one that popped into his head:

—Can I take my midget to a strip club?

—Eduardo will go wherever you go, but I doubt they'll let him bring his alcohol into the club.

—Some of them do, said a voice from below. It was a low voice, both confident and calm; the voice of someone who has seen many things.

—I am Eduardo, your personal martini bartender.

He wore a small black dinner jacket and a paisley cummerbund and bow tie. His cola-colored hair was impeccably combed and he had a certain glinting hardness to his look like that of a miniature assassin. He shook the Colonel's hand.

—You can call me the Colonel, said the Colonel.

Then the Colonel jerked his head toward the door and said in the friendly demeanor of a kidnapper or prison guard,

—Let's go.

When they got in the caddy together, the Colonel noticed how Eduardo's feet didn't reach the fuzzy floor mats. The Colonel reached across Eduardo and popped open the glove box. Inside was a Panasonic handheld video cam. The Colonel didn't take it out, he just pointed to it.

—You know how to use one of these?

—Yes, Colonel, said Eduardo.

The Colonel eyed the bartender, waiting for him to ask a question. When no inquiry was made, the Colonel decided that Eduardo was his man.

—That's for later, said the Colonel, shutting the glove compartment with a snap of his wrist.

The Colonel started up the caddy. Its behemoth V-eight engine growled like a yacht's.

—Would the Colonel like a drink to start? asked Eduardo. The Colonel nodded to the affirmative. Eduardo unpacked his kit.

HITTING THE TABLES

Gallagher and Milt approached the craps tables. There were six of them. They formed an oblong circle with a table at each end that was stationed perpendicular to the others. The setup was for the pit boss; so nothing was out of even his peripheral vision. The theory behind it was not unlike the pioneers circling the wagons against the Indians.

Gallagher walked the floor around the tables twice. Finding a hot table was the key to beating the numerical odds: that was strategy. Tactics was beating the dealer once you got onto the hot table.

When gambling Milt would often take on the dealer, put him out of his zone so to speak. Without Milt it was best to go for quiet tables. But with Milt, who liked to work a table, interact, it was good to have high energy.

—This table here, said Gallagher.

—You feel it? asked Milt.

—This one.

They split up: Gallagher at one end of the table, Milt at the other. There was a quiet nondescript shooter who looked like a computer technician. On his second pass, Gallagher knew he was a killer and bet big out of the gate. The key for Gallagher was betting large sums as the table became hot, not after it had boiled over. The computer technician had five passes and Gallagher was up eleven hundred. Milt had made four hundred dollars and was ecstatic. However, Milt had not been served alcohol. Two brothers from California, bearded, and in the wine business, provided decent rolls and Milt hit his first snake eyes hardways.

—I thought drinks were free around here? Milt began shouting. —I don't want to besmirch your casino but the drink service is a joke.

The gamblers laughed at Milt, they liked his use of the word "besmirch." The dealer rubbed his thumb on his black vest and gave Milt a smug look. Milt, fearing the thumb on the vest was a heads-up to security, threw a five-dollar chip on the table in front of him. Just when the dealer thought Milt would shut up, he rolled three consecutive first-roll sevens. Milt had doubled down on the pass line each time.

—Free money, Milt was yelling at the top of his lungs. —Don't bring that drink now, you cheap bastards. You'll change my luck.

Milt held the dice for three passes. Everyone was printing money and happy. Ray peered down at Milt's end of the table. The computer technician was still not smiling.

The pit boss, who was kind-looking like an Italian grandfather, soon came over and took the dealer aside, patted him on the back and pulled him. They brought on another dealer, an attractive Asian woman with a beauty mark on her chin. She wore a bright red vest and had a genteel patter. The dice immediately cooled. One of the bearded brothers breathed out a sigh like he was tired. Gallagher noticed a lull in the table run, but it was not over. The waitress made the mistake of finally delivering Milt his drinks, two of them, bourbon straight up.

—You're a real cooze, aren't you? he asked, zeroing in on the woman dealer. —You think you're going to deal me right down the toilet, but I got news for you, baby. Uncle Milty is hot tonight.

Milt's angry serenade fueled tempers. The killer computer technician got the dice and worked a streak of five more passes. If the dealer had been a bully, she could have shattered his focus, but she was too incensed with big, red, ugly, loud, blurting Milt to notice. The table began to win. The bearded men shouted and high-fived. The woman dealer was a notch above the first, but she lost the table. A bald man with wide, calloused longshoreman hands, who had crapped out every time without scoring a pass, finally won one on a hard twelve; the payout was six to one. Soon after a man who looked like a professor, unoffensive, bespectacled, and soft-spoken, tried to nudge in on the table next to the computer technician, who was polite enough to let him slide into a spot. Gallagher watched and marveled how Milt's nose ferreted out the scene.

—They're bringing in a goddamn cooler, yelled Milt, pointing at the professor. —Lock hands. Keep this guy out. He's a cooler.

Gallagher saw the pit boss's friendly brown Italian grandfather eyes ice over with cold rage. Gallagher had never seen a cooler. Even though Gallagher believed in mathematicians like Fibonacci, Sir Isaac Newton, and Ptolemy, the killer computer technician crapped out on his first roll. He then smiled in defeat. When the killer dice roller smiled, Gallagher picked up his long roll of chips and made his way over to Milt.

—Let's go, said Gallagher. —We're done.

—Fuck that. This table is just getting started, said Milt. —I've spotted the cooler, beaten down the dealers, and am crushing it.

—I'll be at the bar reading a book, said Gallagher.

Milt waved him off, angry.

—That's nonsense. Cowardice. You're abandoning the table, cried Milt.

Gallagher thought how Milt had missed his place in history: the Alamo, Little Bighorn, the Confederate Army at Gettysburg.

—I admire you, Milt.

—Just bring me a drink, he said. —I need a drink.

And then shouting at the dealer at the pit boss at the table at anyone who would listen, Milt, in a high-pitched battle cry, yelled:

—Taste it, bitches!

THE MARKSMAN

Eduardo was on the deck of the Desert Café Bar & Grill off Gold Rush Avenue, making his specialty: a Hendrick's gin martini with a single ice cube and a slice of cucumber. The Colonel had worked it out with the Desert Café bartender that he would pay for every drink Eduardo made. The bartender didn't understand the arrangement at first, but when he saw the trio of women flocking to admire Eduardo's handiwork he took notes.

The Colonel sat back and let the midget sell him.

—Yes, ladies, said Eduardo in a ceaseless patter, as he shook his martini mixer, —I am in the employ of this fellow. He calls himself the Colonel and we've been driving around all day in his Cadillac. That beautiful red car out there in the parking lot. And I've been making him martinis all day. And he has been drinking them *all*. Quite a tolerance the Colonel has.

—Just make Lilly her drink, said the Colonel. He was very good at remembering women's names.

Lilly Brasfield was a hairdresser from Dayton. She wore a black Luxor casino golf shirt that made her pale Midwestern skin seem even whiter. Lilly had chosen the seat closest to the Colonel. She took a sip of her cucumber gin martini.

—Delicious, she said.

The Colonel patted her on the leg.

—What did I tell you? he said.

—You didn't lie, said Lilly. —This is the best martini ever.

Then Lilly turned to Eduardo, her auburn bangs hiding a large, pale forehead the shape of a half moon.

—Thank you, Eduardo, she said.

Eduardo bowed slightly and clasped his hands together. Then, with his palms facing up, he motioned to the Colonel as if presenting him:

—The Colonel never lies, he said.

The three women laughed and then kept on drinking. The cutest of the three, a petite brunette and also a hairdresser, noticed the Colonel's hair.

—Look at his hair. Can I touch it?

She reached over and the Colonel bent his head forward.

—Ohhh. It's like black felt. Feel that, Doreen.

Doreen, who was tall, sallow-complexioned, and the owner of the salon back in Dayton, had good instincts.

—More like Brillo pad, she said. —Too steel wool for my taste.

But the Colonel stayed loyal to Lilly, the girl who sat next to him, not the most attractive but the odds-on favorite.

—What do you think? he asked, bending his head toward her.

She massaged his scalp with strong, professional hairdresser fingers.

—It feels nice, said Lilly.

After another round of martinis, the Colonel got up from his deck chair and announced:

—Me and Eduardo are leaving.

He had touched Lilly's leg and thigh throughout the drinking session and toward the end of the last martini, a blueberry vodka concoction, he'd slid his finger behind her panty waistband. Then he spoke directly to her:

—Lilly, are you coming?

Lilly looked at her two friends. She wasn't usually the one to get hit on, so Lilly's friends were happy for her. Even Doreen nodded for her to go.

The Colonel opened the front passenger side door for Lilly Brasfield. Eduardo scrambled into the backseat. The Colonel got in and started up the car.

—I like sushi, said Lilly. —Do you like sushi?

—I know a cool place, said the Colonel.

The conversation had waned from the highs of Eduardo's sales pitch. The Colonel turned on the radio.

The road going south out of Vegas was lined with brown, sick-looking cacti and dry, yellow sable brush coated in dust. A vulture or a hawk floated in the distance, a black speck above the burnt orange desert horizon. The Colonel took a turnoff onto an exit that was more of a dirt path than a road.

—We're almost here, he said, looking at a map by his side.

The Colonel pulled the car into the parking lot. A large sign announced: LAS VEGAS GUN CLUB AND FIRING RANGE. The clubhouse was built in the Pueblo style, complete with the wood beams sticking out of the clay, sun-baked brick.

—You ever shot an assault rifle before? he asked Lilly Brasfield. She had not, she answered, although she had fired her brother's shotgun once.

—You're going to love it, said the Colonel.

Eduardo was smiling in the backseat. He had never made martinis at a firing range. This would beef up his already strong résumé.

The Colonel bought them all protective glasses and earplugs. He rented an M-16 and a Heckler & Koch S-39 assault rifle. The club manager was an ex-cop who'd never shaved his sideburns from the seventies. He went through some precautionary measures and then showed the Colonel how to load and unload the cartridges.

—I'm a marine, said the Colonel politely. The manager relaxed. He had no idea that Eduardo's black briefcase held copious amounts of alcohol.

—Semper fi, eh? he said.

Then he gave the trio another glance and shook his head apologetically.

—One thing, though. We don't have the facilities for little people, he said, eyeing Eduardo in his tuxedo.

—Can he watch at least? asked Lilly.

Not many pretty girls came to the LVGC and the manager waved Eduardo through with a chuckle.

The range looked out onto the Nevada desert. The targets, standard bull's-eye and human print, were sent out on a pulley system a hundred yards downrange. A wall of bullet-peppered Pueblo bricks was set up behind the targets to limit the number of stray shots.

The Colonel showed Lilly the proper stance and how to squeeze, not pull, the trigger. He let her hold the Heckler & Koch, the lighter of the two assault rifles. The Colonel positioned himself at her back and had his cheek against the nape of her neck as he showed her how to keep the stock of the rifle snug in the sweet spot where her shoulder met with her upper pectorals. He then stepped back and said:

—Fire when ready.

Lilly popped off a few rounds with the Heckler & Koch. After her fifth shot, she looked back at the Colonel and smiled boyishly. The Colonel recalled the target from downrange.

—Not bad, he said, inspecting it for bullet holes. —You have potential. He then took the gun from her perspiring hands. Lilly rubbed the shoulder that had braced the rifle stock.

—That's why they make the rifles these days with a bit of rubber here on the stock, explained the Colonel, as he sent down a new round of fresh targets. —Helps reduce the brunt of the recoil.

—It was a rush, said Lilly. —I can't believe I hit it.

—Eduardo, make this woman a drink, commanded the Colonel.

—Right away, Colonel, said Eduardo with muted glee.

The Colonel picked up the H&K and the M-16, one in each hand. He hemmed and hawed and then shouldered the H&K. With a controlled precision, he squeezed out ten rounds from the smaller assault rifle.

—This thing is a light little bitch, isn't it? he said to his audience, weighing the gun in his hands.

The Colonel brought the target back. Eduardo and Lilly Brasfield watched as he pulled it down from the frame. He held it up for them to see: a tight cluster of holes right in the bull's-eye at the center of the chest on the human target.

—Almost perfect, said the Colonel, putting his finger through one hole that was two inches outside the bull's-eye. His cell phone rang. The Colonel raised a hand, excusing himself. It was the Ghost.

—It went fine, said the Colonel. —He got his money. A happy ending.

The Ghost spoke for a bit and the Colonel listened.

—No, said the Colonel into the phone. —He won't do it again. It's too risky.

The Ghost was speaking louder now, threatening.

—I won't do it, said the Colonel.

The Colonel closed his own phone.

—He's a greedy fucker, he said in the hot dry desert air.

The Colonel put the cell phone in his belt holster and walked back over to Lilly Brasfield. Her lip was perspiring in the sun and a fine coating of dust had beaded up on the droplets of sweat, making them visible.

—You've got to shoot with the M-16. The big gun. Just one time, he said.

—It'll hurt and feel good at the same time.

By the end of the afternoon the Colonel and Lilly were drunk and her shoulder was very sore. She rubbed it and complained. When they left the firing range, the Colonel put Lilly in the backseat so she could relax. It was almost dinnertime but the Colonel wanted her to see the suite at the Bellagio first. Gallagher would be at dinner. There would be plenty of time to do what needed to get done.

Eduardo sat in the front passenger seat with a pout on his face. His tuxedo was covered in dust and he had a rash on his inner thighs from sweating and working his craft under the hot sun.

—Am I working a party tonight, Colonel? he asked, wondering about his suit.

The Colonel ignored Eduardo. He hadn't liked his tone. Lilly again asked him about dinner and the Colonel turned on the radio. He reached across Eduardo, nudging him out of the way with his elbow. He opened the glove compartment and put the handheld video camera in Eduardo's lap.

—You can start filming now, he said.

THE WIVES

On Friday the Colonel, Churchill, and Gallagher went to the Day of the Trader in Vegas. On Saturday the Ghost took some traders and their wives out on a rented boat. They cruised for four hours into Narragansett Bay and then down one of the estuaries.

Celina was sitting in the bow with two other trader wives. Both of them had been born in Oklahoma. To them Celina was an outsider but they still included her in their conversation. They were nice about it. They asked Celina about her husband and let her respond to their complaints on the many ways in which Boston was inferior to Tulsa. Gauging her response, they tried to discern if she was a Northeast "liberal." Celina noticed that neither Jenna nor Tammy smoked. They wore fancy wide-brimmed beach hats and Gucci sunglasses. Between beers they applied sunblock to their noses and shoulders. They're concerned about their skin, thought Celina, as she smoked, calculating that both women were most likely nearing forty.

—That was nice of him to give us a lime in our beers. Did you notice that, Jenna? He didn't give the boys a lime but he has a whole bag of them cut up and he gave them just to the ladies.

—He's got very nice manners. Is he from Texas? asked Jenna, whose chicken-bone-thin legs were all gooseflesh and shivering.

—No, said Celina. —I believe he's from Seattle.

—Seattle, huh, said Tammy, pronouncing the word "Seattle" carefully like it was the name of a foreign country.

—Well, for a California boy he has nice manners anyhow, repeated Jenna.

—Mine, said Tammy, —he needs work. We've got a belching problem.

—That's a beer consumption problem, laughed Jenna. It was obvious that their families spent a lot of time together.

—It's worse in the fall. You know? Football season. He's absolutely useless for three months. Now with that fantasy football, he's always online. Basically, he ignores me and the kids.

She pulled her beach hat down on her head, so that the shade from the brim covered her face.

—I've decided I'm going to have an affair next fall, she said.

The ladies from Tulsa both giggled at this joke. Then they leaned back and let the motion of the boat surging through the waves lull them into an easy summertime stupor. Finally, Jenna broke the silence.

—Randall seems like he just wouldn't be that way. Just watching football all the time. He seems like he has other interests.

—Jenna, darling, said Tammy. —He's blind. He probably listens to football on the radio. He's just different because he's considerate. You can tell. He's a gentleman.

—You can tell from the limes, added Jenna.

Both wives lifted their beers at the same time and took heavy pulls from the bottles. Tammy caught Celina staring.

—We like to drink, said Tammy. —We're Sooners.

Celina had always told Gallagher that she would resist being lumped in as a "trader's wife." After all, she was a painter, an artist. However, Celina felt herself wanting to be accepted by these women. She picked up her beer and drank.

—Where's your husband today? asked Jenna.

—He's in Las Vegas, said Celina.

—That's another problem, laughed Tammy.

—Still, said Jenna. —If the men didn't have gambling problems we probably wouldn't be on this boat.

—I'll drink to that, said Tammy, lifting her bottle and then sucking down the dregs of her beer.

Celina listened as Tammy and Jenna talked more about their husbands' boss, Randall Jennings. She was fascinated as they not only spoke about him in a complimentary way, but also seemed to assess him, as if he was an available prospect as a mate. Celina had heard from Gallagher how common divorce was among traders from Houston and Tulsa. Traders leaving their betrothed for trophy wives and the wives getting a 50 percent payout, taking on younger men, tennis pros and personal trainers. Celina listened to the two women talk and realized as they discussed Randall Jennings that what they prized was wealth *and* attention. Celina noted the fact that Randall could barely see didn't seem to play into their discussion of him as a potential husband. And it occurred to her that these women too, were traders: assessing the value of men analytically, as a horse trader considers the breed of a stallion.

Celina flicked her cigarette overboard and grabbed her beer bottle by the neck. She smiled at the women from Tulsa and wondered what they would say if she told them that her husband, Gallagher, never watched football. He only watched boxing.

SAM'S

When they docked the boat at the marina the traders and their wives thanked the Colonel for the trip, waved good-bye, and left. Only John Shuggs and Celina Gallagher remained and they went with the Ghost to Sam's on the bay. It was the Ghost's favorite bar in Boston, because the owner, Sam Strohmier, had been a sailor and he only talked about boats.

The bar itself had none of the nautical artifacts, the mermaid maiden-heads, old buoys, scrimshaw, or miniature ships in bottles like the other campy seafaring bars that bordered Sam's in neighboring Long Wharf. Sam's was close to the marina and had large bay windows that allowed patrons to admire the harbor.

The Ghost was telling Celina and Shuggs that Sam's was a nautical bar, a true nautical bar. Sam discouraged boaters, but people who liked to talk about boats and the sea, he made their drinks the right way. He was fasci-nated by the Ghost, that a blind man could be so genuinely taken by the sea. Every time Sam saw the Ghost he asked him if he was planning any boating trips. It was no longer a test between them, just a few spoken words about their shared mistress, the sea. That was all that was necessary. It was a nautical bar because of Sam's passion, and the Ghost had seen him give poor service to people who were loud and foolish and who were not true boaters.

After two of Sam's rum specials, the Ghost's helmsman, Shuggs, glazed over.

—Don't fade on me, warned the Ghost.

Celina was looking out the window.

—I enjoy this view, looking out at the water, she said. —It's restful.

—I like it how you said that, said the Ghost. —Because I think you're right. I've heard people say it's peaceful or it's soothing but it's not really those things.

—I'm going to order a Red Bull, said Shuggs.

The young trader stumble-walked toward the bar.

—I like it how you never say you're going to paint things, said the Ghost when Shuggs was gone. —I always imagined a painter would see a nice view and then say something like "I'd love to paint this." I haven't known you too long but you've never said anything like that.

Celina laughed.

—What would you say to me if I did say things like that?

—I wouldn't say anything.

Celina threw back the rest of her drink. Then she rubbed her hand across the back of her neck feeling for any hint of sunburn.

—Do you have to tolerate a lot of people? she asked.

He sat there, staring out the window with his dark glasses tilted forward down the bridge of his nose. His head bobbed up and down comically, forming his face into a scowl, not answering, until Celina laughed.

Afraid she might glimpse his nystagmus-afflicted eyes, he pushed his glasses back up on his nose and said:

—I don't tolerate. I utilize.

When Shuggs came back from the bar, the Ghost said:

—Call my car service, I'm going home.

Then to Celina:

—I can drop you off first.

Sometime during the ride, the Ghost convinced Celina to come up to his apartment so he could show her where he'd hung her painting. She could also see the view that he, himself, couldn't enjoy. The Ghost asked Mr. Carey, the driver, to come along. Mr. Carey often helped the Ghost, earning some extra dollars as the Ghost's factotum, whether it was pouring him drinks or fixing him a late-night omelet. As an ex-corrections officer he was extremely versatile and the Ghost made use of his many talents. The Ghost figured his presence would allay any of Celina's fears of impropriety.

The apartment was modern but spare. Celina and the Ghost discussed *Waiting* and its place on the wall for several minutes and then she took in the rest of the apartment. His bookshelves were empty except for CDs on one shelf. The rest of the wall-hangings were all framed posters: photographs of the Seattle seaside shot in black-and-white that Celina could've done without. She said they were nice. Dominating the room was a piano that looked very expensive.

After showing off the sound system, the fifty-bottle wine storage refrigeration unit, and his forty-gallon turquoise-lit fishtank swarming with aquatic life, including a sea anemone, the Ghost said:

—My housekeeper takes good care of the fish.

He finished the tour by pushing a button that electronically pulled back the blinds, revealing a bird's-eye panorama of Boston Harbor, now a black pool dotted with boats whose lights shimmered across the water, liquid pearls. Celina stood at the window, her hand held aloft without touching the glass.

Mr. Carey poured the Ghost a glass of Middleton's.

—Mr. Carey will get you a drink.

—I've had too much wine. But I'll take a Gewürztraminer, if you have it.

—Mr. Carey, a glass of the Trimbach.

When Carey went to pour Celina her wine, the Ghost almost let his glass of Scotch slip out of his hand but caught it right at the rim. Steadying the heavy bottom of the tumbler with his other hand, he regripped the glass and let out a satisfied, drunken: *ahhhh.*

—Nice catch, boss, said Carey.

—I have tons of my ex-wife's DVDs. If you want to stay and watch something, said the Ghost to Celina.

—But that wouldn't be any fun for you, Celina said. She suddenly felt very drunk.

—No, I'd love to watch a movie, the Ghost told her. —See what movie Celina wants, Mr. Carey, said the Ghost.

The Ghost's driver responded with a "yes, sir." He showed Celina the DVD collection. She settled on a romantic comedy.

Carey was on the couch drinking a tall glass of ginger ale with ice. He never drank on the job. Celina sat in a black leather chair near the mica-top coffee table. Celina saw the limo driver staring at her without trying to seem obvious. He had pudgy lips and no chin. She found the man unsettling. The Ghost sat on the end of the couch nearer to Celina.

Celina remained seated and watched the opening credits. The Ghost brought his hand up and touched her briefly on the shoulder to get her attention.

—I don't like comedies, you know, he said.

—Then why are we watching one?

—Because I can tell you like them, he said.

—Don't do me any favors, she said, laughing.

Celina watched the Ghost. His morose face was at that moment removed from the physical reality of the room. He was thinking about something beyond his surroundings. The Ghost was lost in it, whatever mathematics of the market he was contemplating. Celina wondered drunkenly what it would be like to paint the man's thoughts. She imagined strings of numbers, and for the background, something cosmic like a black hole.

—I'm just going to sit here and drink myself into oblivion if you don't mind. Is that all right with you? asked the Ghost.

Upon him declaring his intention to drink himself into a stupor, Celina gave him a surprised, questioning look that registered concern. The Ghost read her mind.

—Don't worry. When the time comes, Mr. Carey will put me to bed.

Gas had gotten sold down some in the Asian markets overnight. It was 6:00 A.M. and the Ghost was looking out over the empty trading floor. He had come in early so he could think. He was trying to remember exactly what had happened in the apartment with Celina.

The memory of that woman no longer felt like a trade to him. A transaction. He felt something like a chill. He put the back of his hand to his forehead. *Fever.* And gas, gas was still over eleven dollars.

ATTACK! (DAY 1)

The Ghost sniffed at the air in his office. Usually it was stale, odorless. Office air. Today it was different. Today the smell was tinged with energy, a vibration that made the nose itch. A hunch. A premonition. A feeling. The Ghost had been in the market long enough to trust it, whatever *it* was.

The Ghost peered out at the trading floor from behind the glass wall of his office. His desk had no pictures of family, or memorabilia of his favorite sports teams or any knickknacks or good-luck charms of the sort that populate the desk of so many traders. There was his trade blotter and his five giant flat-screens. The Ghost folded his arms across his chest. He wondered if anyone else on the floor could sense what he sensed.

At ten minutes to ten stout-bodied Rector, the meteorologist, knocked on the door to the Ghost's office. As if he had been expecting him all morning, the Ghost waved him in.

Rector's first few words were unintelligible. He stumbled over himself to report victory. Even as he spoke, his information was old news. Poor Rector, always seconds behind the curve. Natural gas was plummeting on whatever intelligence Rector thought he had the jump on. The Ghost decided to be kind because this was the day he'd been waiting for.

—The WSI hurricane season model just came out, spouted Rector. —Not only did a tropical depression over the Atlantic just break up but WSI agrees with our macro view. The wind shear off the Sahara is going to account for an inactive storm season.

The number eleven was nowhere to be found on the magnified screen. Gas had fallen seventy cents in one minute. $10.30 for the July contract.

They're crushing it.

—Good call, Rector, said the Ghost, his voice stripped of emotion, a leader with an army on the move. —Send out an IM to the trading floor about the news.

When Rector left the Ghost estimated in his head the profit off this price action. The number was big. Not big enough for the executives and the board, yet. Still, according to the K-wave, nine dollars was the target number for natural gas. It still had a ways to go, to soften.

After lunch the Ghost called Andrews into his office. For a moment the Ghost felt a kinship with Andrews. He too had been mauled by the market in the past. But as soon as the big man swaggered into the Ghost's office like an embattled sumo who'd just been thrown from the ring, the Ghost noted there was no sense of defeat or emotion in Andrews's voice, just the trader's professional endurance to pain. The Ghost had been imagining this meeting for a while. He couldn't shitcan Andrews in a one-day drop in the market. He had to maneuver it so that Andrews would disobey his stop-loss limits. Then he would register that insubordination by e-mailing the executives. Then when Andrews thought he was safe, waiting for a bounce in the market, the Ghost would put his plan into action.

The Ghost could sense Andrews sitting there, bent forward, legs spread, hands on his knees, breathing heavily through his nose, and knew he would have to trick Andrews in another way. In his original ploy, he was going to tell Andrews he would eschew the normal stop-loss limits, because Andrews's position was technically a natural hedge to the house short. Andrews, the Ghost realized, would see it as a lie, and maybe cover. Instead, the Ghost decided for the emotional route, the direct assault. It was the more long-shot attack, the one Andrews would not expect, and the one to which he just might bite.

—You're getting killed out there. And it's your own fault, said the Ghost with disgust. —I hope you're covering your position.

Andrews sat there. He'd already calculated the damage. If summer Cinergy dropped another $2.75 he would be stopped out. It was unlikely that it would get there. He'd been bombed but his ship wasn't sunk yet. He breathed in slowly.

—It's not a good day, he said finally.

—You're down over three million?

—Just over three, said Andrews, his voice clinical.

—Don't you think it would behoove you to cover? asked the Ghost, with all the condescension of a third-grade teacher. The Ghost was now on record having told Andrews to cover. And the Ghost expected that he'd been condescending enough that Andrews would do the opposite.

Andrews shifted in his stool. The number wasn't at his stop-loss yet. He'd been here before.

—No, I'm not covering, said Andrews. —Natty will bounce. And electricity will bounce with it.

The Ghost hid his excitement. Always go long on Andrews's pride, he thought, measuring the man before him.

—All right then. You're excused, said the Ghost.

The Colonel was doing sets of ten with his Gripmaster Pro Hand and Finger Exercises that he'd just ordered from *Kung Fu* magazine. Natural gas was coming off due to some weather thing, some desert windstorm. He got the memo from Rector.

—Sand particles in the atmosphere. That's some crazy shit, he said to Shuggs, who sat next to him.

This was good for the Ghost's position. The Colonel thought, maybe this calls for a little Red Door action tonight. The Red Door was a members-only strip club cum brothel out on Route 9. After working out at the gym, the Colonel would show up in his USMC sweat suit, toting a six-pack of Labatt's, and beckon over two strippers, one for each knee. He looked at his IM. His inbox was flashing with a message from the Ghost. All it said was:

Super Bowl?

The code word. The Colonel panicked for a second and then remembered what he was supposed to do: wait until three minutes before the market close and start cracking bids in summer Cinergy, reoffering it at the former bid level, until he knocked it down at least three dollars. The Colonel saw it was almost noon.

■   ■   ■

Around 4:00 P.M. Andrews marked his forward price curve and posted his PNL: down ($2.75M). A bad day, very bad, but he'd been glad he hadn't covered because the market had bounced like he thought it would at the end. He'd avoided being stopped out, although he had to survive tomorrow and the day after. Time for worrying about that tonight over a very large bourbon, mused Andrews. He stood up from his chair and stretched his frame, pushing his chest out, his arms wide, hamhock thick.

—That sucked, he said, turning to Gallagher.

Gallagher had made money on his reduced power short and his weather position was still sitting in Greenblatt's book, waiting.

—What are you going to do? asked Gallagher.

—It bounced at the close, didn't it? I'll trade around it tomorrow. If it still looks ugly, maybe I'll lay some risk off.

He didn't speak of it like it was a thing that could end his career. He spoke of it in a quotidian way like a janitor reciting the parts of a building he would come in and clean the next day.

—The Jack Daniel's is going to print tonight at Casa Andrews, said Miller. He wore a worried look for his old boss.

Andrews acknowledged the comment.

—Yup, he said. —After I put the kids to bed.

Although the books were marked and the natural gas market had closed at 2:30 P.M., the electricity market technically was still open until 5:00 P.M. At quarter to five, the Colonel rung down his broker on the squawk box.

—Where's the bid on summer Cinergy? he asked.

—Shit, most of the bids have gone home, reported his broker.

Silence.

—What a day, huh? asked his broker.

—Shut up, said the Colonel. —Find me a fucking bid or you're in the box.

Andrews had marked the summer Cinergy curve at $77.75. The Colonel did the math. In order to stop out Andrews, he needed to hit it down to $75.

—I got a guy showing a crap bid. So don't yell at me, said the broker.

—What is it?

—Seventy-six.

—Yours! said the Colonel.

—You want to sell that?

—Hit the fucking bid.

—You're done, said the broker, confirming the trade. He was confused by the large selloff. He wanted to ask the Colonel what was happening, why was he crushing the market after hours, but he knew better than to suffer the Colonel's wrath. Instead he just reported details of the trade.

—It's Travista, said the broker. —He only wants one piece. You sell fifty megawatts summer Cinergy at a price of . . .

—I know the price, bonehead, said the Colonel. —Where does that fucker come back?

The broker knew the market was being undervalued, but he liked the commission from the trades, so the tone of his voice changed from one of confusion to excitement.

—Hold on. Hold on, he said. —I'll get you done again at those levels.

The Colonel waited a moment. His palms were sweating. He licked his lips. He'd never traded to stop someone out before. It smacked of irrationality and brutality. The Colonel imagined himself in the Champagne Room at the Red Door spanking his favorite stripper's ass.

—Seventy-five-dollar bid on the follow.

—Hit that bid, said the Colonel. —Hit the bid and tell that son of a whore I come back offered at seventy-five.

—I'll try and get you done. Give me a minute, the broker was saying. The Colonel was entering the summer Cinergy trades in the system. He only needed it to trade at that level one time, so they could mark the books there and drive Andrews's position through the stop-loss limits.

—I got another guy who . . .

—Fuck it. I'm out, said the Colonel. —I'm going home. Pull my offer.

The broker was confused again. His voice had the whine of a disappointed dog, one who has returned from fetching a ball and now finds his master scolding him for doing so.

—So you don't want to sell any more? asked the broker.

But the Colonel didn't respond. He was already walking over to the Ghost's office, letting him know that he'd performed the deed.

Gallagher got called into the Ghost's office at ten past five.

—Where's Andrews? asked the Ghost.

—He left at around four. After he marked the books, responded Gallagher.

—He left too early, said the Ghost. —There's been some late action on the summer Cinergy. I'm going to need you to remark the curve.

Gallagher stood there. After gas had closed all the markets, as if tired from the violent selloff, it had dried up and nothing had traded for the balance of the day.

—Randall, unless this shit got sold off while I was just in the pisser, nothing has traded since gas closed.

—You know better than that, said the Ghost. —That's the rule, right? Whenever you're in the bathroom, that's when the market moves.

—They buy it up some more? asked Gallagher.

—No, said the Ghost. —They sold summer Cinergy down another three dollars.

—Jesus, said Gallagher. —Who the fuck did that?

—I don't know, said the Ghost. —But my broker at FreeBond just quoted it to me over the box. Summer Cin seventy-fives got hit.

—That's cheap, said Gallagher. —We should buy that shit.

—Andrews went home. I just need you to mark the books. We'll deal with trading it tomorrow.

Gallagher walked back to his desk. He looked at the empty seat were Hutch used to sit. It was bare of all his personal effects. Next to Hutch's desk was Andrews's, like a blossoming garden of trader vitality: the family photos of his smiling children, his brunette wife, two Bears v. Patriots Super Bowl ticket stubs framed in glass, and a picture of Andrews on a dock, hauling up a tuna, after a deep-sea fishing trip with his brokers.

Gallagher could feel the Ghost's presence as he sat down. Gallagher pulled up the Cinergy forward curve and marked it where he'd been told. Two numbers. A seven. A five. Two numbers that he was entering into the system: two numbers that would clear out another desk as efficiently as a heart attack. Gallagher stared at the screen and knew the Ghost was sitting in his office, waiting for Gallagher to pull the trigger.

The Ghost opened up his e-mail and sent out a notice to the risk group, that one of his senior traders had violated his VaR and either the trader himself or a third party would work to liquidate the position tomorrow.

ATTACK! (DAY 2)

The Ghost borrowed Shuggs's cell phone and made two phone calls. This was the second prong of his assault. Day one was stopping him out. Day two was about making the market plummet through his stops a second time, making Andrews in violation of the risk committee's regulations. It was all about triangulating: one call was to Dartmouth Collins, his broker at NYMB, and the other was to Jesse Kruger, his broker at FreeBond. He'd spoken to them early in the morning and to both for only a few moments in a low voice that differed from his usual even-keeled business voice. This time the Ghost put an edge on it. He'd let them hear the urgency to it, a commander marshaling his forces, an undeniable request to allies.

He'd said the same thing to both of them and then hung up:

—Someone is stopped out and has to cover summer Cin. Let your customers know this. Have them sell it early. If it goes below seventy-two, you will get paid. That is all.

At the open natural gas was down seven cents, $10.28. Off a touch, thought the Ghost, this is going to happen. The Ghost looked up from his computer screen. He could hear Andrews approaching. Andrews stood in the doorway of the office, shaking with rage. The Ghost considered the possibility that he might charge.

—Gallagher moved the curves last night, shouted Andrews. —Cinergy off three dollars after the natty close. What the fuck is that?

—FreeBond reported the trades. Summer Cin seventy-five dollars.

—Some jackass utility panicked. And now I'm stopped out.

—That's the new law: Sarbanes-Oxley. If it trades there, no matter how stupid the number is, we have to mark there or someone goes to jail, most likely me.

The Ghost glanced at his ICE screen. Summer Cin was getting sold at $74.5. The assault had begun. The Ghost raised his eyebrows.

—They're selling it on the screen, Andrews. You don't want to get stopped out two days in a row. You'd better cover.

—You know damn well if I start hitting bids the market will know I'm stopped out and they'll slaughter it.

Andrews slammed his fist against the glass pane on the door. The frame let out the crunching sound of wood splintering.

—Please, said the Ghost. —Refrain from outburst. Now get back to your seat. You're going to have to fight today to keep your job.

For the next two hours Andrews looked for an opening. Instead of covering his long position like the Ghost and risk management policy requested, Andrews bought more. This was a fight for his trading life. He couldn't let the market fall below $72.25 or he was done. His second stop-loss in two days. Andrews leaned into the market, buying it up. He felt like Atlas trying to hold up the whole fucking world on his shoulders. Even though gas was off just a touch, the market was selling the piss out of summer Cinergy. It made no sense. Summer came off two dollars in the first hour, as if the market knew he was stopped out.

I'll wait for a little pop in gas and buy it up big, Andrews thought. Spook these fools.

The Ghost watched the screen and turned on Andrews's broker on his squawk box so he could hear the play-by-play. Andrews was making a go of it.

Instead of trying to cheat the hangman by trying to sell out of his position quicker than his foes could front-run him; Andrews was doubling down, betting against the trend. The Ghost had guessed Andrews would do this. He was less of a sprinter and more of a contrarian, a gutter-fighter. The Ghost also knew Andrews would need a pop in natural gas to support the energy futures in order to survive. Andrews was wearily buying one piece for every fifty cents the market got knocked down, trying to stave off the run to seventy-two dollars, the number, his number of reckoning.

At eleven forty-five, natural gas perked up and went up nine cents. Andrews took one slurp of his Diet Dr Pepper.

—Mine. Buy the seventy-threes, he shouted down to his broker.

Andrews looked at the gas on the screen. It moved up another tick. He could feel the knees of the market shorts buckling. He needed one solid block from the gas. Then he'd see daylight, and like a fullback running hit the hole.

—They're reoffered there, replied his broker.

—Buy them. Mine, he said evenly. —Where do they come back?

—No offer. Hold on. Come back offered at seventy-four.

Andrews breathed out. He turned to Gallagher.

—Can you go downstairs and get me a bacon double cheeseburger, pickles, onion, and mustard, no lettuce?

Gallagher almost replied that lunch was being delivered in a half hour. But he realized Andrews might not have a half hour.

The Ghost sat in his office, gazing at his enlarged screen. He leaned back and exhaled.

The fucking cowards. They're letting him off the hook.

If it hadn't been his own man he was trying to annihilate, but a counterparty whom the Ghost knew was caught long, he imagined how he would smash it down to seventy-one. It would be elegant violence: a smooth kill with a straight razor, a slice to the jugular. But the way Andrews was, all intimidation: a jackhammer trading style; elbows, fists, headbutt and gutbump, prevented these amateurs from gaining ground on him. On a professional level, the Ghost acknowledged it was entertaining to watch, like a heavyweight prizefight. The problem was the counterparties didn't have the salt to take on Andrews's confrontational, relentless style. The Ghost frowned.

Maybe Andrews lives another day.

The Ghost knew the market didn't have the backbone to stand up to

Andrews. He thought about the language he would utilize to abuse his brokers later on. The Ghost let a disappointed fist fall on his keyboard, as if his Scratch 'N Win ticket came up empty. It was almost lunchtime.

It happened at 2:00 P.M. Gallagher had read Booksteader's book, *A Demon of Our Own Design*. It was about the coming age of tumult, predicting heretofore unseen violent moves in the market. *Volatility.* More money than ever in the history of the world was circulating in the market due to the global economy: Asian tigers, the Indian juggernaut, Russian robber barons, Saudi princes, multinational hedge funds, good money after bad flowing in rivers of unpredictable financial derivatives bursting through the conventional dams and wreaking havoc upon the average American's stock market portfolio. Rape and Pillage was the motto of the day. Random acts of bankruptcy and wealth made in moments by something as innocent as a hedge fund analyst trying to hedge high-yield bonds: Buy the Japanese yen and sell the Brazilian bond against it; economies moving in whirlwinds.

At 2:00 P.M. everything changed. Crude oil traders entered the fray. Crude's motivation? Two scenarios, occurring simultaneously. One: It was the day before Month End and the option traders from the New York banks were trying to smash it down to the eighty-dollar strike price so their July monthly puts would be "in-the-money." Two: OPEC released a statement saying they would be opening up the floodgates of an extra million barrels of crude onto the market. These two acts coupled together made crude drop like an anchor. Four dollars in three minutes. It took a full ten seconds for the natural gas traders in the NYMEX pit to recover from the shock and begin smacking the price of gas down.

Andrews still had his game face on. He pulled his bid and watched the summer Cin get hit down to seventy. It was like watching a building collapse. His broker, who had known him a long time, remained silent until he finally said:

—Hoss. They're killing it. What do you want me to do?

—Nothing to do, said Andrews. —I'll give you a call tomorrow. I'll probably have the day off.

Andrews, his head bent down, squeezed the bridge of his nose to release the tension.

He could feel his protégé, Gallagher, staring at him. Gallagher was on the phone. When he hung up the phone, Gallagher said to Andrews:

—That was the Ghost. I'm being told to liquidate all your positions for you.

—Go ahead and do it then, said Andrews.

Having his own guy liquidate his position was the final dagger to the heart. Andrews, who never felt much, admitted to himself that it hurt.

Andrews saw that Harry Sayers was already in the Ghost's office. The tall, lean, suspenders-wearing risk profile manager stood in almost sentry manner before the Ghost. They were no doubt talking about Andrews's position.

Three minutes later a third robot from legal appeared. Andrews recognized him. He was from upstairs, corporate, and distinguished himself by wearing a tie. Then a young gun with mousse in his hair waltzed into the office. He was the Executioner's assistant.

Every time Andrews turned around it seemed the bureaucrats were multiplying.

—It's like the damn Spanish Inquisition in there, said Miller from across the desk.

Andrews knew he'd be seeing the Executioner soon; his waxen face showing all the human characteristics of a hangman's hood. This go around, it was exit interview. Andrews wouldn't be able to tell the Executioner, "Maybe next time."

LATE NIGHT WITH

MILT HARKRADER

Milt had set aside a four-day vacation to see his son and take in the splendor of West Palm Beach. On the third day he decided to have a little fun. After a pancake breakfast with his boy, Milt spent the remainder of the afternoon looking at properties in Jupiter with Ashley Delacroix, a real estate agent from his ex-wife's office. Even though he was staying at the Wyndham, Milt had Ashley pick him up at the famous five-star Breakers Hotel, for effect. While standing with his hands in his pockets outside the Breakers, being stared at by the bellhops, Milt stood in the parking lot thinking: So you only made fifty grand on the front-running scheme, better than losing fifty.

But he was bullshitting himself. Had Milt stuck out the position for the markets sell-off, he would've cashed in and been able to actually rent a room at the Breakers instead of having to stand out in the parking lot, faking it. It was all Gallagher's fault. The kid had kept buying back his shorts and that had made Milt nervous.

Ashley pulled up in her Volkswagen Jetta and Milt feigned companion-ship with the leery bellhops, waving good-bye to them. Ashley had no idea that Milt had no intention of buying real estate. He was merely using her as female companionship, a way to pass the time. Throughout the day, as the two walked through each property, Milt nodded, saying things like "this is nice" or "not bad." He always walked behind her, if possible, to catch a glimpse of the view. After two hours, three condos, one bungalow on the beach, and one three-bedroom rancher, Milt had gawked enough and decided to make his play, saying he was thirsty, did she know a good bar? Ashley drove them to an outdoor bungalow bar that looked across the jetty at a small island thick with mangrove trees. Upon sitting down, the first words out of her mouth were:

—Look. Porpoises.

The rounded gray fins of a pod of dolphins could be seen breaking through the surf; their sleek gray backs glinting like silver in the sunlight.

—They're beautiful, she said.

Milt did not like to deceive someone who had a genuine admiration for dolphins. He ordered two piña coladas, two shots of Cuervo, and smiled across at her. It felt like he was on a date. He was even a bit nervous. Ashley squinted at Milt. She sat facing into the sun. Her small nose made her seem girlish. Or it could be the frosted blond hair, thought Milt.

Halfway into his first piña colada, Milt began to brag.

—I'm probably looking to buy more than one property, Ashley. Who knows, maybe I'll become a small-time real estate player down here?

—Debby says that you're a broker in New York. For electricity or something?

—We call ourselves power brokers, said Milt, shifting in his seat. —It's a dirty business. Lots of people scheming: dreaming up ways to fleece you out of your last dime. But it's a young man's game, all adrenaline and guts. Not many guys over forty. Take me, I'm ancient.

—You're not *that* old, said Ashley, kicking Milt under the table.

—So you want to come down here and be near your son? she asked in a tone that was back to business.

—That's one reason, he said. —The other reasons are obvious.

Milt spread his hands wide and looked out on the sound.

—Our friends the dolphins, he said.

—I know somebody who does what you do, I think, said Ashley. —He trades stocks, though. He's the head of his own firm and he sometimes is on that TV show on Fox, where they talk about the market.

Milt looked at her, as she sipped her piña colada through a straw. Twenty-six? wondered Milt. How old is she? She brushed back her frosted blond hair and Milt could see a small set of crow's-feet at the corners of her eyes. And then: tiny rows of barely perceptible wrinkles above her mouth. A smoker, thought Milt, and then guessed: She's thirty-two, not too old and not too young either. She was still talking about her rich friend, the trader on TV. Milt could tell she assumed he was rich in that same way.

—Debra says you like lasagna. If you want I could fix you a little early dinner if you're not too busy. Then I'll get you back to the Breakers before eight, so you won't miss your plane tomorrow.

Then, remembering not to give away his charade, Milt added:

—If you have me back by nine, I won't turn into a turnip.

The key, thought Milt, is to never let your lies take on a life of their own.

The kitchen was dark and when Milt opened the door to Ashley's freezer his haggard, pale face was illuminated in a ghostly blue light. He was a hungry ghoul looking for a late-night ice cream snack. There was a quart of Breyer's low-cal vanilla and also, wedged behind some tater tots, a frosted bottle of Absolut vodka. He improvised and made a vodka shake, two scoops low-cal vanilla with freezer burn and four shots vodka. He drank it down and didn't make a face, pretending he was on some cooking show, tasting his newest, greatest culinary invention.

Milt sat down on the couch in the living room and looked out the bay window. Drinking his vodka milkshake, sitting there in the dark, Milt grew serene: Ashley's lasagna had been mediocre, but his performance in bed had been worse. He'd come too quickly and when he was washing himself off in the bathroom he'd belched and had heard Ashley chime "oh, Jesus" from the bedroom. Finishing his awful concoction, Milt decided that he missed his son. He crept back into the bedroom and grabbed his clothes. Like a special ops agent Milt dressed quickly and quietly in the kitchen. Some appliance let out a strange electronic buzz that offered cover sound. Milt then realized he didn't have a car. He went over to Ashley's key rack by the Gnome calendar and lifted the car keys.

THE DORM

It took Milt forty-five minutes before he pulled up in front of Aaron's dorm. It was called Flagler Hall after the Floridian railroad magnate, Henry Flagler. In his day, the magnate had stolen millions of dollars of land and natural resources and workers' paychecks. As Milt figured it, he was only borrowing his date's car.

The proctor, a thirty-year-old bachelor with thinning hair, who taught Earth Science, opened the front door. His hair was askew and he was wearing blue pajamas. He had one eye open, the other squinting from the porch light.

—May I help you?

—I need to see my son, Aaron Harkrader. I'm his father. His real father.

The Earth Science teacher looked at his watch. He was going to say something about visiting hours, when Milt cut him off.

—It's a family emergency. I need to speak with Aaron.

—I'm sorry, fumbled the teacher. —An emergency. Yes. I'll go get him.

His son appeared five minutes later. He was dressed in jeans, flip-flops, and a Limp Bizkit T-shirt. The Earth Science teacher lingered in the background, trying to discern if Milt was drunk or distraught. But before he could make up his mind, the father and son made off into the night.

On their way to the car Milt walked into a tree branch. He swore, and giving it a stiff-arm, he pushed it away from his face.

—*Ixora coccinea*, said his son.

—What?

—That's the Latin name for that bush. It's called jungle flame.

—Hey, said Milt. —Don't push it.

They got into the car without saying another word. Milt turned on the stereo and pulled away from the school.

—Are you kidnapping me or something?

Milt leered at his son.

—Is this an alcohol-induced family emergency?

Milt lashed out with his free hand and flicked his son's ear, hard.

—Ow!

—Hey, said Milt, pointing a finger. —What did I tell you?

His son rubbed at his ear.

—That's right. I said, "Don't push it."

—But Dad, I'm working on my routine. I got an improv comedy class and you've got to learn to deliver spontaneous humor.

Milt pursed his lips. If it was a lie, it was a good one.

—They teach you how to tell jokes at that school?

—Yes, said his son, still rubbing his ear.

—That's good. Telling jokes is very important in business. Good joke tellers go right to the top. I'm starting to like my investment.

Milt put his hand on the back of his son's neck and caressed it.

—Sorry about the ear. Where you want to go eat? Shoney's or Waffle House?

—Dad, is Curt Long allowed to mete out corporal punishment to me?

—Your stepdad hit you?

—He slapped me.

Milt made a face.

—He bitch-slapped you, did he?

—Dad, there's really not a family emergency, is there?

—Yes, there is, son, said Milt, drunk, and, suddenly, smiling and admiring his son.

—What is it?

—We're going to be rich, said Milt.

He turned up the stereo. Then shouted, believing for a moment he might actually buy a condo:

—On real estate!

Aaron sunk into his seat and bit at the skin on the back of his nails.

—Can we go to Mickey D's, Dad? he asked. —I feel like a Big Mac.

The next morning Milt was sitting in Dunkin Donuts reading *USA Today* and drinking an iced coffee. That pain somewhere in the pit of his stomach came on like an attack. Milt pushed against his belly with three fingers.

Is that my liver or my appendix?

His cell phone rang. He answered it, speaking only a few sentences to someone on the other line. He ended by saying:

—I understand.

It had been Gallagher informing Milt he was fired. He told Milt in a friendly way that he thought Milt had loose lips about his short position. He told Milt that he didn't think he was on the up and up.

—Good luck, Milt. I mean that, said Gallagher before hanging up.

Milt felt his forehead. Sweat was beaded up across his brows. Milt took the iced coffee and threw it against the storefront window.

Without Stan Couch and Joe Gallagher, his brokerage business was done. He was toast. Twenty years building up a book, entertaining, fawning, crushing your liver to become the "go to" broker of the two top ERCOT traders: then gone in a week. It was a small sandbox, but it had been his sandbox. The iced coffee dripped down the window in what looked like streaks of dirt-colored water.

—What the hell you think you're doing? called an angry-voiced manager in a Dunkin Donuts orange necktie and brown slacks. He was Indian, from Lahore, and looked indignant and resolute, protecting his slice of the American Dream. When he came a step closer, Milt loomed over him, eyes bulging. When he screamed at the manager, it was so loud that the man flinched. Saliva from Milt's mouth flew onto the manager's cheek. When the manager looked up again, thinking his customer composed, Milt shouted it again even louder, trying to make the windows shake:

—Fuck off!

Milt shoved open the door to the Dunkin Donuts and walked down the concrete path, thinking: That motherfucker has a lot to learn about capitalism. The customer is always right.

HURRICANE (THURSDAY)

The sound of children's high-pitched voices could be heard throughout the trading floor. It was early and the market was quiet. The traders sat at their desks barely stirring, moving slowly: some drank coffee, others studied the six-to-ten-day weather report, while a few posted some wide, two-way markets on ICE. The Ghost was reading the daily gas technical report under his dome magnifier. After he finished moving the domed lens over the last page, he threw the report in the trash. Technicians were calling for natural gas to come off more but it was still hovering just above ten dollars. Jennings heard the voices of children. They were ages eight and up and they stood by their fathers asking questions or calling down the squawk box, saying "hi" to the brokers on the other end. It was Bring Your Child to Work Day.

At eight o'clock Jennifer Cohen from Human Resources came and took the traders' sons and daughters to a film about the company and the energy industry. As if a lever had been switched, the family men sparked up their daily mien of insult and vulgarity.

—Gallagher, you're worse than my five-year-old, said Large. —Whole time my daughter was here you were knuckle deep in that nose of yours.

—Take what you can get, Large, chimed Hobart, the coal trader.

—Yesterday, he was elbow deep down the front of his pants.

Two desks down Bret, the new intern, was complaining to Miller about breakfast detail.

—I didn't go to Brown for this shit, said Bret.

—Goat, Miller said, —it goes like this. You're a goat until you're not a goat.

—You should have chosen accounting. The people there treat each other with respect, said Sami, laughing.

—Stay off the radar, said Miller. —You whine enough you're going to get on someone's radar.

—What's Bret whining about? called out Churchill from three desks down.

Bret shook his head. He was on the radar. He turned to Sami and frowned, as if it was all Sami's fault.

—Yours you, said Sami.

Just before lunch the market became active. The hedge funds were running up natural gas and crude oil. Hobart, who was very short power, began yelling over the box at his broker.

—Fucking Zhao flaked again. I'm fucking hanging you. You fucking shitbird. My pet monkey could broker this shit better than you.

The whole floor grew quiet except for Hobart, red-faced, and still cursing down the box. Finally, Churchill said:

—Hobart.

—You motherfucker. I'm . . .

—Hobart!! said Churchill again, louder, reaching out and touching his desk mate on the shoulder. A line of quiet children stood in a line gawking at the shouting trader. Some of the older ones were smiling. They were on their way to the lunchroom. Jennifer Cohen, hands on her hips, stood amidst the line of children, not smiling. She glared across the trading floor with her heavy, dark eyebrows knitted crossly. Her disgusted gaze seemed to encompass the whole trading floor, as if they were all responsible for the verbal assault on children's ears. The fact that the traders were untouchable made her hatred all the more palpable.

The children were marched off, following Jennifer Cohen down the hall. When they were gone, everyone began laughing. Miller cackled. Large laughed his big, puffing, out-of-breath laugh. Churchill snorted. Even a reticent Brett let out a short, impertinent giggle.

Churchill, between breaths and coughs of laughter, shouted down to his broker over the box:

—Poor Hobart just tasted it. Poor Masshole. He fucked up bad. It's "bring your kid to work day" and he was swearing like a sailor in front of the little ones.

Then sensing that something was wrong or out of place, his trader senses tingling, Churchill stopped short. He turned his large frame around.

—Hi daddy, said Emerson, his eight-year-old daughter, standing behind him. —I'm stopping by to say hello.

Forgetting he even swore, Churchill opened up his arms to her:

—Hello, Princess, he said. —Come give Daddy a hug.

Toward the end of the day, when most of the traders had marked their books and gone home, Gallagher skulked down to the far end of the trading floor and stopped in front of Greenblatt's desk. The Caltech genius was staring into the computer screen and typing code so fast that the sound of his fingers on the keyboard had a machine gun–like cadence. Without looking up at Gallagher, Greenblatt said:

—How's it going, dude? Told you I'd rather be you than Andrews.

He stopped typing and smiled at Gallagher.

—I'm going to see My Morning Jacket tonight.

—Okay, said Gallagher. Gallagher had no idea who the band was and didn't care. He was trying not to betray his nervousness about the market. Greenblatt picked up on it and shifted into market talk.

—You see your weather PNL? Your K5 position is looking good. There's some rumblings in the weather market. Apparently, more than one or two folks out there think this new system creeping across the Atlantic could become something. Dallas is off like five, six ticks.

—Sweet, said Gallagher again. —I'm just worried if the Ghost sees my PNL get too sweet he'll check out my positions and see the Dallas position you basised over to me.

—I can't keep it in my book. I told you as of July 1, it's in your book.

—That's cool, said Gallagher. —But if you don't have any Dallas risk on, can you step off the gas when you mark the position? Make it look less sweet than it is, so I'm off the Ghost's radar?

Greenblatt made a Donald Duck quacking sound in his cheeks. Gallagher took that as a Caltech way of saying he was considering it.

—I'll see what I can do, Greenblatt finally replied. —Dallas is not in my portfolio. I can spare you a little love, but not too much.

—I owe you, said Gallagher.

—No you don't, said Greenblatt.

Greenblatt gave Gallagher a little salute.

—Good luck, drunkard.

HURRICANE (FRIDAY)

Once again the market was slow. Only today there was no one to laugh at. Someone mentioned that it was a beautiful eighty-degree Boston July day outside, only they said it in traderspeak:

—Not a bad day out there.

—Perfect José day, said Large. He was a senior enough trader that he could give the "José okay," and it meant everyone had a free pass to go drink at José Panzas.

Some cheers went up and people began turning off their computers.

A chorus of "Bret, post my PNL," followed. Bret, the new goat, would stay behind and mark the books.

A slight breeze coursed through Quincy Market. The Ghost walked alongside Shuggs. Churchill, Hobart, Miller, and Large strolled alongside them in a leisurely fashion. Gallagher was a few paces behind. Since Andrews's dismissal he'd been biding his time. Gallagher was a trader waiting for something to happen. Like Andrews he was hoping to prove the Ghost wrong. He was hoping to come out alive on the other side of the market, whereas the Ghost would not. But more and more Gallagher had the feeling that the Ghost had powers of discernment above the herd. Gallagher felt the moment was coming and wondered if he would soon be following in Andrews's footsteps.

Approaching the outside deck of José Panzas, Churchill was talking about the potent Patrón Silver margaritas, for which the restaurant was famous.

—A margarita is not a steak, you don't need salt, he was saying.

At around 3:00 P.M. back at the office the European ensembles came out. Rector, the meteorologist, looked at his screen and said "Whoa!" His assistant Sykes shook his head.

—That can't be right, said Sykes. —This has got to be an outlier.

—Outlier or not, the guys got to know what this model run shows.

Rector saw the look of fear cross Sykes's face.

—Don't worry. I'll go down and tell them myself.

He had put the chance of the tropical depression off the coast of Africa at a 1 percent chance of forming into a hurricane. The European ensemble showed the storm strengthening into a CAT 1.

Rector got down to the end of the trading floor and nearly all the desks were empty.

—Where is everyone? he asked Bret.

—At José's. Drinking margaritas.

Rector dialed the Ghost's cell phone number. The Ghost picked up and Rector began talking. Quickly. He stuttered through the first three sentences, explaining about the strengthening of the storm from depression to hurricane. Then Rector switched gears and became confident, doing what he did best: backpedal and placate.

—On the bright side, Randall, the storm, even if it does become a hurricane, which I still peg this outlier at only ten percent chance; this thing is headed up the East Coast and not into the production regions in the Gulf.

—You're sure about that? asked the Ghost. —The threat is on the East Coast?

—This might not even become a hurricane, said Rector. —But, yes, that is correct. The East Coast is the most likely area of impact.

—Good, good, said Jennings.

Gas might go up on fear over the weekend, but when the storm dumped rain over the East Coast, temperatures would dip and prices would shit the bed even harder.

—As long as this doesn't hit the Gulf we're gold, said the Ghost, a little drunk on Patrón.

—You're gold then, said Rector. —The Gulf is a thousand to one.

The Ghost closed his cell phone and put it on the table. As soon as the other traders heard that Rector was on the phone, they stopped talking and tried to make out what was being said. It was like ancient tribesmen waiting on what the witch doctor had to say about his reading of the bones.

—Rector says this system might upgrade into a hurricane. But he likes the direction of the storm into the East Coast.

A wave of palpable relief washed over the table.

—That motherfucker sure knows how to almost ruin a Friday drinkup. How typical would that be, said Miller. —A little old tropical depression one minute, hurricane in the Gulf the next.

—It's not going to the Gulf, said the Ghost. —Didn't you hear me?

—I'm just saying if Rector said that. It would've ruined my margarita.

—Hell with Rector, said Churchill. —That call was just a pure Friday afternoon ass-covering in case the hundred-to-one scenario prints.

—Thousand to one, said the Ghost. —He said it was a thousand to one. Now the next person who says "hurricane in the Gulf" can fuck off right out of my little piece of sunshine.

Gallagher nursed his beer and inside was coveting the news. Gallagher noticed the tension in the Ghost's slightly tensed mouth. Rector said it was a thousand to one, but Gallagher knew that meant it was more like a hundred-to-one odds. As bad as those odds were, now Gallagher's fate had a number and somehow that relieved him. He ordered a whiskey. Miller noticed.

—Joe, ain't you on whiskey probation with momma?

Gallagher nodded.

—Yes, currently in the doghouse with the wife, he said. —The old Chateau Bow Wow.

And the way he said it made the Ghost perk up and turn in Gallagher's direction. The Ghost could feel a secret, a plot, a backstabbing rumor from more than ten yards away.

—Here's to a freaking rainstorm on the East Coast, said the Ghost, raising his glass. The other traders toasted him and when Gallagher's shot glass connected to his the Ghost could feel through the reverberations that something was not right.

HURRICANE (SATURDAY)

It was 10:00 A.M. and Gallagher's stomach was coming up out of his mouth. That was what it felt like. Celina had put him on Whiskey Probation because of his most recent meltdown way back on St. Patty's Day. So last night he had been drinking Gilbey's gin: alone on his rooftop deck. He had listened to the Stooges first album, turned up full volume, blaring it across his neighborhood. He looked at the lights in the windows and the purple-blue color above the city skyline. Gallagher had yelled at a few people as they crossed the street. But nothing bad happened. Gin was the drink that knocked him down before he could get up a head of steam.

—Joe, called Celina from downstairs. —Joe, pick up. It's Miller.

Gallagher rolled his naked body out of bed and walking slow like a B-movie zombie made his way to the phone.

—Hello?

—Hey, stupid, are you standing up?

—What?

—I said, are you standing up?

—Sure. I'm standing up.

—Sit down.

Gallagher was a good soldier. He did as he was told.

—You sitting down?

—Yes.

—Are you short?

—A little. Not much.

—How much?

—Just two pieces of July.

—Dude. Rector is a PNL terrorist.

—What?

—Natty is up a buck twenty. There's a CAT 2 hurricane that's going to be CAT 3 by tomorrow, said Miller like a man who had been handed down a life sentence.

—No shit.

—It's headed to the Gulf, said Miller.

—No shit, Gallagher said again, now smiling.

Miller knew Gallagher was short the power but he had no idea about Gallagher's dynamic weather hedge.

—Shock and awe, stupid. Shock and awe, said Miller and he hung up.

Just like that, thought Gallagher, sitting back down on the edge of his bed.

He lifted one hand into the air and toasted the room with an invisible glass.

—Winner-winner chicken dinner, he said.

Later on in the day Gallagher took Celina to a fancy luncheon. Just before coffee and dessert, Gallagher excused himself. He walked over to the sculpture garden and dialed up Greenblatt, who, as expected, didn't pick up. Gallagher left a message:

—Feel free to mark the Dallas position when you roll in on Monday. The K-wave crew took it in the rear. Time to let my weather hedge come clean.

HURRICANE (SUNDAY)

Andrews was sitting in a lawn chair by his swimming pool. He was on his third Old Style beer. He had seen the storm report earlier this morning and decided to celebrate a little. Some baby-back ribs were roasting on his grill. It was a sunny day with just a few plump white clouds in the sky. The clouds reminded Andrews of the potato salad his wife made from scratch: lumpy with lots of mayonnaise. After a little bit he got up from his chair and opened up the hood of the grill. Andrews took the bowl of apple juice–barbecue sauce marinade and began basting the ribs with a brush. He could smell the juice coming off the bone, helping to simmer the fat.

His six-year-old son, a golden image of Andrews in his own youth, came out onto the deck.

—Is lunch almost ready, Daddy?

—Yes. Yes it is, he sang happily.

—It smells delicious.

—It is delicious, said Andrews. —Do you know what else is delicious?

—Cookies are, said his son.

—No, said Andrews. —What is really delicious is when I am right and everyone else is wrong.

—Why is that delicious, Daddy?

—Because that means even though Daddy has no job, neither do Daddy's enemies.

—Why?

—Because that means you get cookies.

His son looked at him as if he was speaking another language.

—I should be getting paid. But you still get cookies. That's how life works.

—Why? asked his son, still confused.

—Go get your mother, said Andrews. —These ribs are ready.

He bent forward and took a deep whiff. He relished it, that sweet, hickory-smoked, luscious fatty smell of the ribs cooking on the grill. He knew then and there that for the rest of his life that smell would remind him of what it felt like to crush your foes even though you lost your job and were sitting unemployed in your backyard grilling and getting a buzz on.

HURRICANE (MONDAY)

It was early, almost 6:00 A.M. Spiros would be arriving soon. The Ghost had just gotten off the phone with him. Spiros had not been happy.

The Ghost sat at his desk and murmured her name. When he said it in his mind he said it like she was a long-lost love or an unfaithful woman: Katrina. Hurricane Katrina, he said to himself. She was supposed to take a right turn at Florida and head up the East Coast, before fizzling out over the Carolinas. That was her track yesterday at 5:00 P.M.

The meteorologist had, even Saturday, given it a 90/10 scenario. The 10 percent being she got ugly and tracked into the rigs off Louisiana and Mississippi. Now the tide had turned. Her track was now an end run around Miami, a 90 percent chance bull's-eye into the heart of the producing region. The platforms were being evacuated. Natural gas and crude had gone limit bid. Furthermore, yesterday Katrina had been a lively schoolgirl, a mere frolicking category 2 storm; overnight she'd turned into something much uglier, a CAT 4, winds in excess of eighty miles per hour with twenty-foot swells.

Both Katrina's initial rack and intensity proved to be cruel head fakes. The Ghost was processing the information the best he could. There was a ringing in his ears, or maybe just one ear. He couldn't tell. He had done the math and since walking in the door his combined short gas and power position was underwater one hundred and fifty million dollars. The Ghost had a few out-of-the-money upside calls that prevented him from losing more, but really they were token insurance, something to keep the bean counters and Spiros happy, a risk management tool as he told them, which was now exposed as a useless hedge in the face of his overleveraged, massive short position. Now it was doomsday.

The Ghost made his way over to the watercooler and going through his head was not the usual stream of numbers: the gas and power forward curves, unhedged delta and gamma positions, locational spreads and monthly rolls, all swirling in his calculating mind like various circus acts vying for his attention; instead the Ghost was thinking of a small human-interest story, he'd heard it on CNN from a live podcast. A commercial fishing vessel going after yellowfin tuna in the Gulf had been unable to outrun the storm. Jennings couldn't recall the exact names of the men who had perished except for one, the second mate, named Chris Jennings, thirty-nine years old. He wondered what the odds were: same last name, same age. The Ghost wondered if he could possibly be a distant relation. As the Ghost's lips touched the cold water, he thought more specifically that just four hours ago a fisherman named Chris Jennings died from swallowing gallons of seawater that filled his lungs and took him on down to the deep. The Ghost had the taste of rust in the back of his mouth. The Ghost pondered sending out an e-mail to fix the water fountain but then the ringing in his ears came back and he wondered if the taste of rust was a side effect of his ringing ears. The Ghost went to his chair on the floor. He took his twenty-five steps by rote. He listened to the banter across the desk. Everyone had been short, except for Andrews, who'd been fired.

I am short a hurricane, thought the Ghost. And it didn't seem real. Chris Jennings had probably survived for a bit, tossed around by the twenty-foot swells before he was finally brought under. The Ghost closed his eyes and tried to imagine the fisherman's last moments.

PISS POOR

The Ghost had always believed that he did share something with Andrews: the professional ability to withstand a haymaker and not buckle, fold, or cry. The Ghost knew he would find out the truth of this soon enough.

The business was built and dismantled by the same means, numbers, the language of mathematics. The Ghost grounded himself by preparing the portfolio PNL to show Spiros. No doubt it would show that the house wore a completely overleveraged short position. Still, the Ghost would need to break it down by each trader's book. The trader in him loved hierarchies and wanted to see which traders aside from himself had lost the most. He first printed off his own PNL, a massive loss even by his risk-taking standards. He looked at the number like it was a tumor, something malignant born out of bad luck, not entirely his own doing. Then he went down the list adding up the losses by trader.

Spiros was standing up in his corner office and pacing now. Spiros finally stepped out of his office and called the Ghost in, beckoning with a tanned hand that the Ghost could not see. As soon as the Ghost walked inside Spiros's office, the trading floor went quiet. More than a few traders had seen Spiros call in the Ghost. And those that didn't were informed in nanoseconds by the curious way traders have of speaking without speaking, the nodding of heads, the rolling of eyes, the craning of necks, and the flashing of hands. Just as hunters who cannot talk when stalking their prey, so does every trader speak the sign language of the floor. And the traders were charged with exhilaration and fear. They were exhilarated because they were witnessing a kill. Their own trading life was affirmed as they saw another destroyed.

The traders who had only lost a relatively small amount and would survive—each made a note, his own rule or paradigm that he literally jotted down in his trader notebook or simply internalized into his own mental matrix of survival. Each one boiled down to simply this:

—Never short a 'cane.

The Ghost positioned himself in front of Spiros's desk, his hands folded in his lap. The time was now 10:00 A.M. The Ghost felt his manager's fear and that gave him some comfort. A trader could always trade, but a manager once fired must find a new host and spend hundreds of hours working to build relationships. However, the Ghost was taken aback by Spiros's abrupt, harsh tone.

—Piss poor! he shouted. The glass walls of his office seemed to reverberate.

The Ghost scratched the back of his head with his thumb. Piss poor: that was a new one. Spiros had saved it up for a special occasion such as this. The Ghost fought back his smirk.

—My God, Jennings! You're down two hundred million since the opening bell, Spiros continued. Dried spit had coagulated at the corners of his mouth.

The Ghost stretched out his arms. He listened to the tone of Spiros's voice, trying to discern if Spiros was angry or merely scared. The Ghost decided he would find out by refusing to talk until he absolutely had to.

—That's a fucking big number.

The Ghost made a small sound as he sucked his lips in, but otherwise said nothing.

—I realize we bet on the hurricane going into the East Coast. But . . .

Spiros leaned forward on his desk, propped up by two arms, bent slightly at the elbows.

—We're finding out today that this was really more of a gamble than anything else. Am I right to say that, Jennings? A gamble?

The Ghost nodded his head. You never answer a statement with a question, he thought. But instead of feeding off his manager's wavering voice, the Ghost himself experienced a strange sensation, the feeling of being worn thin like an overused brake pad or an old carpet. He had been in this situation before. It was never quite the same, but the emotion in his gut had always been of hard, steely reserve. For the first time, the Ghost felt exhausted. He realized that his jaw, as he stared back at Spiros, had sagged and looked soft.

The Ghost leaned forward and said with a dry throat:

—It looks as if it was a hundred-and-fifty-million-dollar gamble.

—Jesus, Jennings, burst out Spiros, as if the Ghost had just confessed to a crime. —You think I can take that to the board. A fucking gamble. I thought we had hedges in place. Those calls aren't worth a shit. This is really very un-fucking-responsible stuff here. This has become a travesty. A bloodbath. This is going to hit the stock, piss off investors.

—It will, said the Ghost.

His impertinent tone grated on the manager. Spiros decided to vent some more.

—Only one fucking trader made any money off this move. That's how overboard you let the whole portfolio get.

The Ghost gave his manager a quizzical look. When he printed out the PNL sheet off the morning marks every trader had been down.

—Someone was up? asked the Ghost.

—Yes. That troglodyte Gallagher: up four million dollars.

—I checked this morning. He was down two, countered the Ghost.

—It seems he had a weather position that made six million dollars. Short K5 or something, said Spiros. —Greenblatt must have re-marked the weather positions when he arrived, after you'd already run the PNLs this morning.

The last exchange was another slap in the face.

The Ghost looked up at Spiros. His mouth was set in a straight line. Spiros didn't notice anything different about the Ghost's jaw. What Spiros saw was that same nothingness in the Ghost's shaded glasses that he had seen when his head trader was up fifty million only a month ago. Only then Spiros had believed it was a calculating void, a numerically swift killing mind attached to an iron gut—a trader of genius. Now he saw something else before him: frayed wires and a cruel remoteness, a malfunctioning device, a mechanical disaster that brought forth in Spiros a sudden scorn and disdain like nothing he had ever felt for another human being in his life, as if the person before him was a thing and not a man.

Spiros took a breath. He felt the need for composure. Spiros Nikakis had once been in the drama club in high school and he had a flair for the mildly dramatic. He summoned up some acting talent and decided to say it sadly when he said it.

—You're done, Jennings.

Then Spiros picked up the phone on his desk to ring down the Executioner.

Gallagher went to the snack room five times to contemplate the candy selection at the vending machine. Five times without buying anything. When he came back to his desk he drained a pint of chocolate milk. Watching the Ghost stare out at the trading floor with a bored look devoid of spite and loathing, Gallagher wanted to escape. Finally, he broke down and bought a pack of strawberry Pop-Tarts. Greenblatt had entered the marks for weather derivatives curves when he arrived at work around nine o'clock. Surely, the Ghost knew by now about Gallagher's final tally: up four million dollars. Even a small positive number would've been in the Ghost's mind a betrayal to the house position. He would've seen Gallagher's VaR report and discerned the K5, Dallas weather hedge.

Gallagher took in the scene across the desk. Miller, Large, Churchill, Hobart, the Colonel, Rector, Shuggs, Sami, and Bret, they were all quiet, glum, and seemed to move at half speed. They had quickly shed the anger phase at Rector and now internalized their losses, assessing their chances of professional survival. Their turn through the meat grinder with Spiros was not, however, on their minds. Instead, the traders just wanted the day to end.

Large kept shaking his cranium back and forth like he was viewing a bad traffic accident on the side of the highway—trader roadkill. More than once he could be heard murmuring the phrase "taken to the woodshed." However, besides Gallagher, Large had lost the least amount of money. Upon seeing his daughter at Bring Your Child to Work Day, his father's protective instinct for his family made him cover some of his position.

Just before lunch, the Ghost materialized behind Gallagher like an evil tiding. There was no sound, no shadow, no inkling of his presence, he just appeared. Gallagher finally understood the essence of the nickname.

Gallagher almost jumped in his chair.

—You're up today, Gallagher, said the Ghost.

Gallagher had lost the capacity for speech. His throat went dry. He grabbed for his cup of green tea but it was empty.

—I'll make sure you get paid, said the Ghost. —In full.

Gallagher shrank like a piece of fruit in a microwave, withering him to one-tenth his former size. Gallagher felt his mouth move, as if to respond to the charges against him. But the Ghost left as silently as he came, moving down the row of desks as if pushed along by an invisible wind. It took Gallagher a few seconds but he eventually stood up. With the Ghost gone, he felt his courage coming back. Gallagher stretched his neck, rotating his head from shoulder to shoulder.

THE PLACE

The Place was situated at the far end of Chinatown. It was a cut above the few other strip clubs in Boston proper. The Ghost gave the Colonel three thousand dollars in cash and told him to entertain his entourage of traders for one last night out on the town. Half of them had already been fired and the other half awaited their fate.

—Even Gallagher? asked the Colonel.

—Gallagher too, said the Ghost.

Unlike the other clubs, The Place presented itself as a blend of aristocracy and capitalism: a twenty-dollar admission fee to keep out the riffraff. The traders entered the main dance area and headed straight up the plush carpeted staircase with the gaudy brass railing to the VIP Club, yet one more standard deviation away from the blue-jean-wearing masses.

The Place knew its clientele. The design was modern lounge bearing a teak-paneled machismo that took its cue from a cigar bar atmosphere where a Cuban general would feel at home. The Place understood the VIP clientele thought of themselves as earners, a sober, reliable set who would want to be treated with dignity, preferring privacy, fine cigars, a well-stocked bar, polite, accommodating service, and, of course, the highest pedigree of Eastern European talent there was to offer. The actual stage in the VIP lounge was quite small. There was no brass pole. Dancers were not expected to work up a sweat, just have perfect bodies. The one dance they did was actually an aggrandized catwalk. Once their set was over the dancers would go sit down and enjoy a drink with whomever they chose. The Place formula for the VIP was the art of the soft sale. They realized they weren't moving volume. They were selling Mercedes.

The traders skulked into the VIP lounge, their faces brooding and grim. Sika, the burly host, sat them at the Ghost's regular table. He then, as if by magic, produced from behind his back a bottle of single-barrel Jack Daniel's whiskey, placed it among them, and then disappeared. The traders' faces grew less moody, although still no one was smiling. Miller grabbed the bottle and started pouring.

—That dude gets it, he said.

The Colonel threw a wad of dance dollars on the table.

—Have at it, guys. This is on Jennings, he said.

One of Hobart's favorites, Jade, a five-foot-eleven blonde from Vermont, who had been a dental hygienist in Hanover, approached the table followed in tow by Sika. Ignoring the other traders, Jade gave Hobart a kiss on the cheek and then walked him off the floor into the blue, spectral gloom toward the back of the club: the Champagne Room. When he was gone the younger traders all grabbed for the dance dollars at once. The Colonel put his large hand over the wad of bills and barked that he would count it out.

—I could use a Red Bull, said Shuggs to Hobart.

—Why don't you go play in the street, said Miller.

—I like her, said Shuggs, looking out at a stripper waltzing across the stage in a skimpy office suit, wearing librarian glasses. She was on the voluptuous meets large side.

—Damn, my boy, here's a marine, said Miller. —He ain't afraid to jump on a grenade.

Shuggs brought over a bottle of whiskey and placed it in front of Gallagher.

—Boss says no hard feelings, Gallagher. Drinks on him.

—Goat, go bring me a bottle, said Miller to Shuggs. —Me and Gallagher will be done with this by the time you get back.

—How about a bottle of Blue as long as boss man's picking up the tab? asked Large.

They all drank with blank, dazed expressions staring at the plus-sized girl dancing onstage. Miller scoped the floor.

—Crack-head skinny with implants. Is that too much to ask?

Gallagher looked up from his whiskey and said:

—I guess this is "the Last Supper."

—Believe it or not, Stupid is right. For once, announced Miller to the table, his mood improving with each sip of whiskey.

The Colonel was looking out over the floor at a petite redhead cruising the aisle. She wore thigh-high, red velvet boots.

—Fuck that, he said. —Last Supper nothing. This is more like dessert.

A frosty-haired blonde with cat-eye makeup wearing gold sequin panties, who just finished her set, strolled up to their table. The expression on her face was that of the professional stripper: a bored, blasé patrician look, at once intimidating and inviting.

She stood next to Shuggs. He looked up at her and said:

—Darling, I'm warning you. I'm from Steel Town and I like to palm some ass.

THE FEDS

Quiet Doug Lawrence, Allied's head of security, escorted three men in suits down the side of the trading floor. Their countenance was grim and hard. They came with handcuffs on their belts. Two of the men wore dark suits of poor quality and filled them out with athletic frames. The third man donned gray pinstripes and polished wingtips. He had a smaller build and a receding hairline. The two men in the dark suits were merely unsmiling, while chiseled into the third man's face was the superior air of a D.C. corporate lawyer. Churchill tapped Miller on the arm and nodded toward the foursome.

Miller, his eyebrows knitted together, whispered:

—What the fuck?

—You see how shiny those handcuffs are? They must polish them things twice a day, said Churchill.

—FERC? asked Miller.

—Those guys got guns, said Churchill. —They're G-men.

—Jesus, said Miller.

Daniel Haupt was sitting at his desk on the phone with a customer. The trio walked behind Doug Lawrence with a deferential air until he pointed a finger toward Haupt. The larger of the men in dark suits placed his hand on Haupt's shoulder and pulled him up without effort, as if levitating the trader. Haupt let his phone fall to the floor. His face had a stunned look, bewildered and vacant, reminiscent of those interviewed after Katrina, people who'd lost their homes and their whole lives. The metallic clicking sound of the handcuffs ratcheting down on his wrists made him come to. For one last time the Colonel looked around the trading floor at his coworkers, who seemed to stand still in time. They looked back, faces unable to bring themselves to show surprise or pity for the man who'd sat next to them for a decade. As the small man in the gray pinstripes read him his Miranda Rights, the Colonel coughed once and said nothing. Throughout he stared straight ahead, his strong chin pointing forward in a disciplined military fashion, as if he was standing at attention. The Colonel held the exact same pose as they led him off the floor. The small man in the gray pinstripes strode two steps in front of the Colonel and the two men in the cheap dark suits walked close behind, nearly touching him.

—Holy shit, said Miller.

—You're surprised? asked Churchill.

—What you think that bastard did? asked Miller.

—What the fuck didn't he do, said Churchill, turning back to his computer screen with a bored look on his face.

A TRADE

Celina sat at the kitchen table drinking a cup of coffee. It was late in the afternoon and the sky outside her window was overcast, dark grays blending into lighter grays. Celina regretted that her artist's eye made her see the varying hues of lead-colored sky as if each patch bore its own distinct fingerprint of gloom. She sipped at the bitter-tasting coffee and fought back the urge to smoke yet another cigarette. In front of her was a ceramic ashtray made by her six-year-old nephew. She spun the ashtray on the wood tabletop and at length spoke to it. The idea of having a child of her own with her husband, the man-child, Joe Gallagher, made her eyeballs feel numb.

—What am I doing here? she asked the ashtray.

She sat there in silence for a few moments and then stood up. The hollow feeling in the pit of her stomach did not stand up with her.

Celina was at her easel, sketching self-portraits in charcoal, when the doorbell rang. She wasn't going to answer it. After all it was probably a Jehovah Witness or an ADT home-alarm salesman. The bell sounded a few more times, too insistent for a salesperson. Celina got up and walked down the hall into the bedroom where she peered out the window that looked down onto the street.

It was Randall Jennings, standing too close to the doorbell. She threw open the window and stuck her head out.

—I'll be right down, she called. She saw his town car waiting at the end of the street.

Celina opened the door and invited him in.

—Careful. Steps, she said, taking hold of his arm.

Once inside he moved past her into the living room as if trying to escape from what he perceived to be the foyer.

—Would you like something to drink? We have beer, of course, she said.

He was frowning at her and he had his hands on his pant legs.

—No. No thanks.

He looked at her for a few moments before saying anything more. It was as if he was waiting for her to speak but Celina said nothing.

—The company let me go. But you heard about that. Anyways, I'm going away soon, leaving for my house in Belize. It's in the jungle and not too far from the beach, just a nice walk down a little path. It's a very restful place.

He let out a huffing sound, as if this small speech exhausted him.

—I came by to invite you to come and stay and paint there. I think you'd like it. The Mayan ruins are only an hour away.

Celina took a step back and sat down on the couch facing the head trader.

—Anyways, I probably don't have to tell you this. But Gallagher is not invited.

When he moved forward Celina was startled because she was expecting him to reach out and touch her on the arm. Instead, he passed by her and stopped in the antechamber, near the front door. He calmly waited for her.

Celina got up off the couch and guided him gently toward the steps.

—Thank you for the offer, she said.

Once out in front of the house, Jennings turned to face her. In a cavalier tone, he said:

—You know it's kind of like the old days back in the Renaissance when artists had patrons. Think of my offer as something like that.

He raised a hand in the air as if it was a barometer, discerning the humidity. Celina was trying to think of an appropriate response. Then he turned on his heels and walked cautiously down the street. The limo service was waiting for him in a spotless, black Lexus sedan. Celina shut the door.

After the visit, Celina went upstairs and showered. It didn't occur to her until later that the she hadn't bothered to be flattered or offended or even surprised by the Ghost's strange offer.

Celina changed into one of her nicer shirts, a floral silk print, and put on her favorite pair of jeans. The Ghost had been wrong about what would inspire Celina. When Celina wanted artistic inspiration she didn't go to tropical landscapes or museums or ancient cathedrals. Rather Celina haunted urban settings, scenes that she thought gave her an insight into the particular time that she lived in.

She left the house and drove to the Four Seasons Hotel, pulling up at the valet stand. It was a five-star hotel that looked out over the Boston Gardens. It was closing in on 5:00 P.M., happy hour. The hotel bar was packed with businessmen and less well-dressed out-of-towners in for a baseball game. The Four Seasons Hotel crowd reminded Celina of a less-polished, but still hyper-masculine scene out of a Max Beckmann painting. She had been here before at happy hour and had always wanted to paint the row of men at the bar with their half-drunk whiskeys, sad hanging jowls, haggard red faces, and mouths puckering as they blew forth a mist of cigar smoke.

She sat there with her drink at the end of the bar, admiring the rogue gallery of businessmen. It was in the dim blue light, subdued by booze, chatter, and the smell of peanuts, that Celina finally decided that the city of Boston was not for her. It was not her milieu. And although Gallagher was not a bourgeoisie, and not a dullard, his overbearing nature, his ponderous mind coupled with his whirlwind energy; had stolen something from her, sapped her energy. The idea of leaving this city, her husband, flowed through her like an infusion of new blood, a forbidden thing, that, once ingested, seemed to grant her a cruel freedom. Her apology to her husband was that in her mind she had no intention to marry again.

I will give him that for his pride.

After her second vodka and tonic, she was thinking that Gallagher might understand her motives. It's a trade, a risk on my part. He's a trader. He'll see that side of it. She fished in her handbag and produced her silver cigarette case. Before she could even touch the end of the cigarette to her mouth, a tall redheaded man with bright pink bourbon blossom cheeks approached her and in the automatic motion of a practiced cad held out a lighter that instantly blazed into a flickering flame and seemed like the promise of something both seductive and lewd.

Celina thanked him and leaned back so as to have one last view of the hovering forms hunkered down at the bar, holding their drinks like scepters, keeping the world at bay, while their weaknesses and fears for that stolen moment were jammed into their pockets with all their loose change.

I need to paint this, thought Celina.

When Celina arrived home, Gallagher was sitting on the couch in the den, watching a movie on TV. On the screen dune buggies and motorcycles were circling a primitive fortress set in some postapocalyptic desert. The movie cut to a bald, deformed, muscle-bound man wearing what looked like a steel hockey mask. He was speaking into a microphone. His voice sounded threatening but his tone was Shakespearean.

—Just walk away, spewed the grotesque in the steel hockey mask.

Celina saw a bag of potato chips spilled onto the couch.

—Are you asleep down there? she called from the stairway.

—No. Come on down, shouted Gallagher. —Where have you been?

Celina took the first step down into the den delicately like someone testing for a tripwire, as she wondered if she was going to be able to tell her husband what she had decided.

BABOONS

Gallagher stood in Celina's old studio. The sun came through the window in a shaft of light that illuminated the hardwood floor in a strange geometric shape, an oblong trapezoid. Gallagher was sitting on Celina's artist's stool, perusing the empty room and letting the radiant heat of the morning sun warm his bones. The walls were bare of paintings and etchings. All the pasteboard shelves had been cleared of her artist's supplies.

Gallagher couldn't believe she had actually left him. The drunken scene in the den with Gallagher watching *The Road Warrior* in his boxer shorts, spilled potato chips stuck to his belly, as he argued that he was a good husband, the perfect mate. At the point where Gallagher should have broken down and begged for a second chance, he had shouted: "I'm a model husband!"

In the end he listened quietly, not because he agreed, not because he was sad, but because he was confused. She gave one last composed, adult speech about "a second chance" for her art. When she appealed to him as a trader, that if anyone should understand taking a risk, it should be him, Gallagher then sat down on the hardwood floor, as if deflated.

That next morning Gallagher drank a pint glass of almost sour chocolate milk for breakfast and sat on her artist's stool for some time, drifting in between states of thinking and not thinking.

During moments of lucidity it occurred to Gallagher a new age had dawned: the Age of Hedge Funds. Within twenty-four hours of the hurricane Allied stock had plummeted. Several hedge funds had made a seemingly coordinated, aggressive play and driven the value of the Boston trading firm into the ground. A week later those traders deemed responsible for the Hurricane Katrina losses were let go. A week after that Allied Power was bought by a Chinese bank. The new management had little use for speculative trading. The few traders who survived the hurricane debacle were all laid off. Two and a half weeks after Gallagher had made the trade of his life, he was out of a job.

Gallagher wearily got up off the stool and made his way downstairs. Once in the kitchen he opened the fridge: the gallon of expired milk was mostly gone. He was thirsty but decided to leave it be. On Celina's corkboard below the German Expressionist calendar was a Post-it with Howard Schiller's name and phone number. Howard had to be behind Celina's insane departure. Gallagher called the number.

—Schiller Galleries, may I help you?

—Is Howard in today? asked Gallagher.

—He is, may I ask who is calling?

Gallagher hung up the phone.

Howard's in Boston today.

Gallagher had parked the SUV on the third floor of a garage on the corner of Tremont Street. Just across the street was Schiller's gallery. Gallagher was sitting in the Ford Explorer, paging through a copy of *Soldier of Fortune* magazine. He'd read it straight through twice, including the ads for hired killers and survival schools in Appalachia and Idaho. A half-full large Pepsi sat in the cup holder and the greasy wrapping paper of a bacon double cheeseburger and BK onion rings littered the floor beneath him. The streets of the business district were bustling around five o'clock, as the forty-hour-a-week crowd left work. Gallagher surveyed the front door of the gallery waiting for Howard to leave.

Gallagher had liked the cover story in *Soldier of Fortune* the most and began reading it for a third time. It was by a retired cop from Ohio who was a fundamentalist Christian. He found out about the Burmese from his minister who had been on a mission there. Their story of persecution by the

Muslims moved him and so he flew to Burma, smuggling a case of twenty-four Streetsweeper fully automatic shotguns in through Laos. He lived with this tribe, token Christians in a Muslim country, and trained them in combat tactics. He wrote about living in a thatch-roofed hut and sleeping in a hammock made from woven palm fronds. Baboons with orange eyes swung in the trees outside his hut and each morning left half-eaten mangrove fruits on his doorstep. The cop had fallen in with the tribe and thought much of them. Ambushes, training sessions, prayer in the Burmese tongue; the cop, it seemed, did not want to go back to Ohio. But he did and so ended the article. There was no reflection on whether the tribe would survive or perish, just a short sentence about how he missed his family and had to go home.

Gallagher liked the idea of sleeping in a hammock in sweltering heat and living with people who could not understand English. Gallagher also liked the baboons, hooting in the darkness, with their crazed orange eyes and swollen pink asses: they were violence and comedy in the same body. Gallagher realized he had no religious affiliation so it would be strange for him to go on that particular mission to Burma. Muslims, Christians, baboons. *Sold*, thought Gallagher, taking a sip of his large soda.

It never occurred to Gallagher that the story might not be true.

Howard Schiller wore a tan fedora with a black hatband and a beige Brooks Brothers poplin suit with a salmon-colored tie. When Gallagher stepped out of the garage, he spotted Howard Schiller taking the turn to walk up Newberry Street. Gallagher knew that Howard and Celina would sometimes meet for drinks in the High Hat bar. Gallagher assumed that's where the art dealer was heading, but Howard walked by the High Hat and went to a place Gallagher had never noticed.

Gallagher's plan was to first crowd Howard, loom over him, but to be polite, even agreeable. If that method yielded no results, Gallagher was prepared to move into bully and intimidation mode. He didn't have the intent of assaulting him, but Gallagher knew that on the subject of his wife his feelings could become volatile extremely fast.

Sauntering up to the front door Howard had just entered, Gallagher could see that it was a standard oak lounge with professional clientele settling in for happy hour martinis or a glass of red wine. As he grabbed the handle on the front door, Gallagher noticed the sticker of a rainbow posted to the bottom corner of the windowpane. It was a gay bar.

Gallagher suddenly realized he'd had an unconscious fear that Howard had been screwing his wife. That was the only reason he was there, that's why he'd spent two hours in his SUV staking the art dealer out. Gallagher took his hand off the door handle and turned around and walked up the street. There was an Irish bar called Sheenan's on the next block right by the movie theater. There would be whiskey and Guinness there. He would drink until it was time to go home.

TAE KWON DO

Andrews's eleven-year-old daughter, Sarah, was going for her green belt. His wife had taken their two boys to a water park birthday party. They were not good swimmers. That deal seemed like it would be more work, so Andrews volunteered for the Tae Kwon Do, which he privately referred to as Tae Kwon Dorks.

Gallagher was sitting next to Andrews in the stands. The American and Korean flags stood on either side of an electronic scoreboard. Just to the right of the flags was a glass case, exhibiting an array of martial arts weaponry: exotic-looking spears, bo sticks, and kenpo staves. Andrews gave color commentary.

—This ain't optional for some of these nerds. They'll need this shit to survive middle school, said Andrews. —But you'll see some of these kids are actual athletes.

When Gallagher didn't respond, Andrews said with a mocking grin:

—You speak geek. I know you're fluent in nunchaku from your Dungeons and Dragons years.

Just then two boys in the orange belt division were squaring off, wearing the padded headgear, with cup and knee and foot pads. The lean, lanky boy from Sarah's team, the Fighting Tiger Dojo, bowed at the waist to his opponent, a squat, stocky kid with bristly, black hair that stuck up through his headgear like spiky hedgehog fur.

The boy from Sarah's team stepped forward and threw three successive side-kicks. He hopped forward with each kick. The hedgehog kid managed to deflect two of them but the third kick landed squarely in the solar plexus. And he let out an audible *ooofff!*

On the second frame the long leg of the lean fighter snapped out in a praying mantis front kick that sent the head of the spiky-haired opponent back and he fell to the canvas.

Andrews winked approvingly to Gallagher:

—Damn, said Andrews. —That's two points.

Gallagher stopped sipping at his Coke and let out an "ugh" sound.

—See what I mean? said Andrews. —These kids are learning to play for keeps.

After the first match ended in a victory for the Fighting Tigers Dojo, Andrews turned to Gallagher:

—If you want a hot dog now is the time to get it.

—I'm not hungry, said Gallagher.

Andrews frowned at this. He wanted to go get a dog, but sensed that Gallagher wanted to talk about it.

—Have you heard from Celina?

—No, said Gallagher.

—You looking for work? asked Andrews, moving on to the easier topic.

—Not yet.

—You could apply for a job with the new company. Smart guy like you would do well in China.

Gallagher answered Andrews while looking out at the fighting arena, his look despondent.

—I got a call from a hedge fund out west. How about you?

—I have a few things that might evolve into something, little powwow with a firm in Houston. You know, the usual suspects. Until then I'm perfecting my short ribs recipe.

The buzzer sounded and the green belt division stood in a line on the fighting platform.

—Sarah is first up, said Andrews, pointing to his program.

Sarah Andrews was a tall girl with her father's blond hair and gray eyes. Her opponent, a red-haired boy a few inches shorter than her, had a nervous bug-eyed look about him. Andrews clenched his fist like he wanted to make the boy's eyes bug out even wider.

—They're making Sarah fight a dude? asked Gallagher.

—Watch this, said Andrews. —She'll crush him.

The referee blew his whistle. The two green belts bowed and then moved into their attack stance. The boy threw two body punches that Sarah avoided by stepping to her left. The boy was slightly off balance. Sarah had created an attack angle for herself. She took a small hop and then her long leg spun out in an elegant arc of a roundhouse kick that connected right to the bridge of the boy's nose. As he fell to the mat, the boy let out a high-pitched yell that cracked mid-scream, betraying his prepubescence. When he looked up at the stands one woman let out a motherly shriek and called out the boy's name. He was bleeding from his nose. A red stream ran down his lips and chin and spattered onto the blue mat in big, dark droplets. His coach ran out onto the mat and offered the boy a towel. The referee waved his hands, indicating that the redhead had forfeited the match to Sarah Andrews of the Fighting Tigers Dojo.

Gallagher's heavy mood lightened for a moment and he smiled at Andrews.

—Damn, he said.

Andrews let out a low, growling, satisfied laugh like a bear who's found a beehive.

—The food chain, said Andrews, slapping Gallagher on the back.

Andrews laughed even louder. Then he stood up and began clapping for his little girl.

PART THREE

THE BID/ASK ON MILT

In the summer of 2005 after Milt Harkrader was fired from NYMB, he disappeared from New York. Rumor had it that he went bankrupt from a misguided play on Florida real estate after the hurricanes and the U.S. economy in tandem caused the greatest crash in that market's history. The word was out that he had moved to Haddam, New Jersey, and worked in a store that sold office supplies. Another version of the story told of Milt selling out at the high before the hurricanes hit and that he had made a killing and now lived in Bimini. Buy the rumor, sell the fact: One story had even percolated that Milt had been decapitated in a boating accident on Lake Michigan.

Pit traders give everything a name. If you welch on a trade, you're a flake. If you trade scared and exist only to make nickels on guys off their markets, you're a bird. If you're wrong more than you're right, you're a goat. The trader taxonomy defined Milt's disappearance from the trading circuit as "blowing up" or "cashing out." Enemies of Milt insisted that he had experienced the former, while young brokers, still full of optimism and partial humanity, who heard of Milt from the legends liked to espouse the latter theory.

THE LOT

As Milt strolled toward the Lexus dealership, he noticed a yellow banner on the edge of the car lot. It was flapping in the wind. In big black letters, it read: FOR LEASE. Beneath the banner were all the new hybrid models. The executives at Lexus thought that Americans would be more amenable to leasing a hybrid versus outright owning it. As if people didn't want to believe that the high gas prices would last forever. The smooth blacktop seemed less menacing in the morning because the heat wouldn't become oppressive until 10:00 A.M. Behind the hybrids, rows and rows of SUVs, luxury sedans, coupes, and the Performance F sports cars were lined up like troops for inspection, primed and polished. Their windshields glinted in the sun. He gazed out over the merchandise; he knew the stats of each model and make by heart right down to the *Car and Driver* magazine safety rankings. He knew which model belonged with each customer as soon as the pigeons walked through the door of the dealership and, more importantly, what options to push.

Milt wore a light tan muslin suit and a powder blue tie. On his head was a new cowboy hat, not a Stetson, but a more modestly priced Brownsville flatbrim. He leaned into the front door with a shoulder, while balancing his coffee. Milt's boss, Chet Eagle, with his canary yellow suit, and his short red hair parted down the middle along with the freckled forehead, called out his usual intense morning greeting.

—Going to kill it today, Cowboy?

Everyone at the dealership called Milt "Cowboy," because of the hat.

—Yours you, Chet, said Milt, his pat response. He kept some of his broker-speak from the floor. No one understood what it meant and it separated Milt. The other salesmen without knowing it accorded him a degree of respect because of this.

Milt sat down at his desk on the showroom floor. He heaved out a sigh. After his manager, Chet, Milt was the first one to arrive. He looked out at the view beyond the tinted glass windows, beyond the rows of perfectly aligned Lexuses, the palm trees along Clearwater Boulevard swayed in the wind that was coming off the Gulf. It's going to be a perfect day to sell some cars, thought Milt. He opened a desk drawer. He took out one of his Jenny Craig peanut butter breakfast bars and unwrapped it. Inspecting the contents list, he read them out loud to himself:

—Dry roasted peanuts, organic oats, organic evaporated cane syrup, soy, vegetable glycerin, cocoa butter, palm oil.

—Jesus Christ! he said, shaking his head.

Milt missed his breakfast sandwiches but knew that being under two hundred and twenty pounds helped him move more cars. Customers wanted to look at beautifully engineered cars, a feat of art and science brought together. Double chins suggested Cadillac, Ford, beefy, bulky, outmoded cars from dinosaur manufacturers, dying brands. His cowboy hat reminded buyers that he the seller was American even though the car was not, so they could still feel patriotic in the purchase.

Milt shambled up to the untended greeter's station. He contemplated taking a strand of licorice out of the candy jar, but thought the better of it. Instead, he reached over the front desk and grabbed a copy of the *St. Petersburg Times*.

Chet bothered him about the headline story.

—You read about the bank robbers in Miami? They were geniuses.

—Geniuses. Ha! That's a good one, said Milt.

He told his boss about the trading duo who'd made millions in the electricity market by shorting out a transmission line in Minnesota.

—The one guy flew over it in a small glider with an engine and dropped a length of chain on the power lines. Caused a region-wide failure of the grid. They got paid.

—How do you make money off that? asked Chet, confused.

Milt was about to explain the caper in detail, but then stopped himself and said:

—Wouldn't you like to know.

Milt put down the paper on the counter.

—Now those guys were geniuses. Except for one thing. Post nine-eleven they got satellites monitoring the power lines and the Feds nabbed the guy and he rolled on the other who made the trades.

Chet stood there with a confused look on his face, stricken like a cigar store Indian.

—Cowboy, he said finally, shaking his head. —You come up with real doozies.

—I knew one of the guys, said Milt. —He was a trader from Boston. He's going to do twenty years for terrorism to the grid.

—Sorry to hear that, Milt, said Chet. —Was he a good buddy of yours?

—No. But I met him a few times. He looked like Cary Grant.

Chet screwed up his eyebrows, looking confused for a split second, then he flashed Milt a forced smile, trying to send his top salesman some winning vibes.

Milt picked up the newspaper and returned to his desk. He plopped down in his rollaway seat, sat back, and read the article. The bank robbers had posed as window washers. It had been a daytime job. The robbery didn't strike him as overly original. It was something he could've come up with. Of course, Chet was impressed.

—Dumb shit, said Milt.

He put down the paper and looked out the dealership's tinted windows, dulling the white sunlight into an easy, comfortable fuzzy gray. In the distance above the rooftops of residential housing, Winn-Dixies, strip malls, surf shops, gas stations, and bowling alleys, Milt could make out the top of the Don CeSar's pink dome. Majestic was the only word for it. He chewed his peanut butter breakfast bar and stared out at the hotel where he had wanted to live. His current apartment offered a better view of the Don CeSar. At night he would make a 151 rum drink with pineapple juice and sliced oranges and from his kitchen window observe the Don CeSar lit up, glowing against the background of the night sky like the pink ghost of an old Spanish castle.

Milt hadn't spoken to anyone in the energy industry in months. His ex-wife, Debby, told Milt the rumor was that Milt had been hit by a speedboat on Lake Michigan, owing to an obituary that shared Milt's exact name and age. Debby laughed as she related to Milt how she hadn't set the record straight.

—I didn't let Lorraine know you were down here, Milty. I figured I'd let you reveal the legend of Milt.

Milt liked it that Debby used the word "legend." It made him feel mythical.

—Let them think I'm dead, said Milt. —I'm never going back.

The door to the dealership opened and it wasn't one of the slow-moving salesmen but a couple, young, attractive, in their thirties, dressed in his and hers Polo, both with white khaki shorts. The brunette wife with the Chanel shades was pushing a new model of the latest luxury baby strollers. They looked around with an air of blithe excitement. They were here for their first family car. SUV time, thought Milt, standing.

Milt tossed his half-eaten breakfast bar in the wastebasket. He moved forward toward the couple with a smile and an easy, endearing walk that only a big man can pull off. He felt the presence of the Brownsville flat brim on his head. Milt was thinking of sausages, bacon, steaks, and other kinds of red meat as he walked up to them. He was thinking of these things because they made him happy and he knew that happiness was contagious and that beneficent contagion was the very heart of the secret to selling cars.

THE LANES

Aaron sat in the passenger seat of Milt's green Lexus sedan. Milt drove down Clearwater Boulevard tight-lipped, not speaking.

—I like the car, Dad. It's sweet.

Since going belly-up on his real estate properties, the car, courtesy of the dealership, was the only vestige of material wealth that Milt could display to the world.

—Where are we going? asked his son, lowering his window.

—Don't fuck with the windows, snapped Milt. —I got the AC set just right.

—Sorry, mumbled Aaron.

Milt accelerated and sped through a red light. The car horn of a Camry that Milt cut off could be heard blaring and then trailing off into silence behind them. Milt passed by the Winn-Dixie and then his dealership and the Barclays Bank beyond it. Up ahead on the right he spotted the illuminated billboard for Clearwater Lanes.

—This is it? asked Milt.

—Dad, you're not going to do anything stupid, are you?

—He called me a bankrupt, right? And your mother told him about my little difficulties.

—Dad, he's a cop!

—He say shit about you having to go to public school next semester?

Milt took the pint bottle of 151 rum tucked snugly in his lap and lifted it to his mouth. The clear liquid washed down his throat with a mild burn and a hint of mango, reminding Milt he was in the tropics.

—I'm showing you what to do when another man calls you a bankrupt behind your back.

—You're going to go to jail and get raped, squealed Aaron. He knew how much his stepfather would cherish the sight of Milt, drunk and out of control, and how he would look at Milt and squint with his small cop eyes and smile that resentful, predatory smile with just the corners of his mouth turned up.

—I'm not joking, Dad. White guys get made into bitches.

—I'm no bitch, said Milt, reaching over and patting his son on the head. —Your dad isn't stupid. I'm showing you what to do when another man calls you a bankrupt. This shit right here that you're about to see is called honor. Don't you ever forget it.

Milt turned off the boulevard into the Clearwater Lanes parking lot, wheels screeching. Some people crossing the lot yelled at them to "watch it" and flipped them the finger. Milt offered his response and leaned on the horn. He drove the car around to the back of the lanes: It was deserted save a Dumpster filled with debris, the back entryway, and a sole light that staved off the darkness and the overgrown brush at the edge of the lot.

—Get out, said Milt to his son.

The man and boy walked around the side of the building to the front of the bowling alley. The night was thick with a lush, tropical heat. Milt's upper lip was sweating.

—So what's he bowl?

—High two twenties.

—So he's good then?

—He led the league, Mom said. And you know what his teammates call him? The Bowlinator, as in the Terminator.

—The Bowlinator. Hah! I like that. I'm going to use that.

They turned the corner.

—I never was that great an athlete, you know, said Milt, musing. —But I played some baseball.

—But you're big, Dad, said Aaron. —And tough, right?

—No, said Milt. —Just big. But I work hard.

They arrived at the twin-framed front doors to the bowling alley. Milt pushed them open. He looked back at his son, smiling and licking his lips:

—And I'm a little bit mean.

The Clearwater Lanes had faux wood paneling that was peeling off the wallboard in places. A smiling dolphin lit up in blue neon lights greeted bowlers as they entered. The concessions stand had a popcorn machine that was out of order, but the corndogs were double battered and a lanes favorite, as was the sometimes-cold beer.

Curt Long's yellow bowling jersey hung off his wiry frame. Debby Long was watching from the gallery as her husband held his blue marbled bowling ball in front of his face and then took four deliberate strides before releasing the rock down the lane with a backspin that made the ball seem to stand still as it rolled. Curt Long had perfect form that was more disciplined and economical in its movement than graceful. With his bowling hand high in the air, the wrist guard keeping his hand straight, an extension of his forearm, Curt Long watched as his blue marbled ball crashed just inches to the right of the lead pin. He turned around before the pins fell. He had bowled a long time and knew a strike when he saw one. Still, when his wife let out her excited piping tiny shriek, he nodded his head and pumped a fist. One of his teammates gave Curt a high five.

Debby sat on the bench and smiled and raised her eyebrows at her husband. She was not allowed to approach him when he was bowling.

The space around Curt Long's lane grew quiet as he and his teammates waited for his ball, Blue Betty, to come rolling back down the ramp. Curt Long was staring at the electronic scoreboard, waiting for the X registering his strike to appear. All of a sudden there was one man clapping from behind the gallery.

—Go Bowlinator! Go Bowlinator! Go Bowlinator, Milt chanted.

By the third chant heads were turning. All the league members knew the name Bowlinator but had never had the gall to shout the name of the league's most talented bowler in a tone of derision and mockery. The big, saggy, dark-eyed bald man dressed in a tan suit, holding a pint bottle of rum, continued shouting faster and louder, developing a lisp as he cried out in near song.

—Bowlinator. Bowlinator. Bowlinator. Bowlinator.

Curt Long turned around and saw his wife's ex-husband standing there with his boy.

—This motherfucker, shouted Milt to the gallery, spreading his arms wide, appealing to the audience as if he was selling a car. —This Bowlinator told my own kid, this good kid right here, his stepson, that I, his real father, was a bankrupt. This civil servant, bottom feeder, living off your taxes and handing out speeding tickets, slandered me, a working man, behind my back to my own son. Well, you civil servant fuck, I'm here for your apology or a fucking parking ticket. What's it going to be?

The crowd sitting on the benches came to their senses and grew indignant. Curt Long was one of their own. They began to boo Milt. Milt became energized and light on his feet. He skipped backward, beckoning their jeers with his hands like the heel in a wrestling match. Curt Long looked at the big man in the suit and his military face tightened up, his jaw flexed, jutting forward so that his narrow face molded into a V. His eyes became intense, they burned darker, changing from their normal gray to the color of pig iron.

—Milt!

It was Debby, crying out, a plea from the stands. She sounded helpless, knowing the act, the carnival of insult, the parade of booze-soaked rhetoric that would follow. Curt almost sneered when he heard his wife's voice express fear at another man's rage. Curt Long stood there, tall and gaunt, unable to speak, reeling from the taunts. The words, slaps in the face, kept coming.

—Guys on the tit don't have to be sharp, continued Milt. —You got nothing to say because you never had to hustle and sell and work the old brain, did you, government tit boy? Say the words, Bowlinator. I ain't leaving your game until you give me the parking ticket or fucking say it: I'm sorry for being a coward and talking shit to your boy.

The crowd who had been booing Milt grew silent, enraptured and greedy: This was free entertainment, family drama Jerry Springer style.

—That's right, said Milt, winning the ear of the crowd. —This is my boy. And I tried my best to send him to private school and I took some risks and hit a bump in the road. But Bowlinator here is jealous of the entrepreneur, the workingman, the hustling man, and he had to degrade me and my failures to my son. MY SON!

Milt was red-faced, shouting, exposed, deranged . . . he was a root canal without the Novocain.

—MY BOY! Not your boy. MY BOY!

Milt pointed a meaty finger at Curt Long, whose lean form seemed to diminish into a straight line, a bony statue in a bowling shirt.

—You don't fuck with another man's son, cop fuck. Lousy, stinking, non-risk-taking, government-fucking stooge.

Milt paused. Even though he was out of breath, he transitioned into the graceful bowing of his head, spreading out his arms respectfully, as if asking his audience to forgive the intrusion. The crowd was silent and he could feel their piercing eyes now staring at their hero, the Bowlinator, with more than a trace of doubt and an inkling of disdain. The seed planted, Milt, in a fatherly, humble way, grabbed his son's hand and escorted him out of the bowling lanes. When they emerged through the front door, Milt exhaled, exhausted, but still floating high from the adrenaline.

—Holy crap, Dad, said Aaron.

They took a few steps into the night.

—He'll never bowl there again, said Milt.

—I thought you were going to kick his ass, said Aaron, his eyes animated. —That was so much better.

—This is the modern age, said Milt. —It's all about being a salesman.

In the parking lot behind the bowling lanes Aaron danced about throwing little jabs and bobbing and weaving. He moved awkwardly, both stiff and bent at the same time, like a marionette. His sneakers made a scraping sound on the gravel. He had moved away from the single lightbulb that illuminated the space, and was skipping near the thick fronds and mass of vegetation, which loomed like a small jungle at the lot's edge. Milt saw his son, ducking invisible punches, play-fighting in the shadows. A strange fear engulfed Milt. It was as if something was going to emerge out of the dark throng of bushes and descend upon his son.

—Come here, Milt snapped.

—We going to the movies now, Dad? asked Aaron.

—I got something I want to show you first, said Milt.

Aaron walked up to his father. They were standing an arm's length from each other. Milt flicked out a quick jab right in front of Aaron's face, just short of his chin. The boy jerked his head back and, as he did, gave Milt a goofy smile.

Milt glared at his son, dead serious, and said:

—Never fucking flinch.

ATLANTIS

The Ghost sat in his cabana, letting the breeze from the reef caress him.

It had rained for five days straight on the coast of Belize. For the first few days it was a light pattering of rain whipped about by strong winds. The sound of the winds, buffeting against the bamboo shutters and howling through crevasses, was stronger than the spitting rain. Then came the tropical downpour: heavy, pounding droplets. The rain came in waves and made the ceramic-tile roof clatter like someone was hurling dice from above. And now the wind could barely be heard as the drumming of rain on the cabana roof and the staccato, machine-gun sound of it pelting onto the ocean drowned out all other noise, except for the chirping of tree frogs. At night their shrill mating song filled the jungle and the cove beyond.

Later in the morning the storm let up. The sun blazed through the parting gray clouds and the air became thick with an oppressive humidity. There was a knock on the front door of the cabana and the gray-haired Mabry called out "hello, anybody home?"

Mabry was an Aussie expat who lived most of his adult life in Guatemala. But as Mabry told the Ghost, his wife had died and he'd come to Belize to work as a night watchman at the Jaguar Reef Resort. When he was off duty he would show up to try and sell the Ghost his homemade tequila or offer to perform odd jobs. The Ghost opened the door. Mabry stood there shirtless, his wrinkled, sagging belly hanging over his camouflage shorts. He smiled through his dripping mustache and the bottles in the soaked-through cardboard box clanked together. A wet, extinguished cigarette hung from the corner of his lips.

The Ghost bought three bottles of tequila for ten dollars. Then he offered Mabry five dollars if he would fix some loose tiles on the patio. He cocked his head to the side and gave the Ghost a long, puzzled glance.

—Your friend left today, eh, captain?

—She will be leaving. Not yet. She's out taking pictures of the lagoon, said the Ghost.

—You are staying on, though?

—Yes, said the Ghost.

—When she is gone, if you need any company, any local girls, just to hang out and party, let me know.

The Ghost said nothing and nodded his head.

—Very well, Mabry, he said and shut the door. As the Ghost walked the tequila into the kitchen, he was bothered by the fact that Mabry would think he was the kind of man who would hire a prostitute. He decided to tell the Reef management about this tomorrow. He didn't want Mabry coming around anymore.

Soon after Mabry left, Carlos arrived with three filets of grouper wrapped in banana leaves. Houseflies darted in and around his dark, lean form, trying to get a taste of fresh fish. Carlos worked quietly at the kitchen counter. Christine, the Ghost's female companion, had suffered from a four-day bout of diarrhea and had been in a bad mood.

—You want me to cook them now? Or wait for the lady to get up.

—Now is good, said the Ghost. —She's out in the lagoon. She'll be back soon.

—This rain's not so bad, said Carlos. —Very normal for this time of year.

—It's a tropical depression. Is there a danger of flooding?

—I don't think so. Unless we get a hurricane.

The Ghost walked over the smooth blue tile floor through the sitting area and into the back room that he'd converted into a small office. On the wall was one painting, Celina's *Waiting*. Christine thought it was strange that a man who was nearly blind could be so attached to one dirty painting. She was a waitress at the Ritz Hotel in Boston. She'd known the Ghost three weeks before he'd asked her to accompany him to Belize. When they toured Tikal, the couple had stayed for two days in a small, quiet pension near the ruins. The landlady at the pension wore a cross and thought Christine was the Ghost's daughter. At the end of the visit Carlos picked them up in the jeep.

The Ghost was interested in the Mayan mythology, their religion of human sacrifice, their advanced knowledge of astronomy, and their blood sport that resembled a combination of volleyball and basketball. On their visit, Christine had hiked up the temples, their steep grade of stone slab steps, while the Ghost had stayed at the base with the guide, who stood glumly and chewed on a cheroot. The guide said nothing to the Ghost and sat there wondering what a beautiful woman was doing with a man whose eyes vibrated.

The Ghost was eating the grouper filet Carlos had sautéed in lemon juice and butter, when Christine entered the kitchen.

—Good morning, said the Ghost. He motioned to her plate of grouper. —Carlos fixed it especially for you.

—Thank you, Carlos, she said. —Freshly diced mangoes. You spoil me.

The Ghost and Christine sat at the burnished driftwood table eating their meal. Carlos stood at the small kitchen island, watching them. He was only nineteen, but his gravitas gave him the presence of someone more mature than his age. The Ghost could sense that Carlos sometimes stared at Christine.

—He is worried about the big storm, said Carlos. —So I might have to drive you to Belize City tomorrow. Are you feeling better?

—Is there a storm coming? asked Christine. She had a Boston accent. Two days before the Ghost had heard her giggling in the driveway with Carlos. He'd made the decision then and there to send her home.

—Nothing to worry about, said the Ghost. —Just a precaution. Carlos'll drive you to the airport today.

—Yes, Carlos, she said. —I am feeling much better.

—I booked you a room at the Marriot right by the airport. It's pretty nice, said the Ghost. —If this storm dumps more rain there's going to be flooding and you'll be stuck here for days.

Christine put her fork on the plate and looked over at the Ghost.

—What he says is true, said Carlos.

The Ghost didn't want to fire Carlos so much as beat him to death.

When Christine and Carlos were gone, the Ghost went into his small office and turned on a live broadcast of the ball game. The Mariners were down two to zero in the battle for the pennant. Also, crude oil was up to eighty-five dollars. The Ghost checked his online stock portfolio. He was up 9 percent on the year.

The Ghost then scrolled through more news at the online *New York Times*. Everything bored him. Except for the Mariners—they just made him angry, losing the night before to Oakland. He stretched out his right hand and removed his shaded glasses. He shook his head and let out a sigh.

The Ghost took careful steps into the living room, and opened up a big coffee table book with photos of Tikal. He opened to his favorite shot, the Temple of a Hundred Warriors. He took out his dome magnifier and let it glide over the picture of the temple. It was a sprawling stone edifice, while at its base ancient columns stood, each one representing the fighting men who dwelled in its living quarters. He slowly scanned once more at the abandoned pyramid, with its stark, rectangular shape and serpentine mosaics.

Monuments to dead things, he thought.

He walked out of the room, moving in silence.

Just yesterday when the rain had stopped and the light burst through the clouds to dry the puddles on the patio, the Ghost had missed seeing a heron with a long, daggerlike beak fly overhead. The bird had made a tight turn at the jungle tree line and then swooped back down toward the house. The Ghost sat on the deck, not seeing the bird. It landed just yards from the edge of the patio and with its straight beak and thin, leathery stick legs struck at something in the grass. The Ghost, hearing something, had moved toward the edge of the patio. Lashing out with its spiked tail and pinching claws was a small scorpion. The heron, in one violent step, pinned the scorpion to the ground with its clawed foot. Then with mechanical precision the bird pecked at the ground until the scorpion's tail with its poison stinger fell away from the armored trunk of its body. In the next moment the bird plucked the insect up with its beak and threw back its head. The scorpion disappeared down its gullet.

The scorpion's tail was gone. The ants had carried it away in the night.

That evening the Ghost sat on the living room couch and listened to the chirping of frogs and the squawk of the wild parrots. The sounds relaxed him. He drank Mabry's tequila. The drink washed over him. He decided the tequila was good enough that he wouldn't report Mabry to the Reef security.

The rains started up again. The deep, pungent smell of wet jungle wafted in through the blinds. It was very good tequila. The Ghost was thinking about his comeback. He had one more fight in him. A piano was arriving tomorrow. He'd have plenty of time to think.

The Ghost came awake suddenly. He thought at first that he'd been dreaming about the hurricane. The deluge descended on the roof in waves. But it was not a dream or the rain that woke up the Ghost. It was an open shutter that was banging against the side of the cabana. The winds would rip it off if he didn't latch it shut. The Ghost rolled out of bed and was hoping he wouldn't have too hard a time securing it in the dark. His soles hit the cold tile and it was then he heard it: the slapping of feet on the parquet floor.

Someone had unlatched the blind. The Ghost had some valuables in the cabana. Two rolls of gold coins he kept in a lockbox, a few thousand dollars in American bills, his computer, sound system, and TV. He had but moments. An attempt to escape in the dark would be too clumsy. The Ghost reached under his bed and grasped the baseball bat he kept there. It was an undented, varnished Louisville Slugger. The Ghost moved soundlessly across the floor until he felt his back pressed against the stucco wall. He was positioned just to the left of the door to his bedroom.

The Ghost waited for what seemed minutes. He heard what could've been men whispering on the other side of the door. Between the howl of the storm and the hum of the air conditioner, the Ghost, disoriented, couldn't be sure. The Ghost grabbed the pine baseball bat and raised it above his head.

The Ghost wrapped his hands tighter around the bat. The fear went out of him. The Ghost assessed the angles and curvature of the swings he would inflict upon on the intruders when they walked through the door.

He stood there in the dark, waiting.

THE SPORTING ELEMENT

It was mid-January, the height of ski season in Vail. A blizzard had descended on the Rockies and dumped near twenty inches of snow on the resort town. The U.S. real estate bubble had gone bust in October and since December Europeans and South Americans of every variety slithered into Colorado to take advantage of the declining dollar and fresh powder.

Gallagher took his New York clients out to dinner at an overpriced restaurant in Vail. All the industry talk had been about gold. Although Gallagher was portfolio manager of the Alternative Energy Desk at a Chicago hedge fund, the topic that consumed the New York investors was gold. Afraid for their dollars, the natural flow of cash during periods of uncertainty was to the yellow stuff: the ancient flight to wealth in times of fear as far back as the Pharaohs. One of Gallagher's analysts had argued that at a thousand dollars an ounce, it was nearing the top. No one gave a shit about wind power, solar, hydro projects, at least not yet, not with an oil-loving Texan in the Oval Office.

The next morning Gallagher's clients left for New York early. He had a day of skiing to himself. He shook off the vodka hangover and headed once again for the superior powder and shorter lift lines of the back bowl. Outer Mongolia. Even the name of the back bowl lift appealed to Gallagher. It conjured up Genghis Khan and his army of horsemen. The Khan had ravaged the lands as far west as eastern Europe. Gallagher had some Czech blood from his paternal grandmother, and harbored the belief he might be of direct relation to Genghis. Gallagher was convinced enough that he had bet a few traders on the floor at Allied. They'd paid the five hundred dollars for the DNA kit that supposedly connected your genes to the conqueror who at one point could declare himself as the father of one out of every five men who'd lived in the time of the Dark Ages. Gallagher had taken the test and his bloodline showed up negative. He could not claim ancestral ties to the Great Khan. He'd been sorely disappointed.

Gallagher rubbed his eyes. The lift line gave out an electrical hum as the quad chair came to a halt. Sitting there above the mountainside, the chair began to swing slightly as the winds coursed around it. Gallagher hugged himself, as the cold cut through his jacket. With nothing to take his mind off his surroundings, Gallagher couldn't help but listen to the couple next to him on the chair. They were talking about a pending lawsuit against some contractors.

—They didn't finish the sunroom to code, said the wife. She was blond, attractive, in her late forties.

—I got Alex on it. He's a leg biter. They don't know who they are fucking with.

The man's weather-beaten face was both craggy and puffy. Beneath the dark lenses of the ski goggles Gallagher imagined him as having a pair of small, raisin-sized nut-brown eyes. It was a mean face; one that spoke of excess and of victories. His outfit was a loud purple and yellow Spyder ski parka and pants. It was an ensemble look because his skis were also yellow, only a brighter shade.

—They think because the house is in Greece they can fuck us. Well, that BlackBerry message was from Alex. And guess what? We've got ourselves a fucking Greek lawyer.

—Good, said the wife. —I have the interior for the room all planned out.

—Just give me a day on this before you send in the decorators, all right?

—It's been two weeks . . .

—Eight days, corrected the husband.

Gallagher let out a groan. The wind swung the chair and stabbed at the back of Gallagher's neck, which was exposed to the elements. The couple hesitated for a moment. Gallagher in one forceful motion lifted the safety bar to the quad. The malfunction of the lift was timed just right for Gallagher's purpose. The chair was beneath a lip of snow that was only a sixteen-foot drop instead of the twenty- to thirty-foot drop that was the lift's average.

Gallagher looked over at the wife, who sat next to him. He glanced at the corner of her perfectly formed mouth and said:

—I'm out of here.

Then with one bump of his hips, Gallagher hopped off the chair and sailed through the air toward the powdered snow below.

Immediately, Gallagher knew he'd done something to his left ankle. A sharp pain shot through his heel into his whole foot. Nothing had snapped, but he'd torn something, a ligament maybe.

Gallagher sat there and lay back in the snow. The sun was hidden by cloud cover. Gallagher noticed the creeping cold. The snow that was jammed up the back of his jacket when he landed made him start to shiver. It wasn't supposed to work out this way. He'd wanted to hop off the lift and ski down the mountain. Now the ski patrol would come along and pick him up in the sled. They'd punch his pass for the season. At worst the couple from Chicago would press charges of reckless endangerment. But maybe the ski patrol would be an attractive girl who would take sympathy, see Gallagher's side of it. Maybe, he'd get to stare at her all the way down the mountain. Maybe, he'd leave Colorado and go to the real Outer Mongolia. After all, nobody had ever found the grave of Genghis Khan. He had his elite guard bury him in a secret location somewhere out on the steppes. When the elite guard returned from their burial detail, they were executed upon the Great Khan's posthumous orders, so that no one would ever know the location of his gravesite. It was said that anyone who discovered the remains of Genghis Khan and dug up his armor would then accomplish the unfulfilled destiny of the Mongolian lord, that of World Conquest.

Now that, thought Gallagher. That would be nice.

Gallagher looked up the slope. He saw the distinct red jacket of the ski patrol approaching, bearing a medevac sled behind him. Gallagher could make out a brown beard on the skier with the sled. Gallagher raised his poles in the air and pumped them as if staving off an attack. Enraged, in pain, he began screaming, as if he was on horseback, invading some village from a thousand years ago. Even though it was well documented through a DNA test that Gallagher had absolutely no relation to the Mongol hordes whatsoever.

The triage unit in the Ski Patrol building diagnosed Gallagher's injury as simply a mild sprain. Gallagher's ankle remained swollen and his face was sunburned. Back at the condo, Gallagher showered and took a nap. When he awoke Gallagher found himself in pain. Still, he was determined to enjoy one more night on the town in Vail Village despite his injured status. Gallagher put on some clean clothes and hobble-walked out the door to the nearest après ski bar.

The crowd at The Club consisted of the rough-and-tumble, middle-class players on the circuit, whose ages ranged from twenty to fifty years old. The entertainer was a cowboy ski bum who went by the stage name "The Good Times Guy." He told dirty jokes and sang Jimmy Buffet-esque boozing-ski ballads. A brass bell hung by his head on stage and more than one drunk trying to impress a lady or his clients rang it and was forced to buy the entire bar a shot. Toward the end of his act the Good Times Guy honed in on a small crowd of well-dressed ski bunnies. Upon being interviewed they let out that they were actually airline hostesses. The Good Times Guy razzed them, calling them "sky sluts" and eventually got one of them to remove her overgarments, exposing her bra.

Gallagher, slightly buzzed, less sore, and in a good-times-guy frame of mind, headed out to a good restaurant to put a dent in the corporate card. He ate at the bar, which was lit by one hazy yellow lamp that created a somnambulant mood. Sitting next to him was an elderly gentleman: silver haired, black turtleneck, and immaculate blazer. He addressed the bartender very carefully and politely. It turned out the man with exquisite manners brokered islands. However, his manners weren't so good that he couldn't resist trying to sell Gallagher a five-acre plot off an atoll in the Azores. Once Gallagher had listened to and respectfully declined the offer, the island broker said:

—Well, I made one sale tonight at the bar. Can you blame me for going for a second?

When the island broker left, Gallagher's meal arrived and he got after it; wolfing down a dozen blue point oysters, a plate of Alaskan king crab legs, and a rack of lamb. He washed it all back with four or five glasses of Glenmorangie 18.

After dinner Gallagher wandered out of the restaurant in a haze that seemed to him as friendly and pleasant as the snowflakes that fell throughout Vail Village.

Two bars later the sensation in Gallagher's ankle moved from shooting pains to a numbed aching. There was an altercation at one bar, the local dive for the ski instructors and other mountain employees. Someone who was French was shouting in his native tongue at a guy wearing an off-hours Ski Patrol jacket. When they came to blows Gallagher headed for the door.

At some point two girls in their twenties were doing shots of something with him back at The Club. Gallagher invited them to his condo's pool. They marched alongside the limping Gallagher through the snowy street of the ski village. Suddenly, a gang of young men on the prowl walked toward Gallagher and his two ladies. One of the men in the group was the Good Times Guy, wearing his black cowboy hat rimmed with rhinestones and sporting a quail feather.

Gallagher studied the Good Times Guy's face. Up close he could see the music man's visage was etched with deep lines and the skin was more slack than rugged, in a way that spoke more of alcohol abuse and old age than a partying bard who had managed to weather the storm. Still, the swarm of younger men and the Good Times Guy surrounded Gallagher's two ladies and co-opted them, although they were kind enough to point at Gallagher like he was an afterthought and offer:

—And you can bring him too if you want.

Gallagher stood alone in the street and watched the crowd move away, as the falling snow obscured them until they became blue shadows. His condo was in the same direction, so Gallagher followed the group at a distance, still able to hear their voices and one of the girl's laughter.

When her laughter was finally lost in the wind, Gallagher might have thought of his ex-wife and become maudlin, but he did not. Instead, he imagined himself to be some bleary-eyed, drunken monk moving through an Arctic leper colony who had just passed along angels to the stricken.

When Gallagher turned the corner by the restaurant he saw that some poor soul had passed out, face-first, in a snowbank. The laughing crowd had walked right past him. There was a cold bite to the air and Gallagher thought that at the very least if no one came to his aid the person's nose would get frostbitten. He grabbed the man by his shoulders and flipped him onto his back. The drunk's face wasn't discolored blue and he wasn't shivering, so Gallagher figured he must have just fallen into the snowbank.

—Buddy, you okay? asked Gallagher, wiping snowflakes off the man's face with a gloved hand.

Even without el Jefe Gallagher recognized him at once.

—Jesus, Milt, he said. —Milt Harkrader, are you okay?

He shook Milt violently.

Milt said at last:

—Listen, guy. Leave me alone. I don't feel so good.

Milt opened his eyes. Then he blinked twice, situating himself. He put his hands against the snowbank and attempted to stand. He looked up at his rescuer.

—Hey, he asked. —How did you know my name?

—It's me, Gallagher. Your old client from Allied Power.

Milt smiled.

—God damn, he said.

Then he held out his frozen hand.

—Help me up, Joe, will you? I need a cab back to the hotel.

Despite some pain in his ankle, Gallagher was able to steady Milt. He grabbed his ex-broker by the arm and walked him toward the square where the shuttle service was still running.

—What the fuck were you doing passed out in a snowbank?

—I don't know, said Milt. —All I know is that I bought an island tonight: a beauty, right off the coast of British Columbia.

—You got the money for that? asked Gallagher.

—Hell, no, said Milt. —I just said I'd buy it for shits and giggles. Gave the guy my old boss's business card.

A cutting wind blew down Vail Village Way. It gave a whistle that grew into a sinister howl and then faded. Gallagher suddenly realized he was cold again. The snow began to fall in what seemed like a sudden, endless curtain of white, as if God blinked and another blizzard had begun.

When the shuttle pulled up, Gallagher managed to help Milt off the bench and guide him over an icy patch on the sidewalk. When Milt boarded the bus he turned and thanked Gallagher.

—Hey, Milt, asked Gallagher. —What are you up to these days? I heard you were in Michigan.

—Fuck that, said Milt. —I'm back in the City. Back in the game.

—What are you doing?

Then the tortured gravel and hungover sound in Milt's voice faded away, and his words rang out with innocence and pride:

—Gold, chanted Milt, spreading his arms wide. —I'm brokering gold. And I'll tell you what, Gallagher, take it from me: That shit is going to the moon!

NOTES ON TRADING;

OR HOW ENERGY TRADING WORKS

In the world of energy trading, there are two species of animal: traders and brokers.

A trader's job is to speculate on the future prices of energy products—coal, natural gas, crude oil, or electricity. In doing so a trader buys (gets "long") or sells (gets "short") futures contracts of any one of these products. The goal is to try to make money by buying at a lower price than they sell or selling at a higher price than they bought. The product that they trade is megawatts, which trade in a standard fifty-megawatt block. The traders make their transactions through a broker, to whom they shout down their market orders on a direct line called a squawk box. More recently, traders can also transact their orders through an electronic trading platform called "ICE," or the Intercontinental Exchange, an electronic market.

A trader usually earns about 7 to 10 percent of their book, the year-end profit they make trading off their firm's financial resources. You don't make money, you're fired.

A broker's job is to bring transactions to traders, or "make" markets. A broker puts a buyer (or a bid) together with a seller (an offer) and a deal is transacted at an agreed-upon price. In essence, the broker is a middleman who has no financial risk unless a trader welches on a trade. This is called "flaking." When one trader breaks a trade after it has been executed, the other trader, who was "flaked" on, has the option of making the broker wear the risk of the bad trade. This is called "hanging" the broker.

While traders get paid by predicting the directions of the markets, brokers do not care about the direction of the market, they are only concerned about "volume," or the number of deals they close. A broker gets paid a commission on each deal he transacts. If the trader is a poker player, then the broker is the card dealer, making his kitty from the tips of the various players. As long as there are gamblers at the table, the broker is getting paid.

While a broker works for a brokerage firm, an energy trader works for one of three entities: a utility or power company, an investment bank, or a hedge fund. A utility trader takes less risk (and gets paid less) than traders at investment banks and hedge funds. This is because a utility trader is trading the excess energy from his assets, which are power plants like coal, nuclear power, and natural gas units. A utility trader is selling megawatts from a power plant, whereas hedge funds and banks have no power plants and are purely speculating, which is known as going "naked short." Some utilities do "short" above and beyond their unit capacity and if prices go up in an instance of external circumstances (like a hurricane or a heat wave) can find themselves financially ruined.

Among energy traders there are two groups: financial traders and physical traders. Financial traders are the type described above who transact futures on the commodities exchanges. Using sophisticated financial tools they speculate in the futures and options electricity markets. Their analysis is a lot of times based on what is called "technical analysis." Technical analysis is the term given to various methods of reading the price charts and analyzing the trends in an attempt to predict future price movement. There are many forms of technical analysis ranging from "candlestick analysis" (the first technical analysis developed by Japanese rice traders in the 1700s) to more modern forms like Elliott Wave Theory, the K-wave, stochastics, and Bollinger bands. Technical trading is sometimes referred to as "chart trading" and "trend trading."

The second type of energy trader is the physical trader. Physical traders are the used car salesmen of the power industry. Unlike a financial trader who buys and sells financial futures, the physical trader buys actual megawatts off his client's power plants. He then buys space on the transmission lines so he can move his cheap megawatts from one energy hub, called "the source," across the grid and sell them to a client at another energy hub, called "the sink." Buying megawatts cheap, moving them across the transmission lines, and selling at a profit is known as physical arbitrage or "hub trading." The physical trader's only risk is that his power gets "cut" as it moves across the transmission lines.

This book is about the individuals involved in this game

TRADER'S GLOSSARY

Accrual Desk: The generation and load side of the electricity business based on cost accounting, not associated with speculative trading.

Bal week: Term for balance of the week, or the remaining days of a given week.

Balmo: Balance of the month. Also known as the "BOM."

Black-Scholes Model: A mathematical model used by energy traders to solve for volatility, which gives the implied volatility of an option at given prices, durations, and exercise prices.

Bid: The term for the value at which a trader wants to buy.

Bid/Ask or "Two Way": The price at which one counterparty will buy and sell a given commodity, i.e., the market.

Big book: A slang term for the size of a trader's portfolio that is large and allowed to take on a lot of risk.

"Boxed": When a broker gets "put in the box" or temporarily fired by a trader.

Candlesticks: In the mid-1700s in Sakata, Japan, Munehisa Homna took one hundred years of data from the world's first futures market, the Dojima Rice Exchange in Osaka, and compiled it into the candlestick charting technique. His trading off this method made his family the richest in Japan. At one point he had over one hundred successive winning trades. The candlesticks had war-like language in their trend predictions: dark clouds, doji shooting stars, hanging man, hammer, engulfing patterns, etc.

Cash traders: Financial traders who trade futures from next day out to the end of the month, also known as "the balance of the month" or the "BOM."

Collusion: When traders or brokers get together and attempt to manipulate a market by agreeing to fix prices and coordinate buy and exit strategies ahead of time.

Congestion, or Transmission Line Congestion: The value of certain nodes on the grid changes as megawatts move to and from points of supply to points of demand. Congestion is essentially what happens when too many megawatts flow on a single line, causing prices to spike in the load pocket and decrease in the supply node. A megawatt traffic jam, if you will.

Corn Crush: The CBOT corn crush measures the difference between the sales value of finished fuel ethanol and the price of corn.

CQG: An electronic technical analysis tool, charting platform and news service for the commodities markets.

Cuffing: When a broker misrepresents a market by tightening the bid/ask, so as to give the appearance that he holds a better market than he does. A very risky maneuver in which the outcome sometimes is the broker gets hung (see *Hang*).

Delta Positions: The Greek symbol used by traders to value how long or short their positions are.

Dispatcher: Utility worker who ramps up and down the units, "dispatching" the electricity to the power grid from an energy company's various power plants: gas, coal, nukes, etc.

ERCOT: Electric Reliability Council of Texas. Or the electricity market for Texas.

"Flaking on trade" (v. to flake): When a trader refuses to accept a given deal once it has already been transacted and confirmed by the broker.

Front-Running: The act of selling or buying in front of one's client or fellow trader to assure oneself a lower buy or higher sale.

Futures (contract): An agreement between a buyer and seller to exchange a commodity or security at a set date in the future (the delivery date) for a price set now. The futures buyer agrees to pay the price and receive the underlying commodity; the seller receives the fixed price and must deliver the underlying commodity. The buyer, who is said to be *long*, hopes that the price of the underlying commodity rises before the delivery date so he can receive the commodity for the cheaper fixed price that he has agreed to pay. The seller, who is said to be *short*, is hoping that prices fall between now and then instead. For example, the buyer and seller agree, in March, to transact on a futures contract for August PJM electric power at a price of eighty dollars (per MW). If the price in August is actually one hundred dollars, the buyer has made twenty dollars by locking in a cheaper price in advance—the seller must still furnish the electricity but, instead of paying the current price of one hundred dollars, the buyer only had to pay the contractually obligated price of eighty. If the seller did not already have electricity to give the buyer, such as by owning a power plant that generates electricity, the seller must go on the open market and buy it for one hundred dollars—taking a loss of twenty dollars since he is only receiving eighty from the buyer.

Futures are much simpler to trade than actual physical commodities. In some cases, such as electricity, the underlying commodity cannot even be stored for use at a later date, making futures the only feasible way to quickly get in and out of positions or to take a bet on the direction of prices. Futures sellers do not need to own the underlying commodity in order to sell futures (such as those who short-sell stocks being required to "borrow" shares of the stock they wish to sell, or at least ascertain there are shares available to borrow) nor do futures buyers need to be capable of actually taking delivery of the commodity when they buy futures. Actual physical transactions only happen when the futures contract expires on the delivery date. The vast majority of futures traded contracts on commodities, such as electricity and natural gas, do not actually result in delivery of the underlying commodity. Traders usually exit their positions before the delivery date simply by selling their futures contract if they were long or buying it back if they were short, leaving themselves with the financial profit or loss but no obligation to receive or deliver a commodity. In addition to speculative trading for profit, futures are widely used by market participants called hedgers who wish to reduce their risk, such as someone who owns a power plant wishing to sell electricity futures to lock in current prices and reduce uncertainty about future revenues.

Gamma Risks: Gamma is the change in volatility.

Heat Dome: A ridge of high-pressure air that usually indicates above-average heat for a given area.

Hammer Patterns: Bullish pattern on Japanese candlestick chart.

Hang: Means to stick a broker with a bad trade, making the broker, not the trader, financially responsible.

HPL: Houston Power and Light, an electric utility.

ICE: Intercontinental Exchange, an electronic trading platform for commodities markets.

Illiquid: When a market is illiquid, it lacks liquidity, or volume. In other words it is not actively traded and makes it difficult for traders to get in and get out of positions.

ISO: Independent system operator.

Kondratieff, Nikolai: Russian economist who theorized the concept of a sixty-year economic time cycle. A proponent of the New Economic Policy (NEP), Kondratieff was drafted by Stalin to prove academically that communism was superior to the messy boom-bust western capitalist system. His economic research suggested that a major weakness of a centrally planned economy was that it does not have any way to periodically weed out inefficiencies. Although he predicted the deflationary collapse of capitalist economies, an event that occurred on schedule in the form of the Great Depression, he was executed by a firing squad for his basic capitalist leaning.

K-waves (also called **supercycles, surges, long waves,** or **Kondratieff waves**) is a time cycle described as regular, sinusoidal-like cycles in the modern capitalist world economy. Averaging fifty and ranging from approximately forty to sixty years in length, the cycles consist of alternating periods between high sectoral growth and periods of relatively slow growth. Unlike the short-term business cycle that in various forms has been familiar since the nineteenth century, the long wave of this theory does not belong within current orthodox economics and is sometimes categorized as part of heterodox economics (a catch-all term for alternative ideas to economic ideologies in force). Subscribers to the K-wave believe the economic life of mankind is cyclical in nature. Expansion follows contraction, boom follows bust, inflation follows deflation, bear markets follow bull markets.

Limit Up/Limit Down: When a market spikes or falls the Exchanges protect the participants by limiting the amount a market can rise or fall in the period of one day.

Long: Or "getting long" is the act of buying any *futures* contract or underlying commodity, hoping the price of that product goes up in value. Futures traders who are long have agreed to pay a fixed price in exchange for receiving a commodity at a later date. If the price goes up between now and then, the long futures trader can make money, either by taking delivery of the commodity and immediately reselling it for a higher price in the market than he agreed to pay for it or simply selling his futures contract for a higher price.

MW: Symbol for "megawatts." The standard valuation of electricity futures is traded in 50MW "blocks" or "pieces."

Nat Gas Ring: Natural gas trading pit on the exchange (**NYMEX**).

"Natty": Natural gas.

NQ: Symbol for July and August in the futures markets. Known as the "summer package."

Offer: The term for the value at which a trader wants to sell. Also known as the "asking price."

Options: A financial derivative that represents a contract sold by one party (option writer) to another party (option holder). The contract offers the buyer the right, but not the obligation, to buy (call) or sell (put) a security or other financial asset at an agreed-upon price (the strike price) during a certain period of time or on a specific date (exercise date).

OTC Market: Over-the-counter market. OTC securities and commodities are traded through brokers or dealers who negotiate with traders (who provide bids and offers) over telephone or computerized networks instead of through a stock/commodities exchange.

Physical Deal: Moving actual physical megawatts, or electricity, through the transmission lines from one hub to another for a profit. Also known as "hub trading."

Pit Traders: Traders that work on any one of the worldwide financial exchanges in the trading pits of certain equities and commodities markets.

PNL: Profit and loss. A trader's PNL indicates how much money they are up or down.

Polar Pig: Meteorological term designating an Arctic air mass descending from the North Pole.

"Printing": Printing refers to a high price that ticks or prints real time on the electricity grid. As in "that shit is printing," meaning in trader slang that the thing referred to has high value.

Reuters: Commodities futures news service and charting tool.

Sarbanes-Oxley Regulations: Laws requiring full disclosure of trading information.

Short: or "getting short"/ The act of selling a *futures* contract or commodity, hoping the price of that product goes down in value and can be bought back for a lower value at a later date. Futures traders who are short will receive a fixed price, agreed upon now, in exchange for delivering a commodity at a later date to the buyer. Futures traders who are short can make money if the price drops between now and the delivery date, either by buying the commodity more cheaply than the fixed price on the market and delivering it when the contract comes due or simply buying their short futures contract back for less money. For example, in March, futures trader A has sold a PJM electricity contract for delivery in August to futures trader B for eighty dollars (per MW). If it is now August and electricity is only worth sixty dollars, futures trader A, who is short at eighty dollars, has made twenty dollars. He can either buy actual electricity on the market for sixty and deliver it to B to fulfill his futures obligation, who must still pay A eighty dollars as per the futures contract, or A could simply buy back his futures contract for sixty dollars from either B or anyone else in the market, locking in his profit and eliminating the need to actually deliver electricity.

Shorting futures markets has more risk than being long. The underlying assets cannot generally be worth less than zero so the trader who is long futures only has to worry about losing all the money he paid up front in the catastrophic event prices fall to zero (commodities are rarely given away for free). The trader who is short can lose a theoretically unlimited amount of money if prices keep rising. This is a particular concern in electricity, an energy commodity subject to severe price spikes.

Squawk Box: The voice-activated box by which brokers call down and communicate markets to traders, and by which traders call down to brokers and execute on those markets in real time.

Stopped Out: When a trader loses so much money that he violates his risk parameters and has to be shut down or "stopped out" by the risk group.

Stop Loss: The actual numerical loss amount in dollars where a trader becomes "stopped out" (see *Stopped Out*).

Term Traders: Financial traders who trade futures one month out and beyond.

Transmission or "tranny": Transmission lines and the act of owning a line or the ability to move physical power "megawatts" across that line for potential arbitrage.

VAR: "Value-at-Risk." How much money a company gives a trader to risk.

"Vol" or volatility: The degree to which a market can change or move in value. High volatility is associated with high risk.

"Yours you": Yours means "sold." "Yours you" directly translated means you are selling somebody's future potential. More prosaically it means: "You suck."